THE
ONLY
WITNESS

Pamela Beason

WildWing Press
Bellingham, Washington, USA

ALSO BY PAMELA BEASON

CALL OF THE JAGUAR

SHAKEN

ENDANGERED

This is a work of fiction. Names, characters, places, and incidents are products of the author's imagination or are used fictitiously and are not to be construed as real. Any resemblance to actual events, locales, organizations, or persons, living or dead, is entirely coincidental.

WILDWING PRESS
3301 Brandywine Court
Bellingham, Washington 98226

Copyright © 2011 Pamela Beason
ISBN 978-0-9798768-6-8
www.pamelabeason.com

Printed in the U.S.A.

I dedicate this book to my brother Larry.
I wish you could have stayed longer.

Chapter 1

Brittany Morgan knew she was a good mother, no matter what other people said.

She parked her old blue Civic around the corner from the main entry, in the shade of the grocery store so the car would stay cool in the early evening sun, maneuvering it into the middle of three empty spaces. She couldn't get or give any more dings or she'd have to listen to her father's going on and on about the deductible again. When she pulled on the hand brake, it squawked like a Canada goose, interrupting her favorite song. She *had* to figure out a way to make her parents buy her a better car. She was, to quote her English teacher Mr. Tanz, 'biding her time.' At first she'd thought it was 'biting her time', which made a lot more sense, because you could see how people might want to bite off minutes and hours and spit out the boring parts to get to the good ones. But Tanz made her look it up. It meant, like, waiting.

She'd been biding, putting off asking for a new car for almost a year. All because of Ivy. She looked at the baby, sleeping in her carrier in the passenger seat, backwards like they said, so she wouldn't get a broken neck if the air bag went off. But then, this junkmobile probably didn't even have an air bag on the passenger side. She'd have to remember to ask her father, who you would think would show a little more concern for his granddaughter.

The last strains of *Love Was* faded away and Radio Rick started talking about the upcoming news. She turned off the engine. When the car did its death lurch like it always did, Ivy jerked in her sleep, waving her tiny butterfly stockings in the air. An iridescent bubble formed in the bow of her lips, broken almost instantly by the sucking motion her lips always made as she drifted back to sleep.

Brittany's breasts tugged in response. She pulled out her tee-shirt and inspected the lavender cotton fabric. If anyone saw her with big wet blotches over her boobs, she'd just die. But the pads were working. Plus, they made her look at least a cup size bigger. Maybe she'd keep using them after she quit nursing. Her stomach got flatter every day and she knew her boobs would follow once she quit feeding Ivy.

Everyone had been wrong about what it'd be like to have a baby. How could anyone not adore Ivy Rose Morgan? Only two months old, she was already prettier than any baby in the ads, with her long lashes curled against her ivory cheeks and her soft peach-fuzz hair. She was a sure bet to win the photo contest.

Diapers were disgusting, it was true, but she changed them herself, even at night. And here she was, planning ahead, going to the store after school to get Huggies even before she'd used the last one. If that wasn't responsible, what was? As soon as she graduated from high school, she'd work on her clothing design business but she'd also get a job at Sears, because then she'd be able to get anything she needed for the apartment she'd have. Just her and Ivy. And her friends, too, of course, whenever she wanted them to come over. And maybe Charlie would come around sometimes, too. After all, he was Ivy's father, and once he saw her, he might decide that he really wanted to take care of his family instead of staying away at college.

Before Brittany got out of the car, she made sure all the windows were down a couple of inches. Not so much that people could stick their hands in, but just enough for good airflow. When she turned the key in the driver's door, she heard the locks click into place all around the car, but she walked around to double-check Ivy's door, like any responsible mother would.

She glanced at the tall gray van parked in the space to the right. It had those weird rock-star windows, mirrored so you couldn't see inside. It didn't look like the sort of ride that a rock star would be caught dead in, though; it was kind of faded with white lettering on the side. *Talking Hands Ranch.* Sounded like a camp for deaf kids. The mirrored windows were probably so people wouldn't make fun of the little boys and girls signing instead of talking.

Turning back to her car, she leaned down, moved her lips close to the opening at the top of the passenger window, and whispered, "Mama will be right back, Ivy Rose."

Chapter 2

Neema pressed her face close to the inside of the van window. Her broad hands fluttered in the air, signing *soft soft*. The girl's hair was red-gold, long and swishy. She wanted to touch that hair, press it to her nose to smell it, maybe even taste it just a little. But the girl walked away around the corner and then she couldn't see the sunset color any more.

Neema turned to watch the baby. It slept curled up in its chair, just like a baby cat in a basket. She wanted to play with that baby. She wanted its eyes to open and see her. She hooted softly, her breath briefly steaming up the dark glass. The baby didn't move.

Neema slapped the window with her open hand, making a hollow noise that was loud in the closed van. The baby woke, opened round blue eyes, and put its fist in its mouth. *Hello*, Neema signed. The baby's face wrinkled. Was it going to cry? She wanted to open the window. But the window buttons didn't work when Grace wasn't in the van. Neema ducked her chin and made a rocking motion with her arms, holding a pretend baby close to her stomach. She smacked her lips, gave it a pretend kiss. She knew how to be gentle with babies and things that could break.

A shadow moved past the van. When she looked out, a man stood between her window and the car. He watched the baby through the car window for a minute. Then he turned around toward the van.

Neema backed away from the glass. The man leaned closer. His face was mean. Neema tried to look fierce. She showed him her teeth, but he didn't even see her.

He stepped back and looked around the parking lot. Next he pulled a plastic bag from his pocket and stretched it over his hand.

Glove hot, Neema signed to herself. Gloves were for cold.

He turned to the car, pulled a long metal thing from his pants.

She signed *Long knife*. What was he going to cut? Not the baby! She hooted softly, signing *bad bad*.

He stabbed the knife down the window. Then he opened the door and reached for the baby. His long sleeve caught on the seat belt. It slid up, and there was a flat blue snake around his arm, its head on the back of his wrist. A snake! So close to the baby! *Snake bad snake arm*, she signed, hooting with fear. *Snake!*

He lifted the baby in its chair and grabbed a blue bag. With the baby under one arm, he shut the door with his glove hand.

The baby cried. The man shook off the bag-glove, and holding his snake hand over the baby's face, he walked to a green car parked behind the van. Neema scrambled to the back window. Snake Arm gave the baby to a woman in the car, then got into the driving seat. The green car got small and smaller and finally disappeared far away. Neema pressed her hand to the window. *Bye baby.*

A bug crawled up the window on the other side. Neema moved her hand to watch it. She pressed her lips to the glass. How would the bug feel on her tongue? Would it taste good? Most tasted bad. She didn't taste red and black ones anymore.

The side door of the van opened suddenly with a loud screech. Neema jumped and banged her head on the roof. Grace thumped two bags of groceries into the box on the floor. When she saw Neema in the back of the van, she signed as she said, "What are you doing?"

Neema hung her head, avoiding Grace's eyes.

"Get back into your seat now, please."

Neema squeezed down the narrow aisle and climbed into the rear passenger seat, sticking her feet carefully out in front of her. She looked for bugs between her bare toes. She found a grain of sand.

After Grace closed the side door, she walked around to climb into the driving seat. She put a banana up by the window and turned to look at Neema.

Neema gestured the peeling sign and patted her own chest. *Give banana.*

"Put your seat belt on. We wear our seat belts in the car."

Neema remembered the other car. She signed *baby.*

"You're not a baby, you can do it yourself," Grace said.

Neema signed *baby* again, and then *car.*

Grace signed as quickly as she talked. "Neema, no pretending now; you're not a baby. You promised you'd be good if I let you come. Josh is waiting for us. And Gumu. Don't you want to play with Gumu?"

Neema signed back.

"Snake make baby cry?" Grace's eyebrows rose. Neema loved those thin black eyebrows. Like flying birds. Now one flew higher than the other. "Are you calling me a snake?" Grace asked.

Neema hated the word *snake*. The sound was bad. And the sign was like a snake moving. Scary. *Baby cry, bad blue snake.*

Grace looked down at her blue shirt and laughed. "That's pretty creative, Neema. Good use of words."

Give banana.

"I'm no snake and you're no baby. Put your seat belt on before the banana." She pointed to the dangling buckle.

Neema shoved the seatbelt parts together.

Grace reached back to pat her leg. "See, you can do it by yourself."

Neema breathed in. The banana smelled like candy and sunshine. It was for her, she knew it. It had brown spots, just the way she liked it. *Give banana Neema*, she signed.

Grace turned the key and reached for the stick, trying to wiggle it into its place. The van made grinding noises. "C'mon, damn it," Grace said, shoving the stick back and forth. "Reverse. Is that too much to ask for?" Finally, she seemed happy and put both hands on the wheel and turned to look out over her shoulder.

As Grace backed the van out of the parking space, Neema watched the girl with the soft-soft red-gold hair come around the corner carrying a bag of food and a pack of soda. Then Grace pushed the stick to another spot and turned the van away and Neema couldn't see the girl any more.

She stretched her arm as far forward as she could, making big gestures so Grace could see even while she was driving. *Give banana.* She impatiently wiggled her fingers.

Grace finally handed her the banana. Neema raised it toward her mouth. Then she remembered. She tapped her chin lightly and thrust her hand toward Grace. *Thank you.*

"You're welcome." Grace smiled at her in the mirror on the front window. "You're a good gorilla."

Ten minutes after Ivy disappears

Chapter 3

When Detective Matthew Finn turned off the road down the long driveway to his house, he was looking forward to lapsing into a vegetative state for the remainder of the day. He'd traipsed around farm country since first light, consulting with the Kittitas County Sheriff's Department on a corpse found in a wheat field.

Grass had shot up through the driveway again. The tufts of green and gold made an interesting visual contrast against the background of gray-white gravel. He knew his police colleagues would find that thought very odd, and he'd learned not to make observations like that out loud. At any rate, he couldn't leave the driveway like that just because he liked the patterns and textures. He'd have to get out the RoundUp and spray for the hundredth time.

The big house, with its covered wraparound deck and accompanying three acres, cost a fifth of what it would have in Chicago. Wendy had loved the wildlife; the deer and raccoons that prowled through the yard, the coyotes that howled and owls that hooted after dark. These days, Finn mostly thought the house was a pain in the butt to maintain.

Three sets of eyes watched him walk from the driveway to the front door. The mismatched set on the porch—one brown eye and one blue—belonged to Cargo, a black furry mix of husky and some other giant breed—maybe Newfoundland or Rottweiler. The two sets of green eyes in the front window belonged to Lok and Kee, a pair of orange tabbies.

Finn slid his key into the deadbolt. Cargo sighed a barely audible whine as he gently pawed Finn's calf.

"Oh, please," Finn told the dog. "Don't give me the fading blossom routine. You could live for a week on that fat."

Aarrnh, the dog moaned, and pawed him again. As soon as Finn had the lock undone, the giant beast nosed the door open and galloped for the pantry, where he would plant his furry hulk and stare at the cabinet that held the dog chow.

The cats were only slightly more dignified, trailing him through the living room to the master bedroom. They rubbed against his legs and meowed as he took off his jacket and holster and slung them onto the dresser, then kicked off his shoes.

The meowing grew louder as he padded to the kitchen, pulled out a cold IPA from the refrigerator and an iced mug from the freezer. One cat—he thought it was Kee—jumped onto the counter to *rraow* at him, while the other sank its teeth into the tender flesh above his right heel. He peeled open a can of tuna and practically threw it at them in self-defense.

"Drama queens, that's what you are. You'd think you hadn't been fed for a week." He took a long swallow of his beer and watched the cats delicately lick the chunks of fish before they picked them up with their teeth. With such dainty maneuvers, it seemed like Lok and Kee should be neat eaters, but the two cats always managed to lick more onto the floor than into their mouths. Maybe he should just dispense with their dishes altogether.

A loud bark echoed in the pantry.

"For chrissake," he groaned. The only pets he'd had as a kid growing up in Chicago were a couple of fantails in a glass bowl. He had no idea that animals could be so demanding. And so vocal. He took another sip and went to feed the black beast. Cargo wolfed down the mountain of kibble before Finn had even finished shoveling it into the dog's stainless steel bowl.

Now that the animals had quit nagging him, Finn walked the few steps to the open door of his den and flicked on the overhead light. He paused in the doorway to study his half-finished painting on the desk. Sailboats racing on Lake Michigan, a scene he'd often witnessed from his condo in Chicago. He missed that wide-open vista over the water.

At one point during happier economic times, the Chicago police department decided to fund a recreation course for its officers, supposedly to promote better mental health among stressed-out cops. Most of his colleagues chose bowling or racquetball or martial arts lessons. Finn chose painting. Studying art had taught him to look at the world in a different way. Now he noticed hues and patterns of light and dark that he'd overlooked before. Oddly enough, his painting hobby made his surroundings seem more three-dimensional and colorful, whereas before he remembered the world as largely flat with shades of gray. He'd learned to live with the razzing at the office.

Although the painting was remarkably similar to the photo that he'd tacked onto the bulletin board, there was something lifeless about his composition. The shadows needed work, he decided; he'd used too much flat Prussian blue. Shadows were never just one color; that was one thing his painting instructor had drummed into the class. Beads of burnt sienna gleamed along the closest
boat's trim; maybe if he added a hint of that warmth to the shadows?

A wet dog tongue washed his fingertips. Cargo's mismatched eyes gazed at Finn's face, then shifted to his empty food bowl and back again.

"No way," Finn said, drying his fingers on his thigh. "One cup of chow twice a day, that's it. You're too fat."

At least that was what Wendy had told him. *The vet said Cargo's too fat.* Odd how he remembered what she said about the dog when he obviously hadn't registered most of what came out of his wife's mouth.

Dinner before painting, he decided. Finn flicked off the den light and walked back to the kitchen, followed by the click of four sets of toenails on the hardwood floor. He had to find the time to take these critters to the animal shelter, and soon. It couldn't be here in Evansburg, though, there was already too much talk. He'd try the next county over. Let some unsuspecting family with plenty of time on their hands take on these furry burdens.

He nuked a frozen dinner—turkey and dressing and the works. While he waited, he thumbed through his mail on the counter. Cargo hovered hopefully, a dark hulk breathing hotly on Finn's elbow.

One envelope was addressed to Gwendolyn Finn. The return address was the university alumni association, where she'd met up with her old friends once a month. He stuck a *No Longer at This Address* label onto it and tossed it into a stack with several others. The microwave dinged, and Finn hauled himself and his dinner to his recliner. He turned on the local news just in time to catch a report about a missing baby in Oregon. He'd seen the story before; the kid had disappeared at least a month ago, hadn't she? Sitting forward in his chair, he pumped up the volume. Yes, it was the case he remembered: six-month-old Tika Kinsey had vanished from a playpen on the front porch when her mother, a freshman just about to start college, had gone inside to answer the phone. According to the newscaster, there were no leads in the case, but it was the one-month anniversary of the baby's disappearance, so they were running the story again. Aside from the five-second introduction by the newscaster, the footage was exactly the same as he'd seen weeks ago. It was annoying how the news channels played reruns now, too.

He finished his dinner and set the tray on the side table. Cargo nabbed the tray and trotted off with it. After spending a minute and a half on the Tika Kinsey story, the news program moved on to a report about road repairs and then the weather—more above-normal temps to come in the next week.

Finn slid a photo out of the breast pocket on his shirt. Apparently, the Kittitas County Sheriff's Department had succeeded in keeping this story quiet so far, which was actually pretty amazing. Technically, the case was not in his jurisdiction, but he had more experience with dead bodies than anyone in the county, so they called him in. The photo was hard to look at, even for him. The reality had been worse. Before breakfast, the farm wife had found her Labrador retriever chewing on what she thought was a discarded doll from a neighbor's garbage heap. She'd nearly fainted when she took the 'toy' from the dog's mouth.

A tiny corpse, covered in dirt, decayed and brutally mangled. John Doe, once an infant boy, now a miniature mummy: dark, dried skin stretched over a skeleton. Buried for weeks or maybe even months among the wheat stubble.

"Homicide?" Everyone had asked Finn, as if he was a miracle worker who could read mummies.

It was impossible to say if murder was involved. Whoever had buried the naked corpse had done it before the field was harvested; time and heavy equipment had obliterated whatever evidence might have been there. Finn had left the case in the hands of the County Sheriff's department, which would have to get more information from the coroner. Finn had suggested the possibility of a stillbirth to a worker in the country illegally; every year the police across the U.S. ran into a few unclaimed bodies in farm country. That's probably why the discovery had been kept quiet; few people wanted to admit to knowing illegals worked in their community. But babies didn't naturally turn up in farm fields. Or in the family dog's jaws.

A crunch from his own canine drew Finn's attention. Cargo flopped next to the fireplace, with the plastic shreds of the frozen dinner tray at his feet.

"For chrissakes, dog." Finn slid the photo back into his pocket, got up and cleaned up the remnants. He had to play tug-of-war with the mutt over the last piece, ending up with slobber up to his elbows.

"I should let you eat the damn thing." He stuffed the plastic pieces into the trash bin under the kitchen sink. "It would serve you right."

Cargo whined and collapsed onto the rug with a melodramatic sigh.

The television was stuck in commercial break mode. What was this, the fifth ad in a row? He wanted to see the sports scores before he went to the den to paint. He sat back down and raised the chair's footrest. He chose a multi-legged yellow wall-walker from an assortment in the bowl at his elbow and lobbed the toy at the large framed photo on the opposite wall. It smacked Wendy just below her wedding tiara and began the slow crawl on its suction-cup feet down her face. Such a beautiful face. So sweet and unpretentious. Or so he'd thought, up until six weeks ago. Now Wendy was living with her pretty-boy business professor outside of town, and he was stuck here in Podunk, Washington, with *her* dream house, *her* parents, and *her* animals.

His former dearly beloved had bought these sticky toys for the cats, who watched his motions with interest. When the first toy dropped off Wendy's wedding photo, he lobbed another, a green one this time. It glommed onto the bride's perfect little nose and quivered there for a second like a horrendous wart before rolling over onto her upper lip.

An orange furball leapt onto his abdomen. The cat deposited the yellow wall-walker onto his chest. It curled its paws under its body and purred, proud of itself.

He tapped the cat on the head. "So you fetch?" Dark orange stripes across its forehead looked like delicate feline eyebrows. The cat lifted its chin and pressed its head against his palm. He couldn't help but stroke it. The fur behind its ears was so soft Finn could barely feel it against his callused fingertips.

"Nice try," he said. "But you're still going to the pound."

When Brittany saw the passenger seat of the Civic was empty, she screamed and dropped her groceries beside the car. Several people turned around to stare at her, and a kind, fat woman started picking up her groceries up from the pavement.

At first, Brittany had the insane thought that Ivy had crawled off. Leaving the driver's door open, she got down on her hands and knees to peer beneath the car. Only an old plastic bag was moving down there, inching its way across the filthy pavement in the light breeze.

"Are you okay, honey?" the fat woman asked.

Then Brittany saw Jed and Marcus and Madison in their smokers huddle across the parking lot. This was some sort of prank. Stuck-up seniors freak out slut girl. Oh yeah, laugh riot. She stood up and dusted off her hands.

"Yeah, I'm okay. I just ... uh ... saw a big spider run underneath my car."

The woman smiled. "Oh, I hate those, too. But people say they're more scared of us than we are of them."

"Like I believe that." Brittany picked up her groceries and slung them into the front seat before she walked over to the smokers.

"Okay, you fuckheads, what did you do with her?"

They did a good job of acting surprised. "*What* did you call us, Brittany Morgan?" Madison put her hands on her hips just like her mother, the la-dee-da head of the PTA, did when she wanted everyone to know she was outraged.

"You heard me. Where's Ivy?" She looked around, expecting to see the beige car seat with Ivy in it on the ground between the nearby cars.

Jed squinted. "Ivy?"

She peered into the closest cars. "Ivy Rose, my baby." A terrible tightness began in her chest.

Marcus walked over to stand beside her, staring through the window of a RAV4. "We ain't seen no baby, Britt." For some reason, a lot of the preppy kids talked like they'd failed English 101. They thought it made them sound tough or something.

"No shit?" She examined each of their faces. Blank, blank, and blank. Her breath stuck in her chest. Ice water rushed down her spine and raised goosebumps all over her body. "Really, no shit, you don't have her?"

Madison touched Brittany's forearm with her perfectly manicured fuchsia fingernails. "You *lost* your baby?"

"Smooth, girl," Marcus commented. "Real smooth."

Suddenly the scenery got wavy, like air shimmering around hot metal, and a demon inside Brittany's chest clawed to get out. She ran back to her car. *Please God, let me wake up now.* The seat was still empty. No Ivy, no car seat. She tugged on the passenger-side door handle. Still locked. Nothing made sense.

The smokers joined her. She stabbed a finger toward the passenger seat. "I left her right here. She was sleeping in her car seat. Did you see anyone around here?"

They all shook their heads. "I saw you walk into the store," Jed said, "but I didn't see a baby. I didn't even see your car."

"That's because I parked on the other side of the—" She spun on her heel. The van was gone. Had it been there when she came out of the store? She couldn't remember. Choking down the nasty ooze that rose in her throat, she turned back. "Ivy was right *here.* See, I rolled down the windows a crack, and I locked the doors. All the doors. I know I did."

"Omigod. You *left* your baby in the car *all alone?*" Madison's mouth stayed open after she said it.

A brown-skinned woman in an orange sundress heard Madison and brought her shopping cart to a halt. "You left a baby in the car alone?" She stared straight at Brittany.

How could she pretend she hadn't now? Brittany nodded miserably. "And now she's gone." Her heart was pounding in her ears. Oh god, it was true. Ivy was gone. "Someone took my baby!"

The woman pulled a cell phone out of her purse and dialed nine-one-one. Then she made Brittany and the others go back into the store with her, and they talked to the manager and asked everyone in the store if any of them had seen a stranger with Ivy. Several people remembered seeing Brittany—"the girl with the strawberry-blonde ponytail"—but nobody had seen an infant at all. Nope, no baby.

"You left your baby in the car?" everyone kept saying, over and over. "You left a baby all alone in the car?"

Like that was somehow more awful than somebody stealing her daughter.

One hour after Ivy disappears

Chapter 4

Finn's cell phone chimed from the table beside his easy chair. There was a cat in his lap. Crap, he'd fallen asleep again watching the news. The TV, still on mute, displayed a game show. Yawning, Finn flicked the cell phone open. EPD—that would likely be Sergeant Carlisle on the desk this time of evening. He checked his watch. Damn. Officially, he still had ten minutes to go on his shift.

"Detective Finn," he growled.

The cat on his stomach slitted its yellow-green eyes. It looked like it was smiling.

"Get out of those slippers and into your wingtips," Carlisle said. "We need you down at the Food Mart."

"I wouldn't be caught dead in slippers *or* wingtips." Finn groaned. "The Food Mart? You kidding me?"

The small police department had four detectives: two men, two women. Each twenty-four hours was split into four shifts between them, which meant they didn't really work as partners. The shifts overlapped by two hours, which theoretically allowed the detective going off shift to pass information and update the detective coming on about the open cases. Practically speaking, the system meant that most of the time each detective worked solo on his or her own case for however long it took.

The uniforms had a tendency to call the detectives in for every crime in which the perpetrator had not yet confessed. In this economy, there was no overtime pay, just a vague promise of 'comp time' that would probably never happen.

"Some vegan unplug the meat freezer again?" Finn asked. "Can't it wait until morning?"

"This'll wake you up."

Forty minutes after he received the phone call, Finn was in the Food Mart parking lot. The uniforms had taped off the parking spot and kept everyone out of the blue Civic. He walked around the little car now, stopped for a moment to ponder the sticker on the back bumper—*The Dinosaurs Died for Our Sins.* Probably something to do with the school board. There was some silly argument about a resolution to teach all sides of the global warming and evolution debates. Whatever the hell *that* meant.

He studied the scene. A typical grocery store, cars coming and going, shoppers rolling carts up the curbs and through the lot, even now, at eight-thirty in the evening. The breeze was picking up, gusting candy wrappers and plastic bags across the pavement.

An empty soft-drink cup rolled into the taped-off area where Finn had assigned a rookie to collect debris. Scoletti wasn't happy about the job, especially now, when Finn had just told him to scrape up and bag all the chewing gum in the zone. Each wad in a separate bag, he had to remind the kid. Man, he missed having a Crime Scene team on his speed dial.

"Hey, Detective, you want me to get that cup, too?" The rookie's tone was smart-aleck.

"Yep. Bag it. But mark it as from across the lot." Finn ignored Scoletti's scowl and turned back to the youngster in front of him.

The girl, a strawberry blonde with hair falling into her eyes, appeared far too young to be a mother. Brittany Morgan had just turned seventeen, according to her driver's license. "So, Miss Morgan," he said for the second time, "Tell me again why you left your baby?"

"She was asleep. I didn't want to wake her up."

"And where was she when you left her?"

"I already told you, Ivy was in the front seat, the passenger seat," she sobbed. "Why aren't you out *searching* for her?"

"I need a little more information," Finn said mildly. "The baby was lying in the passenger seat in front?"

Brittany shot him a dirty look. "Ivy was in her car seat. What sort of a mother do you think I am?" She waved a hand in the air. "I know she's supposed to be in the back, but have you ever tried to put a baby carrier in the back of a two-door?"

Finn had already examined the interior of the Civic. Crumpled potato-chip bag, two hairclips in the back seat. An empty soda can on the floor behind the passenger seat and a bag of groceries in the driver's seat. There were faint marks on the front passenger seat that might or might not delineate the bottom edges of a baby carrier, and some crusty stripes on the floor mat that might or might not be dried drool or baby barf. No definitive sign that this girl even had an infant.

"Car seat?" he asked now. He turned and stared pointedly at the Civic again. No sign of a car seat.

"They took it! They took it when they took Ivy!"

"They?" Interesting that she used the plural. Just an offhand comment, or did she know more than one person was involved?

"Whoever!" She gestured wildly. "Whoever took Ivy!" She glanced into the car again. "Shit! They took my diaper bag, too!"

"Can you describe the car seat and the diaper bag?" He held his pen poised over the notepad.

She pushed her fingers through her bangs, which immediately fell back into her eyes. He couldn't tell what she was thinking. She looked bewildered. A confused child.

He tried for a more gentle tone. "There are a lot of babies in the area. The car seat and diaper bag could help to identify..." He scanned his notes for the baby's name.

"Ivy!" she yelped. "Ivy Rose Morgan!"

"Ivy," he repeated softly. "What was the brand of the car seat?"

"I can't remember. It was used when I got it." Brittany scrubbed her hands against her cheeks for a minute, her eyes on the concrete sidewalk. "It was this icky color, kind of gray beige."

He wrote down *taupe*. "And the diaper bag?"

"The diaper bag was—well, it wasn't a real diaper bag, it was my old blue backpack, but it had two diapers and a little yellow dress in it, with a duck on the front. And some extra socks, because Ivy's always losing—" At that point her eyes flooded with tears and she made a strangling sound as she clapped a hand over her mouth.

He stared at the lines on his pad for a few seconds, giving her time to pull herself together. "Any other distinguishing marks on the bag—backpack? Any other items of yours inside?" he prompted in a low voice.

She turned back toward him. "I can't remember. I can't think about anything but Ivy. Why are we just *standing* here?" She stared at him, blue eyes pleading. After a second, she dashed over to Scoletti, who was on his hands and knees scraping gum from the pavement with a screwdriver. Grabbing a handful of the rookie's shirt sleeve, she sobbed, "Please, go look for my baby!"

In spite of his determination to stay dispassionate, Finn's heart lurched. When older kids went missing it was bad enough, but infants and toddlers—they were portable and easily disposed of, and they never asked strangers for help. He couldn't get the tiny corpse he'd seen this morning out of his head.

And then there were his missing cases in Chicago—a whole parade of them. Most were resolved as accidental deaths or negligent homicides, which often amounted to the same thing with careless parents. The only cases that ended more or less happily were the ones in which one divorced parent stole the kid from the other; at least those parents had hopes of their kid coming home, even if it was after a court battle. The worst case he'd worked on was the hunt for four-year-old Ashley Kowalski. After a twenty-two-hour search, they'd found her in an old refrigerator in the junk heap her grandparents called a backyard. He'd never forget catching her body as it tumbled out. He still had a scar from where he'd cut the back of his hand on the broken latch. He rubbed it now.

The discovery of Ashley's body had been bad, but it was the autopsy report that had done him in. The girl died an hour before they'd opened the refrigerator door.

He'd lasted two years in Missing Persons before asking for a transfer to Homicide. At least the victims there were already beyond help.

There were no detective divisions here in small-town America. In eighteen months, he'd worked everything from vandalism to hog rustling to armed robbery. Whether this was a homicide or a kidnapping or something else entirely, it was his case.

He walked over to Brittany and pulled the girl gently away from Scoletti. He led her to a bench at the side of the store. "We will look for Ivy, Miss Morgan, but first we need to know a little more. Now, when we arrived, the driver's door was unlocked—"

"Because I was putting the groceries in!"

"And what did you buy?" Sometimes a peripheral question resulted in important details.

"Apples, bean dip, Fritos, oh no—" Her hands flew to her mouth again. "I forgot the Huggies! I need Huggies!"

A dust-streaked tow truck pulled into the parking lot. The driver's window slid down, letting a blast of country rock escape, and the guy's gaze flicked from each uniform to the next. When the driver finally glanced at him, Finn tilted his head toward the Civic, and the driver started maneuvering into place.

"I can't believe I forgot the Huggies," Brittany moaned. A mascara-laden tear rolled down her cheek, leaving a dark trail over freckles on its way to her chin. "That's the whole reason I came." Then she noticed the tow truck driver attaching the hook. Her expression changed to outrage. She jumped up from the bench. "Don't let him take my car!"

One of the other unmarked cars rolled in, and Perry Dawes, the detective Finn most often worked with, got out, accompanied by a middle-aged man who wore blue jeans and a worried expression.

"Daddy!" Brittany threw herself into the man's arms.

Finn listened to the girl's sobs and her father's questions for a few seconds. Satisfied that he'd glean no more clues there, he pulled the sack of groceries from the Civic and placed it on the sidewalk for the girl. Then he pulled Dawes aside. "Did you find the father of the baby?"

Dawes shook his head. "Not yet. Mr. Morgan told me that the baby's father is Charlie Wakefield, age nineteen. Who is in Cheney at Eastern Washington University right now, according to his parents, sharing a dorm suite with three other students. I've got the local PD checking on that. And by the way, the elder Wakefields—I had eyes on both of them—told me there's no proof Charlie is the baby's father."

"Really?" Finn raised an eyebrow. "Wakefield..." The name seemed familiar.

"Yep," Dawes said. "Travis Wakefield—our County Exec. Charlie's his son."

Finn rubbed a hand across his brow. The County Executive wielded a lot of influence, especially in a rural area like this. He and Dawes watched Brittany weep in her father's arms. Her tears were real and plentiful, but Finn had learned long ago that teenagers could be consummate actors. Brittany's father—Noah Morgan—seemed completely lost. His eyes scanned the parking lot as if he could spot the infant out there. Finn made a mental note to get the man alone as soon as possible to quiz him about his daughter and granddaughter.

"Where's Brittany's mother?" he asked Dawes.

"Closing up at Washington Federal Bank. She's assistant manager there. She'll be here any minute now. Dad runs the county recycling center outside of town."

"So all grandparents are accounted for?"

"Looks that way." Dawes raised a hand to cover a yawn, then continued, "I've never had a missing baby. Had kids that wandered off before, had two snatched by the non-custodial parents, but they could all walk and talk. Kids and babies," he grumbled. "They should've assigned Larson and Melendez to this."

"It happened before seven, so technically, it's ours. But don't worry; everyone will get pulled in on this until we know what's going on."

"The women are good for the domestics, but not tough enough with real scumbags. They may be dicks, but they got no balls." Dawes chuckled at his own joke.

Finn frowned. Surely the Evansburg PD required all their cops to take the same gender-sensitivity training he'd had to sit through in Chicago.

"Remember how Larson and Melendez were with the Animal Rights Union?" Dawes continued. "They'd have let those ARU nuts off with a misdemeanor charge. But we nailed 'em."

The way Finn remembered it, Dawes didn't start off with the intention of 'nailing' the radical students who'd freed all the rats and rabbits at the college laboratory. Instead, Dawes had dismissed the event as a hilarious student stunt. He and Dawes were about the same age, early forties, but Dawes, having spent his years on rural police forces in Washington, had less experience with major crimes than Finn. On the other hand, he had a lot more experience in dealing with the local population.

"Now we're going to nail this, right?" Dawes broke off to answer his chirping cell phone, said "Got it, thanks," and snapped the cell shut again. "Shit. Charlie Wakefield's cell phone just goes to voicemail. His roommates said they think he's at the library, but so far the university police haven't confirmed that. They say they'll keep looking."

"We need to ping Charlie Wakefield's cell phone to verify the whereabouts, locate his vehicle ASAP, and we need to verify all the grandparents' alibis," Finn stressed.

Dawes grimaced. "The Wakefields won't like that."

"So what?" Finn challenged him.

Dawes squirmed under his glare for a moment before he extracted his notepad and pen from his shirt pocket. "Okay. I'll follow up on Charlie Wakefield and let you know when we locate him. And I'll ask his parents if anyone outside the family can vouch for their whereabouts."

Finn nodded. "I'll check out the Morgans." A car raced into the parking lot. A woman wearing a blouse and skirt jumped out of it, and ran over to Brittany and her father. That had to be Mrs. Morgan.

Dawes tapped his pen on his pad. "How 'bout the Morgan girl's friends? Could be a prank."

"Are kids that cruel?"

Dawes shrugged.

Finn pointed to the *Dinosaurs* bumper sticker as the tow truck pulled the Civic out of the parking spot. "What's up with this debate on the school board? Are the two sides hot enough to come to blows?"

"So far it's only been a lot of yelling. I don't understand why it's a big deal if they teach intelligent design *and* evolution." He shrugged. "Isn't that what science is supposed to be about? Keeping an open mind?" Dawes tried to slide his pen into his shirt pocket and missed, squinted and made it on the second try. Then he looked up again at Finn. "I don't even understand that sticker. Do you?

It was Finn's turn to shrug. He wasn't about to try to make sense of trading T-rex for absolution.

Dawes watched the tow truck pull the Civic across the parking lot. "Nobody would steal a baby just because of a bumper sticker, would they?"

"People the world over *kill* for their beliefs." Finn glanced at his watch. This was going to be one long night. "I'll talk to Mrs. Morgan, then I'll send a uniform over to babysit the Morgans while I fill in Melendez and Larson. Can you get all available uniforms out searching dumpsters?"

"Dumpsters?" After a second, Dawes's brain caught up, and he made a face. "Oh, jeez. Ya think?"

Finn rubbed his brow. "I've seen it before. We need to do three zones to begin with. Here, the girl's school, the family home. Spiral out from all three starting points."

Dawes ran his fingers through his thinning blond hair, his eyebrows kinked in a frown. "We've never had one of *those* cases in Evansburg."

"Keep an eye out for a baby's car seat, too, and an old blue backpack used as a diaper bag, a baby dress with a duck on it, and any other baby stuff. Have the uniforms make a list of the checked locations to compare against the garbage company's tomorrow; we don't want to miss any."

Dawes groaned. "Tomorrow's garbage day."

"Good. So everyone's putting their bins out tonight. Check regular family cans, too," Finn added.

"No way we can cover the whole town by morning."

"Then get trash pickup called off until this is resolved," Finn told him. His head was starting to throb. Delaying trash pickup meant the whole town was going to find out about this.

"Garbage duty—the guys are gonna love this." Dawes rubbed his bony hands together and strode toward the trio of patrol cars clustered in front of the store.

A KEBR TV News van careened into the parking lot, screeched to a halt right at the yellow tape. Two female reporters dashed in his direction, microphones in hand. "Allyson Lee!" the one in the lead yelled. "Detective Finn!" He had been ambushed by Lee before. The cameraman behind her was already rolling.

"Rebecca Ramey!" the girl trotting behind Lee blurted, waving, as if he might pick her because of an alliterative name. Another camera operator, a girl this time, followed on her heels.

Damn. Most towns the size of Evansburg had no television news coverage, but the local college offered a degree in broadcast journalism, and the students used the community access channel to do nonstop coverage. Eager journalism students constantly trolled the streets for stories, and they all came from the sound bite generation. Finn straightened his shoulders and tugged the hem of his jacket to smooth out the rumpled fabric.

A blur of red-blonde hair streaked past him.

"Help me!" Brittany yelled at the reporter. "Tell everyone to look for my baby right now!"

Finn watched the girl's manic behavior. She clung to the reporter's arm as if Lee were her best friend. Had she been waiting for a news crew? Could this be a media-hound version of Munchausen's? Lee tucked Brittany in close beside her, wiped the teenager's face with a tissue and pushed the hair out of the girl's eyes, and then began to question her under the spotlight of the camera. Brittany's parents watched from the sidelines.

Rebecca Ramey, resigned to second place, shrugged at her cameraman and gestured him toward the cluster of onlookers.

Finn's turn would come soon enough. He pulled the horrible photo out of his pocket and looked at it again. He had a bad feeling about why Brittany Morgan had forgotten the diapers. He hoped he was mistaken. He'd really like to be proven wrong this time. But he feared that Ivy Rose Morgan had already met the same fate as Baby John Doe.

Chapter 5

Tickle, Neema signed. Gumu chased her, bowled her over in the sagging middle of the web and, cackling like a mad scientist, continued his gallop to the highest corner. The rope webbing creaked ominously as the two gorillas frolicked in the heavy net stretched between steel posts. The silhouettes of the two apes against the tangerine sunset made a strange and beautiful tableau. Someday, Grace McKenna vowed, she would watch gorillas in their natural environment, nestled amid lush African vegetation, backlit by an African sun.

Josh LaDyne dug the sharp point of the shovel he carried into the soil beside Grace's foot. Sweat streaked his copper-colored face. "That net's not going to hold 'em much longer."

"Don't I know it. Gumu weighs almost twenty pounds more than he did when we moved in." Grace pushed her hair up off her sweaty neck. Even at sundown in early September, it had to be eighty-five degrees out.

Josh watched the gorillas tumble across the webbing. "Neema still doesn't want to sleep in the barn with Gumu? They're still just playmates?"

"Apparently." Grace sighed. "As best I can figure it out, Neema seems to regard Gumu as her brother. She says she wants a baby, but I don't know if she really understands how to go about it. I've shown her films of mating and giving birth."

"Among gorillas?"

She shrugged. "Chimpanzees. That was the closest I could find."

"In the wild, other gorillas would show her how babies get made, right? So you really should demonstrate for her." He paused, his brown eyes solemn. "As a fellow scientist, I'd be willing to help."

She feigned a right hook to his jaw. Laughing, he took a step back to avoid her fist. "Just a suggestion, Dr. McKenna," he said. "Or maybe I should have a man-to-man talk with Gumu."

"Since he's learned only four signs so far, that might be difficult." Gumu had been orphaned in Africa, and had been kept in a cage from babyhood until he grew into the huge hulk he was destined to be. He had joined them a year ago, a traumatized ten-year-old ape who was only now learning to trust a few humans.

Josh ticked Gumu's signs off on his fingers. "*Give. Banana. Gumu. Neema.* With a little rearranging, we could work with that." He thrust out his arms and beat his chest like a male gorilla.

Grace laughed. "Quit that. You're confusing them."

Inside the fenced enclosure, the gorillas had stopped their gymnastics to stare at them. *Joke*, Grace signed. Neema knew the sign and she certainly had her own childlike sense of humor, but there was no way to be sure if a gorilla understood the true meaning of the word.

Banana, Gumu signed back.

"See, what did I tell you?" Josh said. "I bet male gorillas think about their bananas even more often than male *Homo sapiens*."

"Impossible." Grace counted herself lucky that Josh had been willing to stay with the project after they'd been shuffled off to Evansburg. He was twelve years her junior, a grad student working on his dissertation; he could have chosen to finish in Seattle instead of coming to the sticks with her. She enjoyed his company, but sometimes his teasing banter made her uneasy. She was in charge of the gorilla sign language project, he was her protégé. But it wasn't a normal academic situation by any stretch of imagination. They basically functioned as gorilla parents to Gumu and Neema. Their relationship was often misconstrued by observers, especially because Josh was a very attractive specimen of African American manhood. To get off the subject of sex, she asked, "How's the new enclosure coming?"

"I dug the last post-hole this morning, so it's ready whenever the fencing crew gets here." He ran dirt-smudged fingers through his hair, leaving a trail of red dust through his tight black curls. "Thanks for all your help, by the way."

What a waste of talent, to have a Ph.D. candidate digging holes. She had to get more help around the place, more assistants to observe and teach the gorillas. She longed for the good old days, when she had to turn volunteers away. The days when ape sign language was totally new and astounding, before the wackos crawled out from under their rocks and politicians somehow gained control over university funding.

"Sorry," she groaned. "Neema wouldn't quit begging to go for a ride, so I took the van to the grocery store. I thought I'd never get it into reverse to get out of the parking lot. Then halfway home it wouldn't go into third, so I had to crawl back in second gear."

"You need to get the transmission fixed."

"Gee, ya think?" she retorted bitterly. "It's on the list. After building the fence and heating the barn and finding more help."

The project definitely needed at least one more pair of hands, preferably a volunteer pair fluent in American Sign Language. She was spending all her time in animal care and property upkeep instead of writing research papers; that would not earn her any credit with the grant givers. Did she dare approach the biology or psych or special ed departments at the local college for volunteers? Was there a deaf students association?

No, talking to any of those groups would alert the whole community to their presence. From what she'd observed of the residents so far, it seemed a pretty conservative place. Signing gorillas might be more than the locals could take. The project had been very public in Seattle and they'd paid the price.

Neema still mourned for silverback Spencer, Gumu's predecessor. As did Grace.

It would be better to lure another grad student for a semester. Better yet, two grads for two semesters. She could probably find another single-wide at a bargain price if only she could get a little more grant money.

She sighed. Right. Additional funds were unlikely. The downturn in the economy couldn't have come at a worse time. The annual check from the grant foundation was due any day now and it couldn't arrive too soon; she was dipping into her meager savings to pay for supplies and groceries. The van would have to stay parked for awhile.

She glanced around at the half-finished compound. "I'll help move rocks tomorrow, Josh."

"All moved." He yawned. "I found a baby rattler underneath one of 'em, too."

"Yikes. I'm glad Neema didn't see that. Did I tell you that she called me a snake this morning?"

"At least three times."

"Sorry." Surely he was exaggerating.

"I forgive you; it *was* very creative of her. I'll watch for that insult from here on; 'snake' will be a nice change from 'poop head'."

Both the gorillas now had their long black fingers woven into the wire mesh of the fence, their liquid red-brown eyes fixed on Grace and Josh. The sight of those intelligent eyes jailed behind wire mesh always gave Grace a pang of guilt. It's no different than using a playpen to corral toddlers, she told herself. These two youngsters were plenty capable of mischief.

Neema and Gumu studied humans just as intensely as Josh and Grace studied them. Like human children, gorillas learned by watching. They could open cabinets and refrigerators, punch computer keys, wield tools with much greater strength than humans. They understood a vast amount of human dialogue, whether or not they'd learned the signs to show it. Right now the gorillas were clearly eavesdropping, because

Neema, her eyes round with anxiety, pulled her fingers from the mesh to sign *Where snake?*

No snake here, Grace signed.

Snake make baby cry, Neema signed back.

Grace frowned. Was Neema so often referring to babies now because she wanted a baby? Her favorite film was a *National Geographic* special featuring a gorilla family of five adults and three infants. Neema sometimes invented an imaginary baby or pretended her doll was a baby. Or referred to another animal as a baby. Or even to herself.

You baby? Grace flicked an index finger toward Neema's chest.

Neema huffed and signed *here fine gorilla.*

Josh laughed. "No problem with self-esteem in that cage."

Neema fine gorilla, Grace agreed. *Grace fine woman, not snake.*

Neema stared at her for a second, then signed *Josh snake. Gumu snake.* She hooted at her own jest and then leapt onto Gumu's back. The two gorillas chased each other across the netting again.

"Speaking of snakes," Josh said, *"I'm* fine. Thanks for your concern."

Grace jerked her thoughts back to him. "Oh god, I'm sorry. Are you okay?"

"Yep. I'm still three-dimensional. I can't say the same for the rattler. But I feel like a field hand. Next you'll have me pickin' cotton bolls."

"Get real. There's no cotton in the northwest. You'll have to stick with moving rocks."

The sun had set as they talked. Dusk triggered the security lights, which glowed dimly, outlining the perimeters of the three trailers set into a U-shaped formation—hers, Josh's, and the study trailer, where they worked with the gorillas and where Neema usually slept. The old horse barn with its attached fenced enclosure loomed in the forth corner, the gorillas dark shadows in the webbing.

"Let them play," Josh said, reading her thoughts. "I'll put them to bed in an hour or so and lock up."

"Have you had dinner, Josh? I have enchiladas we could share. It's the least I can do for all your work today."

"Add a beer and I'll forgive you. But, none of that lite crap, you hear?"

"Amber ale, iced mug, slice of lime?"

"Sublime." He jerked the shovel out of the dirt. "Hey, I rhyme."

"I swear, you're twenty-six, going on twelve."

"And you're thirty-eight, headed for sixty." His hand landed on her shoulder. "Do us both a favor; relax the frown lines and lighten up for awhile."

Headed for *sixty*? That hurt. Somebody had to worry about all the picky little details like bills and future funding, didn't they? Still, *sixty*? Did she really seem like an old lady to him? She swallowed painfully and gestured toward her personal trailer. "I'll try, Josh. Ditch the shovel and wash your face and come on in. We can discuss tomorrow's lesson plan for Neema and Gumu."

He shouldered the shovel. "What the hell is a cotton boll, anyway?"

Fifteen minutes later, Grace turned on the television in her living area as she poured their beers. She shoved the enchiladas into the microwave and settled at the counter on a kitchen bar stool next to Josh. On the television screen, police cars flooded the Food Mart parking lot. Grace turned up the sound as a female reporter stuck a microphone in front of a wild-eyed girl with a strawberry blonde ponytail.

"My baby! Someone kidnapped my baby out of my car!" the girl sobbed.

Grace grimaced. "That poor kid. She doesn't look old enough to even have a baby, let alone lose one." Having grown up in southern California, Grace was accustomed to hearing about all sorts of horrific crime, but babynapping seemed extreme for small-town Evansburg, Washington. Her eyes widened when the reporter estimated the time of the kidnapping.

Josh noticed. "You know that girl?"

Grace shook her head. "No. But Neema and I were parked in that same area just a few minutes earlier. Thank god we were gone before this happened."

Brittany looked like a lunatic on the ten o'clock news, with hair sticking out everywhere and her face blotchy with tears. But wouldn't any mother whose baby had just vanished look a little psycho?

Then, after watching her interview in the grocery store parking lot, Brittany stared at the image of their neighbor, nosey Mrs. Kay, talking to a reporter in their own neighborhood.

"Well, I don't like to speak ill of the poor girl. Brittany's only a child herself. But once I walked into the house and the baby was lying on the carpet in the living room. Anything could have happened." Mrs. Kay pursed her lips like she was proud of all those old-lady cracks around her mouth.

Brittany threw her pillow at her tiny bedroom television set. "You damned old crone! Ivy was sound asleep. It's not like she can fall off the floor!" And she'd been just on the other side of the wall, getting a soda. This was just like the car thing. It was unbelievable how everyone kept harping on that. Some maniac had kidnapped Ivy and people were talking about *her* like she was a criminal.

Ivy's photo and statistics filled the TV screen. At least that was something; everyone would be watching for her baby. Her friends already knew; Cynda and Joy and Karleen had called to tell her the cops had visited them. All her friends had promised to get the word out about Ivy's kidnapping on Twitter, too.

She muted the sound on the television and walked to the window. So dark. She should be out there, searching for Ivy. But where? How could you know where to start looking? In her mind, she could hear a faint wailing. Was Ivy crying in hunger? Was she all alone in the dark? Brittany's stomach clenched again as horrible images raced through her head, but she'd already thrown up everything, there wasn't anything left down there but acid. Her breasts were another story. They hurt, so full that she should go use the pump but that would mean that she believed Ivy wasn't going to be home any time soon.

She couldn't think of anyone who hated her so much they'd take Ivy. Nobody could hate a little baby, could they? Okay, maybe Charlie was a little cold right now, but that was because he was away at school. He hadn't even seen Ivy yet, and guys weren't that much into babies anyway. No matter what Joy said, Charlie didn't hate her and he didn't hate Ivy. Nobody hated their own flesh and blood.

"Such a beautiful baby," people said, every time they saw Ivy. The kidnapper had to be some deranged woman who was walking by and saw this beautiful baby and wanted Ivy for her own. Probably one of those poor women who couldn't make their own babies. Like all the other pregnant girls, Brittany had gotten the lecture about the "selfless gift of adoption" from the school nurse. How could any mother do that? Her daughter could never be anyone else's daughter.

Brittany pressed her hand to the window pane. The glass was so warm that her fingers didn't even leave an impression. Like she really didn't exist. Maybe this wasn't really happening. Maybe Joy's brother Clay had slipped her some acid like he had at Joy's party a couple years ago. Then she'd seen butterflies everywhere. Everyone still laughed about it. She closed her eyes; opened them again. No butterflies. And her mind seemed to be working fine, because now she remembered that Clay had been sent off to juvie jail a year ago for peddling X at parties.

There was a soft knock at her bedroom door. The door opened before she could ask who it was, and Detective Finn walked in. Her dad stopped in the doorway behind him.

Finn's clothes were wrinkled and his graying brown hair was messed up. He made it worse by running his fingers through it. "Okay if I look around your room a little?"

He walked around the changing table and pulled open the louvered closet doors. He studied the folded stacks of baby clothes in the cubbies and glanced back at her, probably surprised that she was so neat with Ivy's clothes. Hers were another story—she'd tossed a pair of stretched out jeans, a stained T-shirt, and yesterday's bra and panties in the far corner. Her peasant blouse had slipped off the hanger again and now lay on top of her running shoes.

The police officer downstairs had taken photos of the whole house and told Brittany not to move anything in her room, like *she* was a criminal. She found the remote on her bed and clicked off the television. Did Detective Finn have the right to paw through her underwear and criticize how she didn't hang up her clothes?

"What if I said it wasn't okay?" she asked.

"Britt." Her father filled the doorway like he was blocking her escape to the hallway.

Finn shut the closet doors and turned to smile at her. "It's just routine; we always do this. Your parents already gave us permission." He stared at her sewing machine in the corner, closed up in its cover. Next, he studied the Diaper Genie for a minute as if trying to figure out what it was. Wrinkling his nose, he moved on to her bulletin board, where he looked over her colored pencil sketches of baby dresses and rompers. "What are these?"

"Designs by Brittany." She was especially proud of the yellow and black numbers—they made the girl babies look like butterflies and the boys like sweet bumblebees. "I design 'em and sew 'em. I design matching outfits for us moms, too."

"You're good," Finn said.

Like a police detective would know anything about fashion. But it was nice to hear anyway. "I'm going to go to design school after I graduate." She felt her father's glare land on her when she said that, so she added, "At night, probably, because I'll be working during the day."

"I see." The detective focused on her desk and then her laptop. "We'll have to take your computer." He walked toward it.

"What?!" She could understand the car because of fingerprints and all that, but why take her computer? "I need it to tell everyone about Ivy. I need it to print flyers."

"Looks like you already did that." Finn tapped a finger on top of the stack on her desk. "How'd you do it so quickly?"

She barely kept herself from saying *duh*. It had been *hours*. "It only takes a minute—just paste in the picture and type."

"I see." He snapped her laptop closed and jerked the cord out of the surge protector. "We'll need it just for a little while. It's all routine. We'll need your cell phone, too."

"I don't have one." Turning, she frowned at her father. She'd had one for six months, but he refused to replace it when it disappeared.

"No cell phone?" Finn asked. "Droid? Blackberry? I-Pad?"

She rolled her eyes at him. "I wish. I can't even text, if you can believe *that*. This isn't one of those rich houses, in case you haven't noticed. The computer's all I've got; I really need it for school." Not to mention it was her only lifeline to keep up with what was going on. "Why isn't everyone out looking for Ivy? Why are you treating *me* like I'm a criminal? Why do you need *my* computer?"

"We're all working to find Ivy." Finn stopped coiling the computer cord long enough to meet her eyes. "Brittany, someone might have been spying on you through the computer."

No way. "I hardly ever use the camera thing."

"You don't have to," he said.

Now there was a creepy thought. She'd heard about moles and spyware that could record your keystrokes and find your passwords and credit card numbers. Could someone out there read all her email?

"It might help us get Ivy back, Brittany. You want us to check, don't you?"

He made it sound like she was being selfish or something. Her cheeks were hot. "Yeah," she said. "Check."

Downstairs, the doorbell rang. A minute later, footsteps climbed the stairs. Could it be Charlie? Or maybe Joy? She could really use a friend right now.

"I know it's late, but I've asked someone to come along, someone I think you'd like to talk to." Finn gave her another smile.

And then in walked her mother with the very last person on earth she needed to see right then—Micaela d'Allessandro. Wearing a cop uniform, no less. Brittany stared at the tall black-haired girl and clutched Ivy's plush pig more tightly to her boobs, which were starting to feel like petrified wood and were probably already leaking through the pads.

"Brittany! You poor thing." Micaela plopped down on the twin bed next to her, throwing an arm around her like they were best friends.

"Is this her?" Micaela picked up the photo of Ivy that Brittany had taken off the wall. "You were lucky to have such a sweet baby."

She made it sound like her baby was in the past. "I *am* lucky. Ivy *is* sweet," Brittany hissed.

Finn squirmed like his jockeys were too tight. "I understand you two went to school together," he said.

Like that meant they had to be friends? Brittany dropped her gaze to the floor. Had Micaela told him that they were exact opposites? Micaela d'Allessandro had been a big star on the soccer team when she was a senior and Brittany was a sophomore who practically flunked out of phys ed. Worse, Micaela was the originator of Virtue Inc., the holier-than-thou club where everyone promised to abstain from sex until they got married. Virgins on Ice, everyone else called it. Brittany checked Micaela's left hand—yeah, that stupid silver promise ring was still there.

While Micaela ran around being Miss Perfect Virgin, Brittany's growing belly proved that she was headed for the blistering tropics below instead of the cool fluff of heaven. Mrs. Taylor, who ran the program for unwed mothers, insisted on calling the program for pregnant girls by the ridiculous name of Sister-Mothers Trust, which Brittany and her friends quickly changed to Sluts on Toast before anyone else could come up with something more awful.

And now here they sat, Slut on Toast next to Virgin on Ice. As opposite as hot fudge on ice cream. Ivy'd be the cherry on top. Brittany raised her hand and bit down on her knuckle. She'd bite off her finger before she'd cry in front of Micaela d'Allessandro.

"I'm here for you, Britt." Micaela gave her a one-armed squeeze. "Whatever you want to tell me."

Brittany shrugged off the arm around her shoulders and slid away. "How'd you get to be a cop so fast?"

Micaela stiffened. "I'm a police tech right now. I work at the station and answer phones and log in evidence and do research. Next year, after I finish my associate degree, I'll go to the academy."

"So I don't have to talk to you." Brittany looked at Finn when she said it, but his eyes were elsewhere. He was still studying everything, pacing in the small space. It was a teensy bedroom with all her and Ivy's furniture and there were way too many people in it right now.

"Britt," her father hissed again from the doorway. "We need their help, don't we?" He held a piece of paper in his hand. A search warrant? On television, that was always the key to the kingdom. But there wasn't anything to find here; this wasn't the house they should be searching. Another house out there somewhere had her beautiful baby girl in it.

Finn stopped in front of the bassinet next to her bed. "The baby slept here?"

She could tell what he was thinking, that the white wicker basket was a shoebox, that maybe she didn't plan on her daughter ever getting to be a big girl. She lifted her chin. "Ivy's only two months old; it's not like she needs a lot of space. My friend Jenn is giving me her crib in a few months when she gets a regular bed for her little boy."

Micaela scooted close again. "What happened with Ivy, Britt? Was Charlie involved?"

Brittany rolled her eyes. "Of course Charlie was not *involved*." Shit, that sounded lame. "He wants to be, of course, but he's at college," she said. Who the hell did Micaela—Miki—think she was, snooping into her personal life? "Why would you think Charlie had anything to do with this? God!"

Micaela pursed her lips. "You shouldn't—"

"—take the Lord's name in vain," Brittany said in perfect unison with her. Micaela might wear a uniform now, but she was obviously the same God-is-Great-and-So-Am-I bitch she'd been in high school.

They locked eyes with each other. Over by the closet, Detective Finn nervously cleared his throat. Micaela shot a glance his way, and then she twitched and forced a fake smile onto her face. She stretched out a hand like she was thinking about placing it on Brittany's thigh, but left it hovering a few inches above as she said in a sickly sweet voice, "Have any of your little Sister-Mother friends ever talked about wanting to hurt their babies?"

"I'm not a rat." It just came out.

She didn't mean that they'd *done* anything. It was just that they'd made a pact to keep their bitching inside their group. *What happens in Sluts stays in Sluts.* Even Mrs. Taylor said that—except for the sluts part—because, like she said, all young moms need to be able to talk openly in the SMT class. Being discrete, Mrs. Taylor called it. Bottom line, it meant you didn't rat on the other girls. But judging by the way both Micaela and Detective Finn perked up like they smelled something good to eat, Brittany knew it was probably the worst thing she could have said right then.

Chapter 6

"Out." Finn gestured at the yard.

The orange cat—Lok?—stood halfway in, halfway out the door, regarding the grass and trees uncertainly. His braver twin, Kee, sat on the porch a few feet away, switching his striped tail.

"You're always begging to go out," Finn told the cat, giving his fuzzy backside a nudge with the side of his shoe. "So go."

He'd been too busy to scoop the litter box poop for a couple of days. He'd stumbled home at three in the morning, after making sure all relevant information about Ivy's disappearance was entered into the Washington State Patrol system and the National Crime Information Center database. When he pushed open the front door, he discovered that the damn tabbies had used the rug in the foyer for their bathroom. After he tossed the whole thing out and put new litter in their toilet box, he collapsed on his bed. The cats insisted on sleeping next to him, pinning his legs in place like small superheated sandbags. Every time he turned over, they'd complain and jump off. Then they would slowly sneak back, all the while purring loudly for some inexplicable reason. He'd tried locking them out of the bedroom, but then they scratched on the door and yowled all night.

Cargo slept on the rug next to the bed, snoring, but somehow managing to wake up and lick Finn's hand every time he let a finger droop over the mattress edge. Now the giant mutt was doing his usual patrol of the yard, smelling every overgrown inch and watering the irises and roses and the half-finished fence with his own brand of liquid fertilizer.

With all the animal interaction, he hadn't gotten more than three hours of sleep. It was a damn good thing Wendy never bought that parrot she'd wanted, or he'd have to listen to a mouthy bird, too. As he locked the deadbolt, he wondered if she had a bird these days. Probably not. He'd checked out her lover; business professor Gordon Black didn't look the parrot type. Maybe she didn't want a menagerie anymore; maybe the right man was enough for her now.

When he let the screen door slam, the cats rocketed into the bushes as if he'd fired a shot at them. Then they turned and regarded him with wary green eyes. "Oh, for godssake, you'll be fine," he grumbled. "Go kill some mice. Eat a bird. Shit outside for a change."

His cell phone buzzed, and he pulled it out of his pocket. He half expected the FBI, but the readout said *Scott Mankin*. His soon-to-be-ex-father-in-law. He didn't want to talk to Scott; they never had more than two words to say to each other now. But if he didn't answer, the dang thing would ring again in ten minutes.

"I'm getting into the car, Scott," he said into the phone.

"It's Dolores, dear. How are you? You're working on that Morgan baby case? You must be exhausted."

At least his mother-in-law had given him an exit line. "Yeah, Dolores, I'm hanging in there, but not getting much sleep. I'm leaving the house now."

"You know what you need?"

A transfer back to Chicago? A good lay? Some peace and quiet so he could finish his painting?

"A home-cooked meal. We haven't seen you in weeks. Why don't you come over tonight? We're having lasagna."

Lasagna sounded good. Having to sit at a table with his in-laws didn't. Soon to be ex-in-laws. "Thanks for the offer, Dolores. But I have no idea when I'll be able to get away."

"Your father says he and your mother are worried about you."

Startled, he said, "My father?"

"We email, dear, remember?"

After retiring from managing a golf course, his father had developed a passion for building miniature landscapes. He volunteered at several museums, building dioramas, and was transforming his basement into a wonderland of hills and valleys and small villages through which a miniature train ran at his command. Finn was still not used to this newfound enthusiasm for all things tiny. But now he remembered that Dolores had instantly hit it off with Michael Finn when they'd come to Chicago for the wedding. Dolores built elaborate dollhouses. She and his father no doubt compared scales and plans and materials over the internet.

"Oh yeah," he finally mumbled. "Tell him I'm fine and I'll call when I can. I really don't have time for anything right now except this case."

"Just come when you can, then, Matt. I can always warm some up for you."

"We'll see. Gotta go now."

"God bless."

"Right. Thanks." He stuck the phone into his pocket and opened the car door. Cargo nearly knocked him over as the big mutt lunged, getting his front feet and head into the driver's seat before Finn could grab his collar.

"No, no, and hell no!" He hauled back on the collar. The dog yelped. His front legs scrabbled against the seat. How could a dog weigh so darn much? A massive paw landed on the driver's wheel and a loud bleat startled them both. Cargo shot backwards into Finn, fell onto the ground and then galloped back to the front porch.

"For godssake, dog." Finn flicked dirt clods from the seat and then folded himself into the car. Sweat already slimed his back under his belt holster; he dreaded putting on his linen jacket in this heat.

He arrived bleary-eyed and rumpled at George Vancouver High School. As he extracted himself from the seat, he noticed that his khaki trousers were covered with black and orange hairs. He brushed his fingers over them. They seemed to be glued to the fabric. *Damn it.* He rummaged through the first aid kit in the trunk until he found some adhesive tape. He wound it around his hand, and standing with one foot on the back bumper of the car, managed to peel some of the fur from his pant legs. How much was stuck to the seat of his trousers? Did he look like a walking furball from behind?

"Detective Finn!"

He straightened, glad the woman hadn't caught him patting his own butt. She was short and plump, with curly blond hair, dressed in beige slacks, sandals, and a short-sleeved plaid shirt.

She smiled. "I saw you on the news last night."

He hated this aspect of small town America, the way everyone knew who everyone else was. If the department ever needed undercover work, they'd have to borrow a detective from another county.

She held out a hand. "I'm Daisy Taylor, the local head of the Sister-Mothers Trust program."

He suppressed a smile as he peeled the tape from his hand and turned to toss the wad into the trunk. 'Sluts on Toast' was what Brittany had called the group. He pulled on his jacket to cover his gun.

The woman walked him toward the building. "Three girls are absent this morning, including Brittany. The other two are seniors who somehow got the impression that they don't need to attend this year. I'm going to have to speak to them. Of course, I didn't really expect Brittany today." She shook her head. "This is all so awful. I can't believe this is happening in Evansburg. I hope the girls and I can help in some way. We want to do anything we can."

"I'll need the names of the missing girls." He'd get the women detectives to locate and interview them.

"Odds are that they're at the outlet mall in Larch Creek; it has a McDonald's." She stopped and turned toward him. "I know this probably isn't my place, but I was sorry to hear about your wife." She put a hand on his forearm. "That just wasn't right."

Did everyone in this burg know his life story?

She blushed. "Sorry, I probably shouldn't have said that. But my brother works out at the college in the business school, and you know, people talk."

Obviously, the whole town talked. Finn cleared his throat uncertainly.

"My sister's newly single, too."

He continued to stare at her. Was she actually trying to set him up on a date?

"Well." She sniffed and then led him down a hallway past a glass case filled with two rows of photos. He stopped. On the top, under the label *Graduating This Year*, were pictures of four smiling teenage girls with babies in their arms. Names were typed and pinned neatly under each photo.

In the lower row, under *Graduating Next Year*, was Brittany Morgan's photo. Brittany wore a yellow blouse and a green headband. Infant Ivy Rose laughed at the camera, her mouth open and her eyes shiny. The baby had a yellow and green ribbon wrapped around her head, with a big bow over her left ear, like she was someone's special present. There could be little doubt that she was Brittany's daughter—same ivory skin, same strawberry-blond hair, same bow-shaped lips.

"Are there other Slu—Sister-Mother programs in the area?" he asked the teacher.

"We're the only one in this county. Two of my girls come from more than thirty miles away. SMT is a nationwide program, though—we get funding for supplies and all our teaching materials from the federal education center in Texas. And we encourage the girls all over the country to communicate through our internet site, YoMama."

"YoMama?"

She smiled. "I know, it sounds silly; but it's catchy, right? We have all sorts of educational materials posted there, and the discussions are monitored to make sure nothing dangerous or illegal is going on. Only girls in the program can join the online group."

"We'll need access, too."

She eyed him doubtfully.

"We need to make sure there's not a predator trolling the site," he told her. "The girls will never know we had access, and we'll be off as soon as this case is resolved."

She nodded. "I guess I can have you invited to join; give me your email address before you leave. Can you come up with a user name that sounds like a teenage girl?"

He blinked at her, taken by surprise.

She fluttered a hand at him. "Never mind, I'll send you a couple of suggestions. Please don't identify yourself online in any way. These girls need access to a site where they can feel safe; the whole idea is to build a support group of teen moms so they don't feel isolated."

It was a little disturbing, imagining all those young girls around the United States talking about sex and stretch marks and breast-feeding.

And then he stood before six of them. One girl's belly was so huge, it looked as if she might deliver by lunchtime. Two bounced infants on their laps. He'd read about a pact among teenagers back east to get pregnant at the same time, and he wondered if such planning had been in effect here. But no, it was more likely that a *lack* of planning was responsible for this particular population surge. Just what the world needed, more clueless parents raising kids. He hoped birth control information was part of the Sluts on Toast curriculum. *Sister-Mothers Trust*, he reminded himself.

One blonde girl clutched a dark-skinned baby to her chest. Unlike Brittany Morgan, who had a sprinkle of freckles across her nose and cheeks, this girl had freckles on her arms and neck as well. The spots didn't cover her whole body, though; he caught a glimpse of the smooth curve of an ivory breast under the infant's rounded cheek. The girl noticed his gaze and pursed her lips into a sly smirk.

The teacher's hand landed on his arm, and he realized she had just introduced him. He quickly jerked his gaze to a neutral spot above the girls' heads and cleared his throat, praying that his face was not as red as it felt.

"As you know," he said, "Brittany Morgan's baby, Ivy Rose, is missing, and the police need your help to find her."

Suspicious glances ricocheted among the girls. Maybe he should have said "we" instead of the "the police..."?

"I know that officers visited a few of you last night. This morning I'm going to ask each of you a few questions. It shouldn't take long. Brittany's not in trouble. Nobody here is in trouble." In his mind, he added the word *yet*. "We need to get a picture of what Brittany and Ivy did yesterday and what was going on in their lives. Any detail you can think of might help."

Daisy Taylor loaned him her class list, and he took the students in alphabetic order into the supply closet where the teacher had set two folding chairs facing each other. The room was claustrophobic, walled on two sides by shelves of erasable markers and paper towels and disposable diapers, a door at each end. He closed the one that led to the classroom and checked the other one—it opened onto a hallway, empty right now. He left that door open a crack for ventilation.

He sat down with the first girl, the hugely pregnant one. Mandy. Their knees nearly touched in the small space. Damn. For his own protection, he should probably have an adult female present or tape these sessions. Mandy clutched her belly with both hands and acted as if this was the last place she wanted to be. If he asked a teacher or set up a camera, the girls would be less likely to talk. He'd have to take the risk.

The diapers gave off a powdery smell, or was that the wipes? What he knew about babies could be etched on the head of a pin. Wendy had told him she wanted to move to Evansburg because it was a good family town. She hadn't ever actually said anything about babies; looking back, he knew he'd made assumptions that she was ready to start a family. Now it seemed like he was destined to be childless.

The first two girls—Mandy and Alex—gave him nothing, except the news that half of the class was married, which he hadn't expected. But maybe teenagers were better suited to long-term relationships than middle-aged detectives. He wished them luck.

Finally, the freckled girl—Brittany's friend Joy Saturno—provided a couple items of interest.

Joy twisted a plain gold wedding ring on her finger as she spoke. "Charlie." She blew out a breath. "Britt likes to pretend that Charlie was her boyfriend, but really she was just an easy hookup for him. I mean, she practically threw herself at him. He dumped her as soon as he found out she was pregnant. And he took a senior to the prom, not Britt."

"How'd he feel about Ivy?"

She rolled her eyes. "In Charlie's world, Ivy doesn't exist. And Britt really doesn't either, you know?"

"But Charlie knows that Ivy's his baby?"

Joy batted heavily mascaraed eyelashes at him. "It doesn't matter what Charlie says. Britt says that Charlie is Ivy's father. And she oughta know, don't you think?"

The Wakefields had no use for the Morgans, according to Dawes. Was there real animosity there? Charlie had finally called in last night just before 11 P.M., claiming to have been studying in the library until it closed. Dawes, with the cooperation of the Cheney PD, was checking up on all the Wakefields' alibis. But so far it sounded as if none of the Wakefields had any interest in Ivy.

Finn had let his mind wander in speculation; he pulled it back to what Joy was saying.

"Britt was always going on and on about how Ivy was the prettiest baby ever." Joy pushed her long blonde bangs aside and rolled her eyes. "Red hair, ivory skin, blue blue eyes—la la la. She was so sure Ivy would win the Pretty Baby contest today."

"Pretty Baby?" Finn asked.

"It's like a modeling contest for babies, you know? They're coming after school. You pay them to take pictures and then they call you back if they want to use your baby as a model. If you win, you get a thousand dollars."

At this point Joy leaned close, wafting a breath of spearmint gum his way and revealing a startling amount of freckled cleavage under her sleeveless blouse. He leaned back, jerked his eyes to the hallway door. Through the opening, he watched a woman scrub a black mark from the wall across the hallway. She wore a blue janitor's coverall with what looked like sergeant's stripes embroidered on the sleeve. A young man with a tie and black hair scraped back in a short ponytail stopped and touched her on the arm, then pointed down the hall. She nodded and they both walked off in the direction the man had indicated.

"But I'm Britt's friend, so I had to tell her," Joy continued, "Ivy wouldn't even come close to winning. They want ethnic now, like my Ruben, not some Ivory Snow baby."

"How did Brittany take it when you said that?" he asked.

"She acted like she didn't believe me. But I could tell she really did." Joy nodded, urging Finn to believe her.

"So she was upset," he said. Was this normal teen girl cattiness?

"Besides, I think they only give prizes to babies of married couples," Joy added. "You know, to set a good example. I told her that, too."

Were the married girls pitted against the single girls? He'd have to ask Mrs. Taylor. Were there other divisions within the class? He noted the tiny gold crosses dangling from Joy's earlobes and remembered Brittany's curious bumper sticker— *The Dinosaurs Died for Our Sins.* "Do you girls ever discuss evolution?"

"Evolution? Puhl-leaze." Joy rolled her eyes. "Like we don't have anything better to do than talk about dinosaurs and Jesus?"

He dismissed Joy and took a break outside before interviewing the next girl. His phone chirped; he snapped it open. "Finn."

The station operator said, "I've got the FBI for you."

He'd been expecting them. The next voice sounded young and female. "This is Special Agent Alice Foster, Detective Finn. I'm with the Child Abduction Rapid Deployment team in Los Angeles."

"Los Angeles? I'm in Washington State."

"Yes, I know. My team is charged with responding to child abduction notifications all along the west coast. I received notice that you posted information about a possible infant kidnapping from..." There was a rustle of paper. "Evansville, Washington?"

"Evansburg."

"Do you have a suspect?"

He quickly reiterated the details of the case, his irritation rising. He'd typed the same information into the FBI record only a few hours ago.

"If it's a murder, then of course we have no role in this."

No kidding. "I understand."

"We'll post the photo and vitals on our nationwide network, and we will send you a profile of similar kidnappers, as well as a list of all known child molesters in your area."

"Good." He resisted the urge to tell her that the Washington State Sex Offenders list was probably more up to date than her lists. Uniforms were knocking on all those doors at this very moment.

"We will send an agent to your location as soon as we can. But until then we have full confidence that the Evansville police will do their best to resolve this case."

He didn't bother to correct her again. "Right."

"Please keep us posted about any developments in this case."

"Of course." He punched End and stuck the phone back in his pocket. He'd covered the bases and done all the legally required reports. Once in awhile the FBI was helpful with their profiles and their maps and computer systems, but often they just created more paperwork. They'd been involved in several of his investigations in Chicago, but in every single case the locals had caught the perpetrator, not the feds.

He paced along the front steps of the school to stretch his legs, thinking about Brittany and her classmates. Would a teenager throw out her baby because the infant couldn't win a beauty contest? Brittany hadn't seemed callous to him. But then he remembered one of his juvie cases from Chicago. A sixteen-year-old girl whacked a friend in the head with a baseball bat, killing the other girl instantly. Her stated reason: her friend had splashed a Coke on her new softball uniform; she hadn't meant to *kill* her. Zero impulse control, a frequent teen problem. Did Brittany fit in that category?

His cell phone vibrated. He checked the readout. Speak of the devil. "Detective Finn," he answered.

"It's me, Brittany Morgan. I just remembered something. You said we couldn't have an Amber Alert because we didn't have a car description or anything. But now I remember— Talking Hands Ranch."

He needed another cup of coffee if he had to follow teenage leaps like this all day. "Talking Hands Ranch?"

"There was a gray van parked next to my car at the Food Mart. It had these mirror windows, and the writing on the side said Talking Hands Ranch."

It wasn't the usual stranger-lurking-in-the-shadows story that most of the guilty invented. He whipped out his notepad and jotted the information down. "Was there a logo?"

"You mean like a picture? Ummm ... no."

"The type of van?"

"Well, it was big and gray, and it had mirror windows. But the writing on the side, that's got to be important, right? I mean, that's a weird name, Talking Hands Ranch, right? Like maybe it's a deaf school or something, Talking Hands? So now can I get an Amber Alert?"

He'd already explained to her that they needed a reasonable suspicion of who the kidnapper was and the vehicle used. "We can't do anything without a plate or a person."

A sob rasped through the phone. Oh great, now he was making young girls cry. "But that's really important information, the Talking Hands Ranch name," he told her. "I'll look into that right away."

His phone beeped the second-call tone, and he quickly ended the call with Brittany and switched over. It was Mason, the department's resident geek.

"It's gonna take a week to sort through all the stuff on this kid's computer, Finn."

"Keep an eye out for any messages from Charles Wakefield—that's the baby's father."

"Is that another kid?"

"College kid now. He's nineteen."

"Okay, still a kid, he's probably on Facebook and Twitter. W-A-K-E-F-I-E-L-D? Any relationship to the County Exec?"

"Son."

"Ugh. Well, like I said, it's gonna take awhile to wade around in all this muck. But I have already come across one interesting item I wanted you to know about."

"What?"

"Brittany Morgan routinely visits this website called YoMama."

"Yes, I found out about it this morning. It's part of the school program for pregnant teens. I've asked for access to their email loops."

"There's all kinds of stuff about losing weight and breastfeeding and diaper rash and what to feed a baby. Can you believe that? They have to be told what to feed their babies?"

"And?" Finn prompted.

"Brittany's user name is Hot-dash-T. Get it—Hottie?"

"I get it." Sounded like a porn name. Why did so many teenage girls act like skanks these days?

"She connected there with someone named SKORGirl." Mason spelled the user name for him.

Finn rubbed his forehead. Daisy Taylor's face appeared at the window. He held up five fingers to indicate he'd be back soon. "Is that supposed to mean something to me?"

"SK, then OR—it might be Serena Kinsey, the girl in Oregon whose baby Tika went missing from her yard a month ago. Brittany was emailing her before that and they were both bitching about how boring it was to be stuck with a baby every night. Then after Tika disappeared, Hot-T's mail is all about how SKORGirl didn't do anything wrong and shouldn't beat up on herself. And then last night, at nine-thirty, Hot-T sent SKORGirl a message: 'Now we're truly like sisters. I know exactly what you're going through. Because now Ivy's gone too.'" Mason paused. "Do you think these girls conspired to get rid of their babies?"

It was at least an interesting coincidence. "Which town was the Kinsey case in?"

Finn heard faint typing sounds, then, "Portland."

"Thanks, Mason. Keep at it." Finn called the station, assigned a tech to research business records on Talking Hands Ranch and call Portland for a copy of the Kinsey case report. With the desk sergeant, he confirmed that the garbage bin detail had so far turned up no human remains or baby items.

"Unless you count a lot of used diapers, of course. We've received plenty of complaints, though," the sergeant said. "The phone's ringing off the wall with people asking why the cops are wasting taxpayer dollars going through their garbage. They also want to know when the garbage *will* be picked up."

In other words, they still had nothing. Finn rubbed his burning eyelids. Ashley Kowalski's limp form falling from the refrigerator flashed though his brain. The farm dog digging up baby John Doe. Tiny corpses. Shit. Why couldn't he turn off that mental video player?

Kidnapping or murder? Where was Ivy Rose Morgan? He remembered a list of special services posted at the station. He made another call to the station, held up another five fingers in Taylor's direction, and keyed in a phone number.

"Mrs. Morgan," he began when he got Brittany's mother on the line.

"It's Ciscoe, actually," she said. "I didn't change it. But never mind; do you have any news?"

"Not yet. We're bringing in a special canine team from Spokane. We'll come to your house this afternoon."

"Canine? A dog? Like a search dog? Ivy disappeared from the car in the Food Mart parking lot, not from our house."

"We tried a dog in the parking lot. It couldn't find anything more than thirty feet from Brittany's car. But now we think it could possibly be useful to bring this other specially trained dog to your house, walk him around the neighborhood. He might pick up a trail we haven't thought of yet. In past cases, missing children have been found at a neighbor's house."

Susan Ciscoe seemed doubtful, but said okay. He didn't tell her that he didn't need her permission. He also didn't volunteer that the missing children he'd mentioned had been found dead, and that this dog from Spokane was trained to sniff out cadavers.

Chapter 7

On the video monitor, Grace McKenna studied the image of a white kitten scampering across the shaggy landscape of a gorilla belly. Neema, lying on her back, threw one huge arm over her head and chuckled in delight. *Snow tickle Neema,* she signed.

Grace moved away from the screen and sat down on the braided rug next to Neema, crossing her legs. She signed *Where snow?*

The gorilla cupped a gentle hand around the kitten. *This snow,* she gestured with the other. Then, *soft baby.*

So Neema had decided to name this kitten Snow. Just to be sure, Grace signed, *Snow is dog?*

Neema's gorilla eyes flashed a look that implied Grace's species was the one with limited intelligence. She signed *Snow dog here.*

Before she had worked with Neema, Grace would not have believed that an ape could be sarcastic. It was great to get this sort of 'talk' on tape to demonstrate that gorillas had rich imaginations and associations and memories, much like children.

"You don't like dogs," she said, simultaneously signing the words. "I'll take the dog away." She reached for the kitten.

Neema clasped the tiny furball to her chest as she abruptly sat up. *Neema's baby.* She hurriedly drew her fingers out from her mouth, mimicking whiskers, thumped her chest and then curled her hand across it, then pulled imaginary whiskers again. *Cat my baby cat.*

"Ah, now you know the difference." *Best cat? Neema keep Snow?*

Neema drew the basket of kittens closer, gripping the wicker rim between her feet. *All cats play.*

"One." Grace held up a finger. "You can have *one*. Which one do you like the best?"

All stay Neema.

"One."

The white kitten squirmed against Neema's chest and mewed softly. The gorilla bent and brushed it with her lips, and then set it carefully on the floor. Next, she gently plucked a calico kitten from the basket and lifted it for a kiss.

What color that cat? Grace signed.

Nest.

Grace frowned and spoke while signing simultaneously. "It's not time for your nest now. Not time for sleeping. It's morning," she said, gesturing a sunrise. "What color is that cat? Blue? Red?"

This nest.

"You want to take the cat to your nest?" Grace asked. "You want to sleep with that cat?"

Play now.

Grace sighed. "Talk now," she insisted. "You must answer when I ask you a question. What color is that cat?"

Nest.

Grace gritted her teeth. Neema could be incredibly stubborn, especially when she was bored with answering routine questions.

"Yellow? Green? Brown?" Grace persisted, flashing signs one after another.

"Dr. McKenna," Josh interrupted from the doorway. "Take a look at Neema's nest."

Grace glanced at him over her shoulder, then turned and studied Neema's nap area in the corner. She'd created a gorilla sleeping nest, but instead of using leaves and grasses as she would in the wild, she'd used an old black rug, a white blanket, and a few orange and yellow towels.

Black. White. Orange. A calico nest. Turning back, Grace regarded the calico kitten in Neema's hands.

"And some people think apes are slow," Josh said dryly.

Neema echoed, signing *slow*.

Josh laughed. "Good thing she doesn't know the sign for clueless."

"She's repeating, not agreeing," Grace retorted. "And the tape is rolling."

He looked at the camera mounted near the ceiling. "Well, Dr. McKenna, you're the Ph.D. *You* would recognize the difference between repetition and agreement."

"Either get lost or come on in," Grace muttered. To Neema, Grace signed, *black white orange cat black white orange nest.*

Nest, Neema agreed.

"So it's finally time for a new pet." Josh knelt on the floor beside Grace. Neema now had both the white and calico kittens in her lap and was laughing her soft huh-huh-huh at the feel of their tiny claws on her legs. A gray kitten from the basket leapt up to bat at the black gorilla toes wrapped around the rim. Neema hooted with delight.

Which cat for Neema? Josh signed.

All cats stay. Play. Neema plucked the gray from the basket and added it to her lap.

"One cat," Grace insisted. Should she make the decision for Neema and remove the rest of the kittens? Or would that touch off a temper tantrum?

Some days it was hard to remember that she had a Ph.D. in Psychology. She should be teaching at a university, be *Professor* McKenna, with a roomful of dewy-eyed students looking up to her. When she'd first taken on this sign language project, she imagined working with Neema for a few hours each day and then retreating to her office or the lecture hall. Teaching gorillas sign language was a fascinating project, but the day-to-day process was grueling. When had she become this drudge, this weird mix of academic, zookeeper, and mommy? She never dreamed she'd be raising two gorilla children for the indefinite future. It was a lonely business. If only there was another gorilla mom to compare notes with.

A soft 'hunh' from the barred area behind Neema drew their attention. Gumu, confined to the 'cage' area for now, stretched his long black arms through the bars toward them. Then he stepped back and slapped himself on the chest.

Neema regarded her gorilla companion for a moment, and then signed *cat Gumu*. Gumu thumped his right hand against his chest, and then thrust the hand through the bars toward her.

Grace turned to Josh. "Do you think Gumu can be trusted w—"

Before she could get out the rest of the sentence, Neema scooted across the floor with a gray tiger kitten in one hand and the calico in the other. She sat down just out of reach of Gumu and cradled the kittens between her legs.

"Uh-oh." Grace started across the floor. Neema had always been gentle with other animals. But Gumu was a huge male, younger, less 'humanized.' And male gorillas had been known to kill smaller animals in their territory.

Josh grabbed Grace's arm. "Wait."

Baby, Neema signed. *Soft soft.*

Give Gumu. The thump the gorilla gave his own chest was so loud that both the kittens and the humans in the room startled at the sound. He insistently held out his hand, the huge black fingers curled upward.

Soft, Neema signed again. *Baby.* Then she held out the gray kitten and gently dropped it into Gumu's giant palm.

Grace groaned as Gumu pulled the kitten back into the cage. He held it up in front of his face. The kitten squeaked. Neema hooted softly, slashed an arm through the air, then held both arms briefly across her stomach. *No snake. Love baby.*

Gumu inspected the mewing kitten, gently holding the tiny animal to his nose and sniffing. He thrust his other hand through the bars toward the calico kitten Neema still held.

Nest soft baby, Neema signed.

Give Gumu.

Grace gasped as Neema handed him the calico kitten.

The male gorilla compared the kittens, one grasped in each giant black hand, blowing on their fur and running his lips gently over their tiny bodies.

Baby soft. Neema hooted softly again as she signed.

"It's as if she's telling him to be careful," Josh murmured.

Gumu set the tiny gray kitten on the floor. It scampered between the bars and pounced on its white sibling next to Neema's leg. Grace could almost breathe again.

Gumu cradled the calico against his pot belly. Its purr was audible. He placed his arm horizontally against his chest, then tapped himself again. *Baby Gumu.*

"When did you teach him *baby*?" Grace asked.

"I didn't." Excitement raised Josh's voice half an octave. "Neema did."

Neema had taught Gumu a word! What other sign language conversations were they having when she wasn't watching? Clearly, she needed to film the gorillas in the barn and play enclosure as well as during their lessons. That meant more cameras and hours of videotape to review. As soon as her grant check arrived, she'd see about buying more equipment and recruiting more help.

Neema turned to Grace and Josh, signing *Nest Gumu.* She scooped up the white kitten and signed *Snow baby Neema.*

Josh expelled a breath. "Think Gumu agrees his kitten should be named Nest?"

Grace shrugged. "No way to tell unless he picks up the sign."

"What was that snake business?"

"Maybe she was telling him not to treat the kitten like a snake, but like a baby?" Grace guessed.

"Or maybe she was telling Gumu not to be mean like a snake."

Snake bad baby cry, Neema signed.

"Well, there you have it," Josh chuckled. "Gumu learned a word from Neema, Neema's obsessed with snakes, and we have two new pets."

Grace laughed. "I think the gorillas made it pretty clear that those kittens are *their* pets, not ours."

Two cats play, Neema agreed. Then she cuddled her ivory bundle of fluff even closer to her chest, pressing it gently to her leathery black nipple as if she expected the kitten to nurse.

"Good session. The Foundation should really appreciate that video." Grace stood up, stretching. "Time for lunch."

Neema's gaze bounced to Grace. The gorilla balanced Snow on her hairy protruding belly as she used both hands to quickly sign her list of favorites: *Jell-O lettuce yogurt banana*.

Gumu too looked up from the calico kitten. *Give banana baby*, he signed.

"How altruistic of him," Josh said.

"Right. Go ahead and feed them, but keep an eye on him to make sure he doesn't actually try to make that kitten eat a banana. I'll take the others back." Grace pressed the three remaining kittens into the basket and tossed a towel over them.

Josh grabbed the basket from her. "You feed, I'll take them. I'm going out, anyway."

"Thanks," she said. "Tell the Canos that we're giving the kittens a good home. Do *not* mention gorillas."

"Will do." He snapped off a salute. "Then I'm heading into town to grab a bite to eat with a friend, okay?"

The friend, Grace knew, would be young and female and pretty. "Go for it," she said.

"I'll be back in two to three hours. Can I bring you anything?"

A winning lottery ticket? A handsome professor bearing a gourmet picnic basket and a bottle of good Chianti? *You're the Ph.D. in charge of this project, Dr. McKenna*, she told herself. Swallowing her self-pity, she answered, "No. We're good, aren't we, guys?"

Jell-o, Neema signed. *Yogurt jell-o*.

As the door closed behind Josh, Gumu grunted and signed *Banana give.*

Grace sighed.

Brittany's mother was dry-eyed, but a deep furrow was carved across her forehead, and her reactions seemed slow. Sleep-deprived. Finn could identify with that.

"You stayed home from work," he observed.

"I went in this morning while Noah stayed here. Now he's out at the plant. It's hard to focus on work, but it's sort of a relief to be able to actually *do* something useful."

He nodded. That was why it was routine to post an officer with a victim's family in the first few hours—they started cleaning house, doing the laundry, cooking, and so forth, just to keep busy, sometimes mucking up a crime scene in the process. A female uniform had spent the night with the Morgans and left at dawn, reporting no unusual activities in the house.

"Brittany's out with friends posting flyers," Susan Ciscoe told him.

Finn hoped that was true. Belatedly, he realized he should have assigned someone to tail the girl. His career had been filled with moms and dads who had no inkling that their Ethan made pipe bombs with his friends, or that their Emily traded sex for the latest fashions from The Gap. In one shocking case in the 'burbs, eight teens had formed a vampire club, drinking each other's blood. The parents had gone blithely about their own lives while their seventeen-year-olds spread HIV around their intimate circle.

He detested this stage of an investigation. Dealing with the initial confusion was like wrestling an octopus. It was hard to keep track of what every arm was doing; hard to constantly juggle all the possibilities in his head. After a clear suspect emerged, building a case would be much more straightforward.

"So Brittany's out posting flyers," he repeated. There was a stack beside them on the front porch, weighted down with a smooth rock from the stone borders along the Morgans' front walk.

"I believe so," Susan said, confirming his suspicion that she really wasn't keeping tabs on her daughter.

"And your son, Danny?"

"I sent him over to our neighbors." She pointed to the white house across the street. "They have an eleven-year-old boy, too."

Eleven. Certainly old enough to get rid of an unwanted squalling niece. Another possibility he needed to check out. He made a note on his pad.

"Is Brittany your husband's child?"

The glare Susan gave him could have melted a glacier. "Of course. Danny, too. Just because a woman doesn't change her last name on marriage doesn't mean she's got a wild past, Detective. Good lord, what *is* it with this town? Is *everyone* stuck in the 1950s?"

Ouch. He knew that the Morgans had moved to Evansburg five years ago from Denver. "I know how you feel," he said. "But I have to ask these questions."

She reached a hand up under her shoulder-length auburn hair to knead the back of her neck. "I didn't mean to bite your head off. I didn't get much sleep last night."

"Me neither," he sympathized.

"We were sorry to hear about your wife, Detective Finn."

He stared at her for a long awkward moment. Did the whole frigging county know? Had he missed an announcement Wendy had placed in the paper? *Hey, Evansburg, I'm ditching my clueless husband Matthew Finn to run off with the love of my life! —Wendy Mankin*

"The police officer, last night..." Susan let the words trail off.

He'd have a word with that female uniform, but he knew it wouldn't stop the gossip. He tapped his pen impatiently on his notebook. "How does Danny get along with the baby?"

She grimaced. "It's hard to get him to notice anything that's not in a video game. Or on a plate in front of him."

Video games. He made another quick note to check out the kid's favorites for violence. "How did you feel when you found out Brittany was pregnant?"

When he looked up from his pad, Susan was frowning. "How would you feel if *your* sixteen-year-old daughter got pregnant?"

It was difficult to imagine being in that situation. Especially now.

Susan continued. "I didn't plan on being a grandmother at thirty-nine. I have an MBA, for heaven's sake; Noah has a degree in mathematics. We never dreamed we'd end up working at mediocre jobs in a small town, let alone have a pregnant teenager who has absolutely no desire to go to college."

"It must be hard," he said.

"Brittany was nearly five months pregnant when we found out, so abortion wasn't an option," Susan volunteered, answering his unasked questions. "I did encourage her to give the baby up for adoption, but I wasn't going to force her. We do insist that Brittany takes care of Ivy..." Her voice caught. "...took care of Ivy...oh, mercy." She raised a hand to clutch at her shirt front, and tears pooled in her eyes. "We might not have wanted a grandchild so soon, but Noah and I love that baby so much."

Both of them glanced at the stack of flyers again, where Ivy Rose Morgan's round baby face smiled at them, her right eye hidden beneath a river rock paperweight.

"I understand that Charlie Wakefield is the child's father?"

Susan nodded, and a tear spilled over from her left eye.

"Have you heard from him?"

"Never."

"Does he pay child support?"

Wiping the tear away, she shook her head. "He doesn't want anything to do with the baby. At first we decided that we simply wouldn't include him in any way in Ivy's life, keep it simpler, you know?"

He nodded again.

"But now that both Noah and I have had our hours cut back, we really need the financial support. So last week we went to the Wakefields."

Finn perked up. "And their reaction?"

"The cold shoulder. They agreed to share responsibility *if* we could prove that Charlie was Ivy's father."

Finn waited for Susan to continue.

She sighed. "Brittany thought that was insulting. She refused to bring Ivy into the clinic for the paternity test. Noah and I were talking to her, trying to bring her around, maybe just do one of those home mail-in jobs, but now..." Another tear escaped and slid down her reddened cheek.

Finn's heart rate sped up. Now that the baby was missing, there would be no paternity test. Unless the techs somehow managed to get DNA from some baby item they'd collected from Brittany's room, there would be no way to prove Ivy was Charlie's child.

A Subaru station wagon pulled up in the driveway. Brittany got out, tottering on platform sandals that curiously were now as popular as they had been when Finn was a kid. His mother had worn lime green leather nailed to stacked wooden soles.

The teen wore her long strawberry-blonde hair loose today. Her blue jean shorts were tight and she wore a yellow halter top that exposed a lot of skin. *Hot-T.* Finn made an effort to lift his gaze to the girl's face and keep it there. Her oval face was puffed and blotchy, but as she approached the front porch, her eyes were bright.

Seeing her daughter's expression, Susan shook her head. "There's no news. They're searching our neighborhood."

"Why?" The look Brittany turned on him was genuinely bewildered. "That's not going to help. Ivy didn't get kidnapped *here.* It's been *twenty-three* hours! Why aren't you searching at the Food Mart, or"—she gestured vaguely at the surrounding suburbs—"out there?"

"The department's doing that, too, Miss Morgan," Finn reassured her. He hoped the patrol officers were doing a good job. A two-month-old infant was a pretty small bundle to look for. The sergeant told him that at roll call this morning the uniforms had been surly. It was bad enough that Finn was the outsider. Now that he was calling the shots on this case, the local boys were openly resentful.

"Did you find that Talking Hands Ranch van?" Brittany's gaze was still fixed on his face.

"Not yet," he admitted. "No business named Talking Hands Ranch is registered in Washington State. There are no rules about registering a sign on the side of a vehicle. It would be easier with a plate number or a make and model."

"Isn't that your *job*?" Brittany asked. "It was gray, and it said Talking Hands Ranch on the side. How many can there be? I *still* don't understand why there's no Amber Alert!"

He stifled a groan. "We're working on finding the van, Miss Morgan. When was the last time you saw Charlie Wakefield?"

"Charlie?" She blinked, surprised. "At the end of school last year? Maybe six weeks before Ivy was born? Why? He's not going to help. Where's the FBI? Whenever there's a kidnapping on TV, the FBI is all over it." She pivoted toward Susan. "Mom, are *we* supposed to call the FBI?"

"The FBI is aware of everything we do. I am sharing all our information with them." He struggled to keep his tone even. It was aggravating to be grilled by a seventeen-year-old who learned about kidnapping investigations from television.

Unlike when he'd first seen her yesterday, Brittany's face was devoid of makeup; she looked worn out and much older than her seventeen years. Desperate mother or desperate murderer? He still couldn't tell. "Brittany," he said, "If Ivy's been kidnapped, she's probably with someone who will take care of her."

"*If?* Why do you keep saying *if?*" The girl's voice was tight.

"That's just the way detectives talk." He hooked a thumb in his belt, trying to look casual. "Where were you this morning?"

Her blue eyes were accusatory. "I was getting *help*. My friends and I are putting up flyers."

"Have there been any tips on the station hotline yet?" Susan asked Finn.

So far nothing but nutcases, according to the operator and the sergeant. "A few," he said. "We're checking them all out."

"Mom and I put Ivy on Facebook," Brittany told him. "And more pictures of her are going to be in the newspaper and on TV again tonight."

"I see." Facebook. He'd forgotten about that possibility. He'd better prepare the switchboard for a flood of calls and set Mason to somehow collecting all the emails or tweets or IMs whatever the heck all those messages were called these days. Who was going to read all that?

"I really need my computer back," Brittany said.

"Soon." Finn sucked in a breath and rapidly scanned the street, searching for antenna-laden vans with television logos on the side. Thankfully, none was in sight. Yet. Reporters were camped outside the station last night, and they'd track him down sooner or later. More coverage would mean more pressure from the public, and then of course, the local politicos would do their grandstanding, so there'd be pressure from the mayor, too.

On the plus side, if this *was* a kidnapping, media coverage might shake loose a few leads. More than one scumbag had been nabbed on a tip from *America's Most Wanted*.

He made a mental checklist: review the interviews of grocery store staff and customers, scrutinize the detritus collected from the area around Brittany's car, retrace the teen's steps from the last two days, check out Charlie Wakefield and friends, discuss findings with patrol officers and other detectives and the men inside the Ciscoe/Morgan house now. Finn rubbed his hand across his cheek, discovered a patch of stubble he'd missed. He was numb with exhaustion, and it wasn't even five P.M.

Brittany was still talking. "I made a list of things that were in the diaper bag for you."

"That could be useful," he said.

"I'll get 'em." The girl clomped up the front steps and into the house.

The canine team arrived a second before Brittany returned. Finn was shaking hands with the canine officer when the girl joined them, a paper fluttering from one hand.

"They are in my room *again*. They didn't even want to let me take this, even when I said it was for you." She looked up at the window, where an officer was observing. She waved, pointed to the paper, and handed it to Finn with a theatrical gesture. Finn flashed an okay sign, and the officer disappeared from the window.

Brittany stared at the dog. "What's the German Shepherd for?"

"This is Hans," the canine officer explained. "We're going to see what he picks up."

Brittany folded her arms across her stomach. "But Ivy didn't go missing from *here*."

The Spokane officer had a soothing way about him. "I understand that, Miss Morgan. But Ivy might be somewhere in the neighborhood. Don't you think that's a possibility?"

"Like, maybe a neighbor took her?" Brittany's gaze moved to the houses nearby.

"If she is in the neighborhood, Hans could find her faster than any human could."

The Shepherd whined softly. He seemed eager to comply.

"I'll get Ivy's blanket," Brittany said.

Finn's face must have registered his confusion, because she added, "So Hans can get her scent, right?"

How could he tell those hopeful blue eyes that the dog was trained to sniff out decaying flesh? "Good idea."

Brittany went back into the house, and Finn left Susan to step down into the yard. "Do the back yard first," he murmured quietly to the dog handler.

The gate on the chain link fence rattled as the canine officer unlatched it. He gave the shepherd a command in German. The dog dashed through the gate opening, his sharp muzzle to the ground. He zigzagged across the dry grass and disappeared around the corner of the house with his human in pursuit.

"Why are you searching the back yard?" Susan asked.

"The trail has to start somewhere," Finn answered vaguely.

As they followed the dog's progress, Brittany came out of the house via the back door, carrying a yellow baby blanket. Halfway across the yard, she bent to pick up something from the grass. A pink pacifier. Her eyes filled with tears as she wiped it on the leg of her shorts.

A sympathetic knot formed in Finn's throat. He swallowed to squash it down. The girl's tears could mean anything: regret, remorse, fear.

A white van emblazoned with *KEBR News* pulled up on the street just beyond the fence. A female reporter and cameraman spilled from the doors even before it came to a stop. Brittany excitedly waved them around to the gate.

He ran a hand over his hair to be sure his cowlick was behaving itself. His cell phone chose that moment to buzz in his pocket. He flipped it open and held it to his ear. "Detective Finn."

"Arrrruuuu!"

"Not now," he growled. It wasn't Dawes. Who the hell—?

"Don't forget our meeting at seven to go over your testimony. We're calling you tomorrow afternoon."

Vernon Dixon, Assistant District Attorney. The Animal Rights Union case. "Look, Dixon. I don't have time, and you don't need me. Detective Kathryn Larson was in charge of the ARU case."

"But you were in on it, too. Larson is too sympathetic to the cause of rodent rights."

"Kathryn Larson is a damn good detective; she'll do her job. Sara Melendez is a pro, too."

"You're the senior dick. And the prosecutor's choice."

The reporter held open the gate for her cameraman. Finn backed toward the clump of people near the fence. "I'm not coming tonight. Urgent police business." Even an hour away from the Morgan case might be too much. If he'd only slept an hour less on the Kowalski case; if he'd only been an hour smarter...

"Then meet me at the courthouse at noon tomorrow," Dixon commanded. "We'll rehearse over lunch; we'll call you first thing when we reconvene at one P.M."

"I'll try." He snapped the phone shut. Hans whined and circled excitedly in the flower bed.

The reporter held her microphone out like a sword as she rushed them. "Brittany! Mrs. Morgan! Detective Finn!"

Allyson Lee again. Damn, the girl was persistent. She no doubt had a bright future in TV journalism. Finn couldn't wait for her to graduate and leave Evansburg for the big time. The red light above the video camera glowed; the cameraman had his eye to the lens. Like it or not, the show was on. The student reporter was tall for a woman, and especially for a Chinese woman, at least five-ten by his estimation. Finn straightened, maximizing his full six feet.

"Allyson Lee, KEBR News," the reporter announced breathlessly as she positioned herself among the cluster of family and officers. She turned to Finn. "What's going on here?"

Near the fence, Hans zeroed in on a clump of marigolds, whining, and pawed the ground. Shouting commands in German, the canine officer ran forward.

A sound somewhere between a grunt and a whimper came out of Susan Ciscoe. Her face went pale.

"You found something?" Allyson Lee's voice rose in excitement as she gestured at the cameraman to focus on the policemen. They positioned their shovels to dig.

Josh didn't return until dinnertime. The kittens named Snow and Nest were asleep in a box Grace had prepared for them. Neema, now sporting her favorite old red muffler around her neck, was gnawing on half a cabbage in the middle of the kitchen floor in the study trailer. Grace prepared sandwiches at the counter in the study trailer.

"Mail. Newspaper." Josh slapped them down on the table. He eyed the sandwiches. "I hope one of those is for me."

Neema, catching sight of *National Geographic*, her favorite magazine, scooted over to grab it from the stack of mail.

"Just look," Grace warned. "No tearing out pages."

"I like your tie, Neema," Josh told the gorilla. Neema glanced at him briefly when she heard her name. *Pretty*, he signed, mimicking a tie around his own neck.

Neck bracelet red pretty, she signed back. Neema plopped down in the middle of the rug, cradling the magazine with her feet and carefully turning the pages with her thick fingers.

Josh pulled out a chair. "You need to teach her 'necklace' and 'ring'."

"I think 'neck bracelet' and 'finger bracelet' are pretty descriptive." Grace screwed the lid back on the jar of mustard. "I may leave it that way to prove gorilla reasoning."

Had she mentioned Neema's word combinations in her latest paper? She needed to put in at least a couple of hours on it tonight, even if she had to stay up until midnight. She was coming up on her journal deadline, and she hadn't hammered out even half the word count she'd promised.

"They're still searching for that baby in town," Josh said, unfolding the newspaper. He held up the front page, which featured a photo of the distraught young mother in front of the Food Mart, and an inset of a fat-cheeked infant.

Neema scurried over to look, signing *go store candy*.

No candy now. Stay here now, Josh signed. He brushed away Neema's hands and shook out the paper. "This poor girl. She left the baby in the car—can you imagine?" He shook his head.

"Yes," Grace said, turning. "She's only seventeen. When I think back on the dumb things I did at that age..."

"When I was seventeen..." Josh mused, leaning back in his chair. Then abruptly he shook his head and sat up. "Nope, I'm not going there."

Baby baby baby. Neema batted at the photos on the page. *Hair soft soft red gold.*

Grace's heart skipped a beat. She signed, *Whose hair red gold?*

Girl red tail hair soft soft.

"OK." Josh raised a carrot stick toward his mouth. "I get the 'tail' because this girl—Brittany Morgan—has her hair in a ponytail. But the photo's black and white."

"Don't you remember? She was on the news last night. She's a strawberry blonde."

"Oh yeah." He settled back to read the rest of the paper.

Grace rubbed a hand across the knot that had formed in her stomach. Josh didn't remember, but she did. Neema had been outside playing with Gumu at the time they were watching the news. She couldn't have seen the story on television.

Red gold soft soft. Snake make baby cry. Grace made herself take a deep slow breath. Neema might have seen the girl walk into the store, or maybe she'd seen someone else who looked similar. Neema often made up stories; she interpreted ideas in creative ways with her limited vocabulary. *Neck bracelet. Finger bracelet. Poop head.*

Snake make baby cry.

Yesterday Neema had clearly called Gumu a snake. And she'd called the kittens babies. Or so Grace had thought. Was Neema talking about something else?

Red gold soft soft. Snake make baby cry.

It probably meant nothing. She took another deep breath, cut the finished sandwiches in two and moved the plates to the small table.

"I almost forgot." Josh pulled an envelope from the batch next to his elbow. "For you."

The return address was the Tolliver Animal Intelligence Foundation. "Thank god." Grace ripped open the envelope. She needed to deposit the grant funds before her credit card bill came due. She glanced at the check. The amount was $25,000. Half of what she was expecting.

"Chips?"

She raised her head. "What?"

"Stellar sandwich, but do we have any chips in here?" Josh rose from his chair.

"Check the cabinet over the sink." Fighting a surge of anxiety, she flipped the check face down on the table and unfolded the letter. Maybe they were sending the money in two installments this year.

> Dear Dr. McKenna,
> We regret to inform you that we can award your project only fifty percent of the funds we gave you last year. The downturn in the economy has precipitated a downturn in donations, so we are forced to reduce awards to all grant recipients this year. We wish you the best of luck and look forward to receiving quarterly progress reports on your important project.

"No! Damn it, no!" Grace slapped her hand down on the letter.

"I take it that's not good news." Josh extended the open potato chip bag.

She waved the chip bag away. "They sent only half my grant money. For the whole year! How am I supposed to house and feed two gorillas and two people for a whole year on twenty-five thousand dollars?"

She sat there, chewing her thumbnail, re-reading the letter, hoping she'd misunderstood. Her sandwich lay untouched on the plate. First she'd been hustled off to the sticks, and now this? She was classified as a research professor at the University of Washington. She received health care benefits and library access and credit union membership and a few other perks, but no salary. The Tolliver Foundation funded her position—their grant money was her entire income and all of her project expense money.

The gorillas' play enclosure was unfinished, the security system had not yet been installed, the barn where Gumu slept was unheated, and winter was coming on. The grocery bill alone for feeding two gorillas amounted to fifteen thousand a year. What the hell was she supposed to do now? Was there any chance the university would come up with the other twenty-five thousand? She had a sinking recollection of news reports about major cuts to higher education budgets.

Josh glanced guiltily at the half sandwich left on his plate. "Guess I'll be using my fellowship money for my food from now on."

If only she had fellowship money, too. A student loan. Anything to fall back on.

He laid a hand on hers. "We'll cope, right?"

Although she couldn't imagine how, she murmured, "Of course."

Reassured, he picked up the remaining sandwich half and went back to reading the paper. It was nice of him to make it sound like they were a team, but Josh was only here until he finished the research for his thesis on animal language. Thank god he hadn't yet chosen his exact focus. She hoped it would take him years to do his research; she needed every second of assistance she could get from him.

Neema scooted over, signing *gorilla good kiss* as she pressed her mammoth black lips to Grace's cheek. When she knuckled back to her *National Geographic*, Grace noticed that half her sandwich was gone. Neema sat with her back to them, hunched over the magazine, hiding her face.

Josh looked up from the paper, grinning as he chewed the last bite of his sandwich. "Feeling ripped off?"

"You have no idea," she told him.

Thirty-eight hours after Ivy disappears

Chapter 8

Finn grabbed the coffeepot and refilled his cup and Dawes's, although he could no longer feel the caffeine. He suspected Dawes couldn't, either. The other detective had dark circles under his eyes and looked at least five years older than he had two days ago. Finn knew he looked the same. He'd fallen asleep in the recliner again last night, woken up to the dog whining to go out, one cat in his lap, the other on the chair back above his head, and cat fur covering his tongue.

"No, ma'am, that's the Hartley house," Dawes said into his cell phone. "That's Addison Hartley with her baby Miranda." He rolled his eyes at Finn. "Yes, ma'am, I'm absolutely sure. Thanks for checking with the police department; we appreciate your help." He flipped the phone closed and made a note on the pad in front of him. "That's the twenty-sixth reported sighting of Ivy Rose Morgan. Did you know we have five other red-haired babies in the area?"

Up to now, Finn had only been vaguely aware of *any* babies in the area. He certainly hadn't paid attention to which ones had red hair. "Could you write down their names and addresses for me? And, uh, thanks for taking all those calls."

Dawes yawned widely, and then said, "No problemo. Makes sense for me to take them. I already know who they're talking about half the time."

Finn summed up his side of the investigation for Dawes, which didn't take long, since most of it had already played on the news for the whole town to appreciate. "Larson and

Melendez are following up on tips, and they'll interview the two girls missing yesterday from Brittany's class."

Dawes took a sip of coffee. "Mr. and Mrs. Wakefield are accounted for—work for him, golf for her and then dinner together with friends at the country club after. And FYI, they're pissed about the attention and the allegation that Charlie is the baby's daddy. Especially Mrs. Wakefield."

Finn quirked an eyebrow.

Dawes added, "Because she's been down this road before?"

Had to be juicy gossip, the way that Dawes was stringing it out. "Just spill it."

"I keep forgetting you're not a native." Dawes leaned forward. Strands of his unruly gray-blond hair slipped down onto his forehead. "There's a gal up in Chelan County who has ten-year-old twin boys who look a lot like Travis Wakefield. And if someone were to check the Wakefields' bank accounts, I do believe they'd find a check headed in that direction every month."

"Ah." So the Wakefield family would know well the cost of illegitimate babies.

Dawes sat back. "On the day Ivy disappeared, Charlie went to track team practice at seven A.M.—they even had their team photo taken that day." He slapped a copy of a photo of the table. "Then he was in classes from ten A.M. until two-thirty. The university police faxed the attendance sheets." Dawes splayed the pages—three class rosters—on the scratched tabletop. "After classes he says he went to the library. According to his roommates, he spends a lot of time there. But so far nobody's been able to vouch for that."

Finn picked up the track team photo. Twenty young women and men, all glossy hair and smooth skin, stood in traditional formation, arranged by height. In the front row, the girls were turned three-quarters with one hand on their hips, appearing more like cheerleaders than track stars. Their uniforms were navy running shorts and a long-sleeved light blue jacket with a navy zigzag design down the forearms.

"That's Charlie." Dawes pointed to a blond kid in the middle row. "He has a track scholarship. They call the team Lightning. How the heck can you cheer for Lightning?"

"There are cheerleaders at track meets?" Finn tossed the picture back onto the table.

"Probably. But what do you yell—zap 'em?"

Finn was too tired to participate in Dawes's pointless tangents. "And the phone company was sure Charlie Wakefield's cell phone spent the day in the Cheney?"

"All calls came from the local towers, including our messages to him."

"But he never answered, so all that proves is that the cell phone stayed at home. Ivy disappeared a few minutes before six P.M.—how long does it take to drive from Cheney to Evansburg?"

Dawes made a face. "Around three and a half hours. Unless you're a teenager—then you can probably do it in less than three. Charlie's racked up a few speeding tickets."

"Where did he spend the night?"

"At his house. He says he was home a little after eleven. His roommates verified that."

"Two thirty to eleven." Finn said. "That's a big hole of time. Is the local PD asking neighbors, library personnel?"

"Supposed to be doing that. But it's a university town, so there's the campus force and then there's the Cheney department, and you know how that goes." Dawes rolled his eyes.

Finn knew what Dawes referred to—universities had their own security staffs that handled most issues on campus, and there were often jurisdiction disputes with the surrounding police departments. Thank god the local college used the Evansburg police instead of running their own show; it made handling cases a lot easier.

Finn groaned at the timeline. "Charlie could have driven here, snatched Ivy, and driven back."

"Could have." Dawes scooped up the fax pages, slid out of his chair and stretched.

"And ditched that baby anywhere in between." Finn thought about the doll baby corpse in the cornfield.

"Let's hope *that's* not the way it goes." Dawes swallowed hard, regarding Finn with weary eyes. "He's coming back tonight; I'm going to grill him then. If I still can't verify where he was when the baby disappeared, I'll take a trip down to Cheney."

"Good idea. Check with the lieutenant."

"Already know what he'll say."

Finn did, too—there was no money in the department budget for travel or overtime or anything else. With tax revenues continuing to drop, the city and county, even the whole dang state, had been running in the red for nearly three years. Now the department was making noises about cutting a couple of uniforms from the force. Just since Finn had arrived, the budget for local government had been cut by a third. Teachers were paying for their own chalk. Dawes would have to eat his own travel expenses if the lieutenant okayed the road trip. There needed to be a big sign posted somewhere—*No taxes, no services.* The Statue of Liberty might be a good spot.

"The list of YoMama users came in this morning," Dawes told him.

"I'll get Miki on matching YoMama users to criminal records." Finn's cell phone chimed and he picked it up. The screen flashed a reminder that he was due in court in thirty minutes. "Speaking of criminals. Damn, I don't have time for court."

"Aarrooo!" Dawes howled, finishing with a grin.

"Shut up." Finn rose from the table and held out a fist. "Back into the fray. Let me know if anything turns up on the Wakefields."

Dawes bumped Finn's hand with a fist of his own. "Ditto on the Morgans. Catch you later."

An hour later Finn was still cooling his heels in the courthouse waiting room. The sound was turned down low on the flat-screen TV stuck up in the corner, but it was still audible. He couldn't believe how quickly the Northwest News Channel had picked up the story from KEBR, not to mention how often they were replaying it.

He paced in the small room. Any minute now he'd be called to the witness stand. Thank god the jurors in the ARU case were not listening to this crap. He hoped none had tuned in during their lunch break.

"...at the home of the distraught mother on Anderson Street, police used a dog to follow what they believed might be an important lead."

The reporter stepped back from the camera, which then zoomed in on the background scene of a couple of uniforms digging up the Morgans' garden. Finn stood at the periphery, slouching a little, his shirt protruding over his belt. Shit, did he always look that sloppy? He sucked in his stomach now, reached down and felt along his waistline, ran his fingers down his trouser zipper. All secure.

Then back to the reporter and the family. Finn had watched it so often he had every detail memorized.

"Goldilocks was our cocker spaniel," Susan Ciscoe explained to Alysson Lee. "She passed away three weeks ago. We buried her there, next to the fence."

Brittany stepped into the frame, close to the camera, blotting out her mother and the reporter behind her. "Why isn't anyone out searching for my baby?" she wailed. "Ivy is only two months old. She's out there somewhere. What are the police doing to find Ivy?"

The shot shifted from Brittany's tearful visage to the KEBR news desk, with its ever-dramatic and interchangeable student Barbie and Ken doll anchors. Ken leaned toward the camera, his blue eyes serious. "That is the question right now—what *are* the Evansburg police doing to find little Ivy Rose Morgan? Officers are reported to be searching trash bins for clues. Why? We called to ask those questions of Detective Matthew Finn, the officer in charge of the investigation. He has never returned our call."

Finn strode angrily from the room. He couldn't tell them that they were looking for a tiny corpse, could he? Still, he probably should have called them back, given them some platitude about how they were pursuing every lead.

The cadaver dog had turned up nothing other than the dead spaniel and a maggot-ridden squirrel corpse a few houses down. Noah Morgan had come home in the middle of the dog excavation. Thankfully, Brittany's parents had stayed mum during the search. They'd pulled him aside as soon as the TV crew and dog team had left.

"Detective." Noah's expression wavered between fury and icy control. "We know you have to pursue every angle, but no one in this family killed Ivy."

"Britt loves that baby with all her heart," Susan emphasized. "She did a stupid thing, leaving Ivy in the car, but it was only ten minutes. She'd never hurt that baby. Never."

He saw nothing in their faces to indicate they were lying. But their innocent gaze could simply mean they didn't know the truth. There was no point in asking them whether their son Danny might have done something awful to his niece.

"What about Charlie?" he asked. "Would he hurt Ivy?"

Noah and Susan regarded each other for a long moment before turning back to him. "Charlie's never even seen Ivy," Noah said.

"Are you one hundred percent sure about that?" Finn asked.

Another long look passed between the parents.

"No," Susan finally admitted. "Not one hundred percent."

So he was back to that frustrating nebulous state. Not one shred of solid evidence or testimony that pointed in a specific direction. Still wandering in circles.

His footsteps seemed loud on the polished floor of the courthouse hallway. From behind the closed courtroom doors, he could hear the low baritone of Jack Fiero.

He could tell from the rhythm that the city's star defense attorney was up to his usual firing-range tactics: zinging multiple questions at whoever was on the witness stand and allowing them no time to answer. It usually left the witness sitting mouth open, unable to get a word out. Eventually the judge would put a stop to it, but the strategy always had the desired effect—to make the witness look like an incoherent idiot.

Two young men came up the stairwell. They wore ties and carried stacks of folders in their arms. Law clerks or paralegals. One wore glossy black shoes that reflected the overhead lights.

"Dumpster diving and digging up dead dogs," Shiny Shoes said. "You know what that means."

"That Morgan girl didn't look like the type," the other responded.

"Do they ever—" When he spotted Finn, the first young man cut himself off. Probably recognized Finn from the television broadcast. They passed in silence and resumed their conversation further down the hall, talking in unintelligible murmurs now.

Finn stopped at the window near the end of the hall to watch the small clusters of demonstrators outside. The two sides seemed evenly matched in numbers, but the animal rights camp seemed to momentarily have the upper hand, having taken up a position closer to the news crew. They strode in a determined circle around their drummer, flashing their hand-drawn signs at the cameraman. *Animals have rights 2. We're ALL God's creatures.* And the inevitable *Animals are my friends, don't torture or eat my friends* with cute photos of rabbits, chicks, and calves. The opposition was older, quieter, and more formal, with neatly printed signs in two variations: *Rat lives ≠ Human lives* and *Animal testing = Lifesaving research.* There was also one loner striding back and forth, carrying a *Next they'll take our guns!* sign.

"Detective Matthew Finn?"

He turned toward the voice. The bailiff stood in the hallway, motioning to him. "You're called to the stand."

The man held open the courtroom door, and Finn strode down the center aisle, not looking at the spectators. He positioned himself on the stand and they went through the usual swearing in and statement of name, position, and experience.

Finn glanced at the three ARU defendants. Two girls, Sierra Sakson and Caryn Brown, and one boy, Jonathan Zyrnek. All of them were pierced—the girls each had an eyebrow ring, Sierra had a nose stud, and the boy had a painful-looking lip ring. The girls appeared to be around nineteen or twenty. Zyrnek had a beard, making his age harder to estimate. Probably misguided students who were liberating lab rats when they should have been in World History class.

Jack Fiero stood up from his chair beside them. He ran a hand over his silver hair. "You were with the Chicago Police Department before coming here?"

"That's right," Finn said into the microphone.

"And you left Chicago because...?"

Was Fiero trying to hint that he'd left in disgrace? Finn said, "My wife wanted to be closer to her parents here in Evansburg."

"And how's that working out?"

In what universe was this relevant? Hell, everyone in this town—probably in this county—knew how that had worked out. "It didn't," Finn snapped.

There was a twitter from the back of the courtroom.

"Do you wish you were back in Chicago?" the defense attorney asked.

Why wasn't Dixon objecting? The judge stared at Finn, waiting. He leaned toward the mike and breathed, "Sometimes."

"I'll bet this is one of those times, isn't it? The Evansburg Police Department has had a hard time solving crimes lately, haven't they?"

"Our resolution rate is pretty standard, I'd say." Not bad; his voice sounded calm and authoritative.

"How do you feel about animals, Detective?"

What the hell? This case was about trashing a research lab. Dixon thumbed through his notes, not looking at him. Finn flicked a glance at the jury. Twelve pairs of eyes watched him.

The three ARU defendants looked interested, too. Caryn flashed some quick finger signs to the boy, and he signaled something back. Sign language? How convenient for having a private conversation in a courtroom. Or for maintaining silence while breaking and entering.

Fiero pressed. "Would you say you *like* animals? Do you have any pets?"

"I have two cats and a dog," Finn said. "But this case has nothing to do with liking animals; the defendants committed multiple property crimes."

Dixon finally rose to his feet. "That's right. Objection, your honor. These animal questions are irrelevant."

About time, Finn thought. But shit, now he'd be stuck with Cargo and Lok and Kee for god only knew how long. He could hardly take them to the pound now.

With film evidence from the lab's security cameras and testimony about how the kids had bragged around campus, there was no doubt in the jury's minds that the trio had committed the crime. The judge didn't seem to take it very seriously though, slapping each defendant with a $500 fine, two hundred hours of community service, and a year's probation.

At four thirty P.M., Finn stood on the grimy sidewalk bordering the Food Mart, studying a memorial of sorts. Bouquets of pink carnations and tiny rosebuds warred for space with stuffed bears and puppies, pacifiers and baby rattles. Pink candles in pebbled glass holders weighed down slips of paper. There were dozens of notes tucked among the items, some in plastic sandwich bags. He snapped on a pair of latex gloves and picked up a few. *We Miss You, Ivy Rose. Where's Ivy? God Bless Brittany and Baby Ivy. We Pray for Ivy. Brittany, did you throw your baby in the trash? Where's Ivy? Where's Ivy?*

A woman wearing a Hawaiian print dress strolled up beside him, her flip-flops snapping against her bare feet. She studied the notes in his hand, and then bent and gently tucked a plastic-encased pink rose into the arms of a tiny white teddy bear. She straightened and glared at him. "How long are you gonna let this go on, Detective?"

"Ma'am?" Did she believe that Brittany was a baby killer? Or that the police were squelching information that would lead to Ivy's whereabouts? She turned and walked away, her footsteps slap-slapping all the way to her car. He picked up all the notes—twenty seven—and slipped them into one of the evidence bags he routinely carried, then called for a tech to come get them. There might be a message from the killer or kidnapper or whoever the hell knew where that baby was. He probably should collect all the toys and flowers and whatnot, too, but he could imagine the public outcry if the police tore down the memorial.

A familiar woman exited the grocery store with a loaded cart. Wendy. A bearded man strolled by her side as they crossed the parking lot. Damn. Finn quickly turned his back, not wanting to acknowledge his wife and her lover. This town was just too damn small. Luckily, his cell phone vibrated at that moment.

"Detective Finn, this is FBI Special Agent Alice Foster. We spoke yesterday?"

"Yes," he said. "How can I help you?" In the reflection on the window, he watched Wendy and the asshole climb into a Lexus SUV and then drive away through the far exit.

"This is more about how we can help you," Agent Foster said. "My colleague and I will arrive at the station tomorrow morning around eight fifteen A.M. Will you be available to talk with us?"

"The station?"

"Your police headquarters, in Evansburg. We've arranged for meeting space with your captain."

Nice of you to coordinate with me, Finn thought. "I'll be there at eight A.M." He headed into the store to do his interviews, trying to decide if he would feel relieved or aggravated to lose this case to the FBI.

Chapter 9

48 hours. That's what the TV show said, the first 48 hours were golden and a crime had to be solved then or else it might never be solved. In one hour, those 48 hours were up. Brittany focused on her feet, watching her pink and silver Nikes march down the sidewalk like they belonged to someone else. She was walking the streets again, like some hooker, like some homeless chick, just watching the cars go by, because she didn't know what else to do. What else *could* she do?

She'd spent the morning on her mom's computer updating Ivy's information on every website she could think of. She'd checked all the messages on her Facebook page and tweeted about how Ivy was still missing. The flyers were up all over; she'd been on the TV news twice and the university talk radio station was repeating her story every hour. The hell with the useless police who wouldn't give her an Amber Alert; she was doing her own Ivy Alert.

But what could she do now? She wanted to call out Ivy's name over and over, like she was a lost cat, like her baby would somehow hear her and cry out for help.

Her back jean pocket vibrated and she heard the first few notes of "Fearless." Her parents had presented her with the new pink cell phone this morning, like it was some sort of consolation prize. Danny had been pissed, of course, so they promised to get him one too. To stay in touch so we can find Ivy, they said. They'd even been able to get her old number. Now if only there was some way to get her contact list back—

she didn't know anyone's number. She'd posted hers on Facebook but she still had to wait for them to call her.

The display on the front of the phone lit up: *WA Cell Phone*. How helpful. "Hello?"

"Brittany."

Finally! "Charlie? Oh, Charlie, isn't it awful? I'm so glad you finally called; I just can't-"

"Britt, what the *hell* have you done?" he asked.

Her voice caught in her throat. "What?"

"The police grilled me in Cheney and tore up my car and my dorm room, and now they're trashing my bedroom here."

"You're here, in Evansburg?"

"Yeah, thanks to you. Look, my parents said they'd get you some money if that baby's mine. Where's the damn paternity test?"

"You *know* Ivy is yours." How could they be arguing about this again now?

"How would I know that?"

"Because you were the only one, you *know* that."

"There are reporters standing outside our house; what the hell do they want? And the FBI just *ordered* me to report for a lie detector test tomorrow. What did you tell them?"

How could he be so angry at *her*? "Charlie, didn't you hear? Someone took Ivy. *Kidnapped* her, right out of my car at the Food Mart."

"*Really*?" he said.

Did he sound sarcastic? She pulled the phone away from her ear and stared at it for a second, wishing she could see his face instead of just his phone number.

"*Really*, Britt?" his voice repeated from a foot away. She pressed the phone back to her ear and heard him say, "Because a lot of people say *you* had something to do with this."

"What people? I wouldn't make that up; someone stole my baby. Someone *kidnapped* Ivy. *Kidnapped* our baby girl!"

"Don't try to drag me into this, Brittany. Whatever you did, you did on your own. And you better make that clear to the police and the FBI, you hear me? You better tell them I had nothing to do with this!"

How could he be so cold? Ivy was his daughter, too. Did he really believe that *she* could hurt Ivy?

"Because, I swear, Brittany, if you ruin my—"

She punched End. How could Charlie talk to her like that? She pushed the phone back into her pocket, thinking about the perfect couple they were only a year ago.

It's all your fault, he'd say as he slid his hand down the front of her jeans. *You're so hot, you set me on fire. You make me crazy.*

In public, he went out with Diana Bluett, one of the country club girls. *She's as boring as history class,* he told Brittany, *but it's the only way to keep my folks off my back.*

I'm not telling anyone about us because I don't want to share you.

You're my burning secret, babe.

And then he'd touch her in all the right places, set her aflame. He rocked her body; he rocked her soul. For three months, they'd done it almost every day. In the equipment shed behind the soccer field, in the hayfield north of town, and a couple of times at her house when she'd skipped school. Their lovemaking was awesome.

But then, because he was a senior, Charlie got busy with the stupid college tests and applications and track, always the damn track team, and weeks would go by before they could connect. She didn't even get the chance to tell him she was pregnant until she was four months along. Well, to be real, she didn't even know for sure she was pregnant for the first three— who knew there could still be blood if you were knocked up? And she couldn't tell anyone before she told Charlie.

She'd dreamed about how he'd say *Now I'm going to tell the world how much I love you. Let's go to Hawaii for spring break to celebrate.*

Instead, he just stared at her for eternity. Then he finally said *No way,* slid out of his car, and left her sitting alone in the school parking lot. She got moved into the Sluts program and they never even passed in the halls. Then he graduated and left town early to go to summer session at the university.

Brittany wiped a tear from her cheek. So she was alone. She'd been alone since Ivy was born, hadn't she? She'd find her baby by herself. She hadn't walked all over this neighborhood yet. Riverside, they called it, although it bordered only a little creek, not a river. Here and there, she heard Spanish floating out through the open windows. Beat-up pickup trucks full of landscaping tools or construction equipment crowded the curbs.

A working class neighborhood, her dad called it. That sounded snotty and it didn't make a lot of sense—everyone worked, so the whole town was working class, wasn't it? But maybe he meant that these people worked hard, sweating outside instead of sitting in some air-conditioned office. Planting bushes or building a house in the sun sounded a lot more useful than filling out forms all day, which was pretty much what her mom did at the bank. She didn't have a clue what her dad did at the recycle plant. Maybe she could get a job at a landscaping company instead of Sears. She stopped walking, looked up, and stared hard around her. How could she be thinking about a job?

Up ahead was a van with dark tinted windows. But instead of Talking Hands Ranch, it said Primero Painting on the side. It was white instead of gray, and the windows were only dark, not mirrored. Inside, she could see cans of paint, rollers, and several buckets.

"Brittany?" A woman dressed in a matching top and pants approached her on the sidewalk. "Brittany Morgan?"

Brittany stopped. "Yes?" she said hopefully.

"You poor thing." The woman spread her arms wide, and then, when Brittany didn't move, threw them around her. Brittany stiffened and tried to pull away, but the woman squeezed her so tightly that she wanted to scream. "You poor, poor thing."

The hug hurt. Her boobs felt like soccer balls, like how she imagined soccer balls would feel if they were so tight-full of air that they could burst under pressure. She had to use hot compresses to keep them from sealing shut like giant pimples. The refrigerator was full of bottles of breast milk and her mother told her there was no more space, but how could she just throw it away? That was like she was throwing away her baby, throwing out motherhood.

The woman smelled like onions. Had she been at home in one of these houses, cooking dinner for her family, and saw Brittany walking by and come out to hug her? It was weird, the way strangers acted like they knew her now.

"Thanks," she murmured, pulling back. The woman finally opened her arms, but her hands stayed on Brittany's shoulders.

"My name's Barbara Sultana, and I live right there." She let go of Brittany long enough to point a manicured finger toward a blue house on the corner. "If there's anything I can do to help, sweetie, just say the word."

Tears blurred Brittany's vision and it felt like she swallowed a peach pit, her throat hurt so bad. The kindness of strangers— that was a famous slogan from some ancient movie or book. The strangers meant to make her feel better, but they always made her want to cry more.

"Just watch out for my baby," she finally choked out.

"I'm praying for you, honey," Barbara said. "Praying for you and Ivy Rose, day and night."

"Thank you." Why couldn't Barbara think of something to *do* instead of just praying? But then, *she* couldn't think of anything useful to do right now, could she? Maybe she should start praying, too. If she prayed for all she was worth, would it make a difference?

Barbara was staring into her face. "Would you like to come in? Maybe have something to eat? A glass of milk?"

"No, thanks." She looked down at the sidewalk. Blades of grass poked up through the crack between the squares of cement. "I need to walk."

"I bet you do, sweetie. Just be careful. And remember that Jesus loves you."

Right. That's why he let Ivy get kidnapped. Oh yeah, God and Jesus were definitely rooting for her. And the dinosaurs died for our sins.

"Well, if I can do anything, you know where I live."

"Okay. Thanks."

Barbara turned toward her house. Brittany walked on. Praying for her and Ivy; a lot of people had told her that in the last few days. Like that would help.

Her family had never been religious. Her mom and dad said that people who wanted to bring religion into school were small-minded. Could losing Ivy be some sort of revenge from God for not being religious? What if she became really devout? Would it bring Ivy home? She stopped and closed her eyes. *God,* she thought in her head, *if you bring Ivy back I'll go to church and I'll pray and I'll even vote with the Virgins on Ice for teaching creationism in biology. OK? Bring Ivy back now and I'll do it.*

She opened her eyes. It didn't look like anything had changed. She turned around to look behind her.

That blue car, parked at the curb a little ways back. She'd noticed it when she'd first started walking, because it had a dent in the front bumper like the driver had driven it into a tree. She'd parked on a different street than this one, and she'd walked at least two blocks. And now the same car was here. A man sat behind the wheel, studying a map that said SEATTLE in great big letters across the front. That didn't make any sense. He looked up. Their eyes met for a second, and then his gaze quickly dropped back to the map.

Her heartbeat sped up. Who the fuck was he? He couldn't be a reporter; if he was, he'd be out on the sidewalk asking her questions. Why was he following her? She stared at him. Should she call 9-1-1?

Down the street, a man and a woman walked toward her, holding hands. The man tilted his head and murmured something to the woman. She'd tell them about the creep in the blue car, see what they said.

When she was nearly up to the couple on the sidewalk, she started, "Hi, maybe I'm crazy, but—"

The woman hissed, "You should be ashamed of yourself, Brittany Morgan. You didn't deserve that sweet baby."

"Aren't you afraid you're going to hell?" the man asked, loud enough for the whole block to hear.

"You'd better pray for forgiveness," the woman added. Then she pulled the man by the hand and they continued on.

Oh god. Her head was ringing. Where had she left her car? Baker Street? She started jogging, but that made her boobs hurt even more, so she slowed to a walk as she approached the corner by the thrift store.

She glanced behind her. The go-to-hell couple was halfway down the street. The blue car was pulling away from the curb. The man stared right at her as he drove in her direction. Was he coming after her? Maybe he'd killed Ivy and now he was going to kill her.

She dashed into the thrift shop and stopped behind the first set of shelves, watching the window through the jumble of toys on the top shelf. She pushed a robot toy to the side for a better view. A princess doll in a ballet tutu fell to the floor.

"Can I help you?" A gray-haired woman positioned herself beside Brittany.

Brittany watched the blue car slide by out front. The man glanced in their direction as he stopped at the four-way stop before driving on. "I think that car's following me," Brittany said.

The clerk turned to the window, but of course the blue car was gone. Brittany stooped to pick up the ballet princess, and then she saw it—her old beige baby carrier, on the floor against the wall. A baby doll sat in it, dressed in a little yellow romper.

Brittany walked to the carrier and jerked it up from the floor, dumping the doll onto the table at her elbow. The clerk turned back to Brittany with an annoyed expression, which Brittany completely got because why was she standing there holding a baby carrier after running into the store like that? She felt like Alice in Wonderland after she fell down the rabbit hole. What was real? The clerk edged around the shelves, barring Brittany from the door. Probably thought she was a shoplifter about to make a run for it.

"This is mine," Brittany told her.

The woman frowned. "We received it in the donation bin yesterday."

"It was stolen from my car."

"Lots of baby carriers look alike."

"See these little stick-ons?" Brittany pointed to a wavy line of green leaves and tendrils that marched down one side of the carrier. "It's ivy. I put those there so it wouldn't get mixed up in class. Ivy—get it?" How could she have forgotten to tell the detectives about the ivy stickers?

Surprise crossed the clerk's face. "Goodness. You're Brittany Morgan, aren't you?" She took a couple of steps backward. So she was probably in the go-to-hell group instead of the praying-for-you group.

And then Brittany saw her blue diaper bag, too, on a table behind the gray lady, with a bunch of other old bags and packs.

"Stay right there. I'll call the police." The woman retreated to the checkout desk.

Brittany picked up the diaper bag backpack. It was empty. Where was Ivy's ducky dress, her socks and diapers? She put the pack inside the car seat and set them down on the floor. She rubbed her hands against the goosebumps on her arms. Who was that creep in the blue car? What did finding the car seat and the backpack *mean*?

It felt scary to find these things without finding Ivy. But finding the backpack and the car seat had to be a turning point, right? There'd be fingerprints or DNA. Maybe her prayer had worked after all.

Three days after Ivy disappears

Chapter 10

Agent Foster was attractive in a buttoned-up way, wearing a lightweight pantsuit with her dark brown hair captured in a plain clip at the back of her neck.

She thrust out her hand to Finn. "Alice Foster, FBI Crimes Against Children unit. And this is Special Agent Dean Maxwell."

"We're here to proceed on the—" Maxwell referred quickly to a notepad—"Ivy Morgan case."

Maxwell's handshake was less firm than Foster's viselike squeeze. Finn chalked that up to the woman overcompensating for being petite and female.

"Proceed in what way?" Finn asked. It came out sounding a little more belligerent than he intended, and he chided himself for letting his frustration show. What he really wanted to say was *Good luck with that.*

"You do know that kidnapping is a *federal* offense," Maxwell said.

Finn folded his arms. "Of course. I've followed all the required procedures."

Foster stepped in front of her colleague. "Yes, we have all your information. We do understand, however, that it's not yet clear whether this is a kidnapping. We need to consult with you about what you've learned so far. And we can provide services that your small department cannot." She pointed to the wheeled case on which Maxwell rested a proprietary hand.

"Agent Maxwell is a trained lie detection expert, and we brought a polygraph."

Finn relaxed a bit. "That *would* be helpful." He'd requested polygraph services from his Captain, but they were still awaiting budget approval from the city council to bring in an outside contractor. Although the tests were not conclusive, at least maybe he could finally get a hint about whether or not Brittany had killed her baby.

"I'll make a list of interviews to do," he told the agents.

"We've got it handled, Detective." Maxwell's gaze met Finn's over Foster's head. "The entire Morgan family will be here at ten thirty A.M.; Charles Wakefield and parents at one fifteen."

"Now, ladies, let's return to the poem. Do you think that Robert Frost was only describing a sleigh ride through the snowy woods?" Mr. Tanz's gaze flitted from girl to girl around the room, skipping Brittany.

Mrs. Taylor hadn't said much to her this morning, either, when she found Brittany standing in front of the photo display. She'd gotten stuck there, mesmerized by the photos of her and Ivy behind the glass. Mesmer-iced was really the right word; for a minute she'd felt frozen in front of the picture of her and Ivy. Like the smiles on their faces, frozen in time.

She felt Mrs. Taylor's hand on her elbow, leading her to her desk, and all the other Sluts had murmured things around her and maybe even to her, but nobody really looked at her before class began. It was like she was one of those giant unicorn-horn pimples that polite people pretended they didn't see. She was the girl who lost her baby.

We have to carry on, Brittany's mother said, try to get back to normal. Was this normal? Feeling like a swollen zit and being invisible?

Beside her, baby Ruben made sucking noises as he nursed, hidden under a blue blanket slung over Joy's shoulder, the way they'd all been taught to breast feed in public.

"The woods are lovely, dark and deep," read Mr. Tanz in his low poetry voice. "How do those words make you feel?"

Brittany thought that words might never make her feel anything ever again. How could words compare with real emotions? Joy switched Ruben to her shoulder and tried to fasten her blouse one-handed under the blanket while patting him on the back. He let out a soft burp, but his brown eyes were already half closed. He was entering the Cuddle Zone—that's what they all called that stage where babies were content and sleepy.

Brittany stretched out her hands. Joy's eyes met hers for a second, and then she handed Ruben over. He was three weeks older than Ivy and heavier, but he was warm and so, so sweet in her arms. She bent her head and pressed her lips to his black wavy hair, choking back a sob. She hoped Ruben would win the modeling contest; if she and Ivy couldn't win, she wanted one of her friends to get the prize. And Joy and her husband had even less money than her family did.

"But I have promises to keep, and miles to go before I sleep, and miles to go before I sleep. Do you think America's favorite poet was simply talking about being tired?" Tanz sounded frustrated now. Most of the teachers thought the Sluts were a little slow. They hated the distracting babies and hated even more how the teachers had to come to the Sluts' room instead of having all students come to them. "Ladies! What other meaning do you think this could have—miles to go before I sleep?"

No response came from the students. Her father was into poetry and that was one of his favorite poems. Brittany knew the answer Tanz wanted, but she wasn't about to say it. Ruben's baby breaths fluttered against her throat like butterfly kisses.

Tanz said it for everyone. "Death! Robert Frost was talking about death!"

The class bell rang, and Ruben jerked but didn't wake. Tanz shut the English book with a sigh. "For tomorrow, read the instructions on page seventy-four and create a haiku poem.

You can choose any subject you like." He strode out of the room.

Joy stood and checked the front of her blouse, folded the blanket and tossed it over the back of her chair. She took Ruben from Brittany's arms and tilted her head toward the hallway. "You could go out there with everyone else now."

"What?"

Joy rocked from foot to foot, cradling Ruben. "You could go back to normal. To the regular classes."

Brittany stared at her. Was Joy trying to get rid of her?

"Because, you know," Joy explained, "Now you don't have a baby, so you don't have to stay in Sluts with the rest of us. You could even try out for cheerleader if you wanted."

Was this was the new normal? Pretending Ivy had never existed? "I never wanted to be a cheerleader. That was you, Joy."

What *would* she do if she didn't get Ivy back? How could she just go on, graduate, get a job, believe that life was turning out the way it was supposed to?

"Brittany!" Her mother stood with Danny in the classroom doorway. That made no sense for a second, and then Brittany remembered—the FBI and the lie detector test. She grabbed her books and ran out of the room, nearly colliding with the incoming algebra teacher.

First up for the polygraph was Danny Morgan, Brittany's eleven-year-old brother. Finn had only spoken to the kid for a few minutes previously; he seemed like a normal little boy, and he clearly thought all the polygraph equipment was fascinating.

"Do you resent Ivy?"

Danny gave Maxwell a questioning look. Maxwell rephrased. "Do you hate Ivy?"

The kid shrugged. "Sometimes. I mean, she cries a lot. And all the money goes for her, and she's just a baby."

"Just Yes or No, Danny. Do you hate Ivy?"

"No." He shrugged again. "I guess."

Maxwell grimaced, made a tick on the page and continued. "Did you kill Ivy?"

Danny snorted. "Like I could do that." He turned toward Maxwell. "You mean, like dead?"

It was going to be a long interview. Finn went to refill his coffee cup.

Noah Morgan and Susan Ciscoe provided no new information and seemed sincere in their statements that no member of their family would hurt the baby.

Brittany was next. As soon as she was alone with the FBI agents, she said, "I think there's someone following me."

"Why would someone follow you?" Foster secured the monitoring strap around the girl's chest.

"I don't know. But there was a blue car last night with a man driving; it was really freaky. Do you think he could be after me? Like maybe he took Ivy and"—she gulped before continuing—"and now he wants to take me?"

Finn winced. Clearly Scoletti needed tailing lessons if he'd been so easily spotted. He hoped the female officer he'd assigned tonight would do a better job.

"Tell the local police about that car." Foster patted Brittany's arm. "Let's get started." She took her seat.

Brittany exploded at the first real question.

"*Kill* Ivy?" Brittany yelled at Maxwell. "Of course I didn't *kill* Ivy. Why would you even ask me that? Why would *anyone* think that? I'm her *mother*!"

Agent Foster, seated at the table across from Brittany, didn't even raise her gaze from her yellow legal pad.

"Just Yes or No, Miss Morgan." Maxwell scribbled a note on the ribbon of paper spewing from beneath the recording pens. "Did you kill your daughter, Ivy Rose Morgan?"

"No," Brittany sobbed, reaching up to rub her eyes.

"Please try to sit still. Did you injure your daughter, Ivy Rose Morgan?"

"No."

"Did you cause anyone else to kill your daughter?"

Brittany leaned forward and covered her face with her hands.

"Please sit up straight. Did you cause anyone else to kill your daughter?"

He had to repeat it again before finally Brittany answered in a strangled voice. "No."

"Did you cause anyone else to injure your daughter?"

Again, a long pause before the girl said, "No."

"Do you know if your daughter is dead or alive?"

Various emotions warred on Brittany's face. Was guilt one of them?

"No," she finally sobbed.

"Did you leave Ivy in the car when you went into the grocery store?"

Finn watched intently. That was one of the questions he'd added to the agents' list.

A tear dripped down Brittany's cheek. "Yes."

"Did you plan for someone to take Ivy while you were in the store?"

"God, no! Why are you treating me like this?"

Maxwell again admonished her to answer only Yes or No and repeated the question, eliciting a "No" from Brittany.

"Did you arrange for Ivy's kidnapping?"

Brittany pressed her lips together and squeezed her eyes closed. "No," she moaned. Maxwell made another note on the recording paper.

"Painful to watch, isn't it?" Dawes stood at Finn's elbow. "But at least the feebies are good for something." He held out a piece of paper. "Thought you might be interested in this. It's a photocopy of a note found at the Food Mart memorial."

IVY IS IN A BETTER PLACE.

All caps. Block letters written with a marking pen. The only aspects that were distinctive were the E's, which were rounded like the left half of the number 8 instead of straight-edged.

"I suppose it's too much to hope for prints?" Finn asked.

"Nothing but smudges."

"Distinctive paper?"

Dawes shook his head. "Common print and copy stock. I'm off to re-interview those teenagers from the parking lot, unless..."

Finn flapped a hand at Dawes. "Go. At least one of us should be out there gathering information. I'll let you know if anything develops here."

"Likewise."

Finn waited until Maxwell finished questioning Brittany, then entered the interview room before Foster detached the polygraph leads. He had a quick whispered conversation with the agents.

"Let's do it now," Foster said, nodding toward the note. Maxwell switched the machine back on.

Finn showed Brittany the photocopy, explaining where the note had been found.

She studied the paper for a long moment, during which she held her breath. Finally she exhaled and raised her tear-filled gaze to look at him. "What does it mean?"

He said nothing, just watched her.

"Ms. Morgan, do you know who wrote that note?" Maxwell asked.

"No." Brittany dropped the page on the floor and stared at it with both hands clasped together. "Who would write that? What does it *mean?*"

Finn wished he had an answer. *A better place.* Heaven? Someone else's arms? Buried in an anonymous grave?

"Ms. Morgan, did you kill your daughter?" Maxwell asked again.

"I told you, no!"

"Ms. Morgan, did you cause your daughter to be killed?"

"The FBI is supposed to help. Why aren't you helping?" Brittany now trembled violently and stared at the window above Foster's head. She quit responding to questions. The FBI agents finally decided to let her go.

As Finn escorted the family out of the building, they passed Charlie Wakefield and his parents on their way in.

All three Wakefields wore identical expressions of icy malice. After a quick glance at Charlie, Brittany kept her eyes down. As Finn passed Travis Wakefield, he heard him mutter, "Incompetent jackass."

If the Morgans heard, they had the decency to pretend they hadn't.

Travis Wakefield and his wife were interviewed first. No new information was revealed. Then Finn observed Charlie's interview with interest. This was the first time Finn had laid eyes on the nineteen-year-old.

"Is Ivy Rose Morgan your daughter?" Maxwell asked.

"Who the hell knows?" Wakefield answered. "Brittany keeps saying so, but she won't do the paternity test." He slumped in his chair. "We're not giving her any money until she does."

"Just yes or no, Mr. Wakefield. Please sit up straight. Do you hate Ivy Rose Morgan?"

Wakefield pushed himself erect again. "I've never even seen her."

Maxwell made a note on the polygraph ribbon. "Yes or no, Mr. Wakefield."

"Then no."

Another note. "Do you hate Brittany Morgan?"

Wakefield hesitated. Finally, he said, "No."

Finn felt a presence at his elbow. Travis Wakefield stood beside him, intently watching Charlie's interview on the video monitor.

"Did you kill Ivy Rose Morgan?" Maxwell asked Charlie.

"No."

"Did you cause Ivy Rose Morgan to die?"

"No."

Finn wondered if he could tell the County Executive to get lost. Probably not; the polygraphs were voluntary, and the guy was his boss's boss.

In the interview room, Maxwell asked, "Did you kidnap Ivy Rose Morgan?"

Charlie answered, "No."

"Did you cause Ivy Rose Morgan to be kidnapped?"

The kid snorted, "Do you mean like did I *pay* someone to take her?"

"Just yes or no. Did you cause Ivy Rose Morgan to be kidnapped?"

Wakefield stared at Maxwell for few seconds as he wiped his hands on his blue-jeaned thighs. "No."

"Do you know where Ivy Rose Morgan is?"

"I wish." That earned him a glare from Maxwell, to which he responded, "No."

"Do you know if Ivy Rose Morgan is dead?"

"No."

"Were you studying at the university library between five and six P.M. last Monday?"

Charlie looked at Maxwell. "I, uh..."

Travis Wakefield strode into the interview room without knocking. Finn followed. "We're done here," the County Exec told the agents. He plucked at the straps on his son's chest and arm.

Both FBI agents jumped up, Maxwell to save his equipment, Foster to ask, "Why the sudden change of heart, Mr. Wakefield?"

Wakefield yanked his son up by the arm. After glancing over his shoulder at his father, Charlie Wakefield approached Finn. "I need to talk to you," the boy murmured in a low voice.

"Go ahead," Finn said.

Travis Wakefield stepped close to them and said, "Charlie and I need a word with you. Alone." He looked pointedly at the two FBI agents.

Was a confession forthcoming? If so, Finn needed a witness. "Agent Foster is attached to this case," he said. "Anything you tell me, she needs to know as well."

The County Executive glared at him and Foster for a moment, then gave in. "All right. But let's take it somewhere more private."

"Back in a minute," Foster said to Maxwell over her shoulder.

Finn led them to the storeroom that doubled as a second interview room when needed. A small table and several folding chairs were sandwiched between shelves of office supplies there, but none of the four sat down. Instead, they stood around the table, shuffling awkwardly. As soon as the door was closed, Travis Wakefield crossed his arms and said to his son, "Tell them."

Charlie pushed his longish blond hair off his brow. "I wasn't at the library when the baby disappeared. I was at work."

Foster put her hands on the back of a chair and leaned on them. "Where do you work?"

Both father and son looked uncomfortable. Charlie said, "I work for a janitorial service. They send us to different places, mostly small businesses. That night I was working at the Ward Building in Cheney from 5:30 P.M. to 10:30 P.M."

"Why did you lie?" Finn asked. "Why did your roommates tell us you were at the library?"

Charlie and his father exchanged a glance. "Uh," the boy mumbled, "I didn't know it was that important to begin with. I told my roommates I was at the library, studying. I really don't need everyone to know that I work as a janitor."

Travis Wakefield said, "I'm sure you can understand how that could be embarrassing for a young man in Charlie's position."

I understand it's embarrassing for you, Mr. Country Club, Finn thought. The Wakefields were clearly on tough financial times if Charlie had to work while going to college.

He said to Charlie, "We'll need the names of your co-workers."

The boy gulped. "I was by myself; the place isn't that big." He pulled a crumpled piece of paper from his pocket and handed it to Finn. "But here's my paycheck stub. See, they put the dates and hours right on it."

Yes, among the list on the printout was the date, along the hours of 5:30 – 10:30 P.M. But Finn needed verification from an actual human being. "Nobody was in the building when you arrived?"

Charlie shook his head. "Everyone was gone, honest. But believe me, if I hadn't cleaned the place, my company would have heard about it the next morning." He apparently thought of what their next question might be, because he said, "I didn't answer my cell phone because I left it in my car. But I called the local police as soon as I got the message."

"I'm sure you can appreciate that good paying jobs are scarce right now," Travis Wakefield told Finn.

"They are," Finn said.

"So we can all agree that Charlie's whereabouts have been documented," Travis Wakefield stated. "I expect you to be discreet about this matter." Taking Charlie by the arm, he walked out the door.

Agent Foster looked perplexed and annoyed. Finn explained the political situation to her. "I'll check with the manager of the Ward Building," he said. "If he can't verify Charlie's presence, maybe there are security cameras that can."

"Let us know what you find out," Agent Foster said. "If you need pressure applied, we can do that."

Finn waited for Agent Maxwell's report, but he was fairly certain of what the polygraph results were going to be.

"The parents and the brother all passed easily," Maxwell told him. "Charles Wakefield's and Brittany Morgan's tests are inconclusive. There was an uptick on Wakefield's graph when we asked about whether he had caused the baby to be harmed and if he knew where she was, but not enough to say he was definitely lying. Brittany Morgan, on the other hand—the graph indicates a probable lie when she said she did not cause her daughter to be harmed."

Had Brittany and Charlie planned something together? According to phone records, they'd talked by cell phone last evening, so they did communicate once in awhile. Did he dare ask the Morgans to let Mason download spyware onto Brittany's new phone?

Alice Foster checked her watch. "We've got a plane to catch. Since we don't have sufficient proof of kidnapping, we'll leave this in your hands, Detective. We'll keep the infant's stats up on the website until the case goes one way or the other. We trust you'll keep us informed of your efforts?"

He nodded. "Of course. Please feel free to send me any thoughts you might have on the case." He was running out of ideas.

"Good luck," Foster said before going out the door.

The clock on the lobby wall reminded him that it was three P.M. He hadn't started on the stack of printouts on his desk. He'd never eaten breakfast or lunch today. *Come back*, he felt like yelling as he watched the agents slide into their car. *The case is yours.*

"Staff reductions will not be announced until the end of the year," the secretary to the Chairman of the Psychology Department told Grace.

"Can you tell me if my name is on a list of possible cuts?"

"I don't have that information, Dr. McKenna."

The woman didn't seem to have *any* information, at least not any that she was willing to share with Grace. If additional funding for her project was not in the works, then it seemed likely her position with the university, nominal as it was, was also on the chopping block. How was she supposed to plan? What was she supposed to do?

"The state has cut funding to all universities, Dr. McKenna; we're all in this together."

Hardly, Grace thought uncharitably; you're not exiled to some backwater where nobody knows you exist.

"Do you have any additional funding sources you can tap?" the secretary asked. "Any private grants you can apply for?"

Grace had been on the verge of asking her the exact same question. Fighting back a surge of frustration, she thanked the secretary and hung up. She tried to push the matter to the back of her mind, and went to join Josh and Neema for Neema's 'social hour' where they didn't work at teaching her new signs, but simply played with the gorilla and recorded her natural sign 'conversation.' Then they'd release her into the outdoor enclosure with Gumu for rambunctious ape interaction.

Josh sat on the floor with Neema, who was trying to give her baby—a plush toy gorilla—a bottle. The two kittens took turns ambushing each other and attacking Neema's other toys strewn around the perimeter of the room.

"I swear, this S-N-A-K-E and baby thing are connected in her furry brain," Josh said. Neema understood far more words than she knew how to sign; often Grace and Josh spelled to each other or used odd synonyms; it was like talking about Christmas around a three-year-old.

Josh continued. "Yesterday, when she talked about that girl who lost the baby, Neema used the S word. Didn't she?"

Grace nodded. "S word, baby, go."

"Man was in there somewhere, too. Along with candy, candy, candy."

Neema looked up. *Tree candy*, she signed around the toy in her arms.

"No candy now," Grace told her. "Josh, don't say the C word again."

"Yes, boss." He went to Neema's toy box and pulled out a set of picture flash cards. He stepped over the kittens and then approached the gorilla. After spreading several flash cards on the floor in front of her, he pulled the plush toy away from Neema, setting it on the carpet several feet away. *Where snake?* he signed. Neema immediately thumped two fingers on the flashcard that showed a zigzagging snake, then reached out for the stuffed baby gorilla. She'd mastered flash cards years ago and was already bored.

Where baby? Josh signed.

Neema rocked the baby gorilla toy in her arms, cradling it in the crook of her elbow as she signed *Baby here. Neema baby want*. The white kitten leapt onto a flash card and then shot off with the calico in hot pursuit. Neema whirled to watch.

"Maybe this is just all about Neema wanting a baby," Grace said.

"Then why does she keep bringing up the S-N-A-K-E?"

Grace knelt on the floor beside Josh, patting Neema's arm to get her attention. *Snake take Neema's baby?* she signed.

The gorilla briefly gazed into her eyes as though Grace was crazy. Then she lowered her head and studiously inspected her finger-like toes one by one.

"Neema thinks Grace is boring," Josh voiced for the gorilla. "Not to mention crazy."

"Not helpful," Grace muttered. She tapped Neema's shoulder. "When did the snake take the baby?" she both signed and verbalized.

Store. Neema looked hopeful again. She laid the baby gorilla toy down on the floor and signed *store candy soda candy.*

Grace ignored the begging. *Snake inside store?*

Neema ignored the question and watched the kittens rocket around the room. *Snow run Nest.*

Josh turned to Grace. "They say caffeine helps kids with ADD. Maybe we should give her some coffee."

"Again," Grace snapped, "Not helpful. I thought you wanted to figure this out."

"Right." He crossed his legs yoga style and faced the gorilla, signing as he spoke. "Neema. Was the baby in the store?"

Baby car. Store candy candy soda.

Where baby now? Josh signed.

Neema glanced around the room as if expecting to discover a baby in a corner. The kittens rolled in a furry ball, Snow thumping Nest with her tiny hind feet. *Cat play,* Neema signed.

Josh persisted. *Where baby now?*

Snake take baby cry, she finally signed.

Snake like this? Grace signed, tapping the flash-card snake. *Snake on ground?*

Bad bad. Neema hooted and looked around the room again, worry clouding her dark eyes. She hated snakes. Even a worm or a caterpillar could send her climbing onto a chair. Species memory, Grace had been told; humans possessed it too.

No snake here, Josh reassured Neema. To Grace, he said, "Is there a sign for 'hypothetical'?" To Neema, he signed *Store snake come on ground, take baby?*

Snake arm man. Baby cry. Store soda go store.

Grace leaned toward her. *Man take baby?*

Man snake arm.

Grace looked at Josh. "What the heck is a snake arm?"

"A mechanical arm?" Josh theorized. "Maybe pincers at the end would seem like a snake head? I used to know a man who had one of those things. Reminded me of Captain Hook. Scared me shitless as a kid."

"Can you draw a picture of one?"

"I'll try." Josh rose and disappeared to the dining area to find paper and pencil.

Grace turned back to the gorilla. Neema had pulled off her red muffler over her head. She chewed the knot for a few seconds, then draped the muffler over one huge black elbow and began twisting the scarlet fabric around her muscular forearm, pulling it tight with her teeth.

"Neema, pay attention." *Where baby go? Where snake arm go?*

Baby go car. Cucumber car.

"Cucumber car?" Grace said aloud.

"A green car?" Josh guessed from behind her.

"Don't put ideas in her head." She turned to Neema. *What color car baby go?*

The gorilla ignored her, seemingly fascinated by the sight of the red muffler twined around her own hairy black forearm.

Josh knelt on the floor next to them, thrusting out his crude drawing of a mechanical arm. *This snake arm?*

Neema dismissed the paper quickly, signing *tongs, give tongs.* She loved Grace's kitchen tongs and often begged to use them to pick up toys or to pinch Gumu.

Grace studied Josh's drawing. "She has a point. Those do look a lot like tongs."

"Cut me some slack; I'm not an artist. That guy from my childhood *did* have tong thingamajigs instead of fingers."

Tongs, Neema signed with her unadorned arm, agreeing. She tugged at the fabric on her other forearm with her teeth.

What snake arm? Grace signed.

Neema waved her muffler-wrapped forearm.

"Duh," Josh huffed. "Ever wonder if she's smarter than we are?"

Grace glared at him. *Snake bracelet arm?* she signed to Neema.

Skin bracelet snake arm, Neema replied. She tore the muffler from her forearm with her teeth, pushed herself to her feet and signed *Coke now*.

Knowing Neema was done with the inquisition for the moment, Grace stood too, signing *juice now*.

"A man with a snake bracelet took that Morgan baby to a green car," Josh summarized. "Are you going to call the police or should I?" His hand was already on the phone.

"Neither one of us. Not yet." Grace took a bottle of apple juice from the refrigerator and poured some into Neema's plastic cup.

"But what about Ivy Morgan?"

Neema gulped the juice down in one swallow, set her plastic cup down on the countertop and brushed her fingertips together, signing *more*.

Grace refilled Neema's cup. "Neither one of us can truly say if Neema saw anything."

The kittens had fallen asleep in the corner. After gulping her juice, Neema went over to investigate, leaning over them silently. She stroked the white kitten's back with a gentle finger.

"You know Neema and Gumu invent stories for their own entertainment," Grace reminded Josh. "And you know how they associate things they see and hear. Remember Lacey?"

Lacey had been one of Neema's favorite volunteers in Seattle. When she took another job and suddenly disappeared from Neema's world, Neema made up a story about how a flock of crows she'd seen flying overhead had taken Lacey away.

Lacey go bad birds, Neema signed now, confirming the memory.

"Neema's been exposed to the television news and now the front page photo, as well as our conversation," Grace reminded Josh.

"But she came up with the S-N-A-K-E on her own, according to you."

Hearing him say it—or spell it—like that gave Grace an unwelcome jolt. "True," she admitted grudgingly. "But you know that Neema's obsessed with serpents."

In the van, in the grocery store parking lot, Neema had called her a snake. And called herself a baby. Clever language usage, Grace thought. She'd even noted that in her daily log. But now...oh god, had she misinterpreted the dialogue? Had Neema been trying to tell her what she had witnessed?

"There was no discussion of a G-R-E-E-N car on the news," Josh said.

He obviously found the prospect of Neema being a witness exciting. Understandable. Under the right circumstances, Neema's story could be dramatic evidence that primates were reasoning, conversational creatures—proof of the validity of their research. *Under the right circumstances.* Did now, at a time when evolution was unbelievably still under debate in local schools, now, when she'd lost her funding and might lose her job, constitute 'under the right circumstances?'

Grace took a deep breath, then swallowed hard. "We need to get her to repeat the same story several times, without prompting. Without rewards."

Neema looked up at the word 'reward,' and brushed her fingers under her chin in the sign for candy.

Josh groaned. "Ever watch that TV show, *The First 48*? It's all about how important the first couple of days are to catching the perps before they're gone. And it's already been longer than forty-eight hours."

Grace frowned. "Calling the cops is the same as calling the media. Especially in this town—witness how reporters are following that poor girl and that detective around."

"So?"

"So you weren't here the last time the media got wind of talking gorillas." A snapshot of Spencer's cold contorted body rose in her imagination. She always saw that vision in black and white, the black corpse on gray cement, white foam drying on the gorilla's lips, black stripes of shadows from the cage bars cutting the horrible scene into long narrow strips. "We're not calling anyone until we're absolutely sure of the truth."

"The attention might bring us more funding."

"Only if Neema's story is true. Otherwise, it will bring us only ridicule."

A grim expression took hold of Josh's face as he considered it.

"So we're not saying anything for now, agreed?"

He sighed, rubbed a hand across his chin. "Agreed."

"Can you take Neema out to the barn and lock them up for the night?"

He went to get Neema's collar and leash. After they'd left, Grace went to her trailer and poured the last glass from her bottle of wine. If she reported that Neema had seen a kidnapping, would she become a hero or the laughingstock of the community? Would increased attention bring more funding and more credibility? Spencer's murder had brought more attention, but the end result was to shuffle the project off to the obscurity in which they now existed. If Neema's story made the news, would any of them be safe afterwards?

When she looked out her bedroom window at seven P.M. and saw the uniformed cop stroll up the walkway to her house, Brittany couldn't decide what to feel. Maybe this was something about Ivy's car seat? The thrift store lady said she had no idea who had put the backpack and the baby carrier in their donation bin. Detective Finn said the baby carrier smelled like the kidnapper had wiped it down with bleach solution, and they couldn't find any fingerprints on it. They did find a partial on the zipper pull of the backpack that might amount to something. Or not. The FBI had taken both the carrier and the backpack to see if their lab could uncover anything more.

It made her want to scream. Didn't they know that *anything* could be happening to Ivy out there? She'd been back through the thrift store neighborhood again after school but hadn't seen anything. She even stopped at the house next door to the donation bin, but they hadn't seen a dark van or anyone with a baby. And this time, as she was driving around, she would have sworn a woman in a silver Subaru was following her. Or was she just going crazy?

That horrible lie detector test—oh god, was that why the cop was here? Would that make the television news tonight? She knew the exact moment she'd failed. *Did you cause your daughter to be killed? Did you cause your daughter to be kidnapped?* She'd said no, but of course the true answer was yes. If she hadn't left Ivy in the car, then she couldn't have been kidnapped. She was responsible for whatever happened to Ivy. On TV, the FBI always helped the family. Why weren't they out searching for her baby instead of torturing her about what she'd done wrong?

They said that Charlie's test was 'inconclusive.' What did that mean? And what the hell did that note mean? *Ivy is in a better place.* It sounded like something a Virgin on Ice or maybe Mrs. Kay would write; they'd think that any other mother would be better for Ivy than Brittany.

The cop was almost at the front door. Oh, god, was this *it*? Maybe they'd finally found Ivy alive and well, or maybe they'd found Ivy—? She couldn't bring herself to think the last word. She felt sick as she galloped down the stairs. The clock had passed that magic 48-hour mark a day ago. Half the town thought she'd killed Ivy; they all thought she should go to hell.

She didn't have to *go* to hell. She was already there. She could barely remember what Ivy's skin felt like under her fingertips. Ivy got diaper rash really bad if she forgot to put on the ointment—did the kidnapper know that?

Last night Ivy woke her up four times. The first time the cry was so loud and real, she got up and wandered around downstairs looking for the baby. Could it have been a premonition of some sort? She was going to take Joy up on that offer of some X. She really needed something that would give her hope.

Her dad got to the door first. The cop framed in the doorway was the one who gave a safety lecture to the Sluts class—use the deadbolt, lock the car doors, don't give personal information to strangers online. She remembered because his name was Morgan, too.

"Brittany Morgan?" he asked, as if he didn't know who she was. Everyone in the state knew who she was now. Just this morning a perfect stranger, an old bitch of a grandma, clamped onto her arm and asked, "Where's Ivy?"

It couldn't be good news if the cop started off that way. "Yes?" *Just spit it out. Whatever it is. I have to know.*

"This is for you." He handed her a piece of paper.

She stared at it through a blur of tears. They notified mothers about their dead babies with a piece of paper now? Cold.

Her father pulled it out of her hands and scanned the page. "She's under *arrest*?" he yelled. "Is this because she failed the polygraph? She *volunteered* to take the test."

Morgan the Cop tucked his chin, making his neck wrinkle. "She failed a polygraph?"

Her father stuck a finger out at the cop's chest. "I happen to know that polygraph results are not admissible in any reasonable court. Failure does *not* mean she's guilty."

How many times were they going to bat that back and forth? She was glad when Morgan the Cop didn't respond.

"Like that notice says, the D.A. has charged Brittany with Reckless Endangerment. For leaving the baby in the car." The cop hooked a thumb in his belt and shifted his hips, like all that gear was weighing him down. "I'm sorry."

He said it to her father, not to her.

"You sons of bi—" her father started.

She put a hand on his arm. "It's okay, Dad, I deserve—"

"Stop!" He threw up his hands like he was fending her off. "Don't say another word!"

Morgan the Cop stepped back out of the doorway and pulled a card from his pocket. "You have the right to remain silent..." He went through the whole thing, just like on TV. "Do you understand what I just said?" he asked her at the end.

She nodded miserably. "I think so."

"You're damn right we want a lawyer," her father said.

"Brittany's old enough to make that decision," the cop said.

She looked at her father. "Yeah, I guess we want a lawyer."

The cop pulled out another card. "Public Defender?"

Her father swallowed as if his throat hurt. "I don't know yet." He took the card.

"There's no shame in it, Mr. Morgan. Your taxes pay for them. We've got some good PDs here."

Brittany stepped onto the threshold and held out her wrists toward Officer Morgan. A flash went off, startling the three of them. The cop turned toward the gate and yelled, "Get outa here, you damn leech!"

"Get off my property!" her dad shouted.

"Public sidewalk!" The photographer trotted away, camera in hand.

Morgan the Cop turned back to her. "No, honey," he said. "I'm not taking you in. But you have to come to court at the time it says on that paper." He glanced at her father again. "You'll see that she's there?"

Her dad nodded, Officer Morgan walked away, and her father closed the door. She trudged back upstairs. Each step was a major effort, like she was wearing ski boots. Did this mean they weren't going to look for Ivy anymore?

At seven thirty P.M., Finn was still at the station, staring at his computer, hoping for a revelation. Dawes had gone to Cheney to talk to Charlie's associates, his boss, and the residents of the Ward Building. Unfortunately, the building had no security cameras, but perhaps one of the companies that leased space could help determine the validity of Charlie's alibi. Detectives Larson and Melendez were interviewing the girls who'd been absent from Brittany's class. After the polygraph test, he'd put in for a subpoena for the Morgans' phone records for the last three months. If Brittany had plotted with Charlie or a friend to do something to the baby, maybe he could catch them that way. Tomorrow, Verizon promised.

Miki materialized beside his cluttered desk, a stack of paper in her hands. Finn sat up. "You're still here?"

"*You* are." She smiled. And was that a wink?

Had to be his imagination. For the first time Finn noticed that her eyebrows were painted on. What kind of nineteen-year-old chose to work overtime for free and painted on her eyebrows?

"About Talking Hands Ranch?" she asked.

"You found it?"

She thrust a few pages at him. "Unfortunately, no. Like I already told you, there's no business registered with that name in Washington State. There's a Helping Hands Agency in Oregon and a Working Hands Co-op in Idaho. Google just comes up with garbage."

"So what is this?" He nodded toward the pages she still held.

"I hope I'm not out of line, but I checked for disappearances of infants across the U.S. in the last five years."

"Good thinking, Miki." He'd checked the Washington cases and read the report about the missing Kinsey baby in Oregon, but had not yet looked beyond that.

She held out the sheaf. "I emailed the files to you, too.

He took the pages from her.

"It's really terrible. Some people just shouldn't have babies. You have to wonder how many of these were born out of wedlock." The phrase sounded odd coming from her young lips. But this was Evansburg, and many young people here were more conservative than senior citizens in Chicago.

A cluster of patrol cops, now in street clothes, were

gathering around the back door at the end of their shift. One turned and yelled across the room. "Hey, Scoletti—want a ride?" Scoletti turned away from the desk clerk he was chatting with. "Nah. I'll be right behind you. Meet you there in five."

The group went out to the parking lot, and a few seconds later Scoletti crossed the room to the back door. Spying Finn at his desk, he paused. "Hey, Finn, a bunch of us are going to Brady's, wanna come?"

He waved. "Can't, thanks."

Scoletti shrugged and left. Finn tapped his pen on his notepad. Well, at least someone had included him this time, even if it had been an afterthought. He missed tossing a few back each week with his Chicago crew.

His cell phone buzzed and he picked it up. Damn—his ex-mother in law again. Probably another invitation to dinner, where he'd have to hear about what Wendy was up to and how they just didn't understand what went wrong between the two of them. He let the call go to voicemail.

An hour later, he was still in his desk chair. Mason was scrambling around at the desk beside him, attaching some gizmo to the computer there. "Working overtime?" Finn asked.

The computer tech's voice answered from under the desk. "Some people have lives; the rest of us have work."

Finn rubbed his forehead, not wanting to think about how depressing that statement was. The list of missing infants on his computer screen—eighty-seven across the U.S. in the last five years—was appallingly long. But knowing the way public records worked, he'd wager that at least a third of those cases had been resolved without updating the records. And some had probably never been missing in the first place. Still, there had been sixteen alleged infant kidnappings nationwide in the last six months, five in the northwest. As well as Serena Kinsey, he had a likely match for one other teenage mom of a missing baby on the YoMama.org users list—a girl in Coeur d'Alene, Idaho named Carissa Adams, whose infant son William had disappeared four months ago from his bassinette during the night. The baby had only been two weeks old at the time.

Coeur d'Alene was only an hour or so away from Cheney, where Charlie Wakefield attended school, and the baby had vanished two weeks after Charlie had started summer session. Was there a connection? Stranger things had happened.

Three teenage mothers, three missing babies, all using YoMama. Coincidence? And there could be more. He'd matched Kinsey and Adams only because their user names—SKORGirl and CariSad—hinted at their real names.

"Mason," Finn said. "How goes the matching of the YoMama user names?"

Mason crawled from under the desk into the chair and touched a button on the keyboard. "I'm working on it. It'll take days to match the names to the class lists. YoMama lets users stay on the site until their 20th birthday, so I've got a mountain to plow through. And naturally the lists are not standardized for easy searches. Two of the teachers *typed* their class lists. On a *typewriter*." He stood up and stomped out of the room.

"Huh." Finn called the Coeur d'Alene police department and asked them to send him the Adams case file so he'd have info on all three cases with the YoMama link.

"We're understaffed, Detective," the sergeant told him. "Although it's still an open case, it's on the back burner. And the detective in charge of that case is on leave at the moment. We'll get that out to you in a week or so."

Fuming, Finn hung up and glared at the phone for a minute. 'In a week or so' was not soon enough. Mason came back, a cable dangling from his right hand, as Finn looked up distances and airline schedules on his computer. "Damn."

"Having a bad hair day?" Mason asked.

"Just a comment on life in general," Finn told him. It was almost a five-hour drive to Coeur d'Alene and he'd have to get up before dawn, but driving would work out better than the plane schedule between small airports. He scheduled the Portland trip for the day after and paid for his Horizon Air flight with his own frequent flier miles.

Chapter 11

Finn left his house a little before five A.M. When he arrived at Carissa Adams' school in Coeur d'Alene nearly five hours later, he was painfully stiff from sitting in the car and his tie was stained with grease from the Egg McMuffin he'd picked up along the way.

He caught up with the head of the local Sister-Mothers Trust program, Marsha Valdez, just before she began her next class. She gave her teaching assistant an assignment, and then she led Finn to the teachers' lounge for bad coffee. He didn't get much useful information. Carissa was not in her class this year, but had seemed depressed at the end of the last school year. Valdez had never heard of Charlie Wakefield.

She walked Finn to the principal's office, where he was told that Carissa was out sick that day, and then she ushered him down the hallway to the outer door, passing a display of photos of girls and babies nearly identical to the one in Evansburg. Probably a requirement in the Sister-Mothers handbook or something. A janitor was polishing the glass on top of the display case. Finn saw no photos of Carissa Adams and baby in the mix.

"Pretty little things, ain't they?" the janitor said, nodding toward the photos. The gray-haired man wore a coverall with three red stripes on the shoulder, similar to what the cleaning lady had worn at Brittany's school. "Especially these two." He pointed to a brown-haired girl with huge earrings and a chubby baby. "'Course I could be a lil' bit prejudiced, 'cause that's my grandbaby. And my great grandbaby."

Finn faked a chuckle for the janitor and then walked out of the building. Had the Coeur d'Alene police interviewed the janitorial staff? Now that he thought about it, he realized that none of the Evansburg detectives had interviewed the school janitors at Brittany's school. He called Dawes and left instructions to remedy that oversight.

Finn drove through the unfamiliar streets to Carissa Adams's neighborhood, which could be described, if one was being unkind, as a trailer park. But these days most of the trailers were manufactured homes and the lots in this park had flowers and fountains. Some even sported tiny patches of grass. The yards looked like a heck of a lot less work to maintain than mowing his three acres of weeds.

The girl's mother welcomed him with a glass of iced tea. It was sweet tea, though, and in Finn's opinion sugar qualified as a pollutant in tea or coffee. After gagging down a mouthful, he set the glass down on the coffee table.

"William was only two weeks old," sixteen-year-old Carissa Adams said to the worn beige carpeting beneath her feet. Her hair, a short spiky weave of maroon and black, did nothing to enhance the girl's blotchy moon face. She didn't seem sick to him, in spite of her alleged stomach virus.

Carissa's mother eyed him like a hen keeping watch on a hawk. A photo of a tiny dimpled smooth-skinned baby surveyed them from the wall. William, no doubt; all black hair and big blue eyes.

Sweat slid down the back of his neck. The windows were open and outside the manufactured home, a handyman was using a leaf blower; he hoped the man would finish soon because Carissa had not yet spoken above a whisper. She sat hunched over like a wilted flower, tears dripping from her face onto her peasant blouse and green cropped pants.

"Tell me what happened to William," he finally said.

"We've been over this so many times already with the local police," the mother complained from her armchair. She tapped ash off her cigarette into the ashtray she held in her lap.

"I know, ma'am. It's not my jurisdiction, but my case in Washington is similar—missing baby, teenage mom in the Sister-Mothers Trust program. We're trying to figure out if there are any connections. It's possible that by solving one we'd solve them both."

"I was sleeping," Carissa finally said. "William was in his cradle. And when I woke up, he was gone." She rubbed her hands over her face, smearing tears and mascara across her plump cheeks. Through her fingers, she stole a glance at his face, then quickly returned her gaze to the carpet.

He asked to see the room that William had disappeared from, and the mother took him to a cramped bedroom. Clothes formed a heap on the double bed, waiting to be folded. Both male and female clothing. The toe of a man's cowboy boot poked through the open door of the closet.

"Who besides Carissa sleeps in this room?" Finn asked.

The mother leaned on the door frame. "Jerome. Carissa's boyfriend."

"Is Jerome William's father?"

The woman nodded.

"When did he move in?"

"About a year ago, after Carissa got pregnant. He's a good boy—I mean, young man—he works on a threshing crew part of the year, and for a security company the rest. He's been real good to me and Carissa."

"He's at work this morning?"

She nodded again. "He's real diligent."

"How did Jerome like being a father?"

"He was proud of that baby. He didn't like the crying, but who does?"

There was an awkward silence for a minute. Then the mother said, "William was in a bassinet over by the window. Which was open, just a crack."

"No screen?" he asked.

"We don't have bugs around here."

Only a wooden stool sat beneath the window now, a hairbrush on the seat.

The mother exhaled a long stream of smoke before she said, "Carissa couldn't stand lookin' at the bassinet anymore. It's in the storage shed out back."

They returned to the living room and Finn asked Carissa a few more questions. "Do you know Brittany Morgan?"

"She's been on TV. The girl with the missing baby, right?"

"Right. How about Serena Kinsey?"

The girl's expression was blank.

"Brittany is Hot-T on YoMama. Serena is SKORgirl."

"Oh," she said. "Then yeah, I used to message them, probably. But I haven't been on YoMama since..." Her words trailed off.

"Do you know this boy?" He showed them Charlie Wakefield's photo. The mother immediately shook her head, but Carissa held the photo for a long minute.

"I think maybe I saw him before."

Finn leaned forward. Now they were getting somewhere. "Where?"

"On YoMama. We were talking 'bout the daddies, you know, and we sent some pictures around. This guy is Ivy's daddy?" She handed the photo back.

"We think so," Finn said. "Ever seen him in person?"

Carissa shook her head.

Damn. "Carissa, what do you think of the Sister-Mothers Trust program?"

"Um." She glanced at her mother. "I think it was a good thing, that girls didn't have to drop out of school just because they're moms too. But since I don't have a baby now, I don't go there anymore."

She burst into tears and buried her face in her hands. "I was such a bad mother," she sobbed.

"I'm sure that's not true," he said gently.

Carissa started crying in earnest, with loud hiccups, and her mother moved over to her, rubbing her back. Finn excused himself, glad to exit that sad household, and left for the Coeur d'Alene police station to question the local officers about the case.

It was after eight P.M. when Finn drove up his driveway. He practically fell out of the car, walking like Frankenstein after driving ten hours in one day. Curiously, the dog and cats were not on the porch to meet him. Half of him hoped they had run off, the other half was disappointed at the lack of a welcome. When he opened the front door, he heard the click of Cargo's nails on the wooden floor. The dog materialized out the dark hallway and pushed his massive head under Finn's hand. "What are you doing in here?"

Cargo barked in response. He heard a low rumble somewhere in the back of the house. Had he left the patio door open? He popped the safety strap from his holster and walked quietly into the living area, one hand on his pistol.

Instead of the stench of the overflowing litter box that he'd left this morning, he smelled ... lemon? The carpet was freshly vacuumed, the piles of paper slithering off the dining room table were neatly stacked, and the oak tabletop gleamed in the light cast by a living room lamp. In the kitchen, the dishes had been washed and the garbage emptied. Lok and Kee were curled up together in his recliner. Kee opened one eye, regarded him for a second, then went back to sleep.

He walked to the sliding glass doors and flipped on the deck light. The back yard lawn had been neatly mowed. Finn took off his jacket and his shoulder holster and laid them on a chair.

The rumbling noise in the utility room stopped. The clothes dryer. Quickly, he checked the bedroom. All neat and tidy. Oh jeez, he'd left a big pile of dirty clothes in the corner, jockey shorts and sweaty socks on top.

For a wild minute, he imagined that Wendy had come back. *I was insane to ever leave you, Matt. Can you forgive me?* But that was crazy. His second leap of insanity was that Miki had somehow copied a key to his house, which was a terrifying thought.

Then he found the note on the refrigerator.

WE WORRY ABOUT YOU.
CALL WHEN YOU CAN.
S & D

Shit, this was embarrassing. But the stroganoff his mother-in-law left in the refrigerator tasted like heaven.

Chapter 12

Josh laid out several pictures of young women in front of Neema. All were in color, two had reddish hair. The photo of Brittany Morgan was cut from the front page of the newspaper this morning, where she'd been pictured holding out her arms to receive handcuffs. Grace had trimmed away the others in the photo and the quality was grainy, but at least it was in color and it showed the girl's face. They'd also cut out Ivy Morgan's image from a poster Josh had picked up at the convenience store.

Grace drew the gorilla's attention to the photos on the floor. She signed, *Where red hair girl?*

Store. Neema signed with both hands. *Go store candy Neema.*

Show me red hair girl. Grace gestured to the photos.

Neema's eyes flicked over them, then she slapped her hand on first a red-haired older woman, and then on Brittany's image.

"Which was the red hair girl at the store?" Grace asked aloud, simultaneously signing.

Go store candy Neema.

"Which girl was at the store?" Grace persisted.

Neema slapped the newspaper photo of Brittany Morgan. She signed *Now candy now hurry.*

Where baby? Josh signed.

Neema looked around the room, and then finally back to them. *Baby cat sleep box.*

"Not the kitten." *This baby*. Grace pointed to the photo of the kidnapped infant. *Where this baby?*

Red hair baby store car. Candy Neema hurry.

Josh exhaled a puff of air in exasperation. "Can we give her a piece of candy so we can get on with the story?"

Grace quickly unlocked a drawer, unwrapped a lollipop and handed it to Neema. The thought that it was unwise to give in to a 400-pound gorilla flashed across her mind, as it so often did. She was a lax parent, raising a spoiled daughter. The trouble was, her 'kid' was capable of throwing her across the room if she so desired. It was hard to know where to draw the line.

Good tree candy, Neema signed. She popped it into her mouth.

Josh smiled. "I still can't get over how she adds the word 'tree' as a descriptor for anything on a stick. I would never have believed it if I hadn't seen it with my own eyes." He watched Neema suck on her lollipop for a minute. "Of course, three years ago I wouldn't have believed that gorillas could comprehend human language, let alone sign it. Nowadays I wonder if the birds are talking about me."

Grace knew the feeling. *Where this baby?* she signed to Neema, then tapped baby Ivy's photo again.

Store. Go store Coke.

"No," Grace groaned. Did mothers of human kids suffer through conversations like this, constantly zooming off on tangents instead of sticking to the topic? "Where is this baby now?" she pressed, pointing to the photo. "Where did this baby go?"

Baby go, Neema agreed. *Snake arm baby cry.* She crunched the candy between her teeth, and then pulled the naked stick out of her mouth and examined it closely to make sure she'd missed none of the sweet.

Snake on ground? Snake in car? Grace signed rapidly, her lips pressed into a grim line.

Man snake arm baby cry. Sensing that this was important, Neema decided to take advantage. *Candy more hurry*, she signed.

Josh leaned forward to connect with Neema's gaze. "Where is the snake?" His hand made a serpentine motion, two fingers pressed out like fangs. "Where is this baby?" He tapped the newspaper photo.

Neema eyed the kitchen drawer, signing *candy candy*.

"Blackmail." Grace reluctantly pulled out another lollipop and handed it over. As soon as Neema had it in her mouth, Grace asked again, "Where is the man snake? Where is the baby?"

Man snake go. Baby cry baby go, Neema signed. Then she clenched her hands into fists, and rolling her lollipop around on her tongue, scooted back to her *National Geographic*.

Josh and Grace eyed each other.

"The snake business, the baby business—is it possible?" Grace stuttered.

Josh glanced at Neema, who now cradled her baby gorilla toy in her arms and held the magazine with her feet. "Sounds like she was trying to tell us what she saw."

Grace swallowed hard. "We *were* in the parking lot around the time that the baby supposedly was kidnapped..."

"Whoa." Josh's face lit up. "I've just found the perfect subject for my dissertation. Signing gorilla vital witness to crime."

Crap, Grace thought. "I so hoped it wasn't true."

Neema scooted back over to them. *Cat baby cat*, she signed. *Want baby cat now now*.

"Good idea. Better than more C-A-N-D-Y." Josh rose from his chair. "I'll go get the kittens."

Grace groaned and leaned forward, resting her head on her arms on top of the table. She couldn't deny it any longer; Neema had likely seen a man take the baby from the store parking lot. She couldn't ignore the fact that her gorilla could be helpful in a criminal case.

But she'd have to be very, very careful. She couldn't risk another nutcase finding out about her gorillas. The kidnapper was out there somewhere. What if *he* discovered that Neema had witnessed the abduction? She couldn't get the image of Spencer's corpse out of her mind.

Spencer hadn't been involved in an important event like this. He definitely didn't want the attention that came after one of her students made a video of Spencer and Grace conversing, complete with subtitles. Spencer had been one contented gorilla learning sign language. Until a zealot named Frank Keyes, outraged that anyone could believe that an ape could 'talk' like a human being, gave that innocent gorilla a cup of cyanide-laced Kool-aid. Keyes had received a sentence of only two years in prison for animal cruelty and a hefty fine for destroying university property.

Keyes was out walking the streets somewhere right now. Grace needed her alarm system in place yesterday. But how could she pay for it now?

Warm leathery fingers softly caressed Grace's arm. She raised her head. Neema sat only a foot away, cuddling Snow in one arm, an anxious look on her face. She signed, *Sad?*

"A little," Grace admitted, holding thumb and forefinger close to show Neema how much. That poor Brittany girl, being arrested, nobody believing her. And her baby was out there somewhere. In whose arms? Snake man's?

Grace knew what she had to do. She needed to get off her butt, climb into her old car, and go do it soon. Lives could be at stake.

Neema leaned forward and brushed her black lips across Grace's cheek in a gorilla kiss, then sat back and held out the white kitten. *Grace love baby cat. Good now.*

Neema was right. Holding the soft fuzzy kitten in her arms did help a little. *Thank you*, she gestured.

Neema Grace love good, Neema signed. *Cat Gumu love. Gorilla love good.*

Grace's heart melted. This giant hulk of a creature was so gentle, so loving. And so completely dependent on her for food, shelter, safety. For her very life.

Serena Kinsey lived with her grandmother Felicia Brown in an ornate Victorian house in Portland, Oregon. The authentic purple, pink, and gold paint colors and the antique rose beds told Finn that Mrs. Brown considered this her castle. Not what he had expected when he'd seen Serena's story on the news, he had to admit. He chided himself for the stereotypes his brain had filed away after so many years as a cop.

"I left Tika right there," the girl said, stabbing a finger at a playpen that still sat on the wide planks of the covered front porch. A lonely pink stuffed pony watched them from one corner of the netting.

Unlike timid weepy Carissa, Serena was dry-eyed and she was *pissed*. "Tika was sleeping, and I went inside to answer the phone, and when I came out, the playpen was empty. I think it was a set-up."

"Why?" He flipped back a page in his notebook. "Who was on the phone?"

"It was a wrong number. Grandma's number is unlisted, so we hardly ever get those."

That information had not been in the police report. Maybe Serena had good reason to be suspicious. "Do you have any ideas about who might have taken her?"

Serena glanced across the street. "At first I thought it might be Adrian's mother."

Adrian was Tika's father, according to the file Finn carried in his briefcase, and he lived across the street. "Why would you think that?"

Serena put her hands on her hips. "She hates me. Always has, always will."

"The woman believes that Serena got pregnant just to trap Adrian," Mrs. Brown said. "As if her precious boy had nothing to do with the baby. He'd always been planning on going to college here, not back east, as he'll tell you himself."

"How about your parents, Serena?" Finn asked.

Her wary brown eyes met his. "What about 'em?"

Mrs. Brown stepped forward. She wore a stern expression that promised she would rap knuckles with rulers if listeners failed to pay attention. "Serena's father died in Afghanistan three years ago. My daughter, Serena's mother, committed suicide six months later."

Now Finn understood why there was no information other than their names in the police report. This family seemed to be cursed.

A young man on a bicycle stopped across the street and laid the bicycle on the lawn. Adjusting the book bag he wore on his shoulder, he trotted across the pavement between the parked cars, and then galloped up the steps, pushing his light brown hair out of his eyes.

"What's up?" He threw an arm around Serena's shoulders and eyed Finn distrustfully. "You're a cop, aren't you?"

Before Finn could reply, the kid stepped forward and thrust out a hand. "Adrian Lomas, Serena's fiancé. And Tika's father. And you are?"

Finn introduced himself and explained he was looking for similarities in child disappearance cases in Oregon, Washington, and Idaho.

"That's more action than we're getting out of the local cops," Adrian said angrily. "Not to mention the press. Between you and me, I think it's because Serena's black."

Finn had no response to that.

"We're going on *America's Most Wanted* next week," he continued. "If the locals aren't going to help, we're going national. Won't the Portland cops look like racist hicks when someone reports they found our daughter?"

Finn held up his hands. "I'm just here to get your story. I'd especially like to hear about the school program, because the other girls belonged to that, too."

"What school program?" Serena said.

"Sister-Mothers Trust?" he enunciated carefully. It was no wonder Brittany had come up with Sluts on Toast. That, or the more natural 'smut,' was much easier to pronounce than the official name.

She made a face. "That's a high school thing they made me go to. I graduated last May. Now I go to the university."

"But you still communicate with other teen mothers via the YoMama website?"

"Sometimes," she said, her face softening into sadness. "They let you stay on until you're twenty. I don't know any other moms close to my age. Not many people can understand what it's like."

"Except for other young moms like Brittany Morgan and Carissa Adams," Finn said.

"Yeah, if anyone can understand what I'm going through, it's Brittany. I don't know Carissa, though." She shook her head, thought for a second, then said, "Oh wait, CariSad?"

He nodded. "That's her user name."

Serena rubbed a finger across her full lips. "I remember something happened to her baby, but that was a while ago."

Finn shifted his weight from one foot to the other. "Last June. Her baby William disappeared during the summer."

"And you think there might be a connection with Tika?" Adrian asked.

Finn turned to face him. "It could be coincidence, but the SMT program and the YoMama website are connections."

"The website? Whoa." Adrian's eyes gleamed. "I'm studying computer science, with an emphasis on security."

Finn studied his young face for a minute, then told him, "Hack away. We need all the help we can get." He shot a look at Mrs. Brown and Serena. "You didn't hear me say that."

"Hear you say what?" Mrs. Brown asked.

Serena fidgeted with one of her long earrings while staring at Adrian.

"What?" the boy finally said.

She looked embarrassed. "We share a lot of girl talk on YoMama."

"You mean bitching about the baby daddies," Adrian guessed.

"Well, yeah," she said. "I guess you could call it that."

He touched her forearm. "I'll cope."

The two of them seemed like a more mature couple than he and Wendy had ever been. Finn turned to Serena. "Speaking of the daddies, do you know Charlie Wakefield?"

"Ivy's daddy, according to Brittany. College student at Eastern Washington U," Serena responded. "I've seen his photo, too. But I've never met him."

"Did Brittany ever say she was scared of him?"

"Nope," Serena said. "He sounded like a no-count to me, but she adored him as far as I could tell."

"Would he know you?" Finn asked.

"Not unless Brittany shared our emails," she said.

Damn. He just couldn't make Charlie fit into the school scenarios. "I'd like to hear about how the Sister-Mothers Trust program worked at your high school. What you got out of it, how it was organized, and so forth. How you communicate on the YoMama site."

Serena, eyes glistening now, stood for a moment with her fingers wrapped around the top rail of the playpen, gazing down at the plush pony inside. Adrian put his hand on top of hers.

Mrs. Brown held open the front door. "Let's go in and chat. I don't know about those other babies, but plenty of people would want Tika."

Finn sat down beside her on a leather couch. "Why's that?"

Felicia Brown twisted, picked up a silver-framed photo from the side table. "Just look at her, Detective."

He studied the picture. The baby girl had black curls, olive skin, shining doe-brown eyes, and deep dimples in both cheeks. Tika was stunning.

William, for a two-week-old, had been a handsome boy. And Ivy was exceptionally pretty. Beautiful babies. "Did you ever enter Tika in a modeling contest?" he asked Serena, suddenly inspired.

Her forehead wrinkled. "No way," she said, dashing his hopes at making that link. "I'd never do that to a child of mine."

Still. Three moms from the Sister-Mothers Trust program, all using YoMama to communicate. Three missing babies. The key had to be there somewhere.

On the bumpy plane ride through sunset-colored clouds back to Evansburg, Finn reviewed the three cases. The other two babies had gone missing from their homes, but the Morgan baby had vanished from a busy parking lot in broad daylight.

How could a kidnapping happen in a public place without a single witness? It truly was mind-boggling. If it truly *was* a kidnapping. His mind kept circling back to that. According to her classmates and teacher, Brittany had left with Ivy at the regular time, 3:45 in the afternoon. Then Brittany and Ivy, freckle-faced Joy Saturno and baby Ruben, and Jennifer and baby Jason, had gone for fries and shakes at the local drive-in. They'd talked about how their babies would do in the Pretty Baby photo contest the next day. According to all of them, Joy had made snarky comments about Ivy not being ethnic enough, and about how the judges wouldn't pick Ivy because Charlie and Brittany weren't married. Brittany retorted that Joy was just afraid that Ivy would win. Then the girls split up, and Ivy's trail went cold.

The stories of all the Food Mart employees had stayed pretty much the same from five days ago. One cashier remembered seeing Brittany that day, and so did the teenage stock clerk and the kids in the parking lot, but nobody remembered seeing Ivy.

Brittany could have ditched the baby carrier and backpack after she'd ditched the baby. Could she have been so upset over Joy's remarks that she'd murdered Ivy? Or accidentally killed her? She certainly acted remorseful. The newspaper image of her, arms extended for handcuffs, tears streaming down her face, could be her confession. Or not.

The baby's disappearance could be Charlie Wakefield's doing, somehow. Or not. Dawes had found nobody to corroborate Charlie's story of working that evening. Finn stared out the window as they passed over the Cascades. On the eastern side of the mountains, the dense green carpet of evergreens below was brightened by slashes of burnished gold. Larches. He'd read about them in a magazine but hadn't yet seen them up close. He and Wendy had talked about making a special trip through the mountains in autumn to enjoy the show.

As the plane taxied to a stop at the little airfield on the outskirts of town, Finn turned on his cell phone and heard the bleep of its message-waiting tone. The first message was from Miki. "The FBI called; they found Talking Hands Ranch. It wasn't the name of a business, but just a nickname for a place where the University of Washington did research. I say *did* because they sold that property almost a year ago. But anyway, we have a VIN and the registered owner's at the UW. I left the printouts on your desk. Hope this helps."

Maybe it was a real clue at last? He checked his watch. The timing sucked. Nobody would answer a university phone after eight P.M. on a Saturday night.

"Next message," the phone announced.

"Someone might have witnessed what happened to that missing baby," a female voice said.

His blood pulsing faster now, he pulled a pen and notepad from his shirt pocket. He startled at the touch of a hand on his arm. The plane had come to a stop and the woman seated beside him gestured for him to get up.

"It was a young female who lives with me." The voice continued. "She's my ward, I guess you'd say."

He unbuckled his seatbelt, grabbed his briefcase from beneath the seat in front of him and then slid into the aisle, the phone still pressed to his ear. He heard the caller take a breath.

"She told me that a man with a snake bracelet took the baby to a green car."

He felt a flare of excitement in his gut. Was this for real? How old was this kid—this young female ward?

It was as if the caller had heard his thought. "My ward is twelve. But she has the IQ of a five-year-old."

Great. A child witness who was mentally retarded? The line of passengers ahead of him finally moved. He walked toward the exit door and descended the stairs onto the dimly lit tarmac.

"She was in the parking lot at the time it happened. I was in the store. I only just now realized what she was trying to tell me."

A mentally retarded child. But finally, someone had *seen* something. He couldn't wait to talk to this kid.

"I'm sorry, but you can't contact her. She's very fragile. That's all the information I have to give. I hope it helps in some way. Brittany Morgan doesn't deserve what's happening to her."

Then the woman hung up. He stood on the tarmac for a minute, the heat radiating up through the soles of his shoes, staring at the caller ID. Crap. It had come in through the department switchboard, who had forwarded it to his cell. But with luck, the switchboard would have it in their call log.

Man. Snake bracelet. Green car. He'd go back to the Food Mart and re-interview the staff; maybe put out the message to the public on the TV station. But...clues from a retarded child? He had to interview that girl and her guardian before he went any further with this.

The station operator was surprised to hear from him, but came up with the phone number and caller ID easily when he supplied the time of the call. He sighed at the result: At Ur Convenience, which he knew to be an odd combo of internet café, gasoline station, and farmers market on the outskirts of town.

He punched in the number quickly. After three rings, a cigarette-rough voice answered. "At Ur Convenience."

"This is Detective Matthew Finn of the Evansburg Police Department. Did you see a woman who used your public phone at seven fifteen this evening?"

A voice in the background asked for change on pump two. "Hold on a minute." There was a clunk, the ching of a cash drawer opening and the thud of it shutting again, and then the raspy voice was back. "Sorry about that; I'm here all alone. Now, what were you saying?"

Finn repeated himself. The guy said, "Nah, the phone's around the corner; can't see it from here. Did something bad go down out there? We got a camera, but it's focused on the pumps."

"I'll need your tape of that time period."

"Huh. It's one of those continuous loop things. I better go turn it off so it won't record over itself; I can't remember when it starts over."

"Go turn it off now. I'll be by in a few minutes to pick up the tape."

"We close at nine."

Finn checked his watch. It was 8:45. "I need you to wait for me with that tape, please. I'll be there in twenty minutes."

There was no response. Finn could feel the hesitation through the phone line. "I'm heading out now, sir. I'll see you in less than twenty minutes."

He hung up and ran to his car, jammed the flasher on top and broke the speed limit on the way to At Ur Convenience. The store lights were off, but the manager was waiting outside in his car, smoking a cigarette. He knocked off the ashes, stood up, and handed Finn the tape. "Long day," he groaned.

"I know what you mean," Finn said. He quickly took down the guy's contact info and then said, "Do you remember a woman in your store at seven-fifteen or so?"

The guy thought for a few seconds, wiping a finger across his bristly moustache. "No, I'm sorry. I can barely remember my name right now. Is this a drug thing? Do I need to be worried?"

Finn sighed. "No, nothing to do with drugs. But it might have something to do with the Ivy Morgan kidnapping."

"Kidnapping? I thought that girl got arrested for killing that baby."

"She was only charged for leaving the baby in the car."

"I figure that's just because you don't have a body yet." The man stared at Finn's face as he took another draw on the cigarette.

God, poor Brittany. What that kid must be going through. But he was as guilty as everyone else; before the tip, he'd been considering the same possibility. Finn sighed and said, "This evening a woman called in a tip from this phone."

"Yeah? Well, I hope she's on that tape, then." He jabbed a finger at the videotape that Finn held. "I should have them take out that damn thing. I mean, who uses public phones anymore, anyway? I'm surprised it even still works."

Finn let the manager leave and walked around the corner. The phone looked lonely, incarcerated in a Plexiglas box under a dim security light. The guy was right; not many people used public phones anymore.

But perhaps that thought offered a glimmer of hope. He called the dispatcher and got forwarded to Guy Rodrigo, who had the misfortune to be certified in evidence collection and on call.

"You've got to be kidding," Rodrigo said when he heard the scene description. "A public phone?"

"I'm not," Finn assured him. "I'll tape off the area so nobody will use it before you get here, but then I've got to head off to watch this security tape. This might be the break we've been waiting for. The clock's still ticking for that baby."

Chapter 13

"Isn't she beautiful?" Brittany asked Charlie. In her arms, Ivy gurgled and smiled, wriggling in the yellow dress Brittany had made for her. "Don't you want to hold her?"

"Of course." Charlie held out his arms, and Brittany felt her heart melt. She was so, so, *so* happy. She handed him their sweet daughter. She turned to pick up the baby carrier. When she looked back, Charlie and Ivy were gone. In front of her stood only a cornfield, the stalks so tall and thick she couldn't see anything but green.

"Charlie!" she screamed. "Charlie!"

"What?" said his voice behind her.

She whirled. His arms were empty. Her stomach lurched. "Where's Ivy?"

"All fixed." He dusted his hands together. "Now I can go back to college and you can be a cheerleader."

She could hear Ivy crying somewhere in the cornfield. But the stalks were so thick, she couldn't get in. Her baby's wails grew louder. She gripped cornstalks in her hands, but they wouldn't budge.

"Don't worry about it." Charlie put his hands on her shoulders. "There's nothing you can do, Brittany. Brittany!"

She woke up suddenly, her father's hands gripping her arms. He hovered over her bed. "Ivy!" she sobbed. "Charlie!"

"It was a bad dream, Brittany." Her father pulled her into his arms. Her mother stood behind him in her nightgown.

She could hear Ivy's wails coming from the closet. "Ivy's crying. Don't you hear Ivy crying?"

Her parents switched positions, and her mother took her into her arms. "Ivy's not crying, Brittany. Ivy's not here."

Brittany sobbed into her mother's neck. "It's all my fault."

"It's the kidnapper's fault." Her mother stroked the bangs back from Brittany's damp forehead. "I'm sure the kidnapper was someone who really, really wanted a beautiful baby. And they're taking such good care of Ivy... She's asleep right now, just like you should be."

Then her father was there, holding out a glass of water and a pill.

"I'm not sure that's a good idea, Noah." Her mom twisted to look at him. "She already had one tonight. She has to go to school tomorrow. We don't want her to be comatose."

Well, *she* wanted to be comatose. Brittany grabbed the pill from her father's palm and choked it down before her mother could win the debate. Her father turned off the light and left the room, but her mother stayed, sitting beside her pillow. Brittany closed her eyes and tried to breathe like she was asleep.

Since they'd put the home phone number on Facebook, the phone rang all day, every day. They turned off the ringer at night, but the answering machine still responded. They didn't even pick up the phone any more, just copied the messages off the old-fashioned recorder several times a day. Some people left messages saying they were praying for Ivy. Some people said they'd seen her somewhere—those always turned out to be some other baby. Some people said God was punishing them. Today, a so-called psychic left a message saying that Ivy's fate was in the hands of a black-haired stranger.

When her mother tiptoed out of her bedroom, Brittany could still hear Ivy crying out there, somewhere in the black night.

Chapter 14

Single-wide trailers, sheds and an outdoor enclosure completely surrounded by a security fence lent 214 Cheyenne Creek Road the air of a hideout. A gray van was parked on gravel near the barn. Yep, it had mirrored windows, and on its side, *Talking Hands Ranch* was painted in fading white script.

The public phone at the convenience store had yielded only fingerprints that weren't in AFIS, but it could very well be that some of the prints belonged to Dr. Grace McKenna. It had taken two days of playing phone tag with the University of Washington to locate Dr. McKenna and the van. It was odd how most people there had never heard of her.

She was setting up a research center on a piece of donated land near Evansburg, the psychology department secretary said. This place looked more like a militia compound than a research center.

Grace McKenna had no record other than an arrest for trespass during a political protest when she was twenty years old. But you never knew what you might be walking into. Finn wondered if perhaps he should have brought some uniforms with him. However, it was broad daylight, and a squad of cops might have been too intimidating for a little retarded girl.

In the leather case under his arm was a tape recorder, a camera, a notepad and pens, and a single red rose in a plastic cylinder. Despite being childless, he was good with kids. McKenna—he was now reasonably sure it had been she who called—had told him her ward was twelve years old, with the

IQ of a five-year-old. No matter her mental status, twelve meant hormones had started to flow. He wasn't a bad-looking guy, old enough to be Romeo's father but more or less fitting the tall, dark, and handsome stereotype. Perhaps he could charm his way into this kid's heart and she'd tell him everything she knew about Ivy Rose Morgan.

A creature moved in the small wooden barn as he passed. The animal sounded big; he heard a snort. The doors were bolted shut. The horse probably wanted to come out into the fenced area but couldn't. The fenced area was completely enclosed, with wire mesh overhead and a rope net stretched up across one corner. Maybe Dr. McKenna kept birds, too? He'd interviewed a veterinarian once who specialized in raptors; their pen had been similar.

A sob caught his attention. A woman, probably late thirties, with long dark hair pulled into a low ponytail, sat on the metal steps of an old single-wide trailer, tears spilling down her cheeks as she read a sheet of paper. By her elbow sat a yellow plastic tub, filled with a cabbage, a loaf of bread, a jug of liquid, and a clipboard standing on end. The woman sobbed again, shook the piece of paper, and said loudly, "Goddamn you, you spineless bastards!"

"Hello?" he said softly, not wanting to startle her.

She bolted up off the step, definitely startled. After eyeing him for a few seconds, she wiped her fingers over her cheeks, inhaled, and said, "Are you lost? Can I help you?" Her gaze darted around the compound, to the barn, and then back to the trailer she'd just left, indicating they were probably not alone. He probably should have asked for backup.

"Dr. Grace McKenna?" She fit the description on the DMV record.

She raised a suspicious eyebrow. "Who are you?"

He pulled his badge from his pocket. "Detective Matthew Finn. Sorry if it's a bad time."

For a second she looked as if she might cry again, but then she waved a hand dismissively in the air and said in a strangled tone, "Have we met?"

"You called a couple of days ago to report a witness to the Morgan kidnapping, didn't you?"

"That was supposed to be an anonymous call."

"Lives are at stake."

"Yes, they are," she said, sounding defensive. Above her reddened cheeks, her gaze was unflinching. "I gave you all the information I had in that phone call."

"Sometimes—"

A loud thump sounded from the barn behind him, and it was his turn to jump. He shot a look at the building. Nothing looked different. He turned back. "What's in there? A horse?"

McKenna pressed her lips together in a quivering line and smoothed her hair back from her brow with her left hand. "Look," she said. "You're right, it is a bad time. I need to get back to work. Maybe I could come to your office tomorrow?"

No way was he going to let her shuffle him off like that. Something fishy was going on here. "Can we talk for just a minute?"

She anxiously eyed the trailer behind her, then turned back to him. Scuffling sounds followed by another snort erupted from the barn, and she put a hand on his arm. "Over here," she said, urging him toward a picnic table under a big cottonwood between the two trailers. She picked up the tub and brought it and the piece of paper with her.

Grace McKenna had ivory skin, hazel eyes, and long dark hair. She might have been pretty except for her watery eyes and a thin scar that ran from her right nostril down through her upper lip. He wondered what she'd been crying about; she placed the paper she'd been reading face down on the picnic table. Another thump and a snort came from the barn.

"What do you have in there?" he jerked his chin over his shoulder to indicate the building behind them. "A stallion?"

"He probably thinks he is." She gestured toward the bench.

"Feel free to let him out," Finn sat down. "I like horses."

"That's okay." She sat down on the other side of the table. "I only have a few minutes, Detective, before I need to get to work. I told you everything I know in the call. There's nothing else I can do for you."

He leaned forward. "Actually, I came to speak to your ward."

"I'm sorry, that's not possible." He sensed she was making an effort not to look at the trailer behind her.

"Is she here?" He studied the single-wide. A dark shape appeared at the rightmost window, then quickly vanished. "I just saw someone at the window. What's her name?"

Grace McKenna stared at the scarred tabletop for a minute, sighed heavily, and then met his gaze. "Her name is Neema. But as I explained, she's got the IQ of a five-year-old."

"Five-year-olds can be pretty observant."

"And she can't speak."

Perhaps the child wasn't retarded, then, but brain-damaged in some other way. "Is Neema deaf?"

"No, but she cannot speak. She uses sign language to communicate."

"Then you can translate."

She shook her head, loosening a wisp of dark hair that sprang forward across her left cheek. She tucked it back behind her ear. "I told you everything she told me."

"I still need to talk to her."

A loud series of snorts and thumps erupted from the barn, and they both turned. The noise grew in volume and intensity. The sides of the wooden building visibly shook with each blow.

McKenna rose from her bench. "I've got to go before he tears the place apart. I can't do anything for you, Detective."

Time for the bad cop routine. He stood up and crossed his arms. "I'm not leaving until I speak to Neema."

She glared at him for a long moment, then took a deep breath. "Guess I can't call the cops to have you thrown off my property, can I?"

Turning, she trotted toward the fenced enclosure, carrying her plastic tub. She pulled out a key on a retractable wire from her belt, and then let herself in through a padlocked gate and closed it carefully behind her. She called out, "Coming, Gumu."

He followed, stopping outside the fence. He was half afraid that Grace McKenna would disappear within the barn, but instead she pulled back the bolt on the wooden door and stood back. A gigantic black hulk rushed out, nearly bowling her over. Slowly Finn's mind shifted from horse to bear, and then, as he blinked in disbelief, to gorilla. *Gorilla?* He involuntarily took a step backwards. Undeniably, it was a gorilla, and a huge one at that. Grabbing the cabbage from the tub, it swung itself up onto the net and curled up, gnawing on the cabbage head as if it were an apple.

McKenna wrote something down on her clipboard, laid the other items on the ground near the barn door, and then retrieved her tub and exited through the gate again, taking care to fasten the padlock. She gave it a tug to make sure it was secure before she turned around.

"You have a gorilla." As soon as the words came out of his mouth, he felt like an idiot. Nothing like stating the obvious to make a professional impression.

She put one hand on her hip and gave him a cool stare. "There's no law against having gorillas here."

He'd have to check on that. He'd never come across this situation before. "Uh, why do you have a gorilla, Dr. McKenna?"

Her expression was guarded. "I do communications research. Gumu"—she pointed at the gorilla in the net—"is an orphan from Africa."

"I've seen the specials on television." Another only slightly less idiotic thing to say.

She nodded and then raised one hand to shield her eyes from the sun. They both watched the big gorilla chew the cabbage for a moment. Grace McKenna came only up to his chin, and she'd gone in that cage with that huge ape. Gorillas in rural Washington. Who would have expected that?

He finally remembered why he was standing there. "I still need to talk to your ward," he said.

She turned to study him for a long moment. Finally, she seemed to make up her mind and gestured toward the trailer. "Might as well get this over with."

The outside door opened into a kitchen. There was a chain and padlock on the refrigerator, and a keyed deadbolt on a side door that led to the rest of the trailer. *What the hell?* McKenna set the tub in the sink, washed her hands, and then picked up her clipboard and, pulling a key out from her belt again, unlocked the interior door. Surreptitiously, Finn reached under his jacket and unsnapped the safety strap on his holster as he followed her over the threshold.

The living room was in shambles. Orange peels, a *National Geographic* magazine, and a toy alligator were strewn across the rug. A huge pile of blankets were heaped in one corner. The place smelled a little funky. McKenna was clearly not the best of housekeepers. But Finn had searched crack houses and homeless squats; this level of grunge was nothing in comparison.

He sat down on the couch, flipping out his jacket tail so it hung loosely over his pistol. Then he unzipped his case and pulled out the rose in its plastic cylinder. "I brought a little present for Neema."

The pile of blankets in the corner suddenly shape-shifted. He found himself staring at another gorilla. In the same room. No more than twenty feet away. With no netting or bars in between them. A gorilla twice his size. He found it difficult to breathe. A blanket hung over the animal's huge black head in an attitude that might have looked funny on another occasion. The creature's eyes were red-brown, and they were locked on his face as intensely as his gaze was locked on the gorilla's. He slowly moved his right hand to the pistol on his belt.

McKenna's hand landed heavily on his shoulder, and he almost jumped out of the seat. "Do *not* pull out your gun, Detective. She's gentle, but that might make her freak out. Just relax. Take a breath."

He tried to relax, but the way the gorilla eyed him made tranquility difficult to achieve. The ape raised its head. Its wide nostrils flared as it sniffed the air. God, was it sniffing him out? He remembered a television show in which wild chimpanzees had killed and eaten a baboon. Why in the hell did his brain serve up trivia like that right now? He swallowed against the dryness in his throat.

"How many gorillas do you have?" he asked. Was it possible that there was a whole gorilla colony just outside of Evansburg?

"Only two." Her hand left his shoulder and she moved to the side of the couch, gesturing to the gorilla as she spoke. "This is a good man. A friend."

"Yeah, friend," he said in the animal's general direction. As if words would keep the enormous creature from ripping his head off. The woman was clearly off her rocker. "Umm, McKenna, is there another room where I could speak to your ward?" *A room without an ape loose in it?*

She gestured to the gorilla. "Come meet Detective Finn." She pointed at him.

The monster scooted forward. Finn leaned back, mashing the cushions against the frame. He wondered how quickly he could vault over the back of the sofa.

The animal's eyes focused on the flower he held. The gorilla moved its huge black hands in the air and then slapped itself on its leathery chest with a small 'huh.'

"She wants to know if the flower's for her," McKenna told him.

His hands shook a little as he opened the plastic cylinder and extracted the single red rose. "This flower is for Neema," he told the gorilla, enunciating carefully. As if that would make it go away. As if telling Cargo that the food was for cats made the dog stop drooling on the floor.

A huge hairy hand snatched the flower from his fingers, and the gorilla scooted backwards as quickly as it had launched itself forward.

"Hey!" he yelped.

The creature twirled the rose between its black leathery fingers in a delicate movement worthy of a flamenco dancer, held the flower to its huge nostrils and inhaled audibly. Then the rose vanished between its rubbery lips, and the bare stem emerged seconds later. The gorilla chewed as it made a motion with its empty hand, first touching its chin and then holding a leathery black palm upward in his direction.

"Neema says thank you."

Neema? This was Neema? He felt as if he'd been booted off a precipice into an alien world. He turned toward McKenna.

"This is how you say 'You're welcome'." She gestured. "Try it, Detective."

He copied her gesture. The gorilla dropped the rose stem on the carpet, tapped its chin and shoved a palm forward again, then brushed its nose as if smelling a flower and ended with a thump on the chest, looking eagerly in his direction. The intensity of those ape eyes was disturbing.

McKenna interrupted their staring contest. "She wants to know if you have another flower for her."

Finn realized his mouth was open and made the effort to shut it without biting his tongue. After another minute of glancing back and forth between the woman and the gorilla, he found his voice. "I only brought one flower."

She signed to the gorilla, which made a huffing sound, picked up an orange peel from the floor and placed it on its head like a tiny cap. It looked ridiculous, but it seemed like less of a monster that way.

Dr. McKenna smiled and turned in his direction. "Well, now that we're all friends, what would you like to ask Neema?"

Feeling as if he were an actor in some surreal play, he reached for his notes. He'd talked to invisible friends of schizophrenics to get information; used puppets to question children who found an adult's questions too intimidating. Perhaps pretending to interview a gorilla was the way to get more information from this mad woman scientist.

Grace McKenna studied Detective Finn. The man didn't take his eyes off Neema except for shooting a few glances in Grace's direction. His neck and jaw were rigid. He'd removed his fingers from his pistol, but his hand remained poised in the air only an inch away.

So it was going to happen; her gorilla was going to have a conversation with an outsider who'd never heard of signing apes. Grace always thought she'd have more time to prepare for this.

"You're telling me that this ape reported the kidnapping?" Finn's gaze shifted sideways to connect with hers. Neema leaned forward to snatch a magazine off the table and Finn's focus shot back to the gorilla.

"I wouldn't use those words. She told me about seeing a baby taken by a man."

He turned his head toward her, but his gaze kept sliding back to Neema, keeping an eye on her out of the corner of his eye. "The Morgan baby disappeared a week ago. Why didn't you report it then?"

"It took me a while to understand what she was saying."

Neema sat on the floor, holding the magazine open with her feet and turning pages with her hands. She stopped on a page that featured a lush bouquet of roses and lilies. She signed to herself, then focused on Finn and gestured.

"What's it doing?" Detective Finn's voice was tense.

"Her, not it. She noticed the flowers in the magazine and said *Good flower sweet eat*. Now she wants to know if you have another flower for her."

"I already said I didn't."

Neema scooted closer to Finn. She tilted her head, intently examining his features and his clothing.

"What?" he said nervously. "What does it—she—want?" He lifted his hand toward his gun again.

Neema hooted and scooted back, signing *Gun bad gun*.

"Please lower your hand. She's worried about your gun."

The connection of Finn's gaze with Grace's was rapid, but long enough to tell her he thought she was crazy.

Gun bad run away, Neema signed. She stood poised on all fours as if she was about to follow her own advice. She was also eyeing a footstool, which made Grace anxious. Neema had thrown furniture at visitors she didn't like. Grace quickly strode to her. She patted Neema on the shoulder, then signed as she spoke. "It's okay, Neema, you don't have to run away."

The whites of Neema's eyes showed, and she was breathing too quickly.

"He won't touch the gun," Grace promised.

Neema looked doubtful, but slowly inched closer to Finn again, her gaze raking him from head to foot. Finn stiffened.

Grace laughed. "Relax, Detective. Haven't you ever had a kid stare at you?"

"Kids, yeah. Not an ape."

"It's pretty much the same. Gorillas have the mental capacity of five-year-old children."

"Yeah?" Finn sounded as if he didn't believe her. He studied Neema while the gorilla stared back at him. "How does she know about guns?"

Grace returned to her chair. "Television. Movies. I usually try to screen out the violent ones, but I've let a couple slip through. The worst was Tarzan. I didn't know it had a scene where hunters K-I-L-L-E-D some chimpanzees."

Where chimpanzee? Neema signed, scraping her hands up and down her sides while she looked around the room.

"No chimpanzee here," Grace told her. "Just talking."

Neema returned to her position on the other side of the coffee table and inspected Finn again for a long moment. Then she signed *Cat where man cat?*

"Neema wants to know where your cat is."

Detective Finn jerked his gaze toward Grace. "Why would it—she—think I have a cat?"

Grace asked Neema in sign language why she thought of a cat.

Neema leaned forward and stretched a black hairy arm across the coffee table. The detective froze as the gorilla's leathery fingers touched down on his khaki-clad thigh. Neema deftly plucked an orange hair from his trouser leg and held it up in front of her nose, signing *cat.*

"There's your evidence, Detective."

"You're kidding." Finn watched as Neema stuck the cat hair on top of her nose and then stared at it cross-eyed.

Grace laughed.

Neema stuck out her bottom lip and puffed out a big breath, blowing the cat hair off her nose. She signed *What man this*.

"Finn," Grace said aloud, frowning.

He turned to her. "Yes?"

"Neema wanted to know what your name was, but I need to come up with a sign for it. She doesn't spell." F? No, Neema's fingers weren't dexterous enough to form the letter.

Neema signed *Gun dog cat man*.

"Okay," Grace said. "Neema wants to call you *Gun dog cat man*."

Finn looked startled. Gun. Dog. Cat. Man. Grace made each gesture slowly, a hand formed into a gun, a hip pat and finger snap for dog, pulled out whiskers for cat, and then a forehead touch followed by a chest tap for man.

"I get the gun and the cat man," Grace said aloud, signing to Neema, "but why dog?"

Neema quickly touched her hip and brought her fingers together in the air and then circled her fingers in front of her nose.

"Really?" Grace sniffed the air.

Finn watched her, frowning. "What?"

"She says you smell like a dog."

"Damn." *Dog*, Neema signed again. He raised an eyebrow. "Am I being insulted by a gorilla? Do you think I smell like a dog?"

Grace said, "I can't smell anything, but gorillas have more sensitive noses than humans. You do have a dog?"

"Sort of," Finn said, still staring at Neema. "Make her do it again."

Grace bristled. "Neema's not a trick pony, Detective."

Where pony? Neema signed. She scooted over to the window and peered out, signing *pony, pony*.

Finn looked at Grace. "Can you ask Neema to sign 'gun' again, please?"

Neema pivoted away from the window, hooting softly as she repeatedly signed *gun bad gun*, her gaze jumping to Finn's pistol in its holster.

"She's doing it now. She's saying *gun bad gun*." Grace did the signs slowly for him, forming her hand into a gun and jerking it in front of her chest as if shooting it, then shoving her hand down for bad, then making the gun sign again.

Finn watched carefully and then looked back at the gorilla. Neema jerked her right hand in front of her chest, hooting softly. Her expression was anxious.

"It's okay, Neema," Grace told her. "I don't suppose you'd be willing to leave your pistol outside, Detective?"

"It stays with me." Finn frowned. "She's not making the same signs you did."

"Gorilla hands are not as agile as ours. Neema's signs are modified American Sign Language; as close as she can get."

Neema continued to hoot softly, her eyes round with worry. Grace could see from the gorilla's body language that Neema was revving up for a tantrum. When she was frightened or angry, she could be destructive, even violent. When gorillas felt threatened, they often attacked the threat. In the wild, this usually came in the form of charging the intruder while shrieking and hurling sticks or leaves or even feces. Detective Finn had no idea what was coming.

"Neema's upset." Grace stood up. "We need to go outside to chat, Detective. Right now."

Finn rose from the couch and took a step toward the door. Neema raised her arms above her head with a screech of alarm. Grace hurriedly moved between them, touching Neema gently. The gorilla wrapped her arms around Grace and tried to climb up her legs as she had when she was a baby; Grace staggered under the adult gorilla's weight.

"What the—" Finn muttered behind her back.

"I'm okay," Grace yelped into Neema's furry shoulder. "I need you to go outside right now. I'll be out in a minute."

Between Neema's increasingly loud hoots, Grace heard the door close behind her. She patted Neema and made soothing noises. After the gorilla finally calmed down, she led her through the door into the cage area, and settled her with a blanket and a carton of yogurt and her favorite ABC book. Finally, Grace went out the side door of the trailer.

Finn whirled as she approached his back, his hand on his pistol grip again. She held up her hands. "Easy, Detective," she said. "I'm still unarmed."

His face was unreadable. The lines around his eyes and mouth were deeply etched into his tanned skin. His eyes were an eerie light blue. Right now, he was handsome in a rumpled, world-weary sort of way; but she could see that he might appear frightening if he failed to shave or comb his hair.

She tried to imagine how he felt; coming to meet a deaf child and finding a gorilla instead. "What's going on inside your head?" she asked.

"Dr. McKenna—" he started.

"Grace."

"Grace," he said. "Tell me about your van. Is this Talking Hands Ranch?"

She winced. "No. The van belongs to the University of Washington. Talking Hands Ranch was a research center they used to own; we did primate language research there. They sold that property and moved us out here. We're sort of in exile. Or maybe swept under the rug," she said bitterly. She'd have to tell him about Spencer and the crazies now so he'd understand the importance of keeping all this quiet.

"When I arrived, you were crying. Can you tell me why?"

Oh god. She'd forgotten about that for a little while. Her thoughts suddenly plunged into a crevasse of emotion. She tried to bounce them out, but her vision blurred and her throat swelled too tight to talk. Moving to the picnic table, she snatched up the page she'd left there. She stumbled back because she couldn't see the ground through the haze of tears. She pushed the letter at him and stood there in the pool of porch light, her arms crossed in front of her chest, sobs overtaking her. She was mortified to be caught blubbering like a little kid.

He squinted at the page. The letter was from the University of Washington. OFFICIAL NOTICE — TO BE SOLD AT AUCTION was the heading at the top, followed by a long list. Lab equipment, quite a few trailers and vehicles, video cameras, dozens of white mice, rats, rabbits, spider monkeys. Somewhere in the middle was:

> RESEARCH SUBJECT 1021 – Female Lowland Gorilla,
> 12 years of age
> RESEARCH SUBJECT 1022 – Male Lowland Gorilla,
> 9 years of age

He stopped reading and looked at her. "Does this mean what I think it does?"

"The university's planning to sell Neema and Gumu," she managed to gasp before she completely fell apart. She suddenly felt dizzy and reached out to grasp his shirt sleeve.

He stepped forward and took her into his arms. She buried her face against his chest. She could feel the heat from his skin beneath his shirt, the muscles of his biceps loosely clasped around her. She smelled his deodorant and sweat. This was insane. Humiliating. She had to pull herself together. Apologize. She raised her chin.

"Detective ..." That was all she managed to get out before she started sobbing again.

Nobody at the university knew her gorillas. Nobody knew that Neema was frightened by the rustle of paper bags, that Gumu adored the color fuchsia. Nobody else remembered how Neema refused to let go of Spencer's cold hand for a whole day after he'd died.

To the university, the gorillas were in the same category as desks and microscopes—surplus equipment. Where would they end up? What the hell was she going to do? She gave way to the horror of it all, sobbing uncontrollably while this stranger stood and held her in his arms.

"You may as well call me Matt," he finally said.

Chapter 15

The regular janitor for the Sisters-Mothers Trust wing was Audrey Ibañez. Dawes had interviewed three other members of the cleaning staff yesterday and gotten little out of them, but Ibañez had been off on sick leave for several days.

"They were full of complaints about having to clean up dirty diapers and baby barf in a high school," Dawes told him. "Guess condoms and tampons are more to their liking? They didn't want to hand over driver's licenses, either."

Ibañez was no different from her colleagues, seeming annoyed at his request for identification, and dragging her heels to her locker. Finn noted that Audrey was actually her middle name—Luisa Audrey Ibañez—as he copied her driver's license number. He handed back her billfold.

"It's just, you know, you never know where that information is going to wind up these days," Ibañez explained, placing the billfold in her lap. "My sister had someone steal her ID and run up a terrible bill on her credit cards."

"The companies can't bill your sister for that."

Ibañez rolled her eyes. "Try telling that to a collections agency."

"We'll protect your information." He slid the report form up and clamped it into his clipboard.

He leaned back, forgetting there was no chair back behind him, almost slipped off the bench and sat up again, feeling foolish. They were sitting on the lowest level of the foldout bleachers in the empty gymnasium; the teachers' lounge had way too much traffic to hold an interview there.

He held his pen poised over his notepad. "You know who Brittany Morgan is?"

"Of course I know who Brittany Morgan is. Who doesn't, now? I see that she's back in class. Poor thing." She tucked a few more black hairs into the braid she wore at the back of her neck. "But of course I knew who she was before this happened. I know a lot of the girls."

Ibañez told him that Brittany seemed like a caring mother. Then her forehead creased. "Most of the time she seemed good, anyway. But you never know what these teenagers can get up to. One time I saw that girl Joy give a marshmallow to her son." She shook her head. "Do you know how quickly a baby can choke on a marshmallow?"

He'd never really thought about it. But now he could imagine how dangerous that could be—soft and fluffy, the perfect thing to fill a little throat that didn't have the strength to swallow it down. No way to grab a glass of water; not even the words or gestures to indicate what was happening. Could Ivy have died from such a simple accident? "Did you ever see Joy or Brittany give Ivy a marshmallow?"

"No. I gave Joy a good lecture about that subject." She shook her head again. "I've seen girls give their babies Coke and potato chips, too. Brittany once, I saw her let Ivy suck on this bird necklace she had. Who knows what that might have been made out of—could have lead or who knows what in it." She made a clucking sound with her tongue. "Sometimes the girls treat the babies more like pets than babies."

The word *pet* made him think of Neema. Although the gorilla hardly seemed in the same category as a cat or dog. Not really a pet. She'd eaten his rose and then thanked him for it. Or at least that's how McKenna had interpreted Neema's gestures. Dr. Grace McKenna, a good-looking, interesting woman. Crying in his arms. *You may as well call me Matt?* What the hell had gotten into him? Damn good thing nobody had witnessed that totally inappropriate scene. McKenna could be a nutcase. He gave himself a mental shake.

No matter whether the tips were the gorilla's clues or McKenna's, he owed it to Brittany and Ivy to give them a shot. Green car. Snake bracelet. He leaned toward the janitor. "Do you know anyone around the school that drives a green car?"

Ibañez snorted. "I know at least a dozen people with green cars. Don't you?"

He shrugged and waited for her to go on.

"Those light green Priuses are real popular; some of the staff and teachers have them. And those lime green Fords; whatever they call those cheap little models—lots of kids have those." She shook her head again. "Lucky devils. I never had a car when I was in high school, did you?" When he didn't respond, she sighed and looked toward the corner where she'd left her mop and bucket. "I really need to get back to work, Detective."

"In a minute." He leaned forward again. "Can you name some owners of green cars?"

She gave him four names: two teachers, a maintenance man, and a student. "I could probably find out some of the others." Her eyes brightened. "Did a green car have something to do with Ivy disappearing? Didn't the police say that baby was probably dead?"

He said carefully, "There have been letters to the editor to that effect in the newspaper. The police have said nothing. We don't know what happened. But a couple of witnesses thought they saw a green car peel out of the parking lot of the Food Mart." Better to make the witnesses plural, he thought; that way it would be harder to pinpoint one person. *Or one gorilla.*

Her eyebrows lifted. "Really? You think someone in a green car kidnapped that baby?"

"A green car was seen speeding away. It may have nothing to do with Ivy, but we've got to follow every lead."

"I should hope so." She folded her arms across the blue coverall she wore. *Jimson Janitorial Service* was stitched in three red lines across the upper sleeve. Was that the name of the company that Charlie Wakefield worked for? He'd have to check.

"You think that someone at the school had something to do with this?" she asked.

"Could be anyone in town." He tapped his pen on the clipboard. "Do you know anyone who wears a snake bracelet?"

Her chin jerked up and her forehead creased into a frown. "What?"

"A bracelet in the shape of a snake."

She lowered her eyes to her clasped hands. "What sort of bracelet?"

Was he reading too much into it, or did Ibañez seem suddenly nervous? Finn kept his face and voice bland. "I don't know much about jewelry," he said.

She studied the floor for a second. Then she sat up and unfolded her arms. "There are wraparound bracelets." She demonstrated, twirling her right hand around her left wrist. "Some of the girls wear those, and they look like snakes. And then there are bangle bracelets." His expression must have been blank, because she explained, "They're circles that you slip over your hand. Some of those might be snakes, too. I used to have one where the snake was biting its own tail—it was supposed to be Egyptian. But that was a while ago. Your best bet would be to ask the girls. Or maybe Miz Taylor."

"Doesn't have to be someone in the pregnant girls' class," Finn said. "How about staff or other teachers? Any of them wear snake bracelets?"

She thought about it for a minute. "I can't remember any offhand."

"Know any men who wear a snake bracelet?"

"Men? With bracelets?"

"Some men wear bracelets," Finn said. "A medical bracelet has the caduceus symbol, which has two snakes in it. Or maybe a watch with a snake design watchband?"

She chewed on a ragged thumbnail and studied her knees for a few seconds. Finally she raised her head. "I can't think of any men who wear bracelets, snakes or any other kind. Who said they saw a man with a snake bracelet?"

What would she say if he told her a gorilla had reported it? He fixed his eyes on his notebook for a second, quelling a smile. "I didn't say anyone saw a man."

"Oh. I guess I just assumed..." She frowned, swallowed hard, and put her hands on her knees. "Well, okay, I'll keep a lookout for a snake bracelet, too."

"Do you know this young man?" He shoved Charlie Wakefield's track team photo toward her.

She took it, squinted at it. "He seems sort of familiar, but I don't know his name. I think he was a student, maybe last year? I haven't seen him around lately. Hey—it's not a bracelet, but how about snaky looking sleeves?" She pointed at the design on the uniform shirts.

Shit, Ibañez was right. The zigzag might be mistaken for a snake. *Especially by a gorilla.* "It's supposed to be a lightning bolt."

"If you say so," she said. "Is this kid a suspect?"

"I can't tell you that."

"Right," Ibañez huffed, insulted. She handed him the photo and glanced toward her mop again.

A figure appeared in one of the windows at the top of the double gymnasium doors. A young man wearing a red tie, his dark hair neatly banded back into a ponytail, peered in, stared severely at them for a moment, then withdrew.

"I need to get back to work now," Ibañez said.

"Is Jimson Janitorial a good outfit to work for?" he asked, thinking about Charlie's Wakefield's job.

"The best." She nodded enthusiastically. "They really believe in their workers."

That seemed an odd way of putting it—how many people would say their employers *believed* in them?

"But they check up on us, too; that was one of our quality control guys just now. So I really gotta get back to work." She pushed herself up from her seat.

He stood and fished a card out of his shirt pocket. "Call me if you come up with more names or think of anything else."

"Course I will." She waved at him over her shoulder as she pushed the rolling mop bucket through the doorway.

He planned to ask the principal about green cars and snake bracelets, too, but first he walked to the parking lot and copied down the licenses of all the green cars there, just in case one of them vanished.

Two hours later, Finn gawked at the scene at Grace's compound. On the other side of the fence, next to the barn, the two gorillas were—unbelievably—painting. Neema's canvas was perched on an easel, and the other, larger gorilla sat on the ground with his canvas between his feet. Or were they hands? Gorilla feet looked like hands, with opposable thumbs and nails on all digits.

Grace and a young black man guarded buckets filled with bright colors of paint. At the moment, both humans and gorillas studied Finn through the wire mesh.

Apes painting. Who would believe it? "I suppose they write poetry in their spare time," he said.

"Only during the winter months," the black man replied.

"Should I come in?" Finn moved toward the gate.

"No!" Grace yelped. "I mean, stay out there, please. Gumu's not well socialized; he can be unpredictable."

The black man said, "I can be unpredictable, too."

Grace made a noise in the back of her throat, then said, "Detective Matthew Finn, this is my colleague, Josh LaDyne. And the other big male is Gumu."

"Dr. McKenna sometimes finds it difficult to tell us apart," LaDyne told Finn.

Grace gave LaDyne an exasperated look. Finn laughed and nodded in LaDyne's direction. "Glad to meet you."

Grace gestured to the gorillas, a sign that mimicked painting with a brush. Neema and Gumu focused on their canvases again. Finn had thought that Neema was big, but

Gumu was nearly twice her size. LaDyne hovered near the giant male but remained out of the gorilla's reach. What exactly did 'not well socialized' mean? Was 'unpredictable' code for *violent*? As in *At any second, Gumu might decide your head would make a great beach ball?*

The gargantuan beast did not appear in the least violent now. Gumu sat, butt against the ground, gripping his canvas from the sides with his fingerlike toes. He reached up to the small table beside Grace and dipped a wide paintbrush into a pail of fuchsia paint. Finn moved around to the side of the pen to view the big gorilla's painting. Gumu froze, paintbrush held in the air. His eyes followed Finn until he stopped outside the fence. After a moment, Gumu added two delicate pink flourishes to his canvas, which was crisscrossed with bold strokes of yellows and greens. Then he sat with his paintbrush held between his teeth for a moment, studying his artwork. His fierce overhanging brow and neckless hunched posture made it difficult to tell if he was pleased or disappointed with his painting.

Fascinating. These apes painted as well as most students in the abstract workshop Finn had taken. What that said about abstract painting or the students, he couldn't decide.

"We're almost done here," Grace told him, hooking her fingers in the fence mesh. "Then we'll take Neema inside."

Balancing on one knuckle with paintbrush poised in front of a low easel, Neema's painting method appeared more traditional, but the results were not. Her canvas bore a block of green with two hook-shaped swishes of purple near one corner, an undulating streak of blue, and a blotch of orange floating in space.

The whole scene was surreal. "Mind if I take a photo or two?" he asked Grace.

"I guess that would be okay, as long as you don't plan to advertise our location."

Finn removed the camera from his pocket and snapped three photos from different angles. Who would believe this? Gorilla artists. He expected at any moment that one or both animals would gulp down a bucket of paint or start slinging it around the pen. "Do they know what they're doing?" he asked.

"Probably as much as most artists," LaDyne said. Then he stepped toward Gumu's painting. "What's that, Gumu?" he asked, pointing and gesturing.

The male gorilla gestured quickly toward his nose with a monstrous hand.

"Flower," Finn said simultaneously with LaDyne. *Incredible.* He had just understood a gorilla sign.

"We're putting these paintings up for sale on E-bay," Grace said. "Maybe I can ransom Neema and Gumu from the University."

"The University won't consider the paintings their property?" Like an employee's work, Finn reasoned.

Grace held a finger in front of her lips in a hush sign. Then she said, "The hell with the University. I am not letting Neema and Gumu go to auction, even if I have to smuggle them to Mexico."

"I didn't hear that," Finn said. He'd hate to have to testify against her in court. "Who knew gorillas could paint?"

"Neema's been painting for years; Gumu, about six months," Grace told him. "E-bay was Josh's brilliant idea. We sold three of Neema's old paintings there just yesterday, made seventeen hundred bucks."

"The buyers know the paintings were created by gorillas?" Finn asked.

"We include a DVD of the artists at work." LaDyne pointed to his left, where a video camera was strapped to the fence.

Gumu let his canvas fall to the ground at his feet and plopped the fuchsia paintbrush back into the matching pail. Then the gorilla dipped a finger in a pail of red, sat back and painted scarlet dots on his toes. Neema scooted over, purple paintbrush between her teeth, to assist in Gumu's self-decoration.

"And the artists, easily bored with traditional canvas, turn to new media." LaDyne stepped to the fence and switched off the camera.

"We're done here." Grace hurriedly grabbed the two paintings and moved them out of harm's way. As she walked toward the paint pails, the gorillas made rapid huffing noises that escalated into shrieks as Neema chased Gumu up into the suspended netting, paintbrush still clutched in one hairy black hand.

Grace unlatched the gate and handed the paintings out to Finn. Above them, the gorillas tumbled in the netting, cackling like hyenas. They bounded from one spot to the next almost as easily as his cats.

"The big guy's going to be purple from head to foot," Finn observed.

Grace handed a pail of paintbrushes out through the gate, saying, "Thank god acrylic paint washes off gorilla fur with soap and water."

"They take baths?"

"They like to spray each other with the hose," LaDyne said. "It's not pretty." He shoved buckets of paint and the easel through the opening.

After Grace carefully padlocked the gate, they carried the paintings and supplies to a storeroom, where LaDyne dumped surplus paint into large plastic jugs while Grace cleaned the paints and brushes.

Finn studied the wet canvasses propped against the wall. "Speaking as a fan of impressionism, I can see the flowers in Gumu's painting." He moved to the other. "But what the heck is Neema's supposed to be?"

"I'm surprised you don't recognize it, Detective," Grace said. "It's Neema's rendition of the kidnapping."

"Seriously?" Now that she had said that, he could see a blue snake streak, a green block that might represent a car. The orange blob—Ivy's strawberry-blonde hair? "Did you ask her to paint this?"

"No. But I told Neema you were coming again to talk to her about the baby and the snake arm man."

"So it was on her mind." It was disturbing to think that gorillas could dredge up memories at will. *The intelligence of five-year-old children*, he reminded himself. It was a hard fact to wrap his head around.

Wiping her hands on a towel, Grace came to stand beside him, facing Neema's painting. "Yes, she was obviously thinking about it."

LaDyne joined them.

The crude splotches of green and purple and orange on the canvas were haunting. Or was that just his imagination because he knew what they represented? "Okay if I get this image on film?" he asked.

Grace nodded, and he pulled out his camera again and shot a few frames of the painting, zooming in on different parts.

They went back to the outdoor enclosure and stood for a minute outside the fence, watching the apes play in the hot afternoon sun. They'd stopped shrieking, but were still rolling around in the netting, cackling and grabbing each other and making huh-huh-huh sounds. If they'd been kids, Finn would have said they were tickling each other.

Grace said, "Now Josh is going to clean up Gumu and give him his signing lesson while we interview Neema."

"How are you ever going to get them in?" Finn shielded his eyes with his hand to watch the gorillas frolicking above them.

Grace stepped toward the fence. "That's easy."

"Snack time," LaDyne said in a low voice.

The two gorillas instantly stopped rolling, sat upright, and turned to watch them. Gumu made a sign like he was peeling a banana. Neema put her fingers to her lips over and over in a gesture that clearly had something to do with eating.

Grace smiled. "See? When it comes to food, gorillas hear as well as bats."

A half hour later, after watching the gorillas consume an odd variety of vegetables and muffins, Finn, Grace, and Neema were inside the study trailer where he'd first met Neema. He announced the time and parties present for his digital camcorder, then set it on the table in the corner of the room to capture the interview. He sat on the couch facing the gorilla, slightly more relaxed than he had been the last time. He trusted Grace, if not Neema.

The gorilla's red-brown gaze scoured his face. Up close, Neema seemed like King Kong, so massive and powerful that it was hard to remember she was female.

"When did you see this girl?" Finn used his right hand to point to the photo of Brittany Morgan that he held up against his left shoulder so the camera could film it. He couldn't make himself stop speaking louder and more slowly than usual, as if he was talking to someone hard of hearing.

Neema stretched out one of her giant black fingers and touched the photo. For some reason it bothered him that she had humanlike fingernails. She flipped both hands at him as if telling him to go away, and then sat there, looking him in the eye. Finn turned to Grace.

"Store," Grace interpreted.

"But the question was 'when.' On what day?"

"Gorillas don't watch calendars, Matt."

Neema's hands flashed. She touched her own chin and stabbed the air in front of her. Next she made several odd motions with both hands.

"Hot banana store red soft tail," Grace translated.

Finn groaned.

"She means that it was hot that day that we went to the store for bananas, when she saw the girl with the red ponytail," Grace said.

"Of course she does." That translation would never stand up in court. He thumbed through the photos he brought, searching for Ivy's picture. Neema continued to wave her hands.

"Store candy candy coke banana yogurt. She's listing all the things she likes to get from the store."

Great. He pulled out the photo of Ivy and faced Neema again. "Did you see this baby?"

Beside him, Grace signed. Neema gestured in response and then scooted away.

"Baby baby go glove hot snake arm." She turned toward Finn. "The very idea of snakes upsets her."

Neema hooted softly and repeated a motion that looked vaguely like a snake striking and then stirred her hands around some more.

"Snake skin bracelet snake bad arm baby cry go."

"*Where* did the baby go?" Finn enunciated loudly, staring into the gorilla's massive face.

Neema knuckled her way to the window and stared out through the glass.

"She's not deaf. Don't yell at her."

"Sorry." He shifted in his seat, tried to relax the knot between his shoulder blades. "This is a little weird for me."

Neema glanced over her shoulder at them. Her mouth opened in a yawn, showing two-inch long canine teeth.

"Ye gods," Finn said.

"You should see Gumu's." Grace got up, grabbed Neema by the hand and led her back to sit in front of Finn. "Deep breath, both of you. Start again."

"Where did the baby go?" he repeated more softly to the monstrous ape face in front of him.

"Baby baby snake arm cry cucumber car go."

"Which means?" he pleaded. He needed some sensible language recorded on the videotape.

"Snake arm made the baby cry and took her to a green car."

"Who is Snake Arm?"

"Snake arm gorilla?" Grace asked, signing simultaneously.

Neema hooted again and waved her arms and pounded on her chest.

"Me fine gorilla."

Neema suddenly swung her bulk toward Finn, stopping only inches away. She swung her gigantic head forward and sniffed before she stirred the air with signs. "Dog cat gun man," Grace said.

Oh good. Now that was on the tape, too.

Grace repeated the question, "Snake arm gorilla?" Neema twirled in a circle and gestured. "Snake arm bad man."

Finn held up a photo of a forearm adorned by a silver snake bracelet, hoping Neema would not notice the arm was female. "This Snake Arm?" Shit, now he was starting to talk like Tarzan, too. He rephrased. "Does this look like Snake Arm?" The gorilla ignored him. He held out an enlargement of the zigzag lightning design on Charlie's track team uniform. "Snake Arm?" he repeated.

Neema made a snake gesture, abruptly shrieked and bounded on all fours for the corner, tipped over the easy chair, then galloped in a circle around the room. Finn bolted up from his seat. Grace grabbed a handful of his sleeve and jerked. "Down!"

He sat. Grace plopped down beside him on the couch and they sat stiffly side by side. Neema ended her tirade perched on top of the toppled chair, hugging herself and hooting.

"Sorry," Grace said, relaxing. "But the calmer the humans stay, the quicker the tantrum ends. You do not want to wrestle with a gorilla; it's no competition, believe me. They hit, throw feces, and even worse—they bite when they're really upset."

Finn blanched, remembering the canines Neema displayed in her yawn. The gorilla had tossed the chair as if it weighed a few ounces instead of forty pounds. He hoped he'd never witness the creature in a full-blown hissy fit.

"Was it the last photo?" he asked Grace. If Neema had recognized the lightning design from Charlie's track uniform, maybe he was really onto something here. "Did she recognize the picture?"

Grace grimaced. "Hard to say. I think she's just had enough for now. Too many S-N-A-K-E-S in this line of questioning."

Neema signed something that made Grace laugh. "She wants a drink. Care to join us in some orange juice?"

"Uh, let's turn off the videotape first, okay?" He reached for the camcorder. "Detective Matthew Finn, two forty-five P.M., interview ending now." He stuck it into his pocket.

This had probably been a complete waste of time.

Chapter 16

There was a new case on Finn's desk when he came in to work.

"Sorry," the sergeant told him. "I know you're still working the Morgan case, but the jobs have been stacking up in the last week. I'm dividing them up four ways."

It was actually a relief to focus on the more straightforward investigation of a drug theft from a clinic. Finn rushed to get there before the clinic opened for patients. The female manager walked him through the building. Besides the two of them, at this hour only a nurse assistant and a janitor were present. The nurse assistant was setting up examination rooms, and the janitor—a young black man in the now familiar Jimson Janitorial coverall—was cleaning bathrooms.

According to the manager, there were no signs of a break-in after hours. They kept the drugs in an always-locked room, and only three people had a key to that room: herself and the two lead nurses.

"Those keys will be the connection," Finn remarked, to her dismay. He'd seen this many times; it was amazing how careless people tended to be with keys. They worked out a schedule for Finn to interview all clinic staff on their breaks over the coming few days.

"That's it." The manager raised her face from her computer screen. "All fourteen of us."

Finn asked, "And the janitor's name?"

She blinked at him, surprised. "His uniform said Marc, didn't it?"

Finn had noticed that the coverall had *Marc* embroidered on the chest pocket. Didn't necessarily mean that the man inside was named Marc. "So you don't know him?"

"I recognize him; I know he works here. Jimson doesn't always send the same ones."

"They have keys to the clinic?"

"Of course—they need to get in after hours. But none of them have keys to the drug room." She frowned. "You don't think—?"

"He's probably not your thief, but I need all the janitors' names to account for everyone."

Unfortunately, the janitor had left, according to the nurse assistant.

"He went out the back door only a second or two ago." She pointed.

Finn rushed out the back door in time to see a white van pulling out of the lot. It had a Jimson Janitorial sign on the back with distinctive purple mops forming the Js.

The manager joined him on the asphalt. "I'll call Jimson and get the names of all the janitors assigned to us."

Four cars drove into the parking lot, one after the other.

The manager glanced at her watch. "We open in ten minutes. See you at one-thirty, right?"

That was his first scheduled interview with a lead nurse. "Right."

He walked to his car. Something about the disappearing Jimson Janitorial van was bugging him. No, it wasn't the van itself; it was the sign on the back of it. The dancing purple-handled J-shaped mops. Whimsical. Memorable. Distinctive.

Where had he seen that sign before?

Wait. Did he remember correctly? He opened his trunk and pulled out his camera, clicked back through the still photos. There. Neema's painting. The green blob—the 'cucumber car.' And in the lower right corner of the green blob, two side-by-side purple J-shaped swishes. He swallowed hard, staring at them, tamping down a surge of excitement. *Stay calm*, he told himself. *Stay analytical*. There were no other repeated patterns in Neema's art. Two purple J shapes. On the 'cucumber car.' The odds against this being a coincidence were astronomical. Weren't they?

Finn slid into his car, found the address of Jimson Janitorial Service with the locator app on his phone, and turned on the engine.

The branch office of Jimson Janitorial Service was a nondescript one-story brick building that looked as if it had been a car repair shop or a gas station in a previous life. The gravel parking lot held only a white Ford van and two cars, a scratched up blue Chevy and a silver Nissan. Only the van had a company sign on the back door featuring the dancing mops of Jimson Janitorial Service. Finn pulled out his camera, squatted on his heels, zoomed in and took a photo of the sign.

"You need something?" A girl leaned against the wall next to the entrance, a half-smoked cigarette in her hand. Her black hair was sawed off into uneven chunks and her fingernails were purple.

Finn stood up, his knees popping. "Detective Finn," he said, pulling out his shield.

"I seen you on television." She sucked on the cigarette and blew a stream of smoke out of the side of her mouth. "Can I help you?"

He thought about it for a minute. "Do you know Charlie Wakefield?"

She shook her head. "Am I supposed to?"

"He works for Jimson in Cheney."

She shrugged. "It's a big company. We got branches all over the place." She blew smoke rings as he pulled out of the parking lot.

When Finn stepped out of his car at the station, a reporter quickly thrust himself between Finn and the employee entrance.

"Reporter Joel Burnby," he said into his own microphone before thrusting it in front of Finn's nose. "Are there any new developments in the Ivy Morgan case?"

The kid looked all of seventeen. So clean cut, so damn eager. "The investigation is ongoing," Finn said. Then he shouldered the reporter aside and pushed open the door.

"But is there any progress?" the reporter shouted behind him.

Finn wished he had an answer to that one. He printed out hard copies of the photos of the Jimson logo and Neema's paintings.

As Finn was leaving the printer room, Dawes entered. "Got something?" he asked, glancing at the pages in Finn's hand.

"Don't know yet," Finn said. "How about you?"

Dawes said, "Today I'm on the rock-throwing out at Bart Quillan's. Looks like it might have something to do with the school board debate."

"Really?"

Dawes shrugged. "Quillan's the science teacher, adamantly opposed to teaching intelligent design. He has one of those dinosaur stickers on his car. The rock that came through his front window had a cross painted on it."

"Nice Christian gesture," Finn remarked. "Ask him what *The Dinosaurs Died for Our Sins* means."

"Already did. He said the kids made it up; they thought it made as much sense as the debate over creationism. He thought it was funny, had some bumper stickers printed and he's been handing them out to anyone that wants one."

"Hence the rock."

"Yep. It's a crazy world." Dawes rubbed the back of his neck. "Any new leads on Morgan? I heard about the tip and the videotape."

But not about the gorilla, Finn hoped. "You know tips; most of them are nutcases. But I'm following a couple of new threads. I'll let you know if they lead anywhere."

"You got the clinic robbery, too, right?" Dawes asked.

Finn checked his watch. Two hours before his scheduled interview at the clinic. "Yes, that one's mine, too. Gotta fly."

He jumped into his car and pulled out his cell phone as he started it up. It took eight rings for her to come to the phone.

"Grace, I have something I need to show Neema."

"What is it?"

"It's a photo of a company logo."

"She doesn't usually recognize letters or numbers."

"It's more of a graphic. It's important. I'm on my way."

As he drove out of the department parking lot, he saw a black Neon pull out and swing into traffic behind him. Damn reporter. He sped up to fifty in a thirty-five mile per hour zone. The black Neon was stuck, flashing its lights at an old pickup turning left ahead of it. Finn spied the marked car up ahead in the regular speed trap, stepped on the brake and spun the wheel hard, turning right into a parking lot. He watched in his rear view as the Neon zoomed past and the black-and-white pulled out behind it, siren wailing and light bar flashing.

Finn grinned as he drove around the block. Then he stuck the flasher on top of his car and drove like a NASCAR racer out to Grace's compound. A quarter mile away, he killed the sound and light show so as not to panic the humans or apes inside.

Grace met him at the door of the study trailer. "Is it something about the kidnapping?" she asked.

"We'll see," he said.

Neema stood watching him, balanced on one fist and her hind legs, looking a little ridiculous with a feather duster in her hand. "House cleaning?" he asked.

"Neema loves to dust," Grace said. "She's good with a sponge, too."

The gorilla sat down, dropped the duster, and made a couple of gestures.

"Cat dog," he and Grace said simultaneously. Grace laughed. He groaned. "Hello to you, too, Neema."

He turned to Grace. "Okay to show her the photo?" He held it up.

Grace glanced at it and raised an eyebrow. "I don't think it'll mean anything to her, but sure, go ahead."

"Can you film this, just in case?" He handed her the department camcorder.

"Okay," she said uncertainly, turning on the camera and flipping open the screen. "Ready."

Finn held the photo of the Jimson Janitorial logo in front of Neema. The gorilla stared at it for a moment, then grabbed it from him and set it on the floor in front of her black toes. Curling her hands to her chest, she hooted softly for a second. Then, her gaze still focused on the photo, she signed.

"Baby go snake," Grace translated as she watched through the camera. "Cucumber bad snake baby go cry. I don't understand—"

"Keep the camera rolling," Finn said.

Neema scooted to the corner and picked up her baby gorilla toy. Finn reached down and picked up the photo, showing it to the camera. "This is a photo of a Jimson Janitorial Service logo," he said for the microphone. "I'm Detective Matthew Finn, Evansburg Police Department. It's October 2nd at eleven thirty A.M." He paused briefly before saying, "Now you can turn it off."

"How did you know?" Grace asked.

He showed her his photo of Neema's painting. "Don't sell that painting on E-bay."

She swallowed. "It's on auction now."

"Well, stop it. Take it down. We may need that painting."

"Okay," she said. "Will it help find the baby?"

"It better. This is the first damn breakthrough I've had in this case." He stuck the photos back into his folder, grabbed the video camera from Grace and shoved it into his jacket pocket. "Gotta run, I'm going to be late for an interview." He headed for the door.

"Matt!" Grace followed him out. "Please don't show that video around without letting me know. Please don't tell the media without talking to me first."

He turned. Her face was tense with anxiety. "You have no idea of what can happen when people find out about talking apes," she said.

"Actually, I think I do." He walked back to her, stuck the folder under his arm and then put his hands on her shoulders.

"I checked you out, Grace. I read about Spencer. I'm so sorry. I promise I will keep you informed."

Finn called Dawes as he was driving back to the station. "Hey, Perry, did you get any weird vibes from Jimson Janitorial in Cheney?"

"Nope. Charlie's boss seemed normal enough. But he didn't lay eyes on Charlie that night and he confirmed that nobody else was working with the kid on that job. He kept showing me the timesheet Charlie filled out and signed the next morning. I found one guy who worked across the street from the Ward Building. He saw a white Jimson van parked there, but he didn't see who was using it. Why are you asking?"

"The anonymous witness called again," Finn lied. "She mentioned that the green car in the parking lot when Ivy disappeared had a Jimson logo."

"The only Jimson vehicle that Charlie checks out is a company van, and it's white," Dawes said. "Matter of fact, all the vehicles owned by the Cheney branch are white vans."

"Maybe Charlie has a friend who drives a green car with a Jimson sign. I'll get a list of employees with vehicles."

"Charlie Wakefield and Jimson Janitorial connected to the high school and a Jimson vehicle seen at the Evansburg Food Mart," Dawes mused. "They are a huge organization. It could just be coincidence."

"We'll see," Finn said.

Brittany set up her sewing machine in the place her laptop would usually sit. She'd already cut out the pieces on the floor, and now she threaded the sea-green velvet under the machine foot. It felt so good to be creative again.

Her mom came into her room, carrying a glass of some glop. "I made you an eggnog. You didn't eat enough at dinner."

"Thanks," Brittany murmured. She pulled the threads through the cutter at the back of the sewing foot, clipping off the ends at the bottom of the seam.

Her mother set down the glass on her bedside table, and then came to hover over her shoulder. "What are you making?"

Brittany tapped a finger on her sketch. "It's a Halloween costume for Ivy. I already made the wings." She pointed to the silver-green creations on her bed. She was especially proud of the gold and black eye shape in the center of each wing.

Her mother looked at the wings for a long moment, then finally said, "A butterfly?"

"A luna moth." Brittany looked up at her. "Remember when we found that one at Gran's in Kansas? Remember how huge and magical it was?"

Her mother squeezed her shoulder. "I do. It *was* magical."

Footsteps thundered up the stairs. "Oh, here you are," her dad said lamely as he walked in. He focused on the wings on the bed.

"Brittany's sewing a luna moth costume for Ivy," her mother told him in the same tone she used to report absurdities like 'Our son says he wants to be a vampire when he grows up.'

Brittany focused on rearranging some pins. She could feel her dad staring at her. He started, "Oh, Britt, do you think that's—"

She cut him off. "It's for Halloween." She pushed the sea-green velvet under the sewing machine foot again. "Because Ivy will be home by then."

She heard him walk closer, but she didn't look up from the seam. "What is *that*?" he asked.

"Mom told you," Brittany said. "It's a luna moth costume for Ivy."

"No," he said, grabbing her right arm. "I mean, what is *that*?" He turned her forearm over.

Her mother gasped. "Brittany?"

For a long minute, they all stared at the gauze pad taped to the inside of her wrist. A few dots of blood had oozed through the white fabric. Her father was frowning and her mother had a hand clamped over her mouth like she might throw up. Shit, what did they think, that she'd cut her wrists? If she was going to do that, she would have done it the right way, the *effective* way, down the arm through the veins so nobody could tape them closed afterwards.

She ripped off the bandage. The tattoo of three ivy leaves was still swollen and raw.

At lunchtime, Joy had given her some X. "To cheer you up," she said, pressing several pills into Brittany's hand. "It's not just for parties, you know, and now that you're not nursing... It'll make you feel better."

She'd swallowed one and put the other two in her pocket. Joy had been right; the pill gave her courage. And strength. Ecstasy was so much more helpful than those stupid anti-depressants. It was not just helpful; it made her feel *hopeful*. After school, she'd gotten the tattoo.

She stood up and gave her parents a hug. "Don't look so worried," she said. She held out her arm and admired the design. "It's what soldiers do," she explained. "To show loyalty to each other and to the cause they're fighting for. I'm a warrior for Ivy."

"More gravy, Matt?" Dolores gestured at the white pitcher on the tablecloth.

"Thank you." He poured an artery-clogging brown river over his roast beef and mashed potatoes. "And thanks so much for cleaning the house and mowing the lawn the other day. You didn't have to do that."

Dolores made a dismissive gesture. "We have time on our hands, dear. And we know you don't right now."

He'd finally given in to his ex-in-laws' requests for dinner. The atmosphere was awkward, but the food was good. He was sick of frozen dinners; the whole chain of events required for cooking took too long; and he couldn't subsist on takeout hamburgers alone.

The Mankins left the television on in the living room while they ate. It was a habit that Finn generally found annoying, but he was able to ignore the sound for the most part. Until he heard his name, and then all three of them turned around to watch the news.

"We called Detective Matthew Finn to ask about new developments in the Ivy Rose Morgan case," the reporter said earnestly into the microphone. "He did not return our call."

The County Executive's face replaced the reporter's. "It's been over a week now since that baby disappeared, and the police are still chasing shadows," Travis Wakefield said. "We are disappointed that Detective Finn has not been able to deliver any results."

Scott jumped up and snapped off the television. "Asshole," he grunted, sitting back down at the table.

Finn stared at the blank TV screen. Was he about to be fired? He really dived off a cliff when he agreed to move here with Wendy. Now he'd been ditched by his wife; soon he'd be canned from a podunk department ... at this rate, pretty soon he'd be living in his car.

"Ignore that, Matt," Dolores said. "Everyone knows you're working hard. Let's talk about something else."

Finn shoveled more roast beef into his mouth. Something else. "Is Wendy still working at the college?" he asked around a mouthful.

A pained expression took hold of Scott Mankin's face, and he brushed a finger across his silver mustache. Dolores rearranged the green beans on her plate.

Finn swallowed. "It's okay, I can talk about her."

Dolores nodded and speared a bean. "She's still there, at least for now. She and Gordon are planning to...er...start a family."

Damn. If *that* didn't show how screwed up the universe was. He'd moved here because Wendy said she wanted to raise kids in a small-town environment. Too bad she'd neglected to mention that the kids she wanted to raise were not Finn's.

"They're moving to Pullman at the end of the year," Scott told him. "Wendy says it's just too hard to start a new life in a small town."

"Good," Finn said. At least he wouldn't have to worry about running into them at the Food Mart or the post office any longer. Then he remembered where he was. Dolores and Scott were losing the daughter they'd been reunited with less than a year ago. "I mean, it's good for me."

"Well, I guess we're back to reality." Dolores patted his fist on the tabletop. "How *is* that Morgan case going, dear?"

He took a breath, unclenched his fingers, picked up his fork again. "We're still waiting for a breakthrough."

Scott wiped his moustache with his napkin. "I always thought the FBI handled kidnappings."

"But it might not be a kidnapping," Dolores said. "Right, Matt? Otherwise, why would the police have searched all the garbage bins?"

Scott frowned. "You've been reading too many mysteries."

Dolores made an irritated noise.

"We have to check out all possibilities," Finn said. "The FBI has all the relevant data on their website. We're keeping them informed. They're waiting for us to generate leads."

The conversation stuck there for a long minute, mired in muck, just like his case. The Mankins had lived in Evansburg most of their lives and knew everyone and everything about the town—what could he tell them that wouldn't come back to bite him in the ass?

They know everyone and everything about this town, his tired memory repeated. *Pick their brains, you idiot.* "We've talked to all Brittany's friends, to the alleged father of the baby..."

"Charlie Wakefield?" Dolores asked. Her cheeks pinked when Finn turned toward her. "Well, word gets around, you know."

"Believe me, I know," he said. "Is there gossip around town that Charlie could have taken the baby?"

Dolores appeared confused. "Why would he do that? He didn't even acknowledge the child, as I understand it." Then she blanched. "Oh. Oh, no."

"Crapola," said Scott.

"There's no proof of anything," Finn quickly said. "And I mean that literally. We've talked to all the parents, to Brittany's teachers, the grocery store clerks, the janitors at the school. Speaking of which, I noticed they work for Jimson Janitorial Service. And I recently found out that Charlie Wakefield does, too."

"Really?" Dolores perked up. "Charlie Wakefield working as a janitor? Isn't *that* interesting; I wonder what happened to all those smart investments that Patricia Wakefield always gloated about."

Uh-oh. "The Wakefields are kind of sensitive about Charlie's job. Please keep that to yourself," Finn told her. "It might be the only thing that keeps me from getting fired."

"I'm sure you're exaggerating," Dolores said.

"I'm sure I'm not. Do either of you know anything about that Jimson company?"

Scott leaned forward. "It's a huge outfit, got offices and contracts all over the place."

Dolores sipped iced tea from her glass. "Isn't that one of those New Dawn companies?"

Finn swallowed. "New Dawn?"

"New Dawn Agency," she said. "From the New Dawn Church."

"*Bright* Dawn Church," Scott corrected her. "*New* Dawn Agency. The New Dawn Agency was the brainchild of Abram Jimson, the founder of Bright Dawn Church—there's about a dozen of those churches around the state. Abram Jimson lives in Spokane, but we've got one of the churches here in Evansburg."

"The Wakefields belong to that church," Dolores contributed.

"So maybe that connection helped Charlie Wakefield get a job," Finn guessed.

"Could be," Scott said. "The church's basic message is that all sinners deserve a second chance to make things right."

Finn quirked an eyebrow. "So they run a janitorial service?"

"Among other things," Scott said. "Jimson's a big believer in ministering to reformed addicts and alcoholics, and to the biggest batch of sinners in the state: the prison population. Bright Dawn preachers hold services at all the prisons. But even if the preachers managed to save their souls, the prisoners had no place to go after they served their time. Businesses wouldn't hire them, neighborhoods blackballed them, you know how it goes—"

Finn nodded and lifted another forkful of mashed potatoes to his mouth.

Scott continued. "They served their sentences but then had no way to turn their lives around. Like most states, the recidivism rate here in Washington was astronomical. Hell, ex-cons were committing crimes to get three squares and a bed again. Then along comes Jimson. He proposes creating the New Dawn Agency and gets a government grant to do it. New Dawn teaches basic skills a lot of these people were missing."

"Like speaking proper English and looking people in the eye." Dolores sat back in her chair and smoothed her short ash blonde hair against her neck. "Not to mention cleanliness and politeness and getting to work on time."

"Not everyone who works for Jimson is an ex-con," Scott said. "There are a lot of regular joes, too. College students, like Charlie. Lots of recent immigrants. You know, your basic unskilled labor." He set his napkin beside his plate. "We use Jimson janitors down at the car dealership. Their workers do a great job. The company guarantees satisfaction. They even send a quality control man around regularly to check up on how they're doing. You don't get customer service like that out of most companies."

"We've got apple pie for dessert, Matt." Dolores rose from her chair.

"That sounds wonderful." Finn smiled. Roast beef, apple pie, and other delicious tidbits—Charlie Wakefield most likely working with felons, and the probability of a pool of felons in the area where Ivy had been snatched.

Chapter 17

From the passenger seat of Joy's car, Brittany watched the strange woman park the SUV in the driveway. There'd been so many false leads; so many babies that were obviously not Ivy. People all over the country were sending her photos of sightings via Facebook; she and her mom or her friends spent hours sorting through them every day. But it was still possible, like Detective Finn said when he brought that dog, that a neighbor had taken her beautiful baby. Someone who'd seen Ivy and wanted her for their own. Ivy might be just around the corner—that was the thought that kept Brittany hopeful. That was what kept her listening for those baby cries.

Today would be the day she'd find Ivy; she just knew it. The X really lifted her mood. Thank god Joy had a good source. Just one pill in the morning made the whole day go a lot faster and smoother. Now she had the energy to keep looking for Ivy, and her mother acted so relieved that Brittany was feeling happier.

In the back, Ruben banged his toy against his car seat and gurgled. He'd come in fifth in the Pretty Baby contest. In spite of what Joy had predicted, the baby that took the prize was a blonde, blue-eyed baby girl. If Ivy had been in the contest, she would have won for sure.

The stranger pulled the baby out of the car seat and cradled her in one arm as she picked up the grocery bag with the other and walked to the door. The woman was fat enough to still be pregnant and her black hair was pinned back with hairpins. A black-haired stranger, just like the psychic had predicted! And living only a twenty-minute drive away from the Morgan house. The baby was the right size.

"See? Red hair," Joy said from the driver's seat. Brittany's parents had hidden her car keys, so Joy had driven her over to this neighborhood.

"Yes," Brittany said. A wisp of red hair peeked from the edge of the baby bonnet.

Brittany startled when her cell phone sang its melody from her purse. *Shit.* Her mother, checking up on her. She grabbed it. "Hi Mom, I really can't talk now," she said in a rush.

"I wanted to call before we went into the dead zone. What are you doing?"

Her parents and Danny had trooped off to a friend's farm near Okanagan for the weekend. Not giving up, just a little break, her mother said, especially since Britt was feeling better. They'd begged her to come, but she'd gotten out of it by saying she had to study for a history exam. As if she'd even cracked a book since Ivy disappeared.

"I'm at Joy's. We're going to watch a movie," she lied. "My phone's going dead; I gotta go." That part was mostly true, the little battery icon was flashing in the upper right corner.

The woman was walking up to her front door.

"No more tattoos?"

"Of course not! Mom, I've got to go—"

"Taking your anti-depressants?"

"Right on schedule, Mom. Like I said, they're really making me feel better. I've got to go."

"I left the Marshes' number on the refrigerator," her mom said. "Call that if you need us, because the cells don't work out there."

"Got it, Mom. The phone's going."

"Don't forget to plug it in to recharge. I love you, Britt."

"Ditto, Mom." She threw the phone down on the passenger seat next to her purse. "I'll be back," she told Joy. She nudged open the car door and scampered across the street, stopping to hide behind a bush.

When the woman fumbled with her keys to open the front door while trying to hold groceries and infant to her chest, the baby gave a little squeak of protest. Brittany's heart leapt like it had been touched with a live wire. Ivy!

Should she call the police? No, they'd never believe her. Nobody believed her anymore. The police would talk to the fat woman, who would probably then disappear forever. Brittany walked around the perimeter of the house, crouching low. She could see the top of a headboard through one window. The headboard was big enough for a queen bed, so she moved on around the house.

There. A decal was attached to the window, one of those Save My __! stickers the Fire Department handed out. Somebody had written *baby* in the blank space in Magic Marker. The window was open a couple of inches. Brittany crouched beneath it, listening to the snuffling of the baby. Then there was a ticking sound and a soft melody began to play—the classical version of Twinkle Twinkle Little Star—and she heard the woman say, "Now sleep, please." After another minute, there was nothing but the melody, playing over and over.

Brittany stood up. She had to stand on tiptoe and mash her face into the window screen to see in. Only the corner of the crib was visible; it was against the same wall that she was leaning on. She had to get in there.

Jamming her house key under the edge of the screen, she managed to pop it out of its track and lower it quietly to the ground. She tried to pull herself up into the window frame, but couldn't make it further than a few inches. She broke a nail and scraped her knees on the siding. "Hold on, baby girl. I'll be right there," she whispered through the window.

Beside the deck she found a plastic bucket and carried it back. Turning it over, she climbed gingerly on top. The plastic sagged under her weight, but didn't completely collapse. She peeked back into the window. Twinkle Twinkle Little Star still played, but the tune moved from one style to another—jazzy, classical, dramatic, light. Ivy would probably like that.

Brittany hoisted herself up on her forearms and wiggled upright until she could reach a leg in. God it hurt, the metal of the window frame and the bumpy wall surface scratching against her bare legs. Why had she worn shorts? She still couldn't see the baby; only the headboard and the little carousel of padded silk stars and half moons twirling above the crib. She slid her whole body inside, landing with a thump on one foot before she could pull the other one inside the window frame. Holy crap, anyone could hear that, couldn't they? She ducked behind the door and waited.

Nobody came. Must have not been as loud as she'd thought, or maybe the thump was covered up by Twinkle Twinkle. She edged out from behind the door and tiptoed to the crib. The baby slept on her back, facing away from her, a pacifier covering the lower half of her face. Ivory snow skin, strawberry blonde hair, long reddish lashes against the plump cheeks. The baby had tiny pink ladybugs on her earlobes. They'd pierced her ears?

"Ivy?" Brittany whispered. Ivy wasn't this big, was she? And she had darker lashes, didn't she?

Could she have forgotten what Ivy looked like in two weeks? Two weeks was like a fifth of Ivy's lifetime, and sometimes it seemed like Ivy changed overnight. Could this be Ivy? Her eyebrows looked familiar. Little red-gold arches. *God, please let it be Ivy.*

Brittany touched the baby softly on the cheek with a finger. "Ivy?" The baby turned her head and regarded her with large blue eyes. "Ivy?"

The baby didn't really look like Ivy and she didn't really *feel* like Ivy, but maybe Brittany didn't remember right. She'd been more than a little whacko in the last two weeks, and the drugs didn't exactly help with critical thinking, as Mr. Tanz would say. At times it seemed like Ivy was only a dream, not a real baby. She heard crying in her dreams.

The kidnapper could have pierced Ivy's ears so that she wouldn't look so much like Ivy; that would be a really smart thing to do. The photo next to Brittany's bed was now a month old. So did she really remember what Ivy looked like?

The mole. Ivy had a mole next to her spine on the left side. Brittany knew that for sure; that wouldn't change. She picked up the baby, held the warm soft body against her chest. God, it felt so right, a baby's weight in her arms again. She pulled up the little pink shirt.

The carousel stopped and Twinkle Twinkle died away. Then there was the creak of a floorboard. Brittany turned. The black-haired woman filled the doorway. Their eyes met, and they screamed simultaneously, just like in the movies. Then the baby started to shriek, too.

After three interviews, Finn was reasonably certain who had stolen the drugs from the clinic. One nurse had a lover with a long record of drug use. Finn had seen this way too often; otherwise smart people in relationships with criminals, so sure that the bad seed would never hurt *them*. He'd met parents who swore that their child would not rob them even after said child had been caught fencing Dad's coin collection. Most likely the nurse had been careless and the dirtbag lover had borrowed her keys and helped himself. Finn was still a few steps from proving it, but he could see the path laid out in front of him like a runway. A couple of uniforms were tracking down lover boy right now to haul him in for an interrogation. He had a warrant for the guy's cell records, and now he held a phone receiver between his ear and shoulder as he scrolled through the guy's criminal history on his computer screen.

"We'll fax those cell records to you within forty-eight hours," the Sprint representative told him.

"Make it within twenty-four if you can." He hung up the phone. Man, it was satisfying to make quick progress on a case. He couldn't wait for the reporters to show up after he had this one in the bag.

Miki materialized in front of his desk. "I called the schools in Coeur d'Alene and Portland like you asked," she said.

"And?"

"They both use Jimson for their janitorial services."

Finn wanted to leap up from his chair and shout "Yes!" He worked hard to keep his expression neutral. "Thanks."

"Is that the answer you wanted?" she asked eagerly.

"Thanks, Miki," he said again.

She pursed her lips and put her fists on her hips, posing like a petulant child. "I don't understand—why those two schools? Does this have something to do with the Ivy Morgan case?"

"Good job." Finn told her. He wasn't about to give a nineteen-year-old assistant any details about a hunch that might or might not lead anywhere. He pretended to study his computer screen.

Miki stood there for a few seconds longer, then turned and walked away.

Jimson Janitorial Service held the contracts at all three schools where babies had disappeared in the last six months. A witness had identified the Jimson logo on the car Ivy was taken to. Next step? Employee records from Jimson to correlate with criminal histories and work locations and dates. With luck, he might be able to track Charlie's movements between Cheney and Evansville, or find an associate that Charlie had hired to snatch Ivy. There could be a not-so-reformed ex-con working at the Evansville high school.

An answering machine greeted him at both the local Jimson office and the company headquarters in Spokane. He checked his watch. Damn. Almost nine P.M. on a Friday evening. He left a message but didn't have much hope of a call back.

"Working overtime again?" Detective Melendez asked as she hung her jacket on the coat tree next to her cubicle.

"You know how it goes," Finn said.

Scoletti and his duty belt clanked to a stop next to Melendez. "Hey, Finn. We've got your dirtbag in Room Two," he said. Turning to Melendez, he said, "Yours is in Room One. And did you hear? The sheriff just hauled Brittany Morgan in for home invasion—some woman out in Briarwood with a red-haired baby." He clanked off down the hall.

It sounded like the Morgan girl was going off the deep end looking for her baby. Now that he had Neema's tips, it seemed likely that Brittany was telling the truth: Ivy had been kidnapped. Finn felt guilty that he hadn't believed Brittany's story in the first place.

"That poor girl," Sara Melendez muttered, shaking her head. "There's never enough time, is there? We're still so far from knowing what actually happened, aren't we?"

"Got that right." Finn stood up, picked up the clinic file from his desk and went to work on the case he could solve today.

"Residential Burglary," Brittany's public defender told her. "That's much better than Burglary I, which they could have charged you with."

"But I didn't steal anything!" Brittany protested.

"Entering a house without permission, that's the legal definition of burglary. You don't have to steal anything."

She pressed her hands down on top of the grungy table in the interview room. The place smelled like old French fries. There was no mirror on the wall, but there was a little camera up in the corner by the ceiling. It didn't look like it was on, though; there was no glowing light like most of them had when they were running.

The cop who brought her had taken her handcuffs off, and the door had clicked shut behind him as he left. There was just a tiny window in the door? Were she and the lawyer locked in this room? It made her feel like screaming to think she couldn't get out.

The lawyer had sandy brown hair and hazel eyes and didn't seem much older than the boys at school. Shouldn't a courtroom lawyer look a little tough? He pressed his lips together and glared at her like he was annoyed to be called here on a Friday night. "This is serious, Brittany."

"Of course it's serious! Why else would I break into a perfect stranger's house?" The baby girl wasn't Ivy, although she could have been her twin. But there was no mole on her back. And her ears were pierced. Three months old and that baby's ears were pierced! Brittany would never do that to Ivy; she'd let her little girl make up her own mind.

But she didn't have Ivy. Maybe someone else was piercing Ivy's ears right now. She could hear a baby shrieking. She pressed her hands over her ears.

"Listen to me." The lawyer pulled one of her hands back down to the table. "You already have the charge of reckless endangerment."

And the failed lie detector test. He thought she was guilty, too; she could see it in his eyes. *Where's Ivy?* She could see the lips of all those strangers, moving over and over. *Where's Ivy?* People who thought she'd done something horrible to her baby.

IVY IS IN A BETTER PLACE.

God, please let that be true. Let her be with someone who wanted a beautiful baby, someone who is taking good care of her.

"How did you get to that house?" the lawyer asked.

"I told you; I hitched." When the police dragged her out of the house, Joy's car was gone. Smart girl, she took off when she heard the screams or maybe it was the sirens. Brittany told the cops she'd hitched a ride out to that address. Nope, she hadn't brought a purse or anything with her. Joy would keep her mouth shut; she still had two months to go on probation for a shoplifting charge last year. Brittany wondered what Joy would do with her purse and phone. She really wished she had that purse. She could envision the little stamped pills of Ecstasy in her coin holder. She was coming down and it was going to be a hard landing, she could tell. Her jaw ached and she felt twitchy. She could really use another X right now.

"We've been unable to contact your parents. Do you know where they are?"

The last thing on earth she wanted was for her parents to find out what she'd done. "My parents went to visit a friend out in the country. They don't have any phones there." She'd already said that at least three times. Did the guy have Alzheimer's, or what?

"Do you know the address?" He opened his notebook to write it down. "We could have the local police drive out to contact them."

She stared at the ceiling for a minute like she was thinking about it. "I don't know the address. It's somewhere near Cheney?" It was the first town that came to her because of Charlie. That shithead.

He looked at her. "The friend's name?"

"Umm." She counted the specks on the table in front of her for a few seconds. "Jones, I think. Tim and Margie Jones. Or maybe Jonas?"

He raised an eyebrow, but scribbled down a few words anyway, then slapped his notebook shut.

A baby was crying, just beyond the green wall there. "Do you hear that?" she asked.

"Hear what?" He scooted back his chair and pulled his notebook into his lap. "I'm sorry, but it's too late in the day to arrange for bail."

The baby was getting louder. The lawyer's voice seemed to come from somewhere far away as he said, "Since it's Friday, you won't be arraigned until Monday."

"I have to find Ivy." Brittany stared at the door, willing it to open. It didn't. She gazed at him through a film of tears. "You have to let me out."

"It's not up to me." He stood up. "The judge will decide that. On Monday."

Chapter 18

It was easy enough to get a DMV list of vehicles owned by Jimson Janitorial. They had quite a fleet; mostly utility vans, but also nine cars. Unfortunately, six were green Tauruses, all the same year and model. The company must have gotten a deal from Ford. All were registered to the company headquarters address in Spokane.

Not surprisingly, Finn got no answer on a Saturday morning at the Spokane headquarters of New Dawn Enterprises.

However, he lucked out at the local Evansburg office. When he arrived in Jimson Janitorial's parking lot, the girl he'd seen before was standing in front of the building, grinding out a cigarette butt with the heel of her sandal. He caught the door behind her and followed her in.

She sat down behind a desk with a gold-colored plaque that declared her to be Linn. At least eight rings and studs adorned her ears. Tiny holes revealed further piercings in one nostril and both eyebrows. The inky head of a bird—maybe a peacock?—peeked from beneath the collar of her plain pink blouse. Finn could easily envision Linn after work hours, hair lacquered into spikes and her face pincushioned to match. He wondered how far down the bird tattoo went.

"Can I help you?" she asked again.

"Does anyone assigned to this office drive a green Taurus with a Jimson Janitorial logo?"

"What?"

Finn repeated the question.

"Mr. Pearson!" she bellowed over her shoulder. Through the open door behind her, Finn saw the corner of a desk surrounded by shelves holding cleaning solutions, towels, and sponges.

Pearson emerged. He could have been a church deacon, with close-cropped gray hair and a button-down shirt. Finn showed him his badge.

"A green car?" he echoed, after Linn repeated the question. He shook his head. "Nope. We got the vans for the cleaning crews, but nobody here has a company car. That's a perk reserved for the big guns, not for us lowly crew managers."

"Do you know Travis Wakefield or Charlie Wakefield?"

"I know who Travis Wakefield is," Pearson said. "Who doesn't around here? Is Charlie the son? I know he has one."

That sounded like a dead end. "May I see your employee records?"

Pearson frowned. "Like what? All we keep here are timesheets and employee phone numbers and such."

"I need personnel files, with home addresses and previous employers." Dates of birth and SSNs were what he really needed to match up with criminal histories, but people tended to freak out when social security numbers were mentioned.

After considering for less than ten seconds, Pearson shook his head. "I can't give you any files without permission from the head office."

"This might help find Ivy Rose Morgan."

The man was adamant; he couldn't give information without permission. "Besides," he said as he handed Finn a business card from the main office in Spokane, "I thought the mama did that baby in; wasn't that why you arrested her?"

Finn explained for the twentieth time that Brittany Morgan had not been arrested for murder and Ivy had not been found, dead or alive. Pearson looked doubtful, as if he suspected that Finn was not telling the truth. He shook his head again. "Sorry, I can't help you without orders from above."

Shit. Finn thought for a minute, trying to conjure up some sort of leverage to make the guy cooperate. He failed to come up with anything. Gritting his teeth, he headed to the station.

Through an online corporate database and a directory information service, he managed to track down Jimson's HR manager in Spokane.

Lisa Dvorak was surprised to be contacted at home. As he spoke with her on the phone, Finn could hear kids fighting in the background.

"I can assure you that we never place employees with records of violence or crimes against children in any school situation," she told him. "That's our guarantee to the school districts."

He repeated his request for all Jimson Janitorial employee records. "They could be of value in one or more criminal cases."

"We've got eleven field offices and cleaning contracts for a hundred and twenty-seven schools in the Pacific Northwest. It would be impossible to compile a comprehensive list of employees for you, Detective."

"You mean you don't have a computerized payroll service?" He failed to keep the sarcasm out of his voice.

Her tone turned icy. "What I meant to say was that it would require a court order. Now I really need to go, Detective." She hung up.

Obviously the woman was not inclined to be cooperative. He'd have to find another way in, or get a court order. Right. *See, Judge, I got these two clues from an ape, and when I tried them out on a cleaning lady, she seemed nervous. And the gorilla painted these J shapes to show it was Jimson.* Finn put the receiver back into its cradle.

Detective Kathryn Larson stood in front of his desk. "Isn't this your day off?"

"Theoretically."

"Why have you been holding out on us, Finn?"

What the hell? Did she know about Neema?

"Sssssssssssss," Larson hissed, forming her fingers into fangs and striking in his direction.

Gossip blew across this town faster than dust from the wheat fields. She'd obviously heard of the snake bracelet he had discussed with Audrey Ibañez. He shrugged. "Might not be anything; it was an anonymous tip."

She tapped on his desk. "Go home. The second string is here. We'll all be watching for babies in green cars, isn't that right? Oh yeah, I thought we'd tail the baby's daddy again, too. He's back in town for the weekend."

"Good thinking," he said. "And check up on the analysis of the stuff we bagged in the parking lot."

She rolled her eyes. "State Patrol won't be done with that anytime in the near future. In case you haven't noticed, this isn't CSI."

He'd noticed. Evansburg had no crime lab, so like most small jurisdictions in Washington State, it used the Highway Patrol lab to process evidence. There were private labs, too, but those were available only when the jurisdiction was willing to pay for their services. "What's the standard processing time these days?"

"I had a homicide that took a year." Larson tucked a strand of curly hair behind an ear. "And they haven't sent us the DNA results yet from an alleged rape seven months ago."

A year? In a year, Ivy Rose Morgan could be anywhere. In a year, Ivy Rose Morgan would look completely different. He'd call agent Alice Foster and ask if there was any way the FBI could process the parking lot collection.

"Go home," Larson told him.

Instead, he went to the Captain.

"Jimson Janitorial Service?" the Captain frowned. "Nobody's going to touch them with a twenty-foot pole."

"Why not?"

The Captain crooked a bushy eyebrow at him in disbelief, then stroked his hand over his bald head. "I keep forgetting that you're new to Washington State. Ever heard of The New Dawn Agency?"

Finn quoted, "The New Dawn Agency was the brainchild of Abram Jimson, the founder of Bright Dawn Church, which has thirty churches statewide. The basic message is that all sinners deserve a second chance. New Dawn wants to give ex-cons jobs, so it spawns Jimson Landscaping, Jimson Oil & Lube, and Jimson Janitorial Service. So now all these ex-cons are gainfully employed and paying taxes."

The Captain nodded. "I see you've done your homework. Everyone hires Jimson because they're cheap and reliable. Hell, they have the landscaping and cleaning contracts at the state capitol in Olympia. They take care of the greens out at the country club here. I think they do most of the state college campuses. Most of the ex-cons go to Bright Dawn Church to get extra brownie points. By the way, at least half the people in this town attend Bright Dawn. Including Travis Wakefield."

So? Finn leaned on the desk. "What if Jimson was involved in the Ivy Morgan kidnapping?"

The Captain looked him in the eye. "You're shitting me."

Finn leaned back and crossed his arms. "I shit you not."

"Involved how?"

"We recently found out Charlie Wakefield works for Jimson Janitorial Service. And we got a tip that Ivy was taken from her mother's car to one with a Jimson Janitorial logo."

"A good tip?"

Neema's hairy visage swam into Finn's mind. "Anonymous," he fudged. "But it sounded credible enough to check out. And Jimson Janitorial has contracts at the schools in Idaho and Oregon where babies went missing."

"Circumstantial," the Captain snapped. "They also have contracts at a hundred schools where babies *haven't* gone missing."

"But it might provide the break we need," Finn argued. He tried for victim sympathy. "You know that Brittany Morgan is in jail right now?"

"I know." The Captain made a face. "The girl's desperate. Or just plain crazy. We can't locate her parents and we can't release her without bail. How could the parents leave her in town on her own?"

That was a good question, but Finn sympathized with Brittany's mother and father. The whole family needed a break. He redirected the Captain back to the subpoena request. "Don't you think we need to follow every lead in this case? Jimson is refusing to cooperate without a court order."

"All you have is an anonymous tip about a Jimson car?"

"And Charlie Wakefield working there."

"Can you put Charlie together in Evansburg with a Jimson car at the right time?"

Finn answered with a heavy sigh.

"That's what I was afraid of." The Captain shook his head. "It's not going to be easy to get any judge to lean on Jimson Janitorial Service, because then some big state honcho is going to be leaning on that judge, you get me? Not to mention leaning on the local police captain. I'm sorry, but I'm not wading into that cesspool."

The Captain turned away, flipped a page on his desk calendar as if dismissing Finn. "However," he said, his eyes still on the calendar page, "a new guy like you might be excused for his ignorance."

Ah. He was going to have to go it alone.

"Try Judge Sobriski," the Captain said softly. "He's new, too."

"Thanks." Finn turned to leave.

As he put his hand on the doorknob, the Captain's voice came from behind him. "Just so you understand, if you muck this up, you'll probably be headed back to your old job in Chicago."

Finn turned. "There are no jobs in Chicago."

"Then you'll just be unemployed."

Now there was something to look forward to.

"Go home, Detective. That's an order. Take the rest of the weekend to think it over. Your shift ended yesterday at five P.M."

A reporter and cameraman were waiting for him at the back of the station. "No comment," Finn snarled as he walked down the steps.

As he approached his car, a blue-jeaned youth stepped in front of him. "Detective Finn?"

"No comment," Finn repeated.

The youth shoved an envelope into Finn's hands. "You've been served," he said over his shoulder as he walked away.

By the law firm's address on the front, Finn knew that he was holding divorce papers from Wendy. Stifling a curse, he tossed the envelope into his car and then slid in. The reporter and cameraman stood by his front bumper, filming. He honked at them and drove away.

It never felt right to go home when he was working a missing person case. It was probably different if you had family, but all he had was the case he was working. And the animals that had taken over his house.

Lok sat beneath the photo of Wendy and watched him expectantly. Finn recognized him now by a diagonal slash above one eye that gave him a skeptical expression. The cat swished his orange tail a couple of times.

All animals communicate, Grace had said. *Humans simply like to pretend they can't understand other species.*

Wishing it were a steel dart instead of a plastic toy, Finn picked up one of the wall walkers and lobbed it at Wendy's photo. It stuck on the glass over her left eye. Lok made a little chirping noise and watched the wall walker intently, swishing his tail. The suckers gave way and the toy began its slow crawl down the wall. The cat crouched and froze, his eyes glued to the toy. When the wall walker had completed its spastic descent to within a foot of the floor, Lok leapt up and batted it off the wall, snagged it with a claw in midair and pinned it to the ground. Picking the toy up in his mouth, the cat trotted over to Finn's feet, dropped the toy on the toe of his shoe, and then widened his green eyes.

"Not again," Finn groaned. But he picked up the wall walker and tossed it again, nailing Wendy on the upper lip this time. Lok leapt after it. He gathered up the rest of the suction-footed toys and slammed them into Wendy's photo, one after another. Cheek. Forehead. Nose. Lok danced below in happy confusion.

He took off his jacket and holster and laid his gun down on the dining room table, loosened his tie. Cargo waited for him in the kitchen, staring at the refrigerator as though he could will it to open. The other cat, Kee, sat on the counter and meowed.

After putting down food for the animals, he changed his clothes, and then retired to his study and his sailboat painting. He squirted water on the little globs of paint in his palette partitions, squeezed a fair amount of burnt sienna into the center of the mixing area, and placed a large container of water on his desk. He picked up a brush and went to work on adding color to shadows in the billowing sails and in the Lake Michigan waves.

Cargo padded in, wedged himself under the desk and lay across Finn's feet with a grunt. A cat—Kee, this time—jumped up on the desk and sat a few inches away, on top of the envelope of divorce papers. He switched his tail, watching Finn paint.

"I suppose you're an art critic now?" The cat watched the brush as Finn mixed the paints on the palette.

Gun cat dog man, a gorilla had named him. Or so Grace McKenna had told him. Unfortunately, the string of words pretty much summed up his life. There wasn't a lot more to add. Detective. Ex-husband. Sap. Amateur painter. Did Neema know signs for those as well as for *cat* and *dog*? He couldn't believe there were gorillas in his life now, too.

Art soothes the mind, a psychologist once told him. Painting was a way to find serenity after a stressful day. The infinite array of colors entranced him. He had dozens of tubes of beautiful paints he had never opened, and every time he cracked a catalog, he wanted more.

Did Neema and Gumu long for colors they had no way to ask for? What would Grace think if she knew that he painted as a hobby, just like her gorillas? Their artwork was already earning a minor fortune on E-bay. Hell, if a gorilla could do it, maybe he ought to give it a try. Might be a new career after he got fired from his current job. Then again, it would be humiliating as hell if nobody bid on his paintings.

He couldn't believe his only witness on the Morgan case was a gorilla. His brain kept circling back to the details. Ivy was still missing. Brittany Morgan was in jail. *Knock it off, Finn*, he told himself. Forget work for a few hours. Enjoy your hobby.

Kee's tail brushed across the manila envelope he sat on. Swish swish, swish swish. The divorce papers. Something else to forget for awhile.

After adding dashes of crimson and cerulean, the sailboats began to appear three-dimensional. Finn held the paintbrush in the air, comparing the painting with the photo. The water was still too flat; if there was enough wind for racing, there'd be more movement to the water. He dipped his brush in a puddle of cerulean and touched the tip to the paper.

Kee attacked, paws out to snag the paintbrush. Finn flung the cat away, caught the water container with his elbow and slopped a spray of water across the desk. Kee landed on the off-white carpet, hissing, and then dashed through the doorway to the living room, leaving a trail of blue and crimson paw prints. Cargo bolted to his feet, barking. Water trickled down the desk drawers to soak into Finn's pant legs.

"Damn it!" Finn padded to the kitchen for a roll of paper towels. The painting could be salvaged, but he wasn't so sure about the carpet. He mopped up the water and emptied the container, dabbed at the paw prints with a folded paper towel.

So much for serenity. His whole life seemed like a farce these days. God, he needed a drink. And someone to talk to.

There was only one person he could think of. He shouldn't contact her. Then again, nobody knew about the connection between them. Heck, she wasn't on anybody's radar as far as he knew. She seemed lonely. And she was the only other human who understood the crazy situation he was in. He picked up the phone and called Grace McKenna.

She was at his house by five, bearing a sack full of steaks, freshly made tabouli, bread, and red wine.

The unusually hot streak of weather had finally broken, and it was bearable to be out under the October evening sun. Actually, it was quite nice in the backyard. He'd have to find a way to spend more time out here.

After a quick perusal of the instruction manual, he fired up the grill like a pro. He found a long-handled fork in his mangle of kitchenware and slapped the steaks on the grill, sprinkling a little garlic salt and Worcestershire sauce on them. God only knew how long the sauce had been in the fridge, but he didn't think it could go bad.

"Sit."

He pivoted to see why Grace was giving him that order. She stood on the deck, holding a piece of dog food, her hand down at her side. Cargo stood in front of her on the lawn, his gaze fixed on her hand. A long string of drool stretched from his massive jaws to the grass.

Finn waited for the inevitable attack. Amazingly, Cargo lowered his hindquarters to the ground and transferred his attention to Grace's face, staring at her intently with shiny eyes. *Aarrnnhh*, he whined.

"Good boy." Grace gave him the piece of kibble. "What a goof." She rubbed the dog's head.

It was the exact same kibble that he poured into the beast's bowl every day. What made Cargo obey her for it? Probably the same thing that made Finn break out the grill when he usually nuked his own dinner.

"What a nice dog." Grace made a fast two-handed slash motion, touched her hip and snapped her fingers softly. Cargo tilted his head, watching. Grace turned pink. "Oh lordy, I'm impossible! You can't take me anywhere." She clasped her hands together to keep them still.

He laughed and picked up the Merlot bottle. "More wine?"

She picked up her glass from the deck and held it out for a refill. Sinking into a deck chair, Grace sighed contentedly as she put her feet up. "A night out. You have no idea what this means to me, Matt."

Her comment sparked a little trill of electricity in his gut. Excitement, or fear? He flipped the steaks and studied her out of the corner of his eye. Obviously, she was pleased; did that mean she was attracted to him? She looked different tonight, scrubbed clean, her hair pinned back at the crown of her head, dressed in a green blouse and white slacks.

She caught him inspecting her and raised a hand to cover the scar on her upper lip. Embarrassed, he turned back to the grill. He hoped she wasn't one of those needy middle-aged women seeking a husband. He wasn't ready to go down that road again, not by a long shot. He shouldn't even be having dinner with her.

"Grace," he said.

"Yes?" She smiled at him.

"This isn't a date."

Her smile faded and her eyes clouded. "Okay," she mumbled.

Oh jeez, now he'd hurt her feelings. "I mean, it can't be. I'm a detective, and we're both involved in an open case."

She pretended to pick a speck of lint from her shirt. "I understand."

Did she? "But if I weren't a detective and we weren't on the same case, then it would definitely be a date."

She met his gaze, looking happier now. "I get it, Matt."

Cargo climbed onto the deck, flopped down by Grace's chair, and laid his massive head on his front paws. Lok appeared, slinking through the open patio door. He examined Grace for two seconds before leaping into her lap.

"Well, hey there." The cat's back rose under her hand and he turned, purring, and butted her arm with his head. She laughed. "What a sweet cat. I had no idea you were such an animal lover, Matt."

He barely stifled a snort. "I like to remain a man of mystery," he said, taking a sip of his wine. "You know what? That cat fetches. Like a dog. Well, like some dogs." He stared pointedly at Cargo.

"I love how animals are such individuals, don't you?" she said. "Each one has a unique personality." She kept one hand on the cat as she sipped her wine.

He turned back to the steaks. Now that he thought about it, the two cats *were* very different from each other—Lok always ready to play and Kee usually ready to complain or to bite him. Speaking of the devil, Kee appeared and now sat beside the lawn chair, switching his tail and glaring at his brother in Grace's lap. One front paw was still blue and there was a red spot on his tail. His mouth opened and an irritated yowl emerged.

"Watch out—that's the bitchy one," Finn said.

"He's probably just frustrated that we're so hard to train." Grace leaned sideways to stroke Kee. "At least *your* animals don't actually tell you you're an idiot." She gazed longingly into the back yard and inhaled deeply. "I love your roses. I can smell them from here."

He followed her gaze to a cascade of yellow roses creeping over the trellis. More pink and lilac roses bloomed on bushes near the back of the yard. All he remembered was blackberries out there. Clearly, Dolores and Scott had done more than simple housecleaning and mowing. How often had they been here?

When the steaks were done, they moved to the patio table to eat. They made a point not to talk about signing gorillas and missing babies, but instead talked about where they'd come from, and how different it was from Evansburg. Finn was surprised to find that for once, he was the expert on the area.

It grew dark while they polished off the wine. In the distance, a lone coyote howled. At 9:30 P.M., Grace checked her watch and stood up. "Jane go back to jungle," she said, signing. He laughed with her.

He walked her to the door, wondering what should happen next. They were—what were they now? Friends, he guessed. Should he hug her? Shake hands? While he was debating, she turned, put her hands on his shoulders, leaned forward and planted a kiss on the tip of his nose. "Good night, Matt. See you tomorrow?"

"Oh. Yeah." They'd made an appointment so he could do a more organized interview with Neema.

"Why are you smiling?" she asked.

"Just thinking about interviewing a gorilla."

"Don't expect too much. Neema has a short attention span." She left him standing on the porch rubbing his nose and feeling that too much wine kept his thoughts from coagulating properly. He stacked the dishes in the sink and turned in. As he pulled the sheet up over his shoulders, first Lok, then Kee leapt onto the bed and positioned themselves, purring, on either side of his hips. Cargo sat by the side of the bed, breathing heavily and eyeing the bedspread as if he was about to join the party.

"Forget it," Finn said. "Lay down."

Amazingly, the dog did. Finn put a hand on each cat. "Good job tonight, crew; way to impress a lady."

Then he flipped over onto his side, rolling Lok off the bed onto Cargo, who woofed and took off in hot pursuit of the startled cat. Kee hung half off the bed. He clawed his way back up and sat on his pillow, switching his tail across Finn's nose.

"Good grief," Finn groaned.

Chapter 19

Brittany lay down on the bunk that wasn't really a bunk, but just a steel shelf that stuck out from the wall. A thin mattress with a plastic covering was all that separated her from the cold metal. She was alternately hot and cold. She pulled the scratchy blanket over herself and rolled onto her back. Her jaws were killing her and she felt nauseous and dizzy; she really needed the tranqs to come down after the X. Especially at night. How could anybody stay asleep with the lights on?

On television, jail looked gross and sometimes dangerous, but they never showed how boring it was. She'd been in this cell for a night and a day. She could see the clock at the end of the hallway if she stood in the corner and looked through the bars. Now it was her second night, and it seemed more like she'd been here for a week. A female guard brought her magazines; she'd already paged through them twice.

But she deserved boredom; she deserved punishment. Every time the jailers brought her a meal, they asked if they could call her parents. "Are you sure you don't know the number?"

Each time, she shook her head. She was sort of surprised her parents hadn't shown up. Maybe they'd called Joy, and Joy had lied for her, told them they were having a good time and Britt's phone was dead. Or Joy had answered Britt's phone and lied for her then.

In any case, she was glad they hadn't found her yet. She wasn't ready to talk to them. What could she say? They'd be so disappointed. They'd never leave her alone again. They'd never trust her again. And why should they? She couldn't do anything right. She was a terrible daughter and a terrible mother. A complete fail, the Sluts would say. A fail-ure, Mr. Tanz would correct.

Her head began to buzz; she rubbed her temples to make the noise go away. She hadn't even known for sure if that baby was Ivy. What kind of mother wouldn't instantly recognize her own baby? She didn't deserve Ivy. That was probably why God took her away.

There was a stain on the ceiling, like a toilet or sink above had leaked. It was a dark rust-red, oblong stain, with a darker spot in the middle. It looked like a mouth. She squinted to bring it into focus. It seemed to be moving.

Did you cause your daughter to be kidnapped?

She put her hands over her ears. A ceiling stain couldn't be talking to her. No, it was just her stupid brain replaying the FBI agent's questions.

Did you cause your daughter to be kidnapped?

If she hadn't left Ivy alone she couldn't have been kidnapped. God knew the truth.

Did you leave your daughter in the car when you went to the grocery store?

God was everywhere. God could do anything, assume any form—that's what Joy always told her. And God could forgive anything.

"God?" She stood up on the bunk to get closer to the ceiling mouth. "Please," she whispered. "I'll do anything. I'll be anything you want. Just tell me what to do. Just bring Ivy back."

Did you leave your daughter in the car when you went to the grocery store?

God wanted a confession? "Yes!" she said to the mouth-shaped stain. "Yes, it's all my fault!"

"Shut the fuck up, bitch!" A man's voice growled from down the hall. "It's three in the fuckin' morning!"

Brittany stared out through the bars into the dim light. Why didn't they ever turn the lights off? The baby was crying again, just down there, just around the corner where she couldn't see. "Ivy?" she whispered.

"Yes, it's all my fault!" the nasty voice mocked in falsetto. "You're right about that, bitch. Now shut up."

"Zip it, motherfucker," another man's voice said. "Leave the girl alone."

Motherfucker was right. It was all her fault. She'd only had one chance to do something right in her life and that was to be a good mother. And she'd blown that. All those people on the street and in the newspaper were right; she deserved hell.

Any good mother should be able to sense if her baby was alive or dead, right? She closed her eyes, tried to feel Ivy. She could hear the baby crying. Was it her baby? Was there even a real baby out there? Or was it a spirit baby? Everyone thought Ivy was dead—was she? Shouldn't she be able to *feel* her baby out there if her spirit was still in this world?

I have promises to keep, and miles to go before I sleep.

She'd wanted to make Ivy those silvery moth wings. Was that some kind of premonition, like Ivy was going to need angel wings?

No! Ivy was an angel, but here on earth. She had to believe that. God had taken Ivy and given her to a better mother, someone more careful, someone who knew how to be a mother. Ivy was with her *real* mother now.

She stared at her arm. Black leaves stamped under her skin didn't make her a warrior. What a stupid idea. As stupid as thinking she could find Ivy. She dug her fingertips into the twining design, but she'd bitten her nails down so close to the quick that she couldn't even tear off the tattoo. She was a loser, a complete and total fail.

Loser.
Stupid.
Fail.
Bitch.

There were horizontal bars as well as vertical ones at the front of the cell. If only they'd left her a shoelace or a belt. But they'd taken everything, leaving her only her underwear, and given her these ugly orange pajamas, a pullover top with no buttons, elastic waist pants.

Reckless endangerment. You left your daughter in the car all alone.

She was afraid to look at the stain on the ceiling. She didn't want to see those rust red lips moving.

Do you know if Ivy's alive or dead?

Did you kill Ivy?

You left your daughter in the car all alone.

Loser.

Ivy was in a better place. She didn't deserve to get her baby back. She knew what she was supposed to do.

Brittany stepped down off the bunk, pulled off the ugly orange pajama bottoms and knotted one pants leg around the horizontal bar above her head.

Chapter 20

Judge Sobriski looked up from the papers on his desk to study Finn. His bushy brows rose to form an inverted V over his bulbous nose. "I thought the police were leaning toward homicide."

Finn grimaced. "Our investigation is ongoing." That was starting to sound like a mantra. "For obvious reasons, we have not shared all facts with the public."

"And what are these facts?" Sobriski folded his hands on top of his antique oak desk. The judge sat ramrod straight. His posture and his gray crew cut were evidence of his JAG corps career. That history probably explained why he'd been elected in this conservative county even though he was originally from the suspect state of California.

"Our principal person of interest is Charlie Wakefield, the alleged father of the baby, and we've recently discovered that he works for Jimson Janitorial Service." Finn gestured toward his report. "Jimson is stonewalling; they won't turn over any personnel records."

The judge examined Finn's written request again. "This says *all* personnel records, and all company car records. But you only need Charlie Wakefield's." He plucked a pen from a polished granite holder on his desk. "So that should be no—"

"No, I want all the employee records." Finn tapped a finger on the piece of paper. "As I noted, we had a tip that Ivy Rose Morgan was taken to a car with a Jimson Janitorial logo." Not strictly true, but close enough, Finn thought. *Snake arm cucumber car baby cry.* He could feel the sweat trickling down his back beneath his linen jacket.

"What made you assume the person taking her was Charlie Wakefield?"

"The witness also reported seeing a snake design on the kidnapper's arm. As you can see in the photo I included, Charlie Wakefield's track team uniform has a zigzag design on the sleeve that might be mistaken for a snake."

Judge Sobriski studied the photo. "This looks like a lightning bolt to me. And as I recall, it was hot on the day of the baby's kidnapping. Why would Charlie wear a long-sleeved track team uniform? Have you confirmed that Charlie was in Evansburg at the time?"

"We can't determine for sure where Charlie Wakefield was at the time of the kidnapping."

The judge shook his head. "Seems a little farfetched to me. Who is this witness that can't tell a snake from a lightning bolt?"

Finn gulped. "The witness has the IQ of a five-year-old. She speaks only in sign language."

Sobriski quirked an eyebrow. "So this information was transmitted through an interpreter?"

Please don't demand an official court interpreter, Finn mentally begged Sobriski. Aloud, he said, "The witness's guardian interpreted for me."

"Even so," the judge said, "There's no need for all the personnel records. The Jimson company will protest that the request is overly broad and burdensome. We're still only talking about Wakefield here."

"Except for the witness's description of a car with a company logo," Finn argued. "Charlie Wakefield doesn't drive such a car, so he either was given access to a car or was with someone in a Jimson Janitorial vehicle. There are six vehicles licensed to Jimson that fit the general description." *Cucumber car.* Finn took a breath. "Jimson won't tell me who drives them."

The judge pointed his pen at Finn. "I'm sure you know that Wakefield is a powerful name in this county. And Jimson is a powerful name in this state."

"I know." Finn pulled out the fact that he hadn't written down. "Jimson Janitorial holds cleaning contracts for three schools from which a baby was kidnapped."

"Three babies?" The bushy brows dipped and then rose again. "I thought we were talking about Ivy Rose Morgan."

"We are. Ivy Rose Morgan," Finn fished the photos out of his coat pocket and laid them out for the judge. "William Adams from Coeur d'Alene, Idaho. And Tika Kinsey from Portland, Oregon."

The judge leaned over his desk to examine the photos.

"All three babies were stolen from teenage mothers enrolled in the Sister-Mothers Trust program in high school—it's a program where teen moms can finish school and bring their babies to class. Jimson Janitorial Service has contracts with all three schools, so their personnel have opportunity to routinely observe these vulnerable girls and babies. And we know that Charlie Wakefield is connected to Jimson Janitorial Service."

Sobriski scoffed, "You suspect that Wakefield kidnapped babies in Idaho and Oregon, too?"

"I agree, that seems unlikely," Finn reassured him. "But as I said, he might have been working with someone at Jimson. It's possible they recruit teenagers in different schools."

"To steal babies?" The judge's tone conveyed his skepticism. The gray eyes behind his glasses bore into Finn's for a moment. When Finn didn't flinch, Sobriski looked back at the pages before him.

"A healthy infant is worth fifty thousand on the adoption market," Finn murmured.

"I see no connection here. All you have is speculation," the judged responded. "Jimson has a duty to protect its employees and its reputation, especially given the history of many of its staff. This state owes a lot to the Jimson companies."

"More than it owes to its citizens?" Finn asked. The glare he received told him he was close to crossing a line. But they weren't in court, so he pressed on. "These are innocent babies and innocent mothers we're talking about here. I'm sure you heard that Brittany Morgan tried to hang herself in jail early Sunday morning."

"Yes." Sobriski nodded somberly. "I presumed that most likely indicated a guilty conscience."

"Or a total lack of hope," Finn countered. He didn't know how the poor kid had remained stable for this long, with the majority of the local populations believing she'd murdered her own baby. He felt guilty for his own suspicions on the matter.

"I cannot believe her parents were so irresponsible as to leave her in jail for so long."

"Apparently they didn't know," Finn said. "A friend of Brittany's texted her mother every few hours, pretending to be Brittany reporting in."

"The jailers should have kept tabs on her." Sobriski shook his head. "This county desperately needs a separate juvenile facility."

Finn clenched a fist behind his back. He needed to get this conversation back on track. "Your honor, we have no evidence that the Morgan baby is dead. Getting these records can help to solve the case one way or another. Our witness ties Jimson and Ivy Morgan together."

"I'm sure you realize what a huge political storm this could cause, Detective Finn." He drummed his long fingers on the desk for a minute, then looked up and said, "I want to speak with your witness."

Shit. "She prefers to remain anonymous, Your Honor."

"I'm not asking her to talk to the press, only to me." Sobriski slid the pages together and tapped them into alignment with his hands. "You're not getting your subpoena with only this." He held out Finn's printed request.

Finn ground his teeth. The truth about Neema had to come out sooner or later. If he could keep it between the judge and himself... If he could just get his hands on those records, maybe Neema wouldn't have to ever go public. He pulled a

DVD out of his pocket. "I have here a videotaped interview with the witness."

Sobriski swiveled in his leather chair and gestured Finn to his desktop computer. "Show me."

Brace yourself. Finn inserted the disk. To his amazement, the judge seemed fascinated by the video. "Intriguing," Sobriski said.

Only a few minutes into watching Finn's interview with Neema, a rap on the door interrupted them. "Jon Ramey with the files you wanted, Judge."

"My law clerk." The judge hit the pause button and swiveled in his desk chair. "Come in."

A young man with an expensive haircut, tailored suit, and shiny shoes stepped into the room, carefully shutting the door behind him. Finn recognized him as one of the gossiping law clerks he'd seen in the courthouse hallway two weeks ago. He shifted to block the clerk's view of the computer monitor.

Ramey sent a questioning glance in Finn's direction. "Excuse me for interrupting."

"The files?" Sobriski prompted.

Ramey stepped close to the judge before pulling out the file folders he carried under one arm. Sobriski took the folders and shoved them into a desk drawer. "Thank you." When the young man hesitated, the judge flapped a hand in his direction. "You can go now."

Ramey exited as quietly as he'd entered.

"Back to this." The judge turned to the computer. The video had stopped on a close-up on Neema. The gorilla looked as if she were sniffing Finn's camera lens. "You're asking me to believe that the only witness to the kidnapping is ... a *gorilla*?"

Finn nodded. "I know, sir. I found it hard to believe, too."

"And you're asking me to believe that the *gorilla* told you this?"

"I am."

"I can see why the keeper would want to stay anonymous. A *gorilla* witness."

Finn felt like the star of a spectacularly bad movie in which every other line would emphasize the word *gorilla*. He opened his notebook and extracted the folder that contained Grace McKenna's resume and academic papers on ape sign language and psychology. "The gorilla communicates in American Sign Language. Her trainer has a Ph.D. in Psychology from Stanford, and is on the faculty at the University of Washington."

The judge picked up the folder and thumbed through the pages, a scowl on his face. Finn waited patiently until Sobriski looked up. "The subpoena?" Finn dared.

"I still want to hear from this—" Sobriski gestured at the computer screen—"this witness ... and the animal's keeper. In person."

Finn stifled a sigh. What were the odds that Neema would behave herself in the judge's presence? If she had to come to strange surroundings, she'd be so distracted that anything could happen. And it was hardly likely he could smuggle a gorilla into the courthouse without someone noticing. Without *everyone* noticing.

"Let's do this on location," Sobriski said, proving he was on the same wavelength. "Tomorrow, at three P.M.?"

Finn nodded, relieved. "I'll arrange it with Dr. McKenna."

The judge lifted the phone receiver to his ear and pressed a button on the desk set. "I need to leave court early tomorrow. Arrange for an adjournment at two P.M., Ramey. I have a field trip I need to attend to." There was a brief pause and then he said, "No, I won't be needing you then. I'll take my own notes."

He hung up the phone and turned to Finn. "I assume I can ride with you, Detective."

"I'll pick you up at two-fifteen?"

The judge nodded. "And I further assume this matter will remain just between the two of us for now, Detective? I would hate for the media to get wind of this."

Thank god. "I feel exactly the same way, Your Honor."

*   *   *   *   *   *

Brittany lay motionless in the hospital bed. She kept her eyes shut, wishing she was comatose like her parents thought. Why wouldn't they give her enough meds to really knock her out? It was too quiet. The overall hush made every teensy noise so irritating. Papers rustled behind her, where her father sat reading the newspaper. Her mother had pulled up a chair beside her, practically in bed with her, stroking Brittany's arm now and then like she was a cat. She wanted to roll over, pull away, but then everyone would know she was awake and want her to talk. She had nothing to say. She'd never have anything to say again.

The door in the hallway outside her room unlocked with its habitual thunk, then swooshed open and shut again with another thunk as someone passed through the locked portal into the psychiatric ward. The footsteps were heavy and hard-soled, not soft like a nurse's. They stopped at her doorway.

"Detective?" Her father sounded impatient, or maybe angry. So it was Detective Finn.

"I'm here to give you an update," Finn said. "We don't have anything definite, but I wanted you to know that we have received a tip from a witness that has resulted in a promising lead."

"Who's the witness?" her mother asked.

Her father stood up. "What was the tip?"

Brittany opened her eyes.

Detective Finn looked right at her as he said, "I can't tell you anything more right now."

What was the point of this, then? He was saying the cops still had nothing.

"I want you to know that I'm still working hard to find Ivy," he said. "I'll keep you posted."

It seemed for a second as if he wanted to say something more, but instead, he just turned and left. She closed her eyes before her mother turned around.

Maybe Detective Finn believed her now, that someone took Ivy, that she hadn't killed her baby. So what? It didn't mean Ivy was coming back; it didn't mean Ivy was still alive. It didn't mean there was a God. If there was a God, he'd fix this somehow. Or maybe he had; maybe she *had* killed herself in jail. Maybe Hell was a too-quiet hospital room she'd never get out of.

As he drove home, Finn debated about calling the FBI. They'd immediately want to grill Grace McKenna, and that was the last thing Grace wanted. He decided he'd call only when the Jimson lead panned out, or if Sobriski refused to issue the subpoena.

Finn turned into his long gravel driveway. The grass on both sides was getting awfully tall. He'd have to find time to mow it, or more likely, weed-whack and bale the dang stuff. Or pay someone else to do it; could he afford that? His bank account was still reeling from Wendy's departure and being suddenly saddled with the entire mortgage instead of only half.

Drinking a cold beer with his feet up sounded perfect. He was too tired to paint. He'd watch one of the brain-dead detective shows where evidence magically appeared, witnesses had perfect recall after twenty years, and the case was solved in an hour. And yes, he had to admit it, when he envisioned his home scene, it included a purring cat on his lap now.

A flash of buff fur shot out of the tall grass in front of his car, and he had to slam on the brakes. After a brief glance his way, the creature vanished into the grass on the other side of the road. Coyote. This one had a splash of blood down its neck. Not a rare animal to see out here in the 'burbs. Once he'd seen one slinking across the road with a rabbit, still kicking, in its jaws.

He heard the yips and howls of the coyote packs almost every evening. Before dawn this morning, they'd been particularly loud.

He drove a hundred more feet before it hit him. The way Cargo stuck to the porch. Why Lok and Kee had been so reluctant to go out in recent days.

After crunching to a stop in front of the house, he leapt out of the car. Cargo heaved himself off the lounge chair on the deck and came to greet him, saliva dripping from his red tongue.

No cats. "Lok! Kee!" Shouting for them made him feel like an idiot. Did the cats even know their names? Or that they *had* names? Cargo whined and pressed his head into Finn's hand.

He looked into Cargo's mismatched eyes. "Where are they, boy?" He walked around the perimeter of the house, saw only birds flitting from tree to tree in the yard. *Damn.* He returned to the porch.

How had Wendy called them? "Here, kitty, kitty, kitty!" Thank god he lived alone; it didn't sound like something a grown man should be yelling. Cargo whimpered and leaned against his leg. He tried again. "Here, kitty, kitty, kitty!"

A strangled mew came from beneath his feet. He stepped down off the porch, knelt in the dry grass and peered beneath the weathered decking. Two green eyes reflected the dim light behind him. "Come on, kitty. C'mon."

Kee pulled himself out from beneath the deck, covered in cobwebs and filth. Finn picked up the cat, then sat down on the porch, cradling the animal in his lap. He ran his hands quickly over the filthy fur. No blood. Kee purred and raised his head so Finn could scratch his chin. Cargo rested his head on Finn's shoulder and blew a huff of hot fetid air into his ear. The wetness he felt oozing down his shirt collar would be dog slobber.

"Where's Lok? Where's your brother?" he asked Kee. Finn slowly scanned the yard for any movement, or god forbid, any scraps of orange fur.

The cat stood up and turned in his lap, peering out into the yard with him.

Chapter 21

Reporter Rebecca Ramey was careful to keep a car between her Civic and the detective's Ford. She was on the tail of an exclusive, thanks to her law-clerk brother. Something big going down; something about a witness in the Ivy Morgan case. She'd borrowed the smallest camcorder available from the studio. This could be her senior project and her big break; then it would be her instead of Allyson Lee standing up in front of the local news cameras. Then she could move on to someplace like Montana or Idaho, and then maybe to a major station like Seattle or San Francisco.

The Ford left the highway and turned down a gravel road. Detective Finn got out, opened a metal gate, drove through, and closed the gate behind his car. Rebecca slowly drove on past like she wasn't in the least interested, noting in her rear view mirror that the Ford proceeded up the gravel road and disappeared into the woods. She circled back and parked on the shoulder. She jammed her cell phone, notepad, and two pens into her pockets. Clutching the video camera to her stomach, she crept across the field toward the thick stand of trees, praying the landowner didn't have any vicious dogs on patrol. The field had been plowed at some time in the not-too-distant past and then abandoned. The ground was uneven, hard to walk on without stumbling, and the blackberries were vicious, reaching out with clawed canes over her head. The weeds came up to her waist, cloaking most of a barbed wire fence at edge of the woods. A rusty sign nailed to a tree declared No Trespassing, but she crawled through the fence anyway. All in all, it took her a good half hour to sneak up on the location. By the time she got there, she had stick-tights covering the legs of her jeans and snarling her hair. This story better be worth it; if she ended up with nothing but poison ivy and blackberry scratches, she was going to kill her brother.

The place gave her the creeps. She stood beside the detective's Ford in the shadow of a small two-story barn, panning the camera around the site. It was not a normal house, but a compound of some sort in a clearing carved out of the woods. Three single-wide trailers were arranged in a U-shape around a patchy square of grass. The barn formed the other side of the square. In front of the barn was a fenced enclosure with wire netting that stretched out and up toward the peak of the roof. Looked like an aviary. The air was ripe with a musky animal smell—manure? It didn't smell like horses or cows—maybe the farmers here kept ostriches? Did ostriches stink? But ostriches couldn't fly, could they? So why an aviary? She peeked through the slats of the fence. The barnyard was empty. Maybe this was some sort of animal rescue place, for eagles or owls or whatever.

Which trailer had the detective and judge disappeared into? She carefully examined the windows of each. There—the trailer on the right. A curtain flicked at the window. She started to move closer, but she'd only taken three steps when she heard a noise above her head. Startled, she glanced up. It was a weird sound, between a growl and a grunt. Beyond the wire mesh she could make out a rope net stretched horizontally above the ground. In the far corner was a tangle of what looked like blankets. Something was moving in them. Or someone? Was that a *hand*?

She couldn't quite make it out. Was there a person sleeping up there in the netting? What kind of psycho place was this that kept people imprisoned? Human trafficking? Now *that* would be a scoop. She had to find a position where she could film this. The hasp on the gate was held shut by a sliding bar. A padlock hung from the ring, but it wasn't quite closed. She slipped the lock out and pulled open the gate and slipped inside. Standing behind the gate in the enclosure, she zoomed her camera on the moving lump up in the net. Finally the camera focused and she could make out the image. In the shadow between wadded-up blankets, a red-brown eye stared back at her.

Finn, Grace, and Judge Sobriski exited the study trailer. LaDyne, leading Neema on a leash, followed a short distance behind them.

Finn thought the interview had gone well, but Sobriski still hadn't rendered a decision on the subpoena. Surreptitiously, Finn checked his watch. If only he could quit feeling guilty about the damn cat at home. He'd stayed up until one A.M. searching for Lok, but hadn't heard or seen any sign of him. He'd shut both Kee and Cargo up inside the house this morning, which meant he'd better be getting back at a reasonable hour or he'd need to hire his own janitorial service to put the place back together.

Grace had started out the interview as a nervous wreck, but Neema had mostly behaved herself. Except for calling LaDyne a poop-head when he refused to give in to her begging for candy. The judge had been appropriately skeptical but surprisingly open-minded. The rose that Finn had provided for him as a gift for Neema had helped win over the gorilla, too.

Sobriski turned to ask Grace, "What did she call me?"

"Scrub hat." Grace made the signs for him, a scouring motion followed by a tap on the head.

"Clever." Sobriski ran a hand over his gray crew cut. "I've read about projects like yours, Dr. McKenna. Years ago, I had the privilege of attending a lecture by Jane Goodall. Fascinating. But I must admit that I never really appreciated these studies until now. I would not have believed Neema had created that painting without witnessing your video."

He glanced at the gorilla, who curled her fingers around her collar and tugged at the leash as a butterfly flitted past. She dragged LaDyne a few steps in the wake of the insect, until the butterfly lifted high above their heads. LaDyne then held out a hand in her direction, and she docilely placed her giant black paw in his and they continued toward the barn.

"Where do you think your research will go?" Sobriski asked Grace. "Will we be able to talk to wild gorillas using Neema as an interpreter?"

"That might be possible," Grace said. "If there were funding to set up that experiment. Right now I—"

She stopped, staring at the enclosure gate, which gaped open a foot. "Josh? Did you leave—"

A series of loud pock-pock-pock sounds caught their attention and they all looked up at Gumu as he raced down the rope net. His descent was accompanied by high-pitched screams, half gorilla, half human. Then a young woman fell through the gate opening, scrabbling on the ground, a video camera cradled in one arm. A huge black mass rolled over her, huffing like a steam engine, and dashed past them in a wave of hot skunky scent. Neema joined in with her own alarm shrieks and leapt after Gumu as he passed, jerking LaDyne to the ground and ripping her leash from his hand. The two gorillas, rocketing forward on all fours, disappeared into the forest.

"Shit!" Grace and LaDyne shouted in chorus. They galloped off after the apes.

Finn's carefully scripted scene roller-coastered from control to total chaos in less than two seconds. As Grace and LaDyne dashed into the woods, the intruder picked herself up and raced down the driveway, her running shoes crunching in the gravel.

"Stop!" Finn took off in pursuit. "Police!" In his dress shoes, he really wasn't prepared for a chase. The girl dashed over the mown strip into the woods and disappeared between the trees. "Stop!"

The intruder clearly knew where she was headed; he, on the other hand, didn't have a clue. She was also at least twenty years younger. She nimbly darted between trees and dove through strands of barbed wire. By the time Finn had climbed over the fence, she was halfway across a lumpy weed-eaten field, and by the time he had extricated himself from the blackberry canes that grabbed his pant leg and shirt sleeve, he heard a car door slam and tires spinning on gravel.

He trudged back, sticky seeds glued to his pants and cockleburs digging into his socks. His shirt was drenched in sweat and he had a blackberry scratch that wrapped around the back of his neck. Pulling out his cell phone, he dialed the college and asked to be connected with their television station.

He identified himself to the news producer and then told her, "Some hotshot girl reporter is going to come in with a video of a gorilla."

"A *gorilla*?"

"That video was illegally obtained by trespassing on private property. If I see it on the air, I will have you and everyone else at your station arrested."

"A *gorilla*?" the woman asked again.

Finn wiped away a trickle of sweat from his forehead. "What is your name? Did you hear what I just told you? Do I need to talk to the station manager?"

"I'm Heather Anderson. No, sir, you do not need to talk to the station manager. I'll take care of it, Detective."

He called Grace's cell. It went to voicemail. He'd seen the phone on the table in the trailer; it was probably still sitting there. He left a message telling her that he'd headed off any news coverage. Small consolation, but it was the best he could offer.

He trudged back through the woods, emerging into the clearing between the study trailer and Grace's living quarters. All was quiet. Grace, LaDyne, and the gorillas were nowhere in sight. No sounds came from the woods. Damn. Thousands of acres of Forest Service land surrounded the compound. How far would the gorillas run?

Judge Sobriski rested in the shade, reclining against the hood of the car. Finn put a foot up on the front bumper and gingerly picked cockleburs from his sock.

"I don't know when I've had such an interesting afternoon," Sobriski said. "But I think I'm ready to call it a day. How about you, Detective?"

Finn snorted. "Amen to that." Unfortunately, he needed to return to the station. He switched feet to pick the burrs out of his other sock. The sticky seeds that covered his trouser legs up to his thighs would have to wait until later.

"Let's go back to my chambers and write up that subpoena duces tecum, shall we?"

Thank god. Finn put his foot back on the ground and grinned at the judge. "Gladly." He pulled the passenger door open for Sobriski.

He couldn't help Grace corral the gorillas, and even though he'd stopped the news broadcast, he had no doubt the girl would spread the word of gorillas loose in Evansburg. But he'd at least be able to go after the Jimson Janitorial records first thing in the morning.

Back at the station, Finn faxed the subpoena to the Spokane Police Department, where tomorrow morning, an officer would deliver it in person to that bitchy HR manager at Jimson Janitorial headquarters. He couldn't wait to see her marching up the steps of the courthouse with the records in hand. Forty-eight hours; that's all she had.

Finally, he was making progress. Now if only the records would lead him to Ivy's kidnapper. And to Ivy. Be nice if they led him to the other two babies' whereabouts, too.

He called Grace's phone again. It kicked into voicemail. He hung up. Damn. Still not back. It was getting dark now. Should he drive back out there to see if she'd recaptured the gorillas? LaDyne was with her; surely they'd be okay. Besides, she was probably more than a little peeved with him right now. She had a right to be. He'd checked his rearview plenty of times. How had he missed a reporter tailing him out to Grace's compound?

He couldn't get Brittany Morgan's hopeless expression out of his head. He called the hospital to check on her.

"She was released this morning into the custody of her parents," the nurse in charge told him.

He thought about going to the Morgan house, but he didn't have anything to tell them. Yet. Maybe in two days, he would have. That was something to look forward to; he really wanted to do something for Brittany. For now, he needed to get home and let his dog out.

Mason strolled up to his desk. "Finn, have—"

"Mason," Finn interrupted, suddenly flashing onto an idea. It was only a little thing, but it was something he could do for the girl. "I want you to release Brittany Morgan's computer back to her."

Mason scowled. "I haven't finished analyzing the hard drive."

"Can't you copy the files?"

"You mean make an image of the hard drive?" Mason said in the scornful tone he used for everyone who didn't speak nerdese.

"I'm pretty sure that's what I mean," Finn replied. "I want to return the computer to Brittany. That girl has been hassled enough."

"It'll take awhile, but I'll put it on your desk later tonight."

"Thanks." Something else to look forward to. Tomorrow, he'd take back Brittany's laptop.

Mason splayed a hand on the top of Finn's desk and leaned toward his monitor. "Seen YouTube lately?" he asked.

"Never," Finn told him. He didn't understand why people wasted their free time watching that drivel. "I'm calling it a day." He started to rise from his chair.

"Wait." Mason stopped him with a hand on his shoulder. He pulled Finn's keyboard toward him, stretching the connection cord to its maximum length. "You'll want to see this." Mason typed for a second, and the screen switched focus to YouTube. Then he grabbed Finn's mouse and clicked on a link labeled

Gorilla Ambush under *Videos Being Watched Now*. The video began to play.

Finn's stomach dropped. He watched Gumu climb out of a pile of blankets and hurtle down the rope net, beating on his chest—pock! pock! pock!—and baring his teeth. A startled voice shrieked, "Omigod, omigod, omigod!"

Gumu hesitated for only a second at the edge of the netting before he leapt toward the photographer. The video showed only the blurry black leather chest of the male gorilla at that point, with the girl's screams as sound track. Then the black blur moved away and from ground level, the camera recorded Gumu galloping past Sobriski and Grace, then Finn, and finally LaDyne. Neema screeched and turned as Gumu went past, dashing out to run after him, jerking LaDyne off his feet and dragging him for a short distance before the leash was torn from his hand.

The screen went black again, and then words appeared: *What do gorillas on the run have to do with the disappearance of Ivy Rose Morgan?* The screen paused on a photo of the baby and the date she'd disappeared, with the attribution *By FirstAmen, Evansburg, WA*. Then it looped back to the beginning and stayed there, on an image of Gumu emerging from his blanket nest.

Finn turned to look at Mason. Now Detectives Melendez and Dawes stood beside the computer tech, as well as a couple of uniforms whose names he couldn't remember. Detective Larson strolled up, late to the party.

Sara Melendez crossed her arms and grinned maliciously. "Got something you want to tell us, Finn?"

"Yeah." He stood up. "My cat is missing, and I'm going home to look for him now." He pulled his car keys out of his pocket and strode quickly from the building.

At first, Grace could hear the gorillas' excited hoots echoing through the forest over her own harsh breathing and yells of "Neema! Gumu! Neema, come!" But the hooting gradually petered out as Neema and Gumu easily outdistanced her and Josh. They must have run close to a mile. Finally, completely out of breath, she held out a hand to signal a stop. They both stood and panted for a long while, Josh leaning against a Douglas fir, and Grace bent over, her hands on her thighs. Sweat dripped off her face onto the fir needle duff below. She pulled a damp tissue from her pocket to blot it.

When she could talk again, she said, "This is a total disaster."

Josh wiped his forehead with his hand and then dried his fingers on his shirt sleeve. "Ya think?" he said.

She straightened, worked some saliva around her parched tongue, and cupped her hands around her mouth. "Yogurt!" she shouted. "Candy! Candy! Candy!"

Josh's eyes widened and his lips twitched as if he were about to laugh, then he joined in. "Banana!" he yelled. "Juice!"

They waited. There was no sound, except for a woodpecker drumming high overhead. They both tried again, but had no better results.

"Damn it!" Grace whined.

"I'll see your damn and raise it to double-damn," Josh countered. He glanced at the sky beyond the treetops. "I suppose you've noticed that it's getting dark."

Grace grimaced. "Hard not to. I also just noticed that while we're leaving a trail—" she pointed to the disturbed duff that marked the path behind them—"we're no longer following one." They both surveyed the ground at their feet. Surely the gorillas, on four feet, would leave at least as much of a mark than two humans had.

"Triple damn," he said. "Plans, boss?"

She surveyed the surroundings. Nothing but the tall straight trunks of firs and hemlocks for as far as she could see. What thoughts were coursing through Neema's and Gumu's minds right now? It was hard to guess. *Wahoo—free at last?* More likely, it was just *Run! Run! Run!* Gorilla panic took awhile to stop once it got rolling. How far would they go? Would they be able to find their way back home? Wild gorillas probably would. But gorillas that had spent their lives in pens and buildings? What would they do if they encountered a cougar or a bear? Or a rattlesnake? What if they reached the interstate? Oh god, she couldn't let her imagination go there.

"I'm sorry," Josh said.

She glanced at him, surprised. "What do you have to be sorry about?"

"Obviously, I didn't close the lock all the way on the barn enclosure."

"That padlock's always been hard to close; I've accidentally done the same thing a dozen times. That intruder opened the gate."

"I couldn't hold onto Neema." He held up his right hand—a deep red groove cut through the palm.

"Nobody could, Josh. She could toss both us around like rag dolls anytime she wanted." She sighed. "The collar and leash were always more of a behavior reminder than real control." She checked the sky overhead again. "C'mon. We'd better get back while we can still see our own path. With luck, Neema and Gumu will find their own way home."

They trudged back in the growing darkness, neither one wanting to talk about what they'd do if the gorillas did not come back on their own.

It was nearly eight o'clock and fully dark when they arrived back at the compound, hungry, thirsty, and gorilla-less. Three cars awaited them, surrounded by a small cluster of people, most of whom appeared to be local college students. Clearly the damn intruder had leaked Grace's address as well as the video.

"Yikes," Josh said. The group turned toward them. A flash went off on a camera.

Grace wearily waded into their midst. "Get off this property. You are trespassing."

More flashes went off.

"Why have you been keeping gorillas out here?" a male voice asked.

A young woman came out of the barn enclosure, a camera slung around her neck. "Where are the gorillas?" she shouted.

"Dr. McKenna asked you all to leave," Josh reminded the audience.

"But why are you keeping gorillas out here?" the male voice asked again.

Now that her eyes had recovered after the flashes, she could see it was a nice looking young man who held out an audio recorder. "The gorillas belong to the University of Washington," she told them, although she hated saying those words aloud. "They are part of a language research project."

"Teaching them English?" a woman asked.

Ignoring that, Grace said, "Now my two lowland gorillas are lost in the woods. They don't know this area, and they will be terrified. If anyone sees them, please call me." She gritted her teeth and recited her cell phone number.

"Wild gorillas loose in the woods?" another young woman asked. "Are they dangerous?"

"No," Josh said. "But they're scared. If you see them, don't approach them. Call Dr. McKenna."

"Now please leave," Grace said.

"Shouldn't the police be notified?" the audio guy asked.

"Why were Detective Finn and Judge Sobriski here?"

"What does this have to do with Ivy Rose Morgan?"

"Go home." Josh waved his arms as if he could scatter them like chickens.

Grace turned toward the study trailer. "I'm going to call the Sheriff to report trespassers right now. C'mon, Josh."

By the time they reached the trailer door, the cars were leaving. But within a minute, Grace's cell phone started ringing with calls about gorillas on the loose. She answered each one with "Did you see the gorillas?" and hung up when the caller said No.

"Should we call the Sheriff?" Josh asked.

"Think they'd help search for gorillas?"

"Maybe Fish and Wildlife Service?" he suggested.

She could see game officers now, patrolling the area with

rifles. Not all would be loaded with tranquilizer darts. "If Gumu and Neema don't come home by morning," she told him. "Then we'll call for help."

Josh came in with her long enough to pour her a big glass of wine. "You can take the first phone calls while I grab a quick shower and something to eat. I'll be back to relieve you in half an hour."

The door slammed behind him. Outside, she heard him call, "Neema! Gumu! Yogurt! Banana!"

Grace saw that Finn had called her cell phone twice. Halfway through his message about keeping the video off the television station, her cell beeped the call waiting signal. KEBR News, the caller ID flashed. She carried the cell phone and the glass of wine to her personal trailer and curled up in the corner of the sofa.

It was going to be a long night.

By the time Finn returned to his house, Cargo had made a puddle in the kitchen. Finn was grateful the dog had spared the carpet. Lok was still MIA. Kee patrolled the doors, begging to be let out into the dark yard.

"No way." Finn scooped the cat up. "At least not by yourself." He went out onto the deck and sat in a chair for a few minutes, calling Lok and listening to the hum of insects and the occasional cry of some nocturnal bird from the surrounding woods. He scratched Kee under the chin while keeping a firm hold on the squirming cat. Neither of them was happy about the situation, and Kee eventually dug his claws into Finn's thigh.

"Stop that!" He stood up, tucked the cat under his arm, and went back into the house. "You never know what's out there," he told Kee. "Could be something that wants to eat you. Could even be gorillas."

He couldn't bring himself to try Grace again, or to watch the late news. He drank two beers and went to bed. Kee slept on his spare pillow.

Chapter 22

By morning, everyone in the area knew that two gorillas were on the loose in the county. Half the residents were out traipsing through the countryside, hoping to catch a glimpse of wild apes careening through the Cascade foothills. The Sheriff called in the Fish and Wildlife capture experts.

"Never dealt with gorillas before," their spokesman said on camera. "But we've got gear we use to capture mountain lions and bears. We'll figure something out."

Grace sat watching events unfold on television with Matt by her side on the couch. The kittens Snow and Nest bounced around them on the floor, attacking Neema's toys and each other. Matt had been with her for nearly two hours, fidgeting, but hanging in there. It was an awkward situation. They barely knew each other, but there was definitely an attraction between them. They were both heavily invested in bringing the gorillas home and salvaging their professional reputations. She knew Matt felt guilty for getting her into this mess, but then, he hadn't, really. She called the tip line; she provided the only lead in his case. Or actually, Neema had. Neema, his only witness, who was out there, lost in the forest.

Grace had no faith in the capture experts. "Half the time these guys injure the animals so badly during a capture that the animals have to be killed," she told Matt.

"At least Josh is there," Matt pointed to Josh on the screen. He climbed into a Jeep with a couple of uniforms.

She saw way too many guns among the crowd on the screen. "Josh can't be everywhere," she moaned. "He can't stop the trigger-happy volunteer who shoots when Gumu panics and rushes him."

The TV station manager remained true to her promise not to air the video, but the reporters kept referring to an 'anonymous YouTube video' that showed gorillas escaping from a compound in the county.

"Want me to subpoena the user record from YouTube?" Matt asked.

"What's the point?" Grace ran her fingers through her tangled hair. Had she combed it since yesterday? Her eyes felt like they were full of sand. "I just don't know what to do," she whined.

He patted her on the forearm. "Did you stay up all night?"

She nodded. "More or less. I took a sleeping bag out into the yard in case they came back. I dozed once in awhile, on top of the picnic table."

The phone buzzed again. Grace picked it up and checked the ID. "Oh lord, it's the University." She stared at the ringing phone for a moment longer. Hell, how much worse could it get? She swallowed hard, then answered, "Dr. McKenna."

"Dr. McKenna, this is Norman Childers from the University Facilities Department. I'm in charge of all physical inventory owned by the university. We've just become aware of the situation in Evansburg. Is it true your two gorillas have escaped?"

There seemed to be little point in explaining that Gumu had been let out of his pen by a trespasser. She said simply, "Yes." She stood up, the phone still held to her ear.

"Those gorillas are valuable property."

"Actually, they are valuable *beings*," she said.

A brief silence ensued. He was probably debating what to say next. "You were entrusted with their care."

"I've cared for them for almost nine years," she reminded him.

"Do the gorillas actually have something to do with this missing baby case?"

"Yes." She wasn't going to explain the complex witness situation to some bean counter.

"Please keep us posted on the situation." He hung up.

"What was that about?" Matt asked.

"My boss wanted to make sure I was suffering appropriately," she said.

"I could vouch for that if you need a witness," he told her.

The phone buzzed in her hand. *McKenna, Maureen.* "Mom," she answered.

"I got your email," her mother said. "How are you holding up? Is there any news?"

"As well as I can," Grace told her. "As for news—I lost half my grant money, my job might be next, and the gorillas are still lost out there." She bit her lip, struggling not to cry like a little girl.

"You could always come back to the Bay area. I know you could get a job teaching at one of the community colleges; get a chance to use your education."

This was a common theme with her parents. They were both full professors; they'd never understood how Grace could do research with animals. A teaching job did sound good right now, clean and safe and easy.

"But what would I do with the gorillas?" she asked.

Her mother didn't respond. They'd had this conversation a hundred times. There was never an easy answer to that question. It hung in the ether between them, even more unbearable now because Grace knew that Maureen McKenna was thinking, maybe even wishing, that the gorillas might soon disappear forever from her daughter's life.

"Well," her mother finally said, "Just remember that coming home is always an option, Gracie."

Grace put the phone on the end table and plopped back down on the couch. She caught herself rubbing the scar on her lip. Matt was watching. Why couldn't she break that habit? She lowered her hand. "Cleft palate repair," she told him. "I had multiple surgeries; I didn't learn to talk properly until I was five."

"That explains the sign language."

"You got it," she told him.

A helicopter cruised low over the compound for the third time, its rotor blades thundering through the flimsy trailer walls. Matt stepped outside to study it, and she followed. Medium-sized, plain black. Probably a rental. Could be a news crew or Fish and Wildlife personnel inside.

"They're like buzzards," Matt remarked.

Like raptors hovering in the sky. Yes. Why hadn't she thought of the opportunity before? She stepped off the tiny porch, waving to the chopper. "Hey!" She galloped to the center of the yard, yelling, "Hey!" She pointed alternately to the helicopter and to the ground. "Come down!" she shouted. "Land!"

She could barely hear her own words over the whop-whop-whop of the blades. After a few seconds, Matt pulled his cell phone from his pocket. Bringing it to his ear, he shouted, "Detective Finn."

Then he trotted to her, holding out the phone. "The chopper pilot. For you."

"I want a ride," she shouted into the phone. She gestured to the ground again and backed away from the open space. Finn followed. She cupped her hands around the phone to shield it from the surrounding noise. "Please land."

To her amazement, the helicopter descended. The Forest Service ranger inside agreed to take her to help spot the gorillas. She piled in. In a cloud of blowing grit and thundering racket, they took off. As they headed for the forest, she saw Matt slide into his car.

Noah Morgan looked surprised to see Finn standing on his doorstep. "Detective?"

"No news," Finn told him. He held out the laptop. "I brought Brittany's computer back."

"C'mon in," the man waved him inside. "Susan's at work. The rest of us are in the living room."

Brittany sat on the couch in front of the television, which displayed a movie. In a chair to the left sprawled little brother Danny, using rapid-fire thumbs to play a game on a small device he held in his hands. Brittany's hands were folded in her lap, her gaze fixed on her knees.

Noah forced a bright note into his voice. "Detective Finn! We saw that story about gorillas last night on the news. What in the world is going on?"

"I can't talk about it," Finn told him. He turned to Brittany and held out the laptop with both hands. "Brittany, I brought your computer back."

She didn't even raise her head. Her hair was clean and combed into a ponytail, and she was dressed neatly in jeans and a T-shirt, but she was as lifeless as a mannequin. Pale yellow and purple bruises still circled her neck.

"Brittany..." Noah said in the low tone that parents used to warn their children.

The girl's gaze rose to meet Finn's. Her blue eyes were as cool and vacant as lake water. Moving robotically, she held out her arms. He placed the laptop in her hands.

"Thanks." She settled it in her lap, folded her hands on top of the computer, and looked up at the television.

On the screen, a girl in a soccer uniform scored a goal and the room filled with raucous cheers of the television crowd.

"Good one," Noah said. His reaction seemed forced.

It was like watching a movie at a funeral. The atmosphere was claustrophobic. Danny was probably oblivious, but Noah radiated anxiety, and Brittany was the embodiment of total despair. This was worse than informing a family about the death of a loved one. At least that was final. This was like awaiting the walk to the electric chair, all the while hoping for a last-minute reprieve.

"Can I talk to Brittany alone for a moment?" Finn finally asked.

"I guess so," Noah murmured. He placed a hand on his daughter's shoulder. "Brittany, why don't you take your computer and Detective Finn up to your room? But remember—say nothing about the case. Just like the lawyer told you."

Finn cringed inwardly. Obviously, Brittany's father thought he was out to convict the girl. "I won't ask her any questions," he said. "I assure you, I have her best interests at heart."

"Right," Noah said.

"Come if you want," Finn told him.

Noah eyed his daughter. She seemed nearly catatonic.

The phone rang three times, and then the answering machine picked up. "If you have a tip about Ivy—"

Noah was clearly straining to listen. Brittany didn't seem interested. Her father flapped a hand in her direction. "Just go," he said. "I'll be up in a second."

The girl stood up, tucked the laptop under her arm, and marched woodenly up the stairs. Finn followed her to her bedroom, leaving the door open behind him.

She put her computer on her desk. There was an odd little winged baby dress lying over the desk chair. Brittany sat on her neatly made bed and pulled a little white teddy bear into her lap. Her eyes watched the floor.

"Brittany, please look at me."

She did. Her expression was as flat as if Botox flooded every facial muscle. She was probably full of tranquilizers. He had to give this poor girl something to think about other than death. "You know that news story about the gorillas?" he asked.

She nodded dully, as if it were an everyday occurrence for gorillas to romp through the woods around Evansburg. He moved the winged green thing from the chair to the desk. Then he pulled out her chair and turned it around, straddled it and crossed his arms on the top of the backrest.

He caught her gaze, and said softly, "You can't tell anyone what I'm going to say to you. It's our secret."

She swallowed, but didn't even blink. She was paying attention, though. He could feel her waiting.

"One of those gorillas—her name is Neema—might have the key to finding Ivy."

Life returned to Brittany's eyes, as if a different person had suddenly dropped into her body. She leaned forward. "How?" she asked.

What had she expected to see from the helicopter? Grace frowned. There was little to view below except for endless treetops, an occasional rock outcropping, logging roads and trailside parking lots. No shaggy black lumps of apes careening through the trees.

Grace tried to visualize the wilderness surroundings through Neema's eyes. Trees everywhere. Neema loved to climb trees, but the straight tall firs with their closely packed branches didn't lend themselves to easy climbing by thick-bodied apes.

The chopper passed above the search parties, lines of volunteers and armed Fish and Wildlife officers, walking in a wave through the forest.

The racket of the helicopter overhead would terrify both gorillas. So would the shouting and crashing of strangers through the underbrush. Gumu and Neema would be seeking places to hide. It had been nearly twenty hours since they'd last eaten. The gorillas would be looking for food and water, too.

"Dr. McKenna?" The pilot eyed her in the rearview mirror.

She shook her head, almost dislodging the too-large headset. She pulled the microphone back into position and said, "I don't see anything useful."

That wasn't precisely true. At that moment, they were flying over an unusual piece of land. At one time it had probably been an old homestead. There was a pile of collapsed and mossy timbers that had once been a cabin. A few gnarled, ancient apple trees were scattered among the evergreens, rotting red fruit visible on the ground beneath them. Near a small stream stood a huge old willow with branches that drooped down to its roots. Good climbing trees, fruit, and a good hiding place.

She quickly glanced between the two forward seats, noted the GPS position on the dashboard readout, closed her eyes and committed the coordinates to memory.

They rapidly passed on, moving over dense forest again. Grace chanted the GPS coordinates in her head as she watched a doe and two half-grown fawns dash up a logging road, spooked by the helicopter. What were the odds that Neema and Gumu would chance upon the old homestead site? The fallen apples and the stream gave her hope. Gorilla noses were keen. And the site was in the general direction the gorillas were heading when she'd seen them last.

Too many people or a helicopter could spook the gorillas into disappearing forever. She'd have to go alone, or with Josh.

"Are you good to land, Dr. McKenna?" They hovered over her compound.

"Yes, thanks for the ride," she said wearily.

They touched down in the yard, and exchanged shouted expressions of regret over the lack of progress. Then she huddled against the side of the barn as the chopper took off in a tornado of flying grit. As the noise faded, she uncovered her head.

"Dr. McKenna?"

Grace startled at the unexpected voice. A young girl stood at her right shoulder. She had long reddish-blonde hair banded back into a ponytail. Her blue eyes were heartbreakingly sad. Grace had seen her before. On television. In the newspaper. *Red tail soft soft.* "Brittany Morgan?"

Brittany nodded. "I want to help."

Grace hadn't seen a car from the helicopter. "How'd you get here?"

"Hitchhiked."

"Do your parents know where you are?" Multicolored bruises darkened the girl's neck.

Brittany raised a hand to her throat, covering the marks. "Please," she said. "I'll call them later."

Grace studied her. T-shirt, jeans. The girl was wan and had deep shadows under her eyes, but otherwise appeared fit. She stared at the flip-flops on the girl's feet.

"I have hiking boots in my pack," Brittany said, pointing to a black backpack leaning against the fence.

"Good," Grace told her. "You're going to need them."

Finn's inbox was full of call slips, most from the press. As he was sorting through them, his desk phone rang.

"Bad news, Detective," the judge said without preamble. "Jimson is fighting the subpoena."

No. It was his only hope. "Can they do that?"

"Just like I predicted, they're alleging that the scope is too broad."

"It has to be," Finn argued. "We have no way of knowing which employees might be involved."

"When they lose on that score, I guarantee they're going to try for invasion of privacy." A slurping noise followed, and Finn envisioned Sobriski sipping tea during a break. "But they won't get it."

"So what happens now?"

"They will report with the records to the Courthouse within 24 hours, or I'll hold them in contempt."

Good.

"Then we'll all have to sit down and go through the records and determine which are applicable and which will be excluded. So clear your calendar, Detective; this is going to take awhile."

Not so good.

Another slurp. "Any news on the gorillas?"

"Not that I've heard."

"Drat. My clerk will call when the records arrive tomorrow, and we can meet in my chambers."

"I'll be there." Finn hung up and stared at the phone with mixed feelings. Sobriski appeared to be firmly on his side, but he was clearly going to pull no extraordinary legal strings to make things work out.

"Don't you have a life, Finn?" Dawes stood in front of his desk.

Finn gave him a look. "Do I really need to answer that?"

"Nope; the answer would be obvious to a blind man. Thought you might like to know that Kittitas County finally coughed up autopsy results on your doll baby." Dawes slapped down a sheet of paper on his desk.

Autopsy? Then he remembered Baby Doe, the tiny corpse found by the farm dog.

According to the coroner, the corpse had been buried for months, and due to decay, the victim's age, time of death, and cause of death were impossible to pinpoint. The baby was somewhere between one and six weeks old. Male. He saw the words "Likely Hispanic" near the bottom of the sheet. So his initial hypothesis was probably a good one; the baby belonged to an illegal, probably a Mexican woman working the farm fields, who couldn't afford to be discovered by immigration authorities. Had the tiny boy been sick from birth, or died in an accident? He hoped that a husband or boyfriend had been by the poor mother's side.

In Chicago, unclaimed corpses were buried in cheap coffins in group graves. Finn had no clue what happened to the unidentified dead in this jurisdiction. He dialed the coroner's office. "What happens to the body?" he asked.

"They preserve pieces in case they need them later for DNA, and then they cremate the rest," the clerk told him.

Finn thought the guy sounded a little detached from his job, but then, if he worked with dead bodies all day, he'd want to detach, too. "What do you do with the ashes?"

"Uh ... it all goes into the trash." There was a pause. "Why? Did you want them or something?"

It just seemed wrong, that an infant could end up as trash. "Yes," he said, surprising himself, "I want that baby's ashes."

An hour later, with Juan Doe's ashes in a small sealed cardboard cylinder sitting in his cup holder, he drove home.

Cargo was waiting for him on the porch, and Kee escaped outside the instant Finn opened the door. Finn fed the monster dog, grabbed a beer from the fridge and took it outside to the deck to watch the sun go down. He walked the perimeter of the yard, half-heartedly yelling, "Lok! Come here, kitty, kitty!" now and then. "Lok!" Was Grace doing this now, strolling through the forest, yelling for Neema and Gumu?

His cell phone vibrated and he pulled it out. Noah Morgan. "Finn," he answered.

"Detective, Brittany snuck out of the house this afternoon after your visit."

Uh-oh.

"We just received a text message from her, saying she was with Dr. McKenna, looking for the gorillas."

Finn blew out a breath. "Then she's safe. Grace will take care of her."

"Did you encourage Brittany to do this? Because if something happens to her—"

"She couldn't be in better hands, Mr. Morgan. I believe that right now, Brittany's better off taking action instead of medication, don't you?"

"You're obviously not a parent. She was taking action when she broke into that house; she was taking action when she tried to hang herself. If anything happens to Brittany—"

"Grace won't let anything happen to her."

"What if they don't find the gorillas? Or if the gorillas don't survive?"

Those possibilities were too horrible to contemplate. "I guess we'll all deal with that if it happens," Finn murmured.

After another few seconds of vague threats, the man finally gave up, and Finn resumed his search around the backyard. The daylight was almost gone. A coyote yipped somewhere to the west and another answered from the south, sounding closer.

His heart skipped a beat when an orange tabby emerged from the bushes, but it was Kee, who followed him into the house through the sliding glass door. Finn sat in his easy chair and flicked on the television. A commercial for some kind of glue that could hold anything together was on the screen, and Finn hit the Mute button. Kee meowed from the floor beside him. Finn picked up a plastic wall walker toy from the basket on his side table and lobbed it at Wendy's photo. It stuck just above her right eye for a second, and then Kee watched it roll on its suction-cup feet down the wall. When it dropped to the floor, he looked up at Finn with confused amber eyes.

Finn reached down and lifted the cat into his lap. "I know," he said, rubbing Kee's ears. "I miss him too."

The room wavered into a blur. No. This was idiotic. He had been involved in cases of missing and murdered people, for chrissakes, and he'd never broken down. Now he was crying over a cat he'd never wanted in the first place?

Arnhh, Cargo sighed, and licked his other hand.

"Don't slobber on the remote," Finn warned. He wiped his nose and eyes on his shirt sleeve and clicked the television volume back on.

The major station out of Seattle had picked up the local news feed and showed the YouTube video, then the footage of Fish and Wildlife and volunteers searching for the gorillas. Grace had to be pulling her hair out now. Then the focus changed to show a rotund silver-haired man standing between the thick white pillars of a church entrance, responding to a group of reporters clustered around. Finn upped the volume.

Silver Hair read from a page he held in his hand, glancing up periodically at the camera. "As you know, our charitable organizations offer the formerly lost a chance to redeem themselves through honest labor. Some of our employees have pasts that are painful to reveal, and such revelations may obstruct their healing process. Now we have been ordered to expose these painful secrets by Detective Matthew Finn, the detective seen in the recent YouTube videos of escaping gorillas."

"Crap." Finn leaned forward. Kee leapt to the floor and disappeared into the kitchen. Cargo studied him for a moment with worried eyes before the dog lay his head back down on his paws.

Silver Hair stared at the camera. "Apparently, from what my organization has been able to piece together, Detective Finn gets his information from a woman who believes that gorillas can talk—Grace McKenna."

"Sign!" Finn shouted at the television. "They can *sign*, not talk, you idiot!"

"This Grace McKenna, this careless keeper of these dangerous escaped apes, has made accusations about our employees. This is yet another thinly disguised attack on good Christians by secular humanists who believe we all descended from monkeys."

"For God's sake," Finn groaned, then snorted at the irony of his own statement.

Silver Hair—no doubt the Reverend Abram Jimson—folded the piece of paper he had read from and lowered his hands. "New Dawn Industries has no choice but to respond to this request, but we urge all our supporters to let the authorities know that we—and you—consider this to be harassment of the worst sort by anti-religious government authorities. Thank you."

The blonde newscaster chirped, "And now for the weather—James, can we expect this wonderful sunshine to continue to the weekend?"

Finn lowered the volume, levered the footrest up, and lay staring at the ceiling for a long moment. He could hardly wait for morning.

"Ow." Brittany stumbled into a depression. In the dark, it was hard to see what was shadow and what was a hole, with only a narrow flashlight beam lighting the way. "Are we getting close?"

They'd been walking through the dark woods forever. She was trying not to complain, but she wanted to stop. Since Detective Finn told her about the gorilla, she'd been spitting out the pills, but she still felt like she had mashed potatoes filling the space behind her eyes. Her head felt heavy and her legs were rubbery; she wasn't used to walking anymore.

Grace, checking her GPS device in the light of her headlamp, stumbled into the same hole. "Damn it!" she muttered.

Putting her palm out to the nearest tree, she rested for a moment while she twirled her foot in the air, testing her ankle. "Sorry," she said, shooting a glance at Brittany. "Yes, we're almost there."

It was interesting and a little scary, hiking through the woods at night. It would have been much easier on a trail, but Grace said they were following the direct route to the most likely place the gorillas would be.

Brittany checked her watch. One A.M. Her parents were probably freaked, in spite of the text she'd sent. The only other times she'd stayed out all night had resulted in...well...Ivy. She hoped this all-nighter would result in Ivy, too.

It had to. She just couldn't go on without her baby. Yeah, she understood now how she'd hurt her parents and the psychiatrist made her promise to try hard for a month, but she didn't want to stay in a world without Ivy.

Brittany shifted her backpack. The water bottle inside of it was digging into her back, or maybe that was the sleeping pad or the rain jacket Grace had made her carry. She wished she had a fancier pack with a waist strap—that was supposed to make the shoulder straps work better. Her shoulders ached already and she had a blister on her left foot. Still, it felt right to be out here, doing something. Fighting. She rubbed her fingers over the ivy tattoo.

Grace stood straight again, and gestured at her to continue. After a few steps, Brittany heard a noise in the woods close by, a sort of snort, followed by cracking of sticks. She stopped. "What do gorillas sound like?"

"That was most likely a deer. Gorillas hoot and whimper," Grace said. "Gumu pounds his chest when he's trying to impress someone."

"Really?" Brittany said. "Like in the movies?"

"Yep," Grace said. "That is real gorilla behavior. Climbing to the top of the Empire State Building to catch planes is not."

Talking helped pass the time. She asked, "What's Neema's favorite food?"

"Hmmm, there are so many." Grace considered. "Oranges. Jell-O. Yogurt. Lollipops would top the list, I guess. Neema calls them 'tree candy.'"

"That's smart." Neema sounded like an especially bright gorilla. She'd be the key to finding Ivy.

They went on walking for another twenty minutes, scrambling over logs and slipping on pine cones and zigzagging among the trees. Brittany occupied her thoughts by trying to imagine Ivy sleeping in her bassinet, her little lips pursing in and out as she dreamed. No, better yet—Ivy sleeping in her arms, her velvet cheek nuzzling against her breast.

"We're here." Grace's voice interrupted Brittany's reverie.

Nothing looked different. Trees and more trees.

"Well, we're close by," Grace corrected, glancing at her GPS device and then at the surroundings. "We'll have to do a big spiral out from here. Look for apple trees, an old homestead cabin, a big willow."

Brittany turned to her left to begin, but Grace's hand stopped her. "Hang on a second."

Grace stared into the darkness and yelled, "Neema! Gumu!"

They waited and listened. Brittany flashed her light around. Just the tall straight trunks of Douglas firs. "I don't hear anything but water," she said.

Grace perked up. "You hear water?"

Brittany nodded. "Like a stream or a waterfall or something."

"Lead on, MacDuff!"

Brittany fumbled her way toward the water sounds. What was a MacDuff? In a few minutes, they found a little stream and followed it until they literally ran into the branches of a big willow. At that point, Grace got very excited and trotted around among the trees while Brittany waited, leaning against an apple tree. Were there gorillas out there in the dark, watching?

Her heart was beating fast. Neema. Then Ivy. When Grace returned, Brittany whispered, "Are they here?"

"Not now," Grace said.

The gorillas were not here? They'd driven that clunky old van, bouncing over miles of rutted roads, and walked all this way in the middle of the night, and the gorillas weren't even here? Oh, what was the fucking point anymore? Nothing worked. She couldn't stand it any longer. The heavy pack, the pitch-black darkness. She slid down to the ground. Bringing up her knees, she rested her forehead on them, wishing she could just disappear. Just stop *being*. Why couldn't she make that happen?

Grace knelt next to her and threw an arm around her shoulders. "Neema and Gumu are not here right now, Brittany, but they may not be far away."

May not? Might as well say Ivy *may* not be far away! The 'Poor Brittany' crowd had been saying that to her for weeks now. The 'Damn Brittany' crowd said Ivy was dead.

"Neema and Gumu *were* here, Brittany. And not very long ago."

She lifted her head. "What makes you say that?"

Grace's headlamp shone in her eyes for a second, then Grace turned away, casting the beam onto the drooping willow branches. She parted the leafy greenery with her hand and shifted her head to light up some broken branches and—

"Is that poop?" Brittany asked.

"Gorilla feces," Grace confirmed. "They're relatively fresh." She shrugged off her backpack and crawled deeper into the shadow of the willow. "C'mon. We're sleeping here."

Brittany pushed herself to her hands and knees and crawled after her, making a wide detour around the poop. "Why? You said the gorillas weren't here."

Grace was already rolling out her sleeping bag. "Because," she said, "I think they'll be back."

Chapter 23

As he walked from the police station to the courthouse the next morning, Finn could see that Reverend Jimson's press conference had been effective. Dozens of people milled about, divided into two factions. The pro-ape contingent was into individual expression. *LISTEN TO THE ANIMALS* read one poster carried by a student wearing an ARU T-shirt. *HUMANS ARE THE ONLY DUMB ANIMALS* read another. The inevitable *I DON'T EAT MY FRIENDS* from the vegetarians. And a few signs held simple marker messages such as *Go Gorillas!* and *Half of My Friends Are Apes.*

On the opposite side of the square, the anti-ape faction was seemingly more organized. Their posters were all the same matching white and came in only three varieties: *I DID NOT DESCEND FROM APES, GOD GAVE MAN DOMINION OVER ANIMALS,* or *TEACH THE CONTROVERSY.*

The college news crew was egging all the protesters on, of course, filming one side and then the other. Then they spotted Finn climbing the steps.

"Detective Finn! Detective Finn!" They all rushed him. "Is it true that you're using testimony from that gorilla lady?" "How is this related to the Ivy Morgan case?" "Why have you targeted Jimson Janitorial Service?" "Are you anti-Christian?" "What's the latest news on the gorillas?"

He wished he knew the answer to the last question. He tried to call Grace several times, but her cell phone just went to voicemail. She no doubt had it turned off to save battery power. Or there was no service wherever she was. According to Josh, she was still out in the national forest searching for Neema and Gumu, with Brittany Morgan in tow.

Finn plowed through the barrage of reporters with one arm upraised, trying not to break his teeth or bloody his nose on any of the outthrust microphones. They didn't belong only to the college news crew; some of the mikes bore ID tags of stations in Seattle and Spokane. *Great. Just great.*

They followed him to the metal detectors, where the security officers pushed them back. Then he was finally through the gauntlet and into the quiet marble hallways.

He'd expected the reverend himself, but instead, Jimson's HR Director, Lisa Dvorak, awaited him in Sobriski's office. She was surprisingly pretty, in a tailored navy suit and heels, her blond hair cut into a chin-length bob. She was, however, just as bitchy in person as she had been on the phone.

"Detective Finn, ape whisperer, I presume," she said on first meeting him.

Finn smiled. "Play nice, this could take awhile." *Barracuda.*

"Got that right." She stepped out of the way to reveal a stack of four white cardboard boxes. "Have fun. When you've identified the records you want to keep, I'll be back."

"Wait!" Finn yelped. "What sort of order are these in? I may need your help."

She bared her perfect teeth. "We have obeyed the subpoena, Detective. We are certainly under no obligation to *help* you persecute our employees."

Finn looked to Sobriski, who shrugged. Damn.

"And the records do not leave the courthouse, correct, Judge?" The woman locked eyes with Sobriski, who said, "I've reserved a room for your use, Detective." Swiveling back to Dvorak, he said, "It will be locked at all times."

"It better be." She turned and abruptly left.

"Sweet woman," Finn murmured. Sobriski pretended not to hear.

A bailiff transferred the boxes to the conference room. Finn opened the first box. Inside were hundreds of personnel records in alphabetical order, each file labeled neatly with name, address, social security, skills, assignments, salary information, and one facial photo. Nothing on criminal history. No names of parole officers.

The records were in alphabetical order, not grouped by work location. Jimson had no doubt done that on purpose. Sweet mother of humanity, this was going to take years. They'd have to match employees to work locations, then match social security numbers to criminal records, and try to find links to vehicles and Charlie Wakefield.

Finn flicked open his cell phone. "Send Mason over here," he ordered.

Brittany woke up to a gentle warm breeze blowing across her face. When she opened her eyes, she nearly screamed. A leathery black face was only inches away from hers, so close she could feel the hot breath coming out of its nostrils. Red-brown eyes burned beneath a heavy black brow. The gorilla was gigantic.

"Grace!" she whispered. The ape hooted and reared back on its hind feet, then bared startlingly long, sharp teeth. Gorillas had *fangs*! Oh god, there was another huge black monster on the other side of Grace's sleeping bag. "Grace!" she squeaked.

Grace finally rolled over, said, "Wha—?" and rubbed her eyes. Opening them, she took a look around. "They're he-re!" she said in a singsong, obviously happy. She sat up. "That's Neema, beside you."

The gorilla tapped herself on her chest and waved a huge black hand.

"Neema fine gorilla," Grace said.

Neema was talking? Brittany pushed herself upright. "Ask her where Ivy is."

The larger gorilla on Grace's left side made what seemed like an obscene gesture. *Fuck? Prick?* Was there swearing in sign language?

"Gumu wants a banana." Grace watched the animals. "And so does Neema."

Banana, not penis. Thank god she hadn't said anything out loud.

Neema leaned close, her breath hot on Brittany's neck. She stretched out a long black finger and touched Brittany's hair where it lay on her shoulder. "They have fingernails!" Brittany said. She looked down. "And toenails!"

"I don't know why that always surprises people," Grace said. "We have practically identical DNA."

Neema was still gesturing. "Yogurt, Jell-O, cucumber, banana, cabbage, milk," Grace translated.

Gumu repeated his earlier sign. Brittany pointed. "He just wants a banana."

Grace laughed. "Oh, believe me, he wants a lot more than that; he just doesn't know the signs for the other foods yet."

Grace pulled her backpack into her lap and extracted two bananas. She was immediately rushed by both gorillas. They snatched the fruit and plowed through the drooping branches.

"Quick," Grace said, "Get dressed and don't—"

A black hand snaked back through the branches, caught Brittany's backpack, and then was gone.

"Shit!" Grace yelped.

They both ran out into the daylight. "Hey!" Brittany shouted. "Bring that back!"

Hooting like jackals, the gorillas vanished into the woods on the other side of the clearing.

By noon, Finn was bleary-eyed after pawing through the files in the four boxes. Mason had come over and set up a computer and a scanner.

"OCR is your only hope," Mason said.

Finn briefly considered slapping him with a file folder to make him speak English, but instead laid the folder on top of the stack.

Mason noted the dirty look. "Optical character recognition," he informed him. "It turns scanned documents into text files that you can use with a word processing system. So, in other words, you can scan these pages and then search for names or terms on the computer."

Finn groaned. "Sounds like a hell of a lot of work."

Mason nodded. "It is. And OCR is notoriously buggy, so it won't work perfectly, but it'll still be faster to match names or social security numbers against NCIC." He made a face at the stack of files on the table. "You want to scan all those?"

Finn had pulled the files of workers at the three schools in Evansburg, Coeur d'Alene, and Portland. "To start."

"Yeah, right." Mason headed for the door.

Finn panicked. "Where are you going?"

"To get another computer, and to shanghai Miki into scanning. Any objections?"

"Good plan." Finn waved him out. He shook his cell phone out of his pocket, speed-dialed Grace's cell and held his phone to his ear as he walked to the window. The demonstrators on the court steps had diminished in number, but when Mason appeared, they became more vocal. A reporter and cameraman, lounging against the side of an SUV, glanced his way with interest.

The computer technician plowed through the crowd, then turned and flashed a sign that looked suspiciously like an upraised middle finger. Thank heavens it was fast and Mason didn't wear a police department uniform.

"This is Dr. Grace McKenna. Please leave a message."

"It's Matt again. Hope you're okay." He flipped the phone closed. Damn. According to Josh, she and Brittany Morgan had not yet returned from their search for the gorillas. Was he going to have to mount a search for the two women, too?

Grace turned in place in the middle of the woods, gritting her teeth in frustration. Neema and Gumu had simply vanished. Again. She'd always been afraid of what the gorillas might do if they were freed, and now she had her answer. They'd run; they'd climb; they'd be wild gorillas within minutes. She couldn't blame them; who wouldn't choose racing through the woods over being locked up in a pen? They might last until their food supply ran out, the first snow of winter fell, or they were killed by a hunter.

She and Brittany spent hours spiraling out from the homestead site, looking for any sign of frolicking apes. Grace was fully dressed and wore her backpack, afraid to leave it behind in case the gorillas raided their campsite in their absence. Brittany wore the T-shirt and shorts she'd slept in, along with her hiking boots. The rest of her clothes were in her pack, wherever that was.

"Along with my new cell phone," the girl reminded her.

A helicopter buzzed overhead, and Grace pulled Brittany into the cover of a Douglas fir. "What are you doing?" Brittany screeched. "Why don't you want them to find us?"

The girl seemed on the edge of hysteria. Grace explained her reasoning. If the media found them, if anyone found them, the resulting barrage of helicopters and people would make the gorillas bolt for new territory.

"If we stay here, I think they'll come back," Grace said.

"But you don't *know* that," Brittany retorted. "You don't know what will happen next. They could be gone for good and then I'll never find Ivy."

Grace had no answer for that. She barely had enough food for herself and Brittany to spend another night in the woods, let alone to lure the gorillas back.

By noon, they'd found Brittany's jacket and water bottle. By dark, they found a pair of jeans and the remains of her backpack. The gorillas had ripped it open, breaking the zipper, to get at the food inside.

No cell phone. That seemed to upset Brittany more than losing the gorillas. The girl knelt by the shredded backpack, sobbing. "What's the use of trying? We're never going to find the gorillas and I'm never going to get Ivy back."

Wonderful, Grace thought. She was stuck in the woods with a teenager who had already tried suicide once. She didn't have any weapons or pills, but she wondered if she should remove the shoelaces from their boots before turning in. Or stay up all night to keep watch on the girl.

"C'mon, Britt," she gestured to their makeshift camp beneath the willow, trying to sound light-hearted. "Let's eat dinner and turn in. Tomorrow will seem brighter." Please let it be so, she prayed.

Grace left the girl under the branches, sitting on her sleeping bag, despondently rummaging through their meager food supplies. Stepping outside of the umbrella of branches, she turned on her cell phone and called Josh. She related the events of the day, and told him that she and Brittany were okay but would not be back today.

"I'm betting Neema and Gumu will show up again tomorrow morning," she said.

He'd been out with the search crews all day, he reported. She could hear television news in the background. Her cell phone blinked, warning that the battery was getting low. She hadn't had a chance to recharge it before hopping on the helicopter yesterday. "Can you call Brittany's parents for me?" she asked.

"Uh," he said.

"Josh? Did you hear me?"

"How far do you think you are from the highway?"

Her heart lurched. "Maybe a mile and a half. Why do you ask?"

Josh's voice was tight. "A semi driver reported hitting two large animals on the highway. The camera is...uh... showing these two black ... lumps in a ditch right now."

"Oh please no," she said, "Are they—?"

"What?" Brittany, eavesdropping on Grace's side of the conversation, had crawled out from under the willow and now tugged at her arm. The girl's eyes were already filling with tears in anticipation of bad news.

"Can't tell," Josh told Grace. "They're filming with a spotlight from a helicopter, and waiting for highway patrol to arrive. And now they've gone to commercial."

Her phone blinked again.

"You have internet on your phone, don't you?" he said. "Check KEBR's website; they'll have the latest." His words were clipped and there was no trace of his usual humor.

"Tell me," Brittany begged at her elbow. "Just tell me."

Grace's cell phone flashed its warning again, then the message *Shutting Down* appeared. "Gotta go, Josh," Grace said. "See you tomorrow, whatever happens." The readout went black. Grace stuck the useless phone back into her pocket. Thank god the GPS was a separate device; she needed it to get them back to the van.

"Just tell me," Brittany moaned. "Is Ivy dead?"

"That was nothing to do with your baby," Grace told her.

"The gorillas are dead, then?"

"No. Neema and Gumu are not dead." Grace hoped she was telling the truth.

Chapter 24

After a day spent pawing through hundreds of files and scanning anything that appeared promising, Finn had a list of Jimson employees who had worked in the last six months at the three schools where babies had disappeared. With the help of Miki and Mason, the pertinent data had been scanned in and compared with police records. True to the New Dawn philosophy, most were ex-cons with records of petty but repeated drug or theft offenses. None was considered violent.

Finn paced the floor of the courthouse conference room while the other two were at lunch. What now? Interview all the staff at all the schools, ask if any of them had snake bracelets and if they knew Charlie Wakefield? Yeah, right. The Captain would go berserk with a request for that much time and manpower. He had to link Jimson employees to Jimson cars somehow.

He stared out the window, willing a solution to come. The protestors had already dwindled to only two on the anti-gorilla side, which he now thought of as the anti-Finn side, because the department switchboard received a dozen calls a day to poke fun at the gorilla man or to complain about Finn's harassment of Jimson.

Finn flicked on the television in the corner of the room. Or maybe it was a computer. He had a hard time telling the difference these days. All he knew was that it received the major television channels and could play DVDs inserted into a slot on its side.

The discovery of gorillas rampaging through the countryside had been the major news story of the year for the local station, and they were still determined to pump it for all it was worth. Last night the mayor and the county executive were on the local news.

"First Detective Finn was after my son," Travis Wakefield had said to the reporter. "And now he's hanging out with gorilla keepers and trying to pin something on Jimson industries? Seems like the police department is 'winging it' instead of doing real police work these days."

On the screen now was a young interviewer deep in obviously scripted conversation with a gray-suited guest identified as Dr. Neville Orburton in a label at the bottom of the picture.

"It's called *anthropomorphic fallacy*," the guest said.

The interviewer appeared fascinated by his statement. "Can you explain that for the rest of us, Dr. Orburton?"

"Anthropomorphic fallacy means attributing human characteristics to animals. This has happened over and over again. There have been many cases where it seemed as though animals could understand language and respond, but it's always been proven that the animal was merely performing a trick in anticipation of getting a treat."

"And how would that be tested?"

"Well, there are many ways, but the easiest is this: if only the animal's usual handler can understand the animal's 'language'"—Orburton put the word in air quotes—"then it's not real language; it's an anthropomorphic fallacy."

"The most famous case is Hans the Clever Horse. He was rumored to be capable of solving math problems and answering various questions, but eventually it became obvious that he was merely responding to his trainer's cues, not actually thinking on his own. The trainer didn't even realize he was giving the horse those cues. That's probably what is going on in Dr. McKenna's so-called language project, too."

"So you believe that Dr. McKenna's research is suspect?"

"I didn't say that. But I'm not so sure that Dr. McKenna can be considered a reliable witness. If she saw something that could help solve the disappearance of Ivy Rose Morgan, why did she wait until now to reveal it to the police?"

"So you think her *timing* is suspect?"

"It's my understanding that Dr. McKenna's research project is on the chopping block right now, and her job may be as well. Choosing to point the finger at a well-known figure like Reverend Jimson guarantees plenty of media coverage."

The host leaned toward him. "You mean that Dr. McKenna might be doing this to gain public sympathy and support for her project?"

Dr. Orburton tilted his head and gave the host a smug smile. "You never know."

Finn snorted. The media obviously thought *Grace* was the witness who had fingered Jimson Janitorial Service. Wait until they found out that a *gorilla* had accused Jimson. But it might be a moot point if Grace didn't get Neema back.

The door squeaked open, and he quickly flicked off the television, expecting Miki back from lunch break. Instead, catty Ms. Dvorak closed the door and then leaned against it. "I hear you've reached the dead end I predicted."

Finn squeezed the television remote so hard it emitted a cracking sound. He relaxed his fingers. He walked to the table, picked up a printed page and handed it to her. "We are requesting detailed timesheets for the last six months on these employees."

She scanned the page. "Timesheets were not spelled out in the subpoena."

"Covered under employee records."

"We'll see what the judge has to say about that," Dvorak replied primly.

Finn had an urge to throw the remote at her. He made himself put it down on the table. "We will also need the names of all the people who had access to these vehicles, and the times at which they had access." He handed her the list of green Jimson-owned trucks and cars.

"Definitely not covered by the subpoena." Her tone was icy. "I'll speak with our attorney, but I can guarantee you're not getting that data without another subpoena. I'm not sure we even keep vehicle checkout information." Without lifting her eyes from the pages in her hand, she turned and left the room.

As soon as the door closed, Finn threw his hands into the air. "Bitch!"

The door opened. Under her drawn-on eyebrows, Miki looked at him through thick mascara and eyeliner. "What?"

"Nothing." He lowered his hands and shoved them into his pockets. "Talking to myself." He paced his well-worn route in front of the windows—seven steps between the squeaky tile and the wall in one direction, eight in the other. There had to be a way around the company's stall tactics. *Snake arm baby go cucumber car...* The green company car was the key.

"Miki," he said. "Can you run the plates of all those green vehicles with Jimson logos against the court records database?"

One painted eyebrow rose. "You mean, like for criminal traffic citations in Evansburg?"

"Like for speeding tickets, accident reports, anything in Washington, Oregon or Idaho." Aside from parking tickets, any report of the vehicle should also carry information about the driver.

She stared at the computer as if considering its capabilities. "That's not a typical query. I don't know if that can be done. I mean, the systems aren't even the same in those three states."

Damn! Finn gritted his teeth. If the public knew how often criminal cases were shot down by lame computer systems, they'd lynch the software CEOs.

"But Mason could probably figure out a way," Miki finished.

By mid-afternoon, the gorillas had not shown up at the old homestead site. Grace's cell phone could not be revived. Could it be true? Were Neema and Gumu the two large animal 'lumps' reported on the news last night? Her gorillas didn't understand what a highway was, and they certainly couldn't anticipate the consequences of running out in front of a semi. How could she ever forgive herself?

Grace spent the morning combing the woods around the clearing, but there were no signs or sounds of apes. Her heart felt like a lead weight in her chest, and she struggled to keep her voice from cracking. "Neema! Gumu! Candy! Banana!"

Brittany had strolled and shouted with her first thing in the morning, but now the girl was so depressed that she sat cross-legged on the damp ground, staring at nothing. Grace didn't want to know what she was thinking. Now she was afraid to take Brittany home, too. This outing had certainly done nothing to lift the poor child's spirits.

"C'mon, Britt," Grace said, holding out a hand. "Let's head back. We've got to hustle if we want to make it before dark." She pulled the girl from the ground, watched as she shrugged on her shredded backpack, and then they began to walk in the direction her GPS device indicated.

Grace struggled not to cry in front of Brittany. If Neema and Gumu were dead, she'd lost everything. Her two gorilla children, her credibility, her career. Maybe even her own reason for living. She was beginning to empathize with the sullen teenager walking behind her. Damn. She picked up the pace, lifted her chin, and bellowed, "Banana! Candy!"

"Give it up," Brittany grumbled.

"I'm not giving up until I *know* the situation is hopeless," Grace said. "Are you telling me you've given up on Ivy?"

The girl shot her a look filled with rage. Brittany ducked her head and walked ahead a few steps before she stopped and yelled, "Neema! Yogurt!"

Brittany was pissed off. They'd hiked all this way and slept out in the cold among piles of gorilla poop for nothing. Absolutely nothing. The gorillas were long gone. "Candy!" she yelled. "Bananas!"

"Gumu! Neema!" Grace yelled. The only other sounds were the thuds of their footsteps and the rustle of their clothing as they moved through the woods.

Grace had heard something awful over the phone last night. She wasn't sharing, but her face was all stiff and it looked like she might burst into tears any second. Maybe the gorillas were dead and Grace was going to pretend everything was all sweetness and light until they got back to town. And nothing would change. Ivy would still be gone, she'd still be the town baby killer, her parents would still treat her like a psycho. If Grace was pretending, maybe her parents were, too? Did they know things they hadn't told her?

A low grunt sounded from the woods behind her, and she stopped and pivoted to look back. Nothing but trees, as far as she could see. She walked another fifty steps before there was another sound...

"Do you hear that?" she asked Grace.

The noise was a rhythmic rumbling wheeze, like a racehorse running for the finish line. Something big, running hard. Getting louder. Coming their way.

Grace looked uptight, like she couldn't decide whether to be scared or happy or angry. "I think we'd better run," she said. And then she took off, leaving Brittany no choice but to gallop after her.

"What is it?" Brittany gasped, pounding behind Grace. A moose, a grizzly—were there grizzlies this far south of the Canadian border?

Grace didn't answer, just kept dashing between trees, her GPS tracker held out in front of her as she ran. Brittany glanced back over her shoulder. Two dark hulking shapes were following, huge black shadows blurred among the trees in the distance. The wheezing was getting louder. She ran faster, catching up with Grace.

Grace looked back over her shoulder. "Gorillas," she panted, an odd sort of half-smile on her face.

The huffing noises were right behind them now. "Why ... are we ... running?" Brittany struggled to get the words out between breaths.

In the next second, her question was answered. She was struck from behind, and went down hard. She screamed. She couldn't help it. The gigantic gorilla rolled over her, but one of his monster hands was clasped around her ankle.

He grabbed her backpack with the other hand. She couldn't get the shoulder straps off, and he was pulling a big hank of her hair in one giant black hand. What was next? Would he rip her head off, or sink those fangs into her neck? She shrieked again. The gorilla jumped back when she screamed, and she scrambled to her feet, pivoting to face him. He rose onto his hind feet and thumped his chest—pock, pock, pock—and bared his teeth like an enraged Doberman. Then he rushed toward her.

"Gumu, no!" Grace shouted, stepping between them to confront him. He rushed past and flung himself into Brittany. She screamed again and collapsed in a heap, the gorilla hovering over her. Gumu grabbed the backpack, wrenched it from her shoulders, and retreated to a safe distance. Neema was sitting on the sidelines, whimpering and gesturing wildly, but now she followed Gumu.

Grace held out a hand and helped her up. "You okay?"

Brittany could feel tears sliding over her cheeks. She didn't want to be a wimp, but she was starving, her feet hurt, and now half of her hair had been ripped out of her head, and she was lost in the woods with violent apes and a crazy woman. "Aren't they supposed to be tame? Are they going to *kill* us?"

Grace pulled her ahead, dragging her by the hand; they stumbled away from the gorillas. "They won't kill us," she said, although she sounded none too sure. "They're only hungry, and Gumu is not very well behaved."

"No shit." Brittany rubbed her left shoulder.

"I've still got food in my pack, so let's hustle. They'll follow." Grace took off again, jogging through the woods, checking her GPS as she ran. Brittany tried to keep up. Running in hiking boots was hard. "I can't...run...anymore," she shouted at Grace's back.

Grace glanced back, looking beyond Brittany. "You can."

A tree limb cracked behind Brittany, and she started running again. She was afraid to look back. The crashes and heavy breathing were right behind her. She ran for all she was worth, expecting to be attacked from behind at any moment.

After what seemed like forever, they stumbled out onto the gravel road and dashed downhill to Grace's van.

Grace rushed to unlock the doors. "Get in," she yelled, pointing to the passenger side. The gorillas were loping on all fours, coming up fast. Grace slid open the side door, shrugged off her pack, opened the flap, pulled out a bunch of bananas and a loaf of bread and tossed them inside. Huffing loudly, the gorillas leapt in, rocking the van with their weight.

Grace slammed the sliding door shut and dashed to the driver's seat, started the engine. She pulled the gearshift, which waggled a little but refused to move from neutral. "Goddamn it," Grace growled. "Not now." She released the parking brake and the van rolled downhill as she continued to jerk at the gearshift. Grinding noises came from somewhere under the front seats.

The van was picking up speed on the downward slope. They bounced into a chuckhole and out again. Grace continued to swear. Brittany's foot stomped a nonexistent brake on the passenger side. Were the brakes in this heap of junk better than the transmission? Was she going to die in a rollover accident, smashed in a van sandwich with two gorillas?

Finally there was a clunk, the gearshift slid into a better spot, and Grace raced ahead in a spray of gravel.

Brittany watched the gorillas anxiously in the tiny mirror on the back of the passenger visor. They were huddled on the floor, stuffing their faces with food. Why wasn't there a wire grill between the front seats and the back of this van, like cops had for prisoners? And she'd thought her Civic wasn't safe.

"They'll settle down now." The way Grace said it sounded more like a wish than a statement, but she was smiling as she watched Neema and Gumu in the rear-view mirror. Grace held up her right hand. "We got 'em, Brittany! Hundreds of searchers couldn't do it. But the two of us found them and we're bringing them home!"

Put that way, it did sound pretty heroic, so she clapped her left hand to Grace's in an awkward high five.

"We're champion gorilla wranglers!" Grace laughed.

Brittany tried to sit up straight in the bouncing van, but she kept sliding around on the slippery vinyl seat and the belt kept getting tighter and digging into her sore shoulder. She dug her fingers into her tangled hair, attempting to straighten out the snarls. Gorilla wrangler. She couldn't wait to tell the Sluts at school. But her cell phone was gone for good, out there somewhere in the woods. The second one she'd lost in less than a year.

Grace startled her by saying, "I'll get you a new cell phone."

So they'd found the gorillas; that was something. But when would they get to the 'finding Ivy' part of this adventure? That was the whole reason she'd come.

Grace's hand landed lightly on Brittany's left shoulder. "I promise that Neema and I will do our best to help find your baby girl."

Apparently Grace could read minds as well as talk to gorillas.

Brittany pulled down the visor and checked the mirror on the back. Big mistake. That dark streak in her hair better not be gorilla poop. She'd lost an earring somewhere. Over her shoulder, she saw a set of red-brown eyes watching her. Neema had buckled herself into a seat belt in the seat behind Brittany's; now that was a freakin' weird thing to see. One of Gumu's hands—or were they called paws?—clutched the back of Neema's seat. Brittany shifted the visor, and now she could see that the male gorilla was sitting on the floor in the cargo area, clutching the backs of both seats in front of him.

Grace hit a washboard of ruts. Brittany grabbed the panic handle over her door. In the mirror, she could see the whites of both gorillas' eyes. This ride couldn't be over soon enough. She closed her eyes and tried to imagine how this would all lead to holding her baby in her arms again. *Ivy, you're never going to believe this...*

A forest of signs had sprouted overnight at the junction of her driveway and the highway. *Save People, Not Apes. We Did NOT Descend From Monkeys. Where's Ivy?* There might as well be a neon sign flashing *Gorillas This Way*, Grace thought grimly. She wondered how Matt was coping. An egg-shaped Honda Insight was parked outside of the gate at the shoulder of the road. That didn't bode well. Grace made Brittany unlock the gate, and after she drove through, lock it again behind them.

The yard was empty when she drove in, but three strangers lounged on the picnic table.

Grace slammed the van to a stop as close as possible to the barn enclosure, and she and Brittany jumped out. "Stay here," she told the girl. She strode toward the strangers. "You're trespassing."

A boy stood up. Or maybe he was a man. The black goatee made it hard to tell. "We know, dude," he said. "But there's no other way to get to you."

The two girls rose. Each had an eyebrow ring, and a silver nose stud gleamed from the flank of one girl's nostril. With their jeans and tee shirts and pierced faces, the three might have been college students from some institution far more liberal than the Evansburg college.

Thankfully, there were no cameras in sight, and the strangers' clothing didn't look like they were concealing weapons. At least not weapons of any size. But there were three of them and one of her, and she couldn't count on Brittany for help; the poor girl was terrified of Neema and Gumu. Brittany stood outside the van now, staring at the gorillas inside. The girl with the nose stud walked toward her.

Gumu pounded on the sides of the van, sounding like he had a sledgehammer. Bam! Bam! Bam! He'd break a window any second now. And then what—run back into the woods?

"Do NOT open that door!" Grace shouted at Brittany and Nose Stud.

The pounding continued, and now she could hear pock-pock sounds of Gumu beating his chest, and Neema's hoots of alarm. How in the hell was she going to get two out-of-control gorillas from the van into the pen by herself? Why couldn't Josh have been home?

"Hey," the studded girl shouted. "This gorilla just signed *milk*." She gestured toward the van, signing *friend*.

Grace's jaw dropped. She turned toward the man/boy.

"Why did you want to 'get to me'?" she asked.

He grinned, stretching the skin of his lower lip tight beneath a lip ring. "To help, of course," he said. "Jon Zyrnek, Animal Rights Union." He held out a dirty hand. Then again, it was cleaner than hers. And he was offering help, so she put her hand into his.

Chapter 25

Bears. According to the paper, the large animals hit by the semi turned out to be a sow bear with a yearling cub. It was sad, but Grace was so grateful that the black corpses hadn't been her gorillas. It had taken two days for Neema and Gumu to settle down, especially with new people in their territory. Both gorillas had terrible diarrhea from all the apples and whatever else they'd eaten during their adventure, but other than that they seemed healthy. And they seemed to have finally bonded during the escapade. Neema now wanted to sleep every night with Gumu in the barn, so Grace had taken the blankets for her sleeping nest out there. The kittens had moved to the barn as well.

As she walked out to the barn to deliver breakfast to her menagerie, she thought about the coming months. She needed to rig up some sort of heat out there, but would any of them still be here this winter? Both Neema and Gumu were still on the university auction list, and the land and trailers were as well. The gorillas' paintings had brought in slightly less than five thousand dollars. She'd have to get the apes back to doing gorilla art, and soon. Now that they were all notorious, perhaps the sales figures would skyrocket. Then again, by now the university was no doubt aware of their little underground art project, and the bureaucrats might very well claim that the money earned on their property by their property was rightfully theirs.

Hell, she'd better learn to create and sell her own paintings; she might be unemployed soon. So far the university had stayed quiet when hounded by the press, other than acknowledging the existence of the ape language project. The fact that they were not defending her in any way did not bode well. The Tolliver Animal Intelligence Foundation had no comment, either. The silence from her supposed supporters was ominous.

Brittany had returned yesterday with her parents, who apparently judged Grace to be at least a benign influence, because she was back today by herself. Grace knew she was hoping for the magical breakthrough when Neema would tell her where Ivy was. No matter how often Grace explained that Neema had no way of knowing that, the girl still wanted to be near the female gorilla, as if the ape was a link to her baby. Now Brittany stood outside the barn enclosure, feeding Neema and Gumu carrots one by one through the wire mesh.

Brittany's hair fascinated Neema. This morning the girl wore it in her usual ponytail and the gorilla kept signing *red tail soft*. From the ARU trio, Brittany had learned the sign for baby, and she signed over and over *Where baby?*

"Baby go snake arm bracelet," Grace translated for her. Unfortunately, Brittany didn't know anyone with a snake bracelet. Now, with the handful of carrots gone, the teenager raised her hands to her head in frustration and wailed, "Doesn't she know anything *more*?"

Grace put a hand on the girl's arm. "Oh honey. Green car, snake arm bracelet. I'm afraid that's it."

Red Tail cry, Neema signed from behind the fence. *Skin bracelet pretty.*

Grace's jaw tensed. *Where skin bracelet?* she quickly signed.

Skin bracelet flower there. Neema thrust out her lips toward the ivy design on Brittany's forearm.

When Neema meant ring, she signed *finger bracelet*.

Skin bracelet.

"I'll be right back," she told Brittany, then dropped the tub of food and ran for her trailer.

In the courthouse conference room, Finn's cell phone buzzed. Mason and Miki had yesterday off, the first day for three weeks, so he'd stayed home and twiddled his thumbs as well. Now they were all back searching for a connection between Jimson employees and Jimson vehicles.

The phone showed Grace's number. "Everything okay out there?" he answered.

"Matt! Skin bracelet!"

"What?"

"It's not a *jewelry* bracelet—Neema signed *skin bracelet*. She means a tattoo! Look for a tattoo of a snake on a man's arm." Grace hung up.

A tattoo was much more findable than a snake bracelet. "We're searching for a tattoo on a Jimson employee," he excitedly told Mason and Miki. "A tattoo of a snake, or something that looks like a snake."

Mason raised an eyebrow. "Another contribution from the gorilla woman?"

Finn chose not to respond.

"You know," Miki contributed, "Tattoos don't have to be permanent." She held out her own arm, which had the word LOVE stamped across the wrist. "My new boyfriend put this one on me last night." She gazed at it fondly.

From Mason came, "Who says that the tattoo was on the Jimson employee? It could have been on a friend, right?"

"I get it." Finn slapped his hand down on the table. "Let's focus on finding information about who drives the Jimson vehicles first." And then he'd look for a tattoo, even if he had to do it himself.

Two hours later, Mason had pulled up a list of traffic records containing the plate numbers for the green Jimson vehicles. There was an accident report in which a Jimson vehicle driven by a Susan Magret had been hit by a pickup near

Seattle; a failure-to-yield ticket for an Oscar Jones in a Jimson van in the Okanagan area. He copied down Magret's and Jones's addresses and dates of birth to run through the computer. There were two speeding tickets near Spokane and another near the Oregon border for Abram Jimson; apparently the guy had a lead foot. A fender bender rear-end collision, also for Abram Jimson.

Looked like the good Reverend was a hazard to public safety. Finn studied the records more closely, searching for times and dates, and saw that one Spokane ticket had Sr. marked after the name. The other two Abram Jimson citations had Jr. noted.

"Does Abram Jimson have a son with the same name?"

Mason and Miki glanced up from their respective computer screens. "Yes," they said in unison.

Finn turned to the boxes of records and flipped through the folders to the Spokane group. Yes, there it was. Abram Jimson Jr. He had been so focused on reading the location of the employee assignments that he'd skipped right over the name. Junior's title was listed as Quality Assurance Officer.

Scott, his ex-father-in-law, had rhapsodized over the janitorial service's performance. *They even send a quality control man around...*

"Mason," Finn said, trying to remain calm, "Does Junior have a record?" If he did, there'd be mug shots.

He paced as Mason tapped a query into the system. Then his hopes were dashed when the computer tech sat back in his chair. "No record."

Damn. Couldn't he catch a break in this case?

"Yes!" Miki clapped her hands.

They turned toward her. "I found his page on Facebook," she chortled.

"Photos?"

She grinned and turned her laptop around. A color photo of Abram Jimson Jr. lounging next to an expensive motorcycle took up most of the screen space.

"Well, hot damn, lookie there," Mason drawled.

Junior had black hair tied back in a ponytail. He was the man Finn had glimpsed with the janitor a couple of times at the high school. In the Facebook photo, Abram Jimson Jr. held his arms crossed against his chest. The arm on top clearly sported a blue ink drawing of a cobra that stretched from his elbow down to his wrist.

Finn grinned and said to Miki, "Print that page for me, would you?"

Mason reached for a notepad. "Guess we'll be asking Jimson Janitorial for more info about Junior's whereabouts on the day that Ivy disappeared?"

"Got that right," Finn agreed.

Miki held out the printed copy of Junior's Facebook photo, and Finn took it eagerly, pulling his car keys out of his pocket as he headed for the door. "Take the rest of the day off if you want. See you later."

"Where are you going?" Mason asked.

"I need to show this photo to a gor.." He only barely managed to change it to "Grace" in the last fraction of a second. The door closed behind him. *A Grace?* Maybe they hadn't noticed.

The protesters seemed to have forsaken the courthouse steps in favor of decorating the county road right-of-way in front of Grace's home. Public property. No laws broken, the Sheriff said, nothing could be done about it. *Where's Ivy?, Stop the Harassment, Save People, Not Apes; God Gave Man Dominion Over Animals; We are not Monkeys; God Loves Reverend Jimson,* and the ever-present *Teach the Controversy.* Grace was right to be worried about her safety. Finn mowed down four signs on his turn into her driveway.

The Sheriff had refused to provide a guard, claiming there was no money for it, but Grace told Finn she had friends helping now. A college kid in a black tee shirt with cell phone in hand had given him a thumbs-up after he drove over the signs. After watching Finn open and close the gate, he held the cell phone to his lips as Finn drove up the road.

"Oh yes," Grace told him minutes later. "That's Jared, one of the volunteers from the Animal Rights Union."

Finn could hardly wait for *that* tidbit to hit the local news. In the study trailer, he was relieved to see that Neema had recovered her quiet demeanor after her adventure. She wanted to know if he'd brought her another flower. He found a mint lifesaver in his pocket, and Grace let him give that to the gorilla.

He insisted that they set up two video cameras, and he took his time making sure the angle of each was perfect. Neema sat in the corner of her training trailer, engrossed in a children's picture book about zoo animals.

"No prompting," Finn told Grace. "No questions."

"We'll just show her the photo and see what she does," Grace agreed.

"Multiple photos," Finn said. "Like a lineup."

One by one, he held up four photos for the camera before placing them on the coffee table.

"Photo 1, Charlie Wakefield." He'd had Mason Photoshop the picture, adding Charlie's face to a torso and arm displaying his track team's lightning design on the sleeve.

"Photo 2, anonymous subject with facial features and dark hair similar to Abram Jimson Jr., no tattoo."

"Photo 3, anonymous subject with blond hair and features similar to Wakefield, twining tattoo on forearm."

"Photo 4, Abram Jimson Jr., sna—serpent tattoo on forearm."

It was far from perfect, but it would do for his purpose today. Finn sat on the couch, and stated his name and the date and time for the cameras. Then he turned toward the gorilla. "Neema."

She raised her head. "Come look at these pictures." She scooted over in his direction.

Neema bent over the coffee table, her nose practically touching the photos, examining each one. Suddenly she screeched and slid backwards, signing frantically.

"Bad bad snake skin bracelet bad," Grace translated. "Bad baby go cry. Bad snake arm man. Baby cry. Baby go."

Grace stepped forward to comfort her frightened gorilla.

"But she didn't identify a photo," Finn groaned. This would never work with a judge.

"Who bad snake arm man, take baby go?" Grace asked Neema, signing the words.

Finn frowned at the Tarzan language being recorded on the tape, imagining what a defense attorney would do with it. Neema sat huddled in the corner, her head bent toward the wall, her face hidden in her hands.

Grace tapped her on the shoulder. "Neema."

The gorilla turned her head. From his position, Finn could see the whites of her eyes.

"Who bad snake arm man take baby?" She pointed toward the coffee table and startled him by switching to actual English as she signed, "Go touch the picture of the bad man who took the baby."

Neema's huge hands flashed.

"Tree candy yogurt," Grace translated. "She's bargaining." She turned to Neema and said, "Yogurt."

The gorilla's big hands moved again. Grace stared at her for a moment. Neema gazed back toward her corner.

"Oh, all right," Grace grumbled, signing her acquiescence. "Yogurt *and* a lollipop, but only after you touch the photo of the bad snake arm man who took the baby."

Neema turned then and inched reluctantly toward the coffee table as if slogging through swamp mud. When she reached the edge of the coffee table, she raised her chin to look, then abruptly rose up on her hind feet and slammed her giant hand down on the lower right photo, slapping it so hard that it slipped from the table onto the floor. She quickly scooted to the door that led to the kitchen, hooting and hugging herself.

Finn recovered from the half-turned retreat position he'd automatically assumed when Neema reared up. He faced forward again, took a breath, and said for the video camera,

"Neema has identified the photo of Abram Jimson Jr. as the man who took the baby. Interview ended."

As Grace went to the kitchen to get Neema her treats, he turned off the camera and retrieved the photo from the floor. "Gotcha," he said to Junior.

Chapter 26

"You have *got* to be kidding," Vernon Dixon said. The district attorney leaned back in his chair as if trying to put as much distance as possible between himself and the video monitor. "You want me to issue an arrest warrant for Abram Jimson Jr. on the basis of hearsay testimony from an *ape*?"

Finn winced and held a finger to his lips. Dixon had shouted it loud enough to be heard down the corridor. "According to multiple citizens," Finn told him, "Junior was in Evansburg making the rounds of Jimson Janitorial clients on the day that Ivy Rose Morgan disappeared." He'd checked with his ex-father-in-law and verified that.

"So what?" Dixon asked.

Which was exactly what Abram Jimson Jr. had said, according to the Spokane detectives who had interviewed him. He hadn't denied being in Evansburg on that day; a stop there was part of his regularly scheduled rounds as a quality assurance officer for Jimson Janitorial Service.

Dixon steepled his fingertips in front of his chest and fixed his steely gaze on Finn. "You've got nothing else?"

"He was also in Portland the day before Tika Kinsey disappeared."

"The day before?"

Junior said he'd gone camping out on the Oregon Coast after doing his quality control rounds; there was no actual record of where he'd stayed the night before or the night after Tika vanished from her front porch playpen. Finn shrugged.

"No." The district attorney swiveled in his desk chair. "There's no way. We'd become the laughingstock of Washington State. Hell, with your current YouTube fame, we'd be the laughingstock of the entire world."

Finn fumed. But Dixon was right, he didn't yet have proof that would stand up in court; he had to find more. Finn's cell phone buzzed as he left the DA's office. Brittany Morgan. She called him several times a day. He didn't answer. How could he tell her that he was fairly certain about the identity of her baby's kidnapper, but he couldn't lay a hand on him? Brittany and her parents would feel even more tormented than they were now. He knew because he was feeling that torment himself.

What else did he have? The baby carrier and backpack had been wiped down, no usable prints. Brittany's car, likewise; all prints belonged to the family. The slimy bastard must have worn gloves. But that didn't seem likely, now that he thought about it; gloves would have covered up much of the tattoo on his wrist and hand.

He dialed Grace as he walked down the courthouse hallway. "Did Neema ever mention anything else about snake arm man?"

"I don't remember anything else. Want me to review the videos I made right after we went to the store?"

"As soon as you can, please." He didn't know what he was hoping for. Some detail he'd missed, something that someone else might recall seeing that day. He pushed open the door and stepped outside. Immediately, two matched sets of reporters with cameramen surged forward. "Detective Finn! Detective Finn!"

Allyson Lee elbowed her competitor to the side and jammed the microphone in his face. "Is it true that the eyewitness in the Ivy Morgan case is not Dr. McKenna, but one of her *gorillas*?"

Her question was immediately followed by a roar of shouts from the small crowd gathered behind the reporters. Several cameras flashed.

Apparently Dixon *had* yelled loudly enough to be heard in the corridor.

He loped back to the precinct with the pack at his heels. He'd barely sat down at his desk when his cell phone buzzed. The readout said *Foster, FBI*. Finn snapped his phone open, feeling a little sick.

"I'm sitting in the Boise airport watching the Northwest News," Agent Alice Foster said. "And I see that you have an eyewitness in the Ivy Morgan disappearance? Why did you fail to inform us of this, Detective?"

"You know how unreliable eyewitnesses can be," he said vaguely. "It's a ... young female ... with the IQ of a five-year-old. All she identified was a green car with a particular logo and a man with a snake bracelet."

"And her identification is linked to this Jimson fellow?"

"The logo belonged to Jimson Janitorial, so we're searching employee records now to see if there's a connection."

"So at this point you *believe* it's a kidnapping?"

Finn thought about that for a second. He did believe it was a kidnapping, but he wasn't ready to say that yet. He still had no idea what had happened to that baby. If the FBI grabbed the case now, he'd lose all momentum. "I've been following up on the lead to see if it's a possibility," he told Foster.

Agent Foster's heavy sigh rasped over the airwaves. "Well, let us know if we can be of assistance. And by the way, the report on your crime scene debris just came back. Lots of prints and DNA on various items, none matched to known felons or to the Wakefields."

Of course, Finn thought bitterly. Nothing about this case could be *easy*.

"Where would you like me to send the report?"

He gave her the department fax number. "Thank you for getting that processed, Agent Foster," he said.

"No problem. Please do keep us informed of any future developments, Detective."

He promised he would, and then ended the call. He wondered when Agent Foster would get the news that his eyewitness was a gorilla.

He stood up to pace, but after his second lap, he noticed everyone else in the precinct was staring at him. "I'm headed home," he told the dispatcher. "Call me if anything comes up."

Twenty minutes later he was out in his backyard, Cargo trailing in his wake as he wandered around his property, shouting over and over, "Lok! Come here, kitty!" The Lost ad he'd sent into the Evansburg Times had run for the last three days, but there had been no calls.

He sat on his deck, feeling exhausted, useless, and depressed. Some detective he was. Didn't know his wife was planning to ditch him. Didn't know a coyote would eat his cat. Couldn't find a way to finger the kidnapper that he knew was out there.

He tried to think from Junior's point of view. Why would the guy be kidnapping babies? He was most likely selling them to perverts or childless couples. What would it take to sell babies? A website? Maybe. There needed to be someplace to display your wares, so to speak.

Wares in this case would be photos, at least to start off with. Finn thought about the photos of mothers and babies in the schools. The same photos were on the YoMama website. But YoMama required an approved user name and password to get in, and neither Adrian in Portland or Mason in Evansburg had detected any unauthorized entries. It was a long shot, but... He called for a fingerprint tech to meet him at Brittany's school, and then he called the principal to come and let them into the building.

"The janitor can do that," the principal said.

"I'd rather that the janitor did not know what we're up to. We'll need private access to the hallway where the photos of the Slu...teenage moms and babies are displayed."

"So you're getting close to solving the Ivy Morgan case?" the principal wanted to know.

"I hope so." Finn flicked shut his phone.

When the principal met them at the side door, he told them, "I closed the doors at the end of the hall and told the night janitor that we were doing maintenance on the fire alarms in this wing."

"Smart thinking," Finn said.

The principal eagerly rubbed his hands together. "So what are we doing?"

"I'm sorry," Finn told him, "But I can't have a civilian here. Police only." He gestured toward the door at the end of the corridor.

The man was clearly disappointed.

"We'd really appreciate it if you could keep everyone away." Finn said. "And make sure this stays hush-hush."

The principal seemed pleased to have an assignment. "You got it. I'll await your call." He headed for the double doors.

"So what are we doing?" Guy Rodrigo, the fingerprint tech, asked after the principal had left.

Finn stopped in front of the photos of all the Sluts and babies, pulled out his camera and took a photo of the collection. Stepping back, he pointed to the photo of Ivy Morgan.

"I want this frame fingerprinted, as well as the back of the photo, and then put right back up."

The tech groaned. "The back of the *photo*? You mean I need to take apart the frame?"

"I'm afraid so." The frame may well have been wiped clean, but if Finn's hunch was correct, there might be prints on the photo of Ivy. "Glove up and get started."

Rodrigo snapped on gloves and dusted the frame. When no prints appeared on the wood or glass, he laid down his brush and powder and then tugged at the frame. "Shit. This is screwed to the wall."

"I noticed." Finn handed him the screwdriver he'd brought. "And just so you know, if I'm right about this one, we'll need to come back and do the rest."

Chapter 27

Unearthly shrieks awakened Grace. She sat up abruptly, reaching for her bathrobe at the foot of the bed. Her bedside clock read 3:29 A.M. The shrieking continued, punctuated by loud crashes. It sounded like the gorillas were fighting with an axe murderer in the barn.

Josh met her in the yard as they dashed to the barn enclosure.

The lock on the gate was intact. Inside, Neema sat hunched in the far corner, while Gumu frantically raced around the perimeter of the enclosure, leaping up to the net, racing across it to touch all corners, then barreling down, pausing now and then to beat his chest and shriek some more.

Inside, just to right of the gate, candy and cookies were scattered on the ground, some crumpled as if they'd been shoved through the fence openings. The fencing was bent outwards near the gate, which told Grace that Gumu had launched himself into the wire mesh toward someone standing outside.

Jonathan Zyrnek trotted up with a walkie-talkie in his hand, panting. "What the hell's going on?"

A second later, Caryn arrived.

"We had a visitor." Grace pointed to the snacks scattered across the ground. She took the key out of her pocket and reached for the lock.

"Shit," Jonathan said. "Caryn reported a car, so we went out to track it, but the driver must have already let someone out down the road."

Grace unlocked the padlock. A second before she pulled the gate open, Neema rushed over to the pile of goodies, grabbed a lollipop, and scuttled up onto the webbing.

"No!" Grace bellowed, dashing after her, Josh at her heels. "No, Neema, don't eat that! No! Give candy to Grace! Not for Neema!"

She struggled to lift herself into the webbing. Josh grabbed her around the knees and tossed her up. Below them, the two ARU volunteers walked toward the sweets, keeping a wary eye as Gumu continued to circle and screech. "Don't touch that candy with your bare hands," she screeched at Jonathan and Caryn. "It's poisoned!"

Josh pulled himself up on the rope webbing behind her.

"No, Neema! Bad candy!" Grace couldn't sign while she crawled across the rope net on her hands and knees. "Candy will make Neema sick!"

But Neema, in typical bad kid can't-stop-me fashion, had the lollipop in her mouth by the time Grace arrived. Grace reached for the stick between her lips, and Neema turned away, chewing. Then she dropped, inert, face down into the netting.

"No!" Grace wailed.

Josh helped her roll Neema's head sideways. The lollipop fell out of the gorilla's mouth down to the ground. Neema's eyes rolled back in their sockets.

"Who should we call?" Josh asked. "I didn't grab my cell phone."

"I have mine." She leaned across Neema and laid her head on the gorilla's furry back. Neema's heartbeat sounded strong, and so did her lungs. So far. Grace sat up and used the corner of her robe to wipe out Neema's mouth. Then she pulled the cell phone out of her robe pocket.

"Who you gonna call?" Josh looked at her.

Grace stared at the phone for another few seconds. She hadn't yet found a local vet for the gorillas. If she called 9-1-1, they'd be invaded by useless uniforms and infuriating reporters. She scrutinized Neema again. The gorilla hadn't twitched a muscle. Would she ever move again?

"I'm calling Detective Finn. I'll stay with Neema. Go check on Gumu." The big male had ceased his shrieking, but still circled the pen, intermittently beating pock-pock-pock threats on his chest. "Pick up that lollipop."

Josh moved off, crawling across the net. "Calm down, buddy," he called to Gumu.

She tapped in Matt's home number and pressed the phone to her ear. He promised to bring a vet with him and get there as soon as he could. After ending the call, she sat in the net, criss-crossing her legs to keep her feet from sliding through the ropes.

She heard Josh's soft murmurs over in the furthest corner as he tried to calm down Gumu. The ARU kids had taken off, flashlights in hand, to track the trespasser.

It was quiet, too quiet. She picked up Neema's giant hand, holding it in both of hers. Was the gorilla's breathing slowing? How could this happen again? Grace bit her lip, trying to keep the tears from coming. Most human beings would never touch one gorilla in a lifetime. Was she going to lose *two* to murder?

The vet Matt brought with him forty minutes later was a surprisingly petite woman named Nan Brewer. She assured Grace that she was a large animal doctor who had volunteered at a zoo while in veterinary school. Brewer seemed unperturbed at having been yanked out of bed at four in the morning to crawl up into a suspended rope net to examine a comatose gorilla. Matt, on the other hand, looked distinctly uncomfortable.

"I was *so* hoping I'd get a chance to see these guys," the vet said, pulling a stethoscope from her bag. "Under different circumstances, of course," she added.

"This is Neema," Grace told her. "The other one, Gumu, is in the barn."

Neema was heavily anesthetized, the vet concluded. Her breathing and heartbeat were very slow, but both were regular. Brain damage was her biggest fear. "Sometimes anesthesia changes animals forever; we don't really know why," she said. "Unfortunately, there's no way to know how she'll come out of it without knowing what she ingested. I'd suggest an IV to protect against shock," the vet said. "Saline and glucose. I'll stay with her for awhile."

"Did you see anyone?" Matt asked Grace, peering out at the yard. "Did you hear anything?"

Of course. He would be itching to do the cop thing. "No," she told him. "We wouldn't have been able to hear the space shuttle launch, the way Gumu was carrying on."

Josh, leaning against the fence below, said, "He kept signing *bad, bad*."

Grace looked surprised. "When did he learn that sign?"

"Guess Neema showed him."

"Cool," said the vet.

Matt crawled toward the edge of the net. "I'll go check the premises."

The ARU kids showed Finn the path the intruder likely took, out through the barbed wire and across that blasted blackberry-filled field, the same way the YouTube reporter had escaped.

"It was a dark pickup," Caryn told him. "I heard it crawling along the side of the road in the gravel and called Jon, and then we both went out to check."

"The headlights weren't on. Pretty hard to make out the plate in the dark, but I think I got a partial." He pulled a small page out of a tiny notebook. "That letter"—he pointed—"might be an O or a D; and that number might be a 3 or an 8. I think I nailed the rest of 'em."

"Thanks," Finn said. So he had four possible combinations to run; it was a good start. It felt weird to get help from two kids he'd testified against less than a month ago.

"Really fucked up on letting the dickhead into the compound," Jon said.

For a second Finn thought the kid was carping about the lack of police protection, but then he realized Zyrnek was criticizing himself.

"You're not an experienced guard," Finn told him. "Don't sweat it."

Caryn frowned. "But with all the ops training we've gone through," she said. "We should have known better."

"Ops training?" Finn asked. "Where'd you do that?"

"Uh." Jonathan pulled at Caryn's shirttail. "We should be making rounds, don't you think?"

She looked at him and then back at Finn. "Oh, yeah. Gotta check the perimeter."

They peeled off in separate directions into the darkness, and Finn walked back to the barn enclosure.

Josh went to bed. Grace and the vet remained sitting in the rope webbing, bonding over the comatose gorilla, discussing eating habits and good and bad behavior like two suburban moms. Brewer still had no prediction on when Neema would wake up.

"Could this affect her memory?" Finn asked from below.

"Hard to say," the vet said. "It could." She turned to Grace. "How would you tell if it affected her memory?"

Grace launched into more Neema stories. He could tell she was more worried than she let on. He wasn't feeling too optimistic, either. It was bad enough to depend on the testimony of a gorilla. What if that gorilla never told the same story again?

Dawn was just beginning to brighten the horizon as Finn drove to the station to look up the license numbers.

Chapter 28

Bad man baby cry snake skin bracelet man come. Bad bad. Gumu scared. Neema scared. Bad bad. Snake arm bad. Candy now.

Neema not only remembered the poisoning event, she talked about it constantly. She reported that *Gumu make bad man go.* From her description, it sounded like the bad man was not the wacko who'd murdered Spencer years ago, but the man who'd taken the Morgan baby.

"Snake arm man?" Grace asked, taping the question session. "The *same* snake arm man who took the baby to the green car?" It was questionable whether Neema truly understood the meaning of the word *same*; Grace hadn't had sufficient time to test the gorilla on that.

Brittany let herself into the trailer in time to hear the last part. Her blue eyes widened as she glanced back and forth between Neema and Grace. "What's going on?"

Bad skin bracelet snake arm candy now, now candy, Neema gestured to Grace. Then, turning to Brittany, she signed *red tail candy Neema candy please.*

"What's she saying?" Brittany asked, signing *where baby?* at Neema.

Red tail give candy good gorilla, Neema signed back. She scooted close to Brittany to touch her hair.

"Neema says good morning and wants you to give her C-A-N-D-Y. Before that, she was describing the man who tried to poison her two nights ago."

"Really?" Brittany's face stiffened. "Could it be the man who took Ivy? How did she describe him?"

Grace sighed. "Bad skin bracelet snake arm."

It had taken her so long to clue in on *skin bracelet*. What else had she missed? She pulled out the videos taken of Neema right after Ivy had disappeared. None of them was safe as long as Snake Arm was still out there.

When Grace called, Finn was staring at several possible matches to prints from the back of the school photo. None of the prints belonged to Charlie Wakefield. Turning away from his computer screen, he answered his cell phone.

"Bag glove," she told Finn. "Neema described Snake Arm as using a bag glove."

"The kidnapper put a bag over his hand?" He was getting surprisingly adept at deciphering Neema's—and Grace's—language. That made sense—the gorilla would be able to see a tattoo through a transparent plastic bag. "Miki," he shouted after he ended the call.

Micaela's head popped up over a file cabinet. "Yes?"

"Can you bring me that report the FBI faxed to me?" He drummed his fingers on the desk in anticipation. She plopped a file folder down in front of him.

He pulled up the common fingerprints from the back of the photos at the school. Ruling out Daisy Taylor's prints—she'd put the collection together—that left only two others. There had been a couple of plastic bags in the collection of detritus he'd had Scoletti scoop up from the Food Mart parking lot. He thumbed through the FBI report, looking for the fingerprint section. If Grace—and Neema—were right, and if his luck had finally turned... Bingo! One of the fingerprints—a male's, judging by the size—from the inside of the bag appeared to match a print from the back of Ivy Rose Morgan's photograph. What were the odds that the same person had his hands on baby Ivy's photo *and* inside a bag found under the car in the parking lot where the baby disappeared? Now all he needed was a set of Junior's fingerprints to compare. The net was closing, he could feel it.

He ran all the license plate combos the ARU kid had come up with for the pickup seen prowling the roadside on the night the gorillas had been attacked. On the third try, he hit pay dirt. *Francisco Ibañez.* Who, he was willing to bet, was a husband or blood relative of Audrey Ibañez, the janitor at Brittany's school.

He had Scoletti pick Ibañez up and bring her in for questioning. He peeked at her through the video hookup before going into the interview room. She sat straight, nervously twisting her hands. Then she noticed what she was doing and made an effort to place them flat on the tabletop. She took a deep breath, as if preparing herself for battle.

He entered the interview room. "Thank you for coming in, Ms. Ibañez."

She smiled. "Of course. I want to help in any way I can."

"Like you helped kidnap Ivy Morgan?" He sat down in the chair across from her. "Like you helped to poison the gorillas?"

She did her best to look shocked. "I would never—"

"We have identified your pickup driving with lights off at Dr. McKenna's compound at three thirty A.M. yesterday, precisely the time her gorillas were attacked."

Audrey's eyes darted back and forth for a few seconds as she thought about it, then her face crumpled. "He made me do it."

"Who?"

"Jimson—the quality control guy. He said he'd report me for smoking meth at the school if I didn't."

"So you've still got a meth habit?"

She shook her head. "No. No way. I'd never touch that stuff again." A tear escaped her right eye and her nose started running; she reached a hand up to wipe the trail of slime away. "Not anything else, either. But I couldn't lose my job; who's gonna believe me?" Her brown eyes bore into his. "I can't lose that job. I can't go back to jail. He made me take that baby to Ireland."

Finn's eyes widened. *Ireland?*

"I didn't have a choice. But those Irish folks were real nice. I could see they wanted that baby bad. I wouldn't ever have left her there if I thought she'd be hurt. Abe was right, Ivy's really in a better place." She nodded enthusiastically, as if transferring Ivy to a nice couple would excuse her actions.

"You left the note at the memorial," Finn said, fighting to keep a grin off his face. It was going to happen. He was going to bring Ivy back to Brittany Morgan.

"I wanted Brittany to know," Audrey said.

"Did you help kidnap other babies?"

Her eyes rounded. "Oh *dios mio*, no. Are there more?" She started sobbing in earnest, and stretched her hands out to him. "Please, please, I can't go back to jail. I'd never see my kids again. He made me do it. He never even paid me one cent."

Finn sat back in his chair. "Tell me everything," he said. "And then we'll see."

"Don't you want me to write it down?"

"It'll all be on the tape," he told her.

She glanced around the room, her eyes searching for the recorder.

"It's recording. Just start at the beginning," he said. "When did Abram Jimson Jr. first approach you?"

A half hour later, Finn called the Spokane Police Department and requested Abram Jimson Jr.'s arrest. An hour after that, he received a call back from a sergeant. "Bad news, Detective. Jimson's in the wind. If anyone knows where he's headed, they're not talking. His BMW is missing." He rattled off the license number and VIN.

Finn called FBI agent Alice Foster, got her voicemail, left a message. He hung up, frustrated. He abandoned his desk chair and walked out to the lobby, just to be in motion. In front of the station, two protestors kept each other company as they paced in a circle. Their yellow signs read *Our Police Believe That Gorillas Talk!* and *Next They'll Take Our Guns.*

He wanted so badly to call Brittany Morgan. He could taste the desire burning his throat. Or maybe it was simply the heartburn that had accompanied him throughout this case. But he couldn't make that call until he knew that Ivy was alive and coming home.

His phone chirped. *Foster, FBI.* He answered as he walked back to his desk. "The Morgan case *is* a kidnapping," he reported, feeling a bit embarrassed that he was chortling about a major crime. "And we need all the help we can get ASAP."

Chapter 29

The next morning, border guards stopped Abram Jimson Jr. as he tried to cross into Canada from Montana. His right index fingerprint matched one on the back of Ivy Rose Morgan's photo, as well as one on the photo of Tika Kinsey. His thumb and middle finger print matched prints found on the inside of a plastic bag from the Food Mart parking lot.

Reverend Jimson Sr. was so noticeably mortified that Finn was inclined to believe his public apologies. With his long-suffering wife by his side, the preacher kept saying, "Abe was the light of our life, so smart that he almost completed law school, but somehow the devil got hold of his soul. Please pray for my son." The law school history went a long way toward explaining how Junior could have pulled off the adoption arrangements.

True to his legal beagle training, Junior wasn't talking. But right after the news broke about Junior's arrest, a Jimson janitor in Seattle had turned himself into the police and made a plea bargain in exchange for information. The guy was on parole for forgery and identity theft, and Junior had blackmailed him into creating false documents for six babies, including a passport for Ivy. He didn't have the real names of the babies, but he'd been smart enough to keep copies of the fake papers.

"Abe had these Jimson checks in his hand," the guy said. "He told me he was gonna say I stole 'em and faked his signature. Who'd believe me? I didn't have any choice."

Through computer records, FBI Agents Foster and Maxwell discovered that Junior had purchased mailing lists and personal information from adoption websites. With the prospective parents' race and physical characteristics and wishful email messages in hand, Junior had very cleverly matched babies to parents who'd find it hard to say no to an infant that looked like them.

The FBI located Ivy in Dublin, Ireland; she was due to arrive in Seattle at eleven tomorrow night. The whole Morgan family was driving over to get her. Tika Kinsey had been found in New York City and would be reunited with her parents and grandmother the day after that.

"And," Agent Foster gleefully told him, "We've located four other babies kidnapped in the last three years from teenage mothers across the country."

"But not William Adams from Coeur d'Alene, Idaho?" Finn asked.

"We found no connection to Jimson there," Foster told him. "And, for the record, Charlie Wakefield never had anything to do with *any* baby, as far as we can tell."

Finn thought Foster had no idea how right she was about that. But now Charlie and Ivy would take that paternity test so their relationship would be on the record; Finn would make sure of that.

"You should be very proud of yourself, Detective," Foster told him. "Jimson had a different accomplice in every school, and as ex-cons they had good reason to keep their mouths shut. Nobody put the pieces together until you did."

He ended the call, indeed feeling mostly proud, trying not to let the Idaho snag dampen his jubilation. He called Grace to suggest a celebration dinner out.

"That sounds great, but how about a potluck here instead, the day after tomorrow, at noon? Some people are coming to meet Neema and Gumu. I want you to be here, too."

He could hear people laughing in the background. Grace sounded happy for a change. After saying goodbye, he stood leaning against the mantle, listening to the clock tick in his empty house. Maybe he'd call Dawes, see if he wanted to go out for a beer. No, that was pathetic; the guy would be at home having dinner with his family, and besides, all the detectives were still pissed that Finn hadn't shared the gorilla connection with them right away.

Restless, Finn drummed his fingers on the mantle. The little cardboard cylinder sitting there vibrated along, moving closer to the edge. He stopped tapping, not wanting to end up with a baby's ashes all over the living room carpet.

Oh god. He grabbed the cylinder. *One to six weeks old. Likely Hispanic. Dug up in a hay field in rural eastern Washington.*

He called the Coeur d'Alene Police Department, asked for the detective he'd spoken to earlier. "Is the father of Carissa Adams's baby—Jerome, I think they called him—by any chance Hispanic?"

"Jerome Lopez," the detective responded. "What do you think?"

"I believe I've located the body of William Adams. Or actually, it was located nearly a month ago, but we didn't know it was him. Lopez worked on a threshing crew, right?"

"Yeah, during the summers."

"I think you'll find that threshing crew passed through Kittitas County, Washington, shortly after William was reported missing."

"You've got a corpse."

"I'll have the autopsy report faxed to you right away; I'll have to arrange to get the ashes back somehow, too."

"Sorry to hear this one is ending this way, but I can't say I'm surprised. Carissa never acted like she believed that baby could come back."

Finn had noticed that, too.

"I hear you're a regular hero, Finn."

"Yeah?"

"That's the buzz. Congratulations."

Finn's phone bleeped the call-waiting signal in his ear. He thanked the other detective and switched over. "It's Scott," the voice informed him. "If you don't have anything better to do, Dolores and I would like to take you out to dinner."

"I'd be honored, Scott. Should I meet you somewhere?"

"Actually," Scott said, "We're right outside your front door. We've got something for you. Well, two somethings."

The first something turned out to be a framed photograph taken in the Cascade foothills in autumn. Brilliant yellow larches flamed against dark green firs, surrounding a waterfall cascading down a gray cliff into a silvery pool.

"It's beautiful." He held it carefully by the frame. Why the heck had Scott and Dolores brought him a photo?

"Scotty took the picture," Dolores said proudly. "It's one of our favorite places. We'd like to take you there sometime."

"I'd like to see that," Finn said.

Scott pulled the photo out of Finn's hands, "I know we're buttinskis, but we thought it was time you made a few changes around here." He turned to the wall, took down Wendy's wedding photograph and hung the larch photo in its place. He handed Wendy's photo to Finn, who stood studying it, embarrassed. There were little smudges all over the glass from the suction cup feet of the wall walker toys.

"Feel free to tell Scotty to go jump," Dolores said. "I told him it was really none of our business."

"No, it's really not," Finn agreed. "But I think Scott is absolutely right." He slid Wendy's photo down between the recliner and the end table.

The second something they'd brought was an odd stack of wood-framed panels covered with wire mesh that Scott unloaded onto the front porch. Finn stared, perplexed.

"We used to have cats," Dolores told him, picking up Kee from the ground. As she rubbed the cat's ears, she said, "And we wanted to keep them safe, but you know cats; they love to go outside, especially at night."

Finn didn't get it.

"It's a cat cage," Scott told him. "Well, it will be after you put the panels together. You can put it outside around that window in the laundry room. Then put a cat door in the window and Lok here—"

"Kee," Finn corrected.

"Kee can go out in the cage whenever he wants, and no varmint will get him." Scott looked proud of himself.

Nothing like locking the barn door after the horse was long gone, Finn thought. But a cat cage was a good idea in coyote country, and he still had one feline to protect. "Thanks, guys," he said.

Scott slapped him on the back. "Let's go eat."

Chapter 30

Finn watched Brittany bravely enter the enclosure with Neema and Grace. Gumu was locked in the barn, snuffling now and then, and probably watching through the cracks in the wall boards.

The girl had brought six pink roses, which she handed to Neema ceremoniously, one by one, using her right hand. In her left arm she cradled Ivy, who wore the strange winged costume Finn had seen in Brittany's room. The baby looked like a giant moth, or maybe a green fairy princess. An odd little crowd had assembled for the occasion, including the three ARU defendants, several of Brittany's friends, her parents and brother, some local officials from Evansburg College, and a red-haired Irish couple that the Morgans introduced as Ivy's Aunt Siobhan and Uncle Sean. The Irish woman wiped her eyes from time to time, and her smile quivered. They had to be the Irish couple to whom Junior had sold Ivy.

Neema, sensing the importance of the moment, gravely and delicately chewed the petals off each rose before holding out her massive hand for another. When Neema had consumed all the flowers, Brittany signed *thank you* several times, flicking her fingers from her chin out toward the gorilla.

Neema signed *baby baby give, red tail give baby Neema*, and then opened both black hairy arms toward Brittany.

When Grace translated, Brittany's eyes widened.

"Up to you," Grace said. "Neema has never intentionally hurt a living creature."

Neema flashed *baby give* again and held out her massive hands.

Brittany took a deep breath and then stepped close to Neema. She clutched Ivy protectively, but stopped only inches away from the gorilla.

"Mother Mary," the Irish woman gasped. Her husband laid a hand on her shoulder.

Neema bent down to the baby in Brittany's arms and studied Ivy's face. Ivy batted her tiny hand against the gorilla's nose.

Neema stiffened and snorted. Brittany stiffened, too. Then the gorilla gave several short huffs that were clearly laughter. The people watching chuckled, too. Then Neema bent and tenderly pressed her huge black lips to the baby's head, giving Ivy a gorilla kiss.

Brittany stepped back, signing *thank you* again.

"Baby come fine gorilla baby," Grace interpreted Neema's next signs.

"No," Brittany said, "Ivy is *my* baby." She planted her own kiss on Ivy's head to make her point.

"She's not talking about Ivy," Grace said. "She's telling you that a gorilla baby is coming."

Dr. Andreasson studied Neema. Grace had introduced him as the head of Evansburg College. She happily told Finn she'd been offered a job teaching linguistics and psychology courses there, and that the position included modest funding for her gorilla language research.

"Is Neema fantasizing about a gorilla baby?" Andreasson asked Grace now.

"No, I told her this morning after the test confirmed it," Grace reported. "Neema is pregnant!"

Silence reigned for a moment as the observers took that in. Finn wished he could hear what everyone was thinking—another ape mouth to feed? A chance to see if Neema would teach her baby sign language? Another gorilla born in captivity instead of in the wild?

Although the county council was clamoring for new restrictions on keeping wild animals, fame had worked mostly in favor of the gorillas. Their paintings sold at a premium as soon as they hit E-bay. LaDyne set up an account for the gorillas at an internet bank, and posted videos of the gorillas and articles about their threatened sale, all featuring prominent Donate buttons. Funds were trickling in from around the world.

Under pressure, the University of Washington removed the gorillas from their list of property going to auction, and they agreed to sell the Evansburg real estate and the gorillas to the new Gorilla Research Foundation. Currently the account had enough money to finalize the purchase and feed and house the gorillas for at least a year. Among the first priorities of the Foundation were security cameras and electric fences.

The court accepted the work of the three ARU kids at Grace's compound as community service, a win-win situation for all parties, although Finn fretted that Caryn, Sierra, and Jon might decide one day that signing gorillas should be as free as laboratory mice. Grace assured him that they'd had a talk about the apes' chances of survival in the wilds of eastern Washington.

After he drove home alone, Finn felt melancholy. He sat on his front porch for a minute, staring at his overgrown driveway. Routine detective work was going to be boring from now on. Then again, he was damn tired; boring might be pleasant for awhile. It would give him time to finish his sailboat painting. His next effort was going to be the Cascades, he decided. He liked the way the new snow on the highest peaks gleamed against the sunset.

He was still on Travis Wakefield's shit list, but his job seemed secure. If no major crimes popped up, he'd have time to go see those larches and waterfalls in the mountains before winter set in. Grace said she wanted to come along.

Something warm brushed against his leg. He put his hand down, expecting to feel Cargo's broad head. Instead, his fingers touched the smaller body of a cat. The creature leapt into his lap. Kee was finally becoming affectionate?

The cat was very thin. His orange fur was filthy and covered with stick-tights and his right ear had a bloody rip in it, but Lok curled his paws under himself and purred as if he was the happiest cat in the world.

Finn stroked his hand over the ratty fur, transferring a few of the sticky seeds to his shirt cuff. He said, "It's about time you came home."

If you enjoyed THE ONLY WITNESS, you won't want to miss a single book in Pamela Beason's new mystery series from Berkley Prime Crime. Look for them in your favorite bookstore and visit **www.PamelaBeason.com** to see what's coming next.

Turn the page for an exciting preview from ENDANGERED, the first novel in the new Summer Westin mystery series.

An Excerpt from

ENDANGERED

by

Pamela Beason

Chapter 1

It was almost time.

This was the man's favorite hour. Dark enough that shadows obscured details, light enough that the campers had not yet gathered all their possessions. Food and utensils and toys and clothes and children were scattered everywhere. People were so careless. He wrapped his arms around his knees and drew himself into a tight ball. In a few moments, the sun would be completely obscured by the western escarpment. Down here in the valley, there was no gentle dimming into peaceful dusk. Instead, a wave of darkness slithered across the canyon, changing light to dark as if someone had closed a door. Campers would crowd into tight knots around their campfires or withdraw into their tents and RVs, fleeing the night as if it were dangerous. Then he'd be free to do what he'd come here for.

He perched in a U-shaped seat formed by two cottonwoods that had grown together. Nobody would notice him under the overhang of golden-leaved branches. Not here in the shadow of the cliffs. He listened to the noise from the campers in the valley, all too audible over the gurgle of the river.

Even from this distance he could hear the drone of RV generators, the crackle of campfires, and even the occasional blare of a television or radio. To his right, he recognized the crunch of gravel as a car pulled into a parking lot. Behind and to his distant left, footsteps rasped rhythmically in the dirt as a jogger slowly approached on the road shoulder. Just across the road, on the signboard at the campground pay station, a warning poster about cougars flapped with each gust of the rising breeze.

At the first campsite beyond the pay station, a small boy, little older than a baby, crawled across an expanse of wind-smoothed rock, his lips pursed as he pushed a toy truck along the miniature sandstone hills and troughs.

Exhaling softly, the man splayed his fingers across his thighs. Under the baseball cap, the toddler's hair was the color of the buttercups that bloomed after the spring rains. He knew that kind of little-boy hair; he knew how silky it would feel under his fingertips. The memory made his throat constrict.

A few yards beyond the boy, the child's dark-haired mother tinkered with a sputtering camp stove. From the thick woods encircling the campsite came the rustle of downed leaves, the firecracker pops of dry twigs shattering underfoot.

The rustling concluded with a sharp crack followed by a dull thump, as if a heavy object had fallen to the ground. A flock of crows rocketed up from a ponderosa's twisted branches, cawing their displeasure at being displaced from their nightly roost. The boy stood up and watched the dark cloud of birds pass overhead toward the river.

His mother took a few steps in the direction the noise had come from. She faced the trees, peering into the growing darkness. "Fred? You sound like a moose out there. That is you, isn't it, Fred?"

The blond boy, one hand outstretched as if to catch the last straggling crows flapping over his head, toddled through the grass toward the road and the river beyond. As the boy came closer, his head tilted skyward, and the sight of that rapt little face under the bill of the cap made the man's heart race. He loved that expression, that mixture of wonder and curiosity that small children reserved for other creatures. But small children should never be left to wander alone. Terrible things could happen to little boys.

The boy's mother left the woods and returned to the picnic table, turning toward the rock ledge where the boy had been playing.

"Zack, it's getting too dark to play on the rock now." Her voice rose. "Zack?"

"Where are the cougars?" Sam Westin held her cell phone to her ear as she lifted one foot to a picnic bench and stretched her cramped leg muscles.

"Hello to you, too, Sam," Ranger Kent Bergstrom chided her. "Weren't you supposed to be here yesterday?"

"Don't remind me," she said. "Did you know there's a bullet hole in the signboard at Goodman Trailhead? A heart shot to the cougar." She lifted her chin to gaze again at the startling beam of sunlight skewering the plywood and Plexiglas. It pissed her off just to look at it.

"Yeah, they nailed that one two days ago. Let's go grab a beer; I'll fill you in."

A frosty mug of anything sounded like heaven right now. Sam squelched a moan of self-pity. "I wish. But SWF is only funding me for four days to do this story, and as you've so tactfully noted, I'm running late. Can you give me a hint where I might find Leto and the cubs?"

"Check Sunset Canyon. I found prints around the river, not more than fifty yards from where you are, just this morning. They were big prints; I'm pretty sure it was Apollo. I followed them up the creek. He was headed for Sunset."

"Is our favorite camp unoccupied?" She referred to a secret box canyon she and Kent had discovered while conducting a wildlife survey two years ago.

"Far as I know. You're going up there now?"

"Yep." She couldn't wait to get into the backcountry.

"It's five forty. The sun's setting."

"Really?" she responded sarcastically. In the time she'd stood there, the sun had sunk halfway behind the escarpment, casting a third of the valley into darkness. In another fifteen minutes, the shadow would cover the parking lot and the skewer of sunlight would disappear from the signboard.

"I just meant that you'd better get a move on."

"I'll jog all the way." While it was still daylight on the plateau above, she had nearly six and a half miles to hike up a steep trail through a sandstone canyon that would already be in purple shadows.

She pressed the End button, then punched in a Seattle number. As she listened to the repeated rings at the other end, she pulled a digital camera from her backpack with her free hand.

In the campground across the road, she heard the faint shouts of a woman. "Zack! Come here right now! Right now! I mean it!"

Probably one of those dog owners who constantly threatened their pets but never bothered to train them. While the woman continued to call out and the phone repeated its high-pitched rings in her ear, Sam snapped a one-handed photo of the light passing through the vandalized board, then stuck the camera into a pocket of her hiking vest.

"Save the Wilderness Fund," a breathless voice finally responded over the airwaves. "Lauren Stark."

"It's Sam. I'm in Utah. I just reached the park."

"Finally!"

"Hey, I'm sorry, I can't help it if this yahoo plowed into my Civic in Idaho. It took forever to get the fender pulled out, and the trunk—" Sam made a chopping motion in the air. "Never mind. You're right, I'm late and we don't have time to discuss why. Are we ready to go?" She paced back to the picnic table and checked the zippers on her backpack.

"The new page is up with the usual information about the fund and your first article of backstory on the cougars. But—oh God—we're running so late, I'm hyperventilating just thinking about it. Adam wants something impressive to show on the news, something you know, like wowee—"

Adam? How had Adam Steele gotten into the mix? Sam had a sudden sick feeling that she'd landed this job only because of some backroom negotiation by the television reporter. A puff of breeze sent golden leaves spiraling down around her. She turned her head to study the shadow creeping across the canyon floor. "Lauren, I promised you a new article today, and I *will* deliver. I'm going to look for the cats right now. I'll send you something by nine o'clock your time."

"We'll be here. And don't forget the chat session tomorrow night."

Sam groaned and pulled a leaf from her hair. "Didn't I have two days in the backcountry before that?"

"That was before you showed up a day late. We've been posting an ad for the chat session for five days; we can't change the schedule now."

"Of course you can't." She'd have to hike back down tomorrow for a dependable electrical connection. Maybe this combo of wilderness and Internet was not going to be so great, after all. She was already exhausted and she hadn't even started this job.

"Tomorrow, eight P.M. Utah time," Lauren reminded her.

"I'll be there." Snapping the phone shut, she stashed it inside another vest pocket, trying to ignore the enticing aroma of grilling hamburgers from the nearby campground. Crackers and cheese would have to suffice for dinner tonight. After hefting the backpack upright on the picnic table, she balanced it with one hand and turned to push her arm through the shoulder strap.

Her hip bumped against a warm body. A small figure stumbled away and banged into the signboard with an audible crack. Sam gasped and let go of the pack, which fell back onto the picnic table with a dust-raising thump. A toddler blinked at her, his blue eyes huge under the bill of a red baseball cap. His lips trembled as he raised a plump hand to his forehead, dislodging the cap. It tumbled to the ground at his feet.

"I'm sorry, honey." She knelt next to him, patted the shoulder of his Pooh Bear sweatshirt. "You scared me."

The urchin jammed his thumb into his mouth and regarded her silently from above a small fist. He couldn't be more than three years old.

"Are you okay? Did you hit your head?"

At the reminder, his blue eyes filled with tears.

"You won't cry, will you?" she murmured hopefully, plucking a pine needle from his honey blond bangs. "Where's your mommy?"

The child jerked the thumb out of his mouth, whirled around and slapped a chubby hand against the Plexiglas-covered notice. "Kitty!" he chortled.

"Big kitty," Sam agreed. "That's a picture of a cougar."

He poked a stubby finger toward the bullet hole above his head. "Hoe."

"Hole," she couldn't help correcting. "Bullet hole. Bad hole. There shouldn't be a hole in the cougar." She sounded like a dolt. Jeez, she didn't have time for idiotic conversations with toddlers. She should be a half mile up the trail to Sunset Canyon by now. Where were the boy's parents? She quickly surveyed the parking lot. Only a ground squirrel scampered through the dusty gravel between the vehicles.

The child turned toward Sam and softly patted her left breast where her T-shirt bore the emblem of a mountain lion on a rock. "Cougie!"

She captured the tiny fingers, slippery with saliva. "That's another cougar," she told him. "And it's also sexual harassment, as you'll find out in a few years."

Gently, she brushed back his fine hair, so soft she could barely feel it against her weather-roughened fingertips. A crisscrossing of scratches marred the toddler's pink cheeks, probably from the blackberry vines bordering the parking lot. She found no lump on his scalp, so he couldn't have hit the board very hard. Recovering his baseball cap from the ground, she slapped off the dust and tugged it back onto the boy's head. The parking area was now completely in shadow. She was running out of time.

The woman still shouted from the campground. Her cries now sounded more distant. "Zachary! Where are you, Zack? Zacharryyy!"

The child ducked his head under the arch of a blackberry bramble and peered down a narrow trail that forked left to the river, right to the road. "Mommy?"

So Zack was not a recalcitrant dog, after all. No wonder the woman sounded so insistent.

"You came down that path, didn't you, Zack?" Sam stood up, moved back to the table, and pulled her pack upright. The boy followed her.

She thrust her arms beneath the backpack's straps and hefted it onto her shoulders. "Go back to Mommy now."

"Zachary! Come here right this instant!" The shouts were faint now.

Sam cupped her hands and shouted toward the campground. "He's over here." Could the woman hear her over the rustle of leaves in the breeze and the babble of the river?

"Mommy mad." The boy's whisper was barely audible.

Sam patted his small shoulder. "She's just worried. She'll be so happy to see you, Zack."

He pulled a circle of black plastic from his sweatshirt pocket and thrust it in her direction. "Twuck!"

The plastic piece was imprinted with a tiny tread pattern and had a center hole for a diminutive axle. "Looks more like a wheel," she said, pushing it back into his hands. "I bet Mommy would help you find your truck and put this wheel back on it."

"Zack!" A man's tone this time, deeper and closer. It sounded like he was only a short distance through the trees, standing on the edge of the road where it overlooked the river's bend.

The child stared uncertainly in the direction of the voice.

"Now your daddy's calling you, too, Zack."

The toddler thrust his thumb back into his mouth. Sam winced, remembering all the places that thumb had been in the last few minutes. She cinched the waist strap on her pack and huffed out an impatient breath. "Okay, we'll go together. But we've got to make it fast."

Taking his hand, she pushed her way through the gap in the blackberries. A thorny branch snagged the netting at the side of her vest, bringing her to an abrupt halt. She let go of the little hand to free herself, and the boy darted into the shadowy cut between the brambles.

"Wait, Zack! Take my hand!"

The toddler disappeared amid the dark foliage. After several seconds of wrestling with the thorny branches, she tore herself free. Sucking on a bleeding knuckle, she took a step down the overgrown trail, squinting into the gloom. She was anxious to be on her way while she could still see the ground under her feet.

His head and shoulders backlit by the glow from a kerosene lantern across the road, a man blocked the other end of the tree-lined path. Zack's daddy.

"Got him?" she shouted.

The rush of the river drowned the man's response, but he raised a hand in thanks. Sam waved back, then hurriedly retraced her steps to the trailhead lot. The hubbub of RV generators, crackling campfires, and excited squeals of children faded as she jogged over the bridge and up the rocky trail to the canyon rim above.

~ END OF EXCERPT ~

Like a little romance and humor mixed in with your suspense? On the next page, you'll find an excerpt from Pamela Beason's romantic suspense novel, SHAKEN.

An Excerpt from

SHAKEN

A Romantic Suspense Novel

by

Pamela Beason

Chapter 1

When the first ripple of earth surged toward her, Elisa Langston stood up and stared, not trusting her eyes. The field around her was quiet; all she heard was the rasp of rubbing branches overhead. Even after the wave had lifted her and set her back down, then rolled on toward wherever it was going, she didn't quite believe it. Was she hallucinating?

But then a second wave, this one more malevolent, roared through the ground, driving her to her knees. Ridge after ridge of earth rolled through her field like breakers surging toward the beach. Car alarms sounded in distant parking lots. Increasing in speed and size, undulations of soil rose and fell around her, tearing landscape fabric, noisily tossing her neat rows of potted plants into mangled piles. Overhead, branches cracked and popped as the taller trees around her shimmied and swayed like crazed hula dancers, showering her with red and gold leaves.

A streak of black-and-white fur flashed past.

"Simon!" she shouted, but the panicked cat was gone. She didn't blame him. If she had four legs, she'd be running, too.

This was the biggest earthquake she'd ever experienced. And the weirdest. It felt as if the planet had suddenly returned to its ocean origins, and the whole world was liquid again. A large wave swelled up beneath her, toppling her backwards, and she was nearly buried by a sudden deluge of rainbow-colored foliage. A tremendous ripping sound came from the north, followed by a thundering crash that reverberated through the ground and rattled her teeth. The old homestead! Elisa dug her fingernails into the dirt, trying desperately to regain her feet and turn toward the noise. Snapping sounds erupted all around her. A sweet gum crash-landed a few feet away, its impact jolting every bone in her body. She flailed wildly, struggling to find purchase in the roiling soil. A rush of cold air blasted her face, and then she felt a crushing blow to her legs and chest. After a brief close-up of speckled bark, her world went black.

When Elisa opened her eyes again, it was dark. How long had she been lying here? Her eyes wouldn't focus on the numbers on her wristwatch. The first stars were out, weak pinpoints of light barely visible among scattered clouds. A gust of wind blew leaves and dirt into her face. Rain would follow soon.

The uneven soil beneath her was cold, and its dampness had soaked through her clothing and hair. Waves of shivering rippled through her. Her head pounded so badly that she would have sworn a freight train rumbled somewhere nearby.

The tree trunk pinning her to the ground was no more than eight inches thick. She was strong, even if she was small. If she could get proper leverage, she should be able to shift it off her body. When her shivering subsided for a few seconds, she tried to move her legs. A lightning bolt of pain shot through her, white hot, then icy, leaving her breathless.

Giving up for the moment on her lower limbs, she fingered the wetness at the back of her head. She'd landed on a rock. When she stretched her hand in front of her face, it was dark with sticky fluid. Groaning, she managed to squeeze her fingers into her front jeans pocket and slide out the penlight she habitually carried. Its tiny beam confirmed the blood on her hand.

She wrapped her arms around the trunk again, pressing the stinging heat of her scratched cheek against the cool bark of the American sweet gum that had nearly killed her. The tree was one of the Festival variety, prized for its brilliant foliage in an area dominated by evergreens.

"I'm never forgiving you," she hissed into a cluster of orange leaves. "I babied you for years, and this is how you pay me back?"

A thin wail drifted on the breeze. A cat crying? "Simon?" she whimpered. "Go for help, buddy. Run to the office. Get Gerald."

Right. As if a cat could rescue her. Her business partner, Gerald, usually left the nursery promptly at five, and for all she knew, Simon needed to be rescued himself. It was an unbearable thought, that her pet might be lying nearby, in pain, waiting for *her* to make things right.

"Anyone! I'm out here!" She slashed her penlight through the air. "Hey!"

Sirens wailed, nearing, then receding. How bad was it out there? A fresh surge of shivers gripped her. She gritted her teeth, picturing buildings reduced to rubble, fires raging from broken gas lines, streets made impassable by wide crevasses and upthrust chunks of pavement.

Her stepmother worked thirty miles away, in Seattle. Had she been on the Evergreen Point floating bridge when the quake hit? Elisa shut her eyes, tried to blank out the sudden, unwanted vision of a giant wave sweeping Gail and hundreds of other hapless commuters into the frigid depths of Lake Washington.

"Hey!" Her shout sounded insignificant, even to her own ears. The sixty-five acres of Langston Green were hardly a wilderness, but they felt like one now. How many times had Gerald begged her to carry a cell phone? If she'd only given in, she could dial nine-one-one now. But instead, she lay here—trapped—clutching only a fading penlight. Her pockets held nothing more than a pair of sharp-edged cutters and a small ball of twine. At best, she could snip twigs away from her face and entertain herself with string games until help arrived. *If* help arrived.

How long would it be before someone thought to look for her out here? They'd check her apartment first, then the office and greenhouse. When they didn't find her, they'd probably think she'd walked the few blocks to the coffee shop or grocery store as she often did in the evenings. Only Timo knew her plans. She chewed on her lower lip, fretting. Did anyone know where *he* was? Was he all right?

Two fat raindrops spattered her cheek, warning her of what was to come. The nighttime temperatures now dipped into the low fifties. Odds were good that she'd expire from hypothermia before dawn. "Anyone out there? Help!"

She wasn't prepared to die. What could anyone say about Elisa Maria Langston in an obituary? Hers was a pathetic life to review. Finding a lost kid on a mountain as a teenager had been her only accomplishment worth noting. She'd peaked at sixteen. How mortifying. No adventures. No great achievements.

Who would miss her? A stepmother and stepsister, an aunt, a handful of colleagues and friends. No Significant Other would cry at her graveside. She always imagined that by now she'd be married, have a child or two. What the heck had happened to that plan? Sure, she'd had dates and even a few torrid sexual liaisons. But embarrassingly few of them, now that she stopped to count. Most men were put off by an assertive Latina who drove a backhoe.

Over the years, she'd been proud of managing by herself. She was strong, self-reliant, and independent. But at the moment, she simply felt alone.

Clouds swirled in the dark skies overhead. Their movement made her nauseous. Closing her eyes, she clenched her jaw to silence her chattering teeth. She couldn't feel her left foot anymore.

Twelve miles away, Jake Street held up one hand to halt traffic in the lane behind the accident, then motioned for the vehicles on the other side to come through. The drivers slowed as they passed, taking in the tragic spectacle of a minivan flattened by a fallen tree. While two firefighters wielded the jaws of life on a van door, another held a woman screaming for her baby. Jake swallowed hard and turned his gaze back to the traffic. A trickle of rain slid down his neck.

A squad car pulled onto the shoulder behind the minivan, and an overweight officer climbed out. He extracted an orange safety vest and hand-held stop sign from the trunk, then approached Jake. "You look like you've done this a few times."

"Plenty." More times than Jake cared to think about. But at least he was just directing traffic this time. The smashed vehicle, the EMTs, and the flashing lights brought back memories of another night that ended with a lot of blood and death and guilt.

"I'll take it from here. Thank you, sir."

"No problem." Jake returned to his Land Rover. His cell rang just as he slid into the seat.

"Where are you, Jake? Are you okay?" It was the secretary at Atlas Security.

"I'm fine. I'm in Kirkland. I was on my way to Langston Green when the quake hit."

"Oh yeah, Langston. Our latest scammer."

Scammer? He flinched at the word, especially as applied to Elisa Langston. His heart had nearly stopped when he'd spotted her name on his list of possible fraud cases.

"Reports are coming in from all over," the secretary said. "I guess it's pretty bad down south. Bill's working on getting the helicopter up. He'll want you to ride along."

Like many insurance companies, Atlas Security had emergency procedures in place to check on their clients and speed recovery in any way possible. It was good for the customers and good for Atlas's bottom line. But if the situation in Seattle was as chaotic as it was here, it could take a while to get a chopper into the air.

"The floating bridges are closed, traffic lights are out all over, and trees are down everywhere. No way I can make it back to Seattle now," he told her. "I'm going to continue on to Langston Green; I can at least see how that client is doing. Call on my cell when you need me."

He stuck the phone in his pocket and pulled away from the accident scene, glad to be gone before the firemen extracted the infant. The only wails he'd heard had come from the mother.

Elisa closed her eyes against the rain and tried to marshal her thoughts. She had to figure a way out of this. She was a problem solver. The tree that pinned her was simply the biggest obstacle she'd had to tackle so far. Not to mention the heaviest.

She moved her legs just to feel the pain, to bring back some focus. It was becoming harder and harder to think. Hypothermia was taking over. With numb fingers, she dug the penlight into the soft dirt at her side, angled the bulb toward the old homestead building in the faint hope that someone might spot the dim glow.

This was ridiculous. She had hidden out here to trap her vandal, her Gremlin; not to get trapped herself. She couldn't die shivering in the mud, pinned under one of her own trees. Shoving the heels of her hands into the dirt, she pushed hard. A black wash of pain rolled through her, so strong that for a few seconds she thought it was an aftershock from the earthquake. After catching her breath, she tried again. This time a dark fog surged up from the agony in her leg to wrap around her head. Her vision dissolved into a swarm of buzzing gnats.

*   *   *   *   *   *

After nearly an hour of detours on back roads, Jake Street finally pulled his Land Rover into the parking lot of the Langston Green nursery. The property was pitch black. He drove slowly toward the remodeled farmhouse that served as the nursery's headquarters. He stared in surprise as his headlights illuminated the enormous root ball of a Douglas fir. The tree's equally massive trunk lay in the crevice it had plowed into the upper story of the building. From a nearby pole, a snapped power line swung in the wind, showering comet-tails of glowing sparks.

Switching on the overhead light, he quickly flipped through the property description attached to his clipboard and found what he was looking for. Gas. The place used natural gas for heat. Crap. He thumbed through the pages, scanning the information for the location of the shut-off valve. Offices downstairs, a one-bedroom apartment on top. Oh God. *Resident: Elisa Langston.* He knew she was the nursery manager, but she lived here, too? He hastily retrieved his all-in-one tool from the glove box, switched on his flashlight, and stuck one leg out into the rain.

His cell phone chirped. He impatiently shook it out of his pocket. "Street here."

"The 'copter's warming up at Boeing Field," the secretary told him. "Bill wants you with them to document damage and secure the sites. They could pick you up at three locations on the east side." She rattled them off.

He chose the closest one. "Hayward Playfield. I'll be there in an hour."

"Bill said thirty min—"

"Tell Bill to go without me if he needs to. I've got to deal with a situation here first." He disconnected before she could object, pulled up the hood of his windbreaker, and ran toward the ruins of Langston Green.

The front door of the old house was locked. The gate in the wooden fence was also locked, but thankfully it was only six feet high and had no barbed wire on top. He managed to climb over it with little difficulty. No guard dogs rushed him from the darkness beyond the sidewalk. He found the gas meter by the back door and turned off the flow.

The door was unlatched. He stepped in. "Hello? Anyone here? Elisa?"

He made a quick sweep through the first floor. Offices, a small kitchen and bath. This story was not too badly wrecked by the tree, but the floor was littered with debris. Rainwater steadily dripped in through the huge hole punched in the ceiling.

He played his flashlight beam on the steep, rain-slick stairs that rose to the second story. The groaning of the downed tree against the house's splintered timbers was ominous. He gritted his teeth. Stable or not, he had no choice but to go up. He grabbed the railing and climbed the steps.

He knocked on the door at the top of the stairs. No answer. He pushed it open. "Elisa? "

The apartment was tiny—and ruined. The tree had taken out most of the roof. He had to crawl under the dripping limbs to shine his light into the kitchen. He quickly scrambled out, avoiding the ragged hole ripped into the floor, and headed for the bedroom. "Elisa?"

His flashlight illuminated the emptiness of the place. She lived alone, judging by the lack of male paraphernalia in the rooms. Her taste was uncluttered: no doodads littered the bookshelves or the dresser, but the bright quilt on the bed and the flamboyant art on the walls spoke of a passion for the exotic. Her open closet door revealed jeans, flannel shirts, boots, coats of varying weights. He measured a small jacket against his six-foot frame. Tiny and tough, that's how he remembered her.

Where was she? He looked out her bedroom window. The wind gusted and tree limbs scraped the walls behind him, reminding him that he needed to get out of here. The file said Langston Green covered sixty-five acres. His gaze roamed the fields to the south. Pitch black out there, except for a dim yellow ember of light in a far corner. What the heck was that?

A voice penetrated the cold fog that claimed her. "Elisa?"

She opened her eyes to the harsh glare of the moon shining directly into her eyes. But then, in a startling maneuver, it retreated upward, its light forming a smoky halo around a man's silhouette. It had been a flashlight, then. But who—?

The Gremlin! Her heart leapt into flight mode. Her fingers dug trenches in the dirt. The pepper spray she'd carried for just this moment lay out of reach somewhere near her right foot. She was a trembling bug on a pin, completely at his mercy.

~ END OF EXCERPT ~

CPSIA information can be obtained at www.ICGtesting.com
Printed in the USA
LVOW10s2147200414

382510LV00009B/86/P